RISE OF THE NIGHTBLOODS

RISE OF THE NIGHTBLOODS

SHANNON HAFFELY

First Printing, 2022

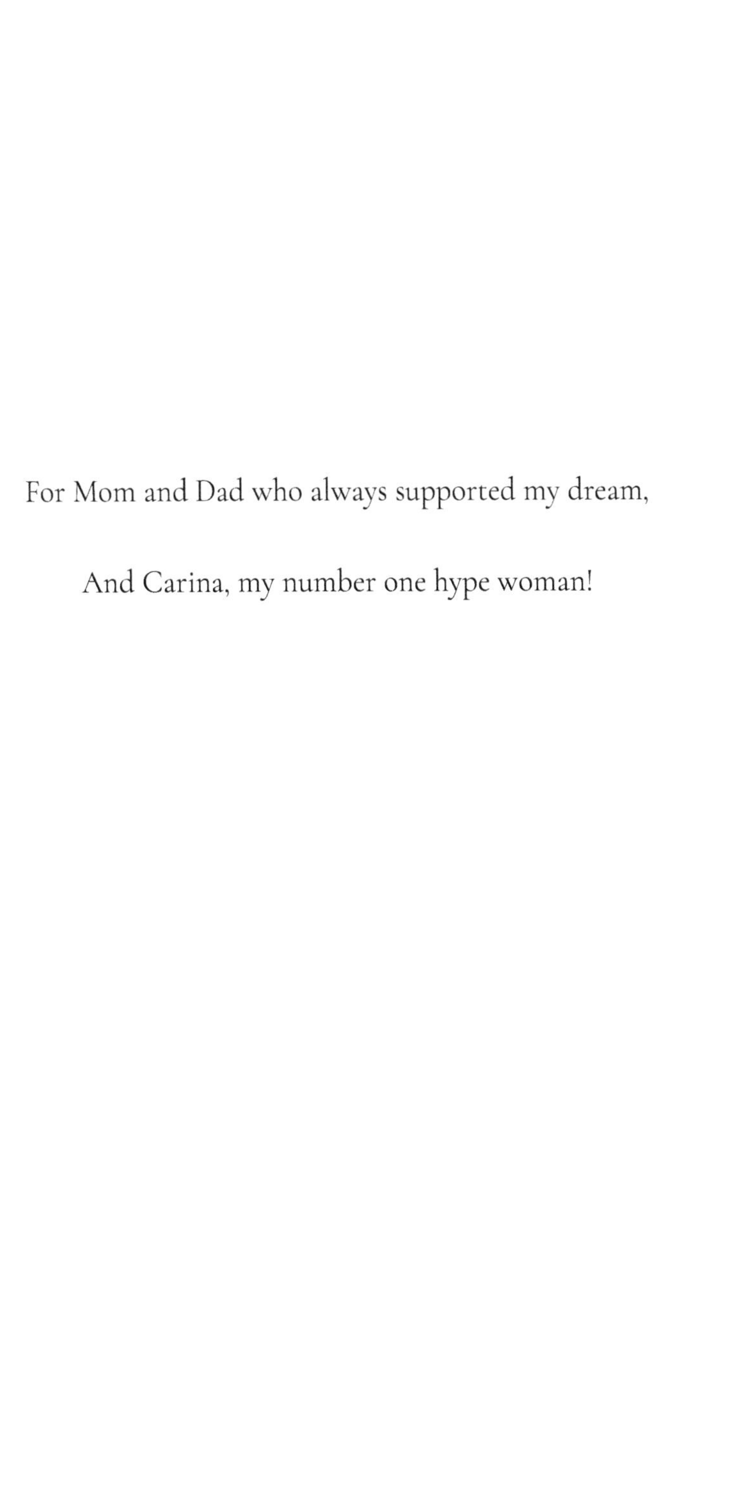

For Mom and Dad who always supported my dream,

And Carina, my number one hype woman!

Contents

II
CONTENTIOUS UNDERTAKINGS

III
VICIOUS MAGIC

IV
LAND FORGOTTEN

I

PROPER PIRACY

I

Raven

Every time I close my eyes, she dies.

Wreathed in the golden light of the setting sun, her full stature is breathtaking. Beneath her, a crate teeters dangerously on cracked cobblestone. Her toes scrape for purchase. A coarse rope grates against her neck as she stands tall, staring defiantly forward. With her she carries purpose. No—commands it, daring anyone to challenge her calm resignation, even as the terror in her luminous brown eyes gives her away.

Her radiant golden hair falls in unruly curls around her face as she meets the glower of a wiry man. Dressed in a prim gray suit, adorned with several medals, he must be a general. I have no love for the soldiers of the king's army, and this woman—her loathing is enough to rival my own.

The crate shifts. Her fear overwhelms my senses. The rope snaps tight.

I gasp, clawing at my throat. Adrenaline courses through me. I pitch forwards into the brown grass, forcing myself to take deep breaths. My fingers dig into rich earth, trying to ground myself. It wasn't real, it wasn't me. I'm alive.

But gods, it always feels so real. And every time it's the same. I know it's a message from the divine. It must be; I haven't had a vision so strong, so clear, since my Awakening at thirteen. The more I try to ignore it, the more it pounds at my skull. Who is that woman? Why her? What do the gods expect me to do about her death?

Bracing myself with my staff, I stagger to my feet. Breathing comes easy, though my head throbs. I groan. Why are the gods so insistent? Even though the connection between the divine and the mortal are faint, they can still be relentless when they want to be.

I just wish they would give me direction towards a cause with real meaning. Magic is dying. I can feel it in my bones as deeply as the woman's death haunting my every waking hour. Energy saps from every corner of the known world. With every passing moon, the familiar warmth of the power that runs through my blood, that gives life to the earth and fervor to the wind, grows fainter. Every breath is like I'm suffocating. Like Oncarii itself is disappearing.

I jam the bladed end of my staff into the ground. It hums in protest, the smooth dark wood warm beneath my fingers. Runes of sight to clear the mind and open the eyes dance across the staff, emboldening my power.

"Please," I murmur, closing my eyes and placing my hands on the rounded top. "Guide me."

Channeling my spirit into the staff, I take a few centering breaths. With practiced composure, I step back into my Sight, begging for it to guide me. All I see is the woman, her skin ashen, her eyes wide and void of life. My eyes flutter open.

With practiced ease, I swing my staff up and tuck it into the scabbard strung across my back.

I mutter, "Completely unhelpful." Casting a fiery gaze to the sky, I throw my arms up. "This is all you can give me? A sacred mission I don't understand?"

"Raven?" My brother's familiar voice calls out behind me, pulling my attention away from the gods who remain silent and impassive. "Screaming to the wind again?"

I try to soften my gaze when I look upon him. It's not him who deserves the end of my wrath. "Just pleading with the gods, Tezin."

Tezin runs a hand through his wild black locks, the only thing similar between us. His pale brown eyes already glinting with a knowing look, he asks, "That vision again?"

I give him a curt nod. "I came out here hoping for some clarity, but it's still the same woman. No direction, nothing to indicate what they want me to do. I just watch her die over and over again."

Tezin pulls me into a hug, firm and yet comforting beyond anything in the material world. Never once have his warm embraces failed to dry my tears and ease my anxieties. It reminds me of the vague memories I have of my papa's gentle embraces. Before the Dividers wrapped him in chains and dragged him into the sea. Even though I was so young, the memory of that has never faded from my mind. It sits there, a painful stain, a reminder of what I am fighting for; to protect Ghzen, my village from suffering the same thing ever again. And to avenge my papa's death.

As long as there is breath in my body, no pirate is safe. Not in my home.

"I think the gods are telling you to save her," Tezin says, pulling away from me.

"Don't you think I've thought of that? I wouldn't know where to begin. I don't recognize her or her surroundings."

"Ah, you think the gods are playing tricks on you?"

"No," I say, drumming my fingers on my arm. "No, they wouldn't do that. I trust in what they're saying. I just wish they would be a bit more obvious. I hate to be angry with the gods, but I just." I huff.

Tezin shakes his head in amusement. Fingers twitching, I resist the urge to hit him. He doesn't have the touch of magic running in his veins. He can't understand the weight of the responsibility that comes with the amazing connection to the world around us. This isn't a laughing matter.

"Take a break. I think to not worry about it will make everything plain."

"Easy for you to say, you never think," I snap.

Tezin moves to punch me in the shoulder. Instinctively, my hand shoots upwards, catching his fist, twisting his wrist. He gasps in pain. I release my grip on him.

"Sorry."

"Raven, take a break," he says, rubbing his wrist. A stroke of guilt washes over me. I hadn't meant to hurt him. "Maybe you should go to the market this time. Give your mind something else to think about."

I consider it. Maybe it would be good for me. "Fine. You're right. I'll go." We dodge a child chasing a seagull through the cobblestone streets. "But only after I visit with Mama. Between training, fishing, meditating, you *know* this is the only time I have with her while..."

My voice hitches. Every day Mama floats a little closer to the afterworld, drifting out of consciousness to wander towards the clouds. I hope when she finally joins the gods they take care of her. For as much as I can't bear the thoughts of losing her, it's worse watching a fraction of her fade away with every rising sun. Already she's forgotten her childhood years. My birthday. Tezin's first trading success at the market. Before long she'll forget my name, my face. But never Papa's.

It's been years since I ventured to Borziau, the national trading bazaar. I long to relive the memories of when Papa brought me along, carried me on his shoulders so I could see above everyone's heads, indulge in the chaotic wonder of the market. I'd never been more ecstatic.

At the far end of Ghzen, on the east coast of the Hebringg Sea, rests our quaint house. Crafted of mud and bricks, it isn't much to look at, but it is the root of my memories, my family, my life.

Gently, I push aside the thick brown cloth that acts as our front door. Vanilla and rosemary incense waft under my nose, accompanied by the sweet, mouthwatering scent of freshly baked gingersnap. I close my eyes and inhale deeply. It's been so long since I've relished in such luxury. Tezin must have been secretly saving up.

A laugh escapes my lips as I head for the stone oven and pick up one of the gooey warm cookies. Popping it in my mouth, a sort of giddiness overcomes me, coaxing out my inner child. Pleasant memories tug at every corner of my mind.

"Oh gods," I say, shoving another cookie in my mouth. "What's the occasion?"

He throws his head back and laughs. It's a hearty laugh that I haven't seen in a while. It fills the air with an addictive euphoria. "I just wanted to see you smile again. Feels like it's been ages. Are you still capable of making such an expression?"

"Oh stuff it," I mumble through a mouthful of gingersnap. Crumbles fall to the cracked wooden floor.

He hooks an arm around my neck and rubs his knuckles in my hair, messing up my neatly wound braid. "Seriously, Raven. That's it."

I shove him off. "I sense an ulterior motive."

"You always do," Tezin says, leaning on the rickety wooden table. His smile falters. "I just wanted to do something nice for you. And Mama."

The rest of his sentence is left unsaid, but I know exactly what he means. If she would eat the cookies if she *could*. Last time I saw her eat was a bowl of gumbo yesterday. And she hadn't finished. My heart sinks.

Picking up the tray of gingersnap, I stride past Tezin into the only bedroom in the house. Mama rests on the bed, her dark eyes glazed over, staring out the window. Light, salty breezes gust through the room, rattling the intricate beaded tapestries on the walls that Mama meticulously stitched together ages ago. I take a seat on the wooden chair beside her bed and put the tray atop the colorful quilt.

"Hey Mama," I murmur, putting my hand on hers. Her dark skin is warm and rough, weathered by long hours working in the brown fields between Ghzen and Borziau before her mind began to stray. "Tezin made gingersnap. It's delicious. You taught him well. You should have some."

Mama remains silent, barely moving, her eyes trained on the window. Her red hemmed gele shifts slightly on her head, but otherwise there's no movement.

"I keep having that vision I told you about. That woman dying. Tezin says the gods are telling me to save her. What do you think?"

Still silence.

I take a deep breath, fighting back the lump in my throat. "Um, well I'm going to the market instead of Tezin today. Finally doing something different. I know you and Papa had fun there. I hope it will do me the same justice."

Mama shakily reaches to put her other hand atop mine. Crinkles line her eyes, glinting with gentle joy.

"Raven," she whispers, her voice calm and soothing. A smile tugs at my lips. My vision blurs. I grip tighter to her hand. "Love."

"I love you too." I can hardly believe she's speaking to me; I haven't heard her voice in months, haven't felt the kindness of her storytelling eyes since I was a child. Is this real?

"Raven!" Tezin calls from the kitchen. "You gotta go now or the bank post will be closed when you get there!"

I sigh. I want to stay here with this Mama, the one emerging from her foggy state, be with the mother I remember from my childhood. But she turns her gaze back to the window, retreating into her shell. Planting a kiss on her forehead, I scoop up the tray and return to the kitchen.

"Mama spoke today." I smile at Tezin. "She spoke!"

Tezin's eyes widen. He sweeps me into a hug, lifting me off the ground. "One step closer to getting her back."

I laugh, unable to stop the joyous tears spilling down my cheeks. "She's going to be okay."

Tezin hands me a basket of rare red-bellied sunngia; a fish delicacy. Hard to find unless you know where to look, which we certainly do. Most people go their whole lives without tasting their tangy, irresistible flavor. Selling these will keep us set for the next few weeks.

I lift the tightly woven basket over my head. "Alright I'm off. Take care of yourself."

"Stay out of trouble."

I flash him a smirk. "I always do."

2

Raven

Excited chatter hums through the air as I near the outskirts of Borziau. A plethora of aromas waft in the wind. My mouth waters. Stepping into the bazaar is like stepping into another world. Ghzen is a quiet coastal town, filled with the gentle laughter of children and the sweeping of brooms on the streets. Borziau couldn't be more divergent.

Everywhere I turn, there is another market stall with a merchant peddling their wares. Vibrant colors burst out from every awning, from every skirt, from every finely made headdress the vendors shove in my face. Reds, blues, oranges, colors I've rare seen so plenty practically hue the air. It's chaos. Entrancing chaos, luring me from one stall to the next, each peddler eager to trade. But it isn't lavish silks nor delectable meats I'm looking for.

Heaving a great sigh, I head towards the banking post. I won't let the king's bankers screw me over as they have always done to

Tezin. Today, I will return with thrice the amount he's ever sold sunngia for. The fair price.

Ducking past a woman balancing silver platters of cinnamon rolls, I finally make it to the opposite end of the bazaar. Out of breath, head pounding from the array of colors and the constant shouting, I step in line at the banking post. Metal spires atop the gray stall stretch towards the cloudless sky. The symbol of a white hyena is stamped on every surrounding blank space, making it clear the bank is run by the king.

I calm my breaths. Even though none of the guards parading around in their steel-gray uniforms can tell I'm a maji by glance, I nervously shift the weight of the staff over my shoulder. I plead they never find out. If they do, I'll end up in service to someone drunk with power, worked until the magic is drained from my spirit, worked until death. Sure, I could fight with my staff, but it would only get me so far. I'm not someone who can control flame or sea, nor earth or wind. Not even a Psychic, one who can peer into the minds of others, travel through their thoughts and dreams.

I'm just a Seer.

Steadily, the line moves forward. I glance at the guards, gaze straying to the sharp curved blades in their belts, accompanied by the sleek black firearms tucked in their holsters. I've never seen a gun fire before, but the stories of what they can do used to keep me up at night. Quick death. Painful. Terrifying.

I exhale slowly, gripping tighter to my basket as the man in front of me sells his wares for half the value they're worth.

"Name?" the banker asks, staring at me with bored, gaunt eyes.

"Raven Zuthrié," I reply. "Here to sell red-bellied sunngia."

He raises a bushy eyebrow. "How much?"

I present the wicker basket filled to the brim with fish stored in brine. His eyes widen, a spark of greed giving life to them.

"Fifty," he says, reaching for his reserve of gold crescents from a shiny tin box.

I scoff. "That's insulting. I'll sell for no less than two hundred."

The teller narrows his eyes, and the guards take a menacing step towards me. My heart pounds a little harder but I don't waver.

"Completely unreasonable."

I grind my teeth. My words fight to slip through. "Sunngia is not in season, and yet I have three pounds. Unless you'd rather I trade to another in my village instead of letting this delicacy fall onto the king's tongue, two hundred."

He glares at me, face a frightening shade of red. "Either you sell for fifty or we'll take it for ten."

The guard closest to me draws his sword. I fight the instinct to back away. Scare tactics are how they rob everyone of their merchandise. Until the blade is against my throat, I refuse to be frightened.

"Two hundred," I repeat, voice level and filled with conviction. "Or I walk."

"Fine," the teller relents. "You drive a hard bargain. One hundred. No more."

I clench my jaw, but yield. It's clear I'm not going to get what it's worth without a blade run through my chest. Reluctantly, I hand over my basket. Dumping the gold crescents into the leather pouch hanging from my belt, I marvel at the weight.

Though I couldn't fetch the true price, it's still better than anything Tezin's ever got.

I glance at the sundials positioned throughout the market, the shadows marking a half hour until sunset. I won't be expected back until twilight. Maybe I can enjoy myself here for a while. I haven't yet been able to revel in the majesty of it all.

Weaving in and out of the market stalls, I come across one that catches my eye. Run by a weathered woman with eyes carrying deep knowledge far beyond this realm is a kiosk of ceramic pots just as wizened as her. Unlike the rest of the bazaar, no one crowds around her stall, clamoring for trade.

Intrigued, I step up to her stall. Trailing my fingers over the earthenware, I sense an arcane, forbearing power resonating from deep within the clay. It's reassuring and familiar. Tranquility flows over me, and the magic within me hums with ecstasy. How unfair that I've only managed such euphoria after hours in mediation.

"Wow," I murmur, picking up a small ceramic goblet, glazed green and gold.

"Magic breaths in your blood," the woman croaks, voice rough but warm.

Fumbling, I unsteadily place the goblet back on the stand. "What? That's preposterous."

"It is alright. You are all the more special for it. The gods have plenty in store for you. I feel it."

A moment of silence passes between us. Slowly, it dawns on me. There's a reason she's so focused on me, not the bazaar, though the possibility is outlandish. "Are you a sage?"

She nods slowly, as if it is painful. "You are intuitive. I sensed you would be."

"Me?" I take a step back, skin crawling. "Have you been watching me?"

She pushes the goblet I'd been admiring towards me, pointedly ignoring my question. Her sleeve hikes up for a moment, revealing a mark inked on her forearm; two black lines curling around each other. She hides it before I can examine it further. "Have you ever channeled?"

I glance around, half expecting a troop of guards to jump out and arrest us both. Hesitantly, I respond, "With my staff."

The sage studies the weapon strung over my back, concealed in its scabbard. "Runes are powerful indeed. Take it from the last practicing sage. Artifacts blessed by a priestess are enlightening."

I pick up the goblet again, running my fingertips over the symbols emblazoned on the sides. Magic is imbued in it, though I'm not sure what kind. If it's truly blessed by a priestess, it's magic I've surely never seen before. All of them were wiped out when King Macos Nazario first rose to power. "What will it do?"

"Sip from it, and you will find yourself grounded. Decisions and visions will be made clear." She says it with a tone that suggests she knows I'm a Seer tortured by a vision. Unsettling to say the least.

The sage pours water from her canteen into the goblet. What was once simple water now shimmers with a faint iridescence. Apprehensively, I lift it to my lips and sip. Shocked at the biting taste, I drop the goblet. It shatters on the ground, drawing a few curious glances. Aware I might have ingested poison, I clutch at my stomach trying to force it back up.

All my thoughts clear. I inhale sharply. Everything lifts from my shoulders. I'm lighter than I ever have been before, like I am a feather drifting in the wind. I close my eyes and find the vision beating down on me again, vivid as if I am living it. Walking through the cobblestone streets, past guards at attention, the breeze caresses my face, mounds of exotic spices tickle my nose. I stop in the center where chaos shifts to tense stillness, a circle gathered around a makeshift gallows.

Pushing through the crowd to the front, I see the same woman I always have standing on a wooden crate, a noose wrapped around her neck. But now I'm struck by every emotion racing through her mind: her terror, determination, a strange sense of relief. I lock eyes with her and then I become her. The noose tightens, searing my skin. Fighting to take a deep breath, I scan the horde of onlookers, searching for help. All I see is myself, staring in horror from the front of the crowd.

A guard with a pin marking him of a higher status, likely a general, struts in front of me. I force myself to look him dead in the eye, and spit. His face twists in rage. I grin. I will go out of this world victorious. He will kill me, but he will not break me.

As chanting fills the square, the general kicks the crate from beneath my feet. Rope tightens around my throat, choking the breath from my lungs. My vision goes dark.

I snap my eyes open, spluttering, clawing at my throat. But there is nothing there. I am not in danger. It is the fate of a woman whose name I don't know, whose face I could never forget.

"What the hell," I whisper, staring blankly at the shards on the ground. "Oh gods, I—I'm sorry, I didn't mean—"

I reach into my pouch and drop a handful of crescents onto the counter to repay for the broken goblet. The woman doesn't reach for the coins. Kind wrinkles crinkle around the corners of her eyes as she studies me.

"What did you see?" she asks, folding her hands in her lap.

"The most vivid vision I've ever experienced. Like I was living in real time, but it hasn't happened. And—oh gods I know where she is!"

The woman leans back in her chair. "Good."

I turn away from her, ready to set my quickly forming plan into motion, but something tugs at the back of my mind. "Who—"

I stop short when I turn over my shoulder to find her gone, vanished into thin air along with the crescents I left. I shake my head. I haven't got the time to wonder about the mysterious intricacies of a sage. The woman is about to be hung. And now that I'm certain she's here at the bazaar, I have a chance to stop her death.

How is the hard part.

Drumming my fingers on my hip, I let my feet carry me quickly through the market. It's still as crowded as when I first arrived, but many people are pushing, shoving, practically stampeding each other to reach the heart of the bazaar. I pick up my pace, squeezing past curious strangers. I pass a market stall with wooden bowls piled high in perfect pyramids of spices ranging from bright blue to the richest brown. Exactly the same as I saw in my mind a few minutes ago. I shouldn't stop to browse, nor even consider buying exotic spices, but I'm drawn to the stand anyway.

Perusing the fine powders, one in particular catches my eye; a pyramid of black spice. It has a scent unlike any I've ever experienced. I swipe my finger across the bottom of the pile and taste it, coughing the moment it touches my tongue. Peppery enough to make my eyes water just by looking at it.

"Ah, the rare nachnuii has caught your attention, I see," says the peddler with a toothy grin. "Comes from the desert at the edge of the world. Possesses a high quality of bite. Enough to make you lose all sense of flavor, if you dare take the risk." He winks and I grimace.

By desert at the edge of the world, I assume he means the scorching sands of the Savach Desert on the other end of Oncarii. Past that, the sea stretches farther than anyone dares travel. Not after those who have tried never returned. It's said to sail past that point is to sail straight into the realm of Luara, goddess of death.

"How much?" I ask, uninterested in his tales.

"Fifteen."

Without hesitation, I hand him the crescents and scoop a handful of the powder into the pouch he gives me. Tucking it into the pocket of my tunic, I continue on my way. Part of me wonders what this mission will accomplish other than saving someone's life and putting myself on the king's radar. I push those doubts away. The gods need me to save her. I can figure out why when the deed is done.

Nearing the central square of Borziau, the hum of chatter grows louder. The undeniable top of a roughly hewn gallows looms high above the gathering crowd. People shoot me annoyed glares, shove me, step on my toes, but I barely notice any of it as I push through.

When I step out in front of the crowd, everyone falls silent. It is as if time stops, and my breaths are the only sound in existence as I stare at the beautiful woman standing beneath the gallows, her wrists bound. Rays of the setting sun glint on her loosely wound coils, giving her hair the appearance that it is spun entirely of gold. She stands tall, commanding the air around her. As her pale brown eyes meet mine, I sense her terror once more. It morphs to resoluteness as the general from my vision strides forward.

Pray tell me how the flaming hells I'm supposed to save her. Of course, now my Sight remains silent.

The general struts up to the woman and hooks the noose around her neck. My heart pounds in my chest. My eyes flicker across the square, searching first for an escape route. There is nothing; every exit blocked by the crowd. But then, perhaps I could use that to my advantage.

"Behold!" The general shouts, turning to the crowd, his face twisted with the same rage I witnessed in my vision as the woman before me. "Rélia Ryan, finally put in her place!"

Most cheer, but some remain stoic like me, anxious with anticipation. Slowly, I pull my staff from its scabbard. Whoever she is, she doesn't deserve the disrespect this man treats her with, that all the guards sneer at her with.

Gods, I have no idea what to do. There's no discreet way to save Rélia Ryan.

"Ready to witness the end of an era, to solidify the king's reign?" the general booms, his lips twisting in a cruel smile.

My heart beats faster. Now I get it. She's a rebel, possibly a leader, heading an insurgency against the king. Something I can get behind.

"Hoo-ah!" the guards shout in response, the cry echoing across the square, beating down on me.

Smugly the general steps towards the crate. And then he kicks it.

I have to act. Now. Or I will see the ashen skin and empty eyes that have haunted me for far too long. Choking back all my apprehension, I dash forward, hand stuck in the pouch of nach-nuii. Shock crosses the general's features. Before he can pull his weapon, I fling the spice in his eyes. He screams and stumbles, collapsing to the ground.

I hurl the bladed end of the staff with skilled precision at the rope hanging from the gallows. My stomach drops. It merely frays the rope. With a deafening clatter, my staff drops to the cobblestone. I scramble to evade the guards rushing at me from all sides. A civilian trips me. Blood erupts in my mouth as my jaw slams hard against the ground. I fight to keep from crying out, lest they see the color of my blood. Too late, I realize, it's already dripped over my lips black as crow feathers.

"A Nightblood!" Someone screeches.

Scrambling to my feet, I make a break for the wooden crate. The general's kick left it splintered and weak. I pray it can hold Rélia's weight. She gasps in relief when I shove it beneath her feet. A small victory to be short lived. Guards surround us on all sides, swords and pistols drawn. Tears spring in my eyes.

"My...boot..." Rélia rasps. Her face is pinkening, though she's only barely conscious.

Without hesitation, I reach into the depths of her brown leather boot. A sharp four-sided metal star slides into my fingers. I toss it at the rope. This time, it cuts clean through. Rélia collapses into my arms. Sweat beads on my palms. My eyes flick around, desperately searching for my staff. To my dismay, I find it in the hands of the red-faced, bleary-eyed general.

One guard roughly grabs my arm, twisting it behind my back. Without me to lean on, Rélia falls to the ground, eyes fluttering closed. I reach for the powder at my side. Another guard catches my wrist before I can grab any nachnuii.

The guards throw me to my knees in front of the general. My hands shake. Gaze glued to the ground, I try to keep the tears from falling.

"Who are you, maggot?" the general crows. "One of hers?"

Before I can open my mouth to respond, he kicks me to my back. Sharp pain cuts across my cheek as he swipes the bladed end of my staff across my face. Instinctively, I try to cover the wound. But the blood flows too freely. Everyone's already seen. They know. And I'm dead.

My voice refuses to obey when I usher it forth. Shallow breaths are all that escape my lips.

The general guffaws. Nausea sends my stomach cartwheeling. Feeble plans born of wild desperation claw through the haze in my mind. None linger long enough for me to latch onto.

"We'll have two executions today!" the general exclaims. "Ryan, and a sully-blood trying her hand at being a hero."

He swings the blade at my throat. Metal on metal rings,

nearly deafening my ear as a dagger catches my staff a moment before it cuts my life short. I take the general's momentary shock to kick him in the knee. A sickening crack echoes across the square. His knee twists at a revolting angle. Howling in pain, he relinquishes his grip on my staff. I catch it before it hits the ground.

"There will be no executions," Rélia says, a grin on her face, beautiful dagger in hand. She saved my life. "At least, not today."

Shooting a wink at me, she grabs my hand and tears off through the crowd. Pounding footsteps echo behind us, the guards rallying, ready to cut us down. Abruptly, Rélia swings down a dark alley, whipping me after her. Chills race up my spine. And I'm not sure what's to blame—the cold stone wall digging into my back or the fact that Rélia has me pinned, sheltering me with her body.

I don't dare move until silence falls. When I'm sure our pursuers haven't found us, I twist my staff between my hands, forcing Rélia's arms away from the wall. "Who are you?"

She gently rubs her viciously bruised throat. "The person who saved your life."

I raise an eyebrow. "I'd say that I was the one who saved you."

"A mutual saving, then." She tucks her dagger into its sheath. Her eyes flicker to the cut on my cheek for just a second. Something like excitement flashes in her amber eyes. I grip tighter to my staff. "If that's all, I really must be going."

I grab her arm. "No. We wait until complete nightfall. Then I can get you to safety."

Rélia considers me for a moment, her eyes shifting between my face and my hand on her arm. She nods curtly, before sliding down the wall. Her gaze falls too often upon my staff, my face, her curiosity burning holes through me. I try to ignore it. But I can't help the sinking feeling that something isn't right.

Knuckles white around my staff, I turn my eyes to the alley entrance.

3

Rélia

Safety. As if this woman could protect me. As if I need protection! Sure, I made one slip up and that bastard General Hroo caught me, but I would've escaped without this stranger's help. My reputation precedes me; if I hadn't escaped, I wouldn't be me.

I brush my fingers across the bruise on my neck. It barely hurts. By tomorrow it'll be gone. But it was too close a call this time. Wrinkling my nose, I try to push away the uncomfortable thought. Close calls are what make life fun. Even if it means acquainting yourself with some stranger whose honey-like voice is strangely alluring despite that the rest of her is as rigid as the king's guards.

Now, though, perhaps the gods have answered my plights, sending her to me. Nightblood, they called her. And the cut on her cheek is damning. She's the key to my freedom. So for now, I will let her think she is rescuing me.

Her dark skin blends into the night around us, and she moves with the swiftness and fluidity of a shadow. Were it not for the silver pins and beads tying her bushy hair back in some semblance of a braid I almost wouldn't be able to see her or the fact that she never tucks her weapon away. No matter which turns we take, or what height of crates we leap over, her staff remains glued to her hand. So she doesn't trust me. Smart. Unfortunate that it won't help her.

"Stop," the woman hisses under her breath as we reach the edge of Borziau. She glances over her shoulder, but there are no guards to be seen anywhere. "We have no cover here on out. Not until we get to Ghzen. It's all open field."

I roll my eyes and get to my feet. "So what are we waiting for? Let's go."

She grabs my sleeve and yanks me back down in the shelter of a crate with a surprising amount of strength. "We need strategy. Unless you'd prefer this end up with both of us dead."

"Obviously not."

Moonlight glints on the silver blade topping her staff. For an annoyingly long moment she grips it with both hands, eyes closed, body rigid. I wonder what maji element ties to her spirit, what fantastic havoc she's about to wreck.

Nothing happens. She slowly rises to her feet. "Alright. We should be clear."

"Should be?"

She nods. "Yeah. We probably won't run into trouble. But no guarantees."

I smirk. "Love those odds. Let's go."

It takes much longer than I anticipated. I thought we'd make it in a half hour run, not half the night walking. Every tree or shrub we come upon, she takes the time to crouch beside. I let her but don't join her. There's no one following us. Not yet anyway. If we don't reach Ghzen soon, my ship will be spotted. Hopefully Penn received my flare and is sailing down the coast. Otherwise I'll have to get creative. Gods, I hate it when the garrison takes my shit.

I'd gone to Borziau with the intention of collecting gold by rather...unreputable means. Perhaps the crew will be upset when I return with a woman instead, but in the long run we'll be set for life. Unfortunately, it's only gonna work if I have a ship docked in Ghzen to escape in. All doubts flee from my mind when I catch sight of a red flare in the distance. It flashes for a moment, barely noticeable against the stars freckling the sky. I quicken my strides. Everything is going to work out just fine.

Finally, shadowed structures rise on the horizon, accompanied by the gentle flickering of lanterns. I haven't spent a lot of time in this village; it's a quaint fishing town that's never done me any harm nor piqued my interest. As we draw nearer to it, I'm glad it hasn't evoked my wrath or drawn the attention of anyone like me. It's as far from the capital as you can get, and the royal influence is faint. Refreshing.

The woman beckons me down the cracked cobblestone streets. She isn't as tense now, walking through her familiar town. She's even sheathed her staff. My step falters, just for a moment. Shaking my head, I regain my composure. No point in longing for my roots. I have a home now. That's all that matters.

"Okay," she says, when we halt in front of a home near the end of Ghzen, close to the pier. "We're here. Try to be quiet. My—"

She stops short as the cloth acting as a front door sweeps aside and a disheveled man steps through. He's scrawny and lighter-skinned than her, the resemblance faint but undeniable. Too young to be her father. Brother, then.

"Raven!" He envelops her in a tight hug, lifting her off the ground. "I was so worried about you. I thought—wait, who's this?"

"The woman from my vision, Tezin," she mutters under her breath, as if unsure whether or not she wants me to hear. Regardless, I do. "But I don't know what to do now. Protect her? I mean, I don't really know her but if the gods sent her to me, then I should trust them, right?"

I snort. Trusting in the gods is naïve. It will only end with broken families and disappointment.

"So...who are you? Why do the gods care about you?" Raven asks, eyeing me with suspicion and a spark of hope.

"They don't. The sooner you learn they care for no one but themselves, the better off you'll be," I say, slowly inching for my dagger. Can't keep stalling. Time is ever ticking. "As for who I am, well."

I step forward, unsheathing my dagger in one fluid motion. Raven's ready for me; her fingers wrap around my wrist with an iron grip and twist. Ignoring the dull pain in my hand, I grab her hair with my free hand. A grunt escapes her lips. She releases her grip on me. In that split-second, I spin her around and press the blade into her throat. Tezin steps forward, eyes wild, but I press harder, drawing a thin line of blood. He stops in his tracks.

In her ear, I whisper, "People generally call me captain."

Raven struggles in my grip. Loathing rolls off of her, practically tangible in the cool night air. "You're a pirate."

"The very best."

"Let her go!" Tezin roars, his voice blowing out the lantern hanging outside their home. An impressive set of lungs for someone so gangly.

I yank on Raven's hair again, warning him not to try anything stupid. "Can't do that. She's the answer to all of my prayers. Don't follow us. Or I'll kill her."

I don't wait for him to make a move. Time is slipping away, and I won't lose a scarce bargaining chip for my freedom.

The walk to the docks is rather short, yet I can almost believe we've walked a league by the time we get there. Raven's a fighter. I can respect that. I hope that spirit of steel aids her wherever she ends up.

"Get off me!" she growls, clawing at my arms, kicking backwards, doing whatever she can to escape.

I tighten my grip as we step onto the fine wood of the largest dock. "If you try to run you won't see your brother again."

Raven, though still tense, relents. Sure to keep the point of my blade trained on her, I unhook the scabbard from around her shoulder and sling it over mine. I allow myself a relieved sigh. One less thing to worry about.

Even as I think that guilt sits heavy like a rock in my stomach, weighing down my conscience. I'm sure she doesn't deserve this, all the hell I'm about to put her through. But if it's her or me, my crew, my ship, the only sliver of happiness I get in this unforgiving world, I will sacrifice her every time. That doesn't make me a terrible person. Just a good captain.

No matter how many times I tell myself that it never gets easier.

Waiting for us offshore is a tall, sturdy ship. Painted on the side in white letters is the name *Anviora*—a word in the ancient magic language of Iquetí loosely translated to the desperation for adventure. Sheltered by the cloak of night, it's almost invisible. Good to know I've taught my crew to have enough sense to keep the lanterns out.

"Penn!" I call, standing on the edge of the dock, searching for a dinghy floating in the calm waters. "Show yourself!"

"How canna be sure it's you?" A heavy, thickly accented voice replies.

I roll my eyes. "No time for your theatrics. Get me on the ship if you want to stay on my good side."

An oil lamp lights the darkness of the pier, revealing a stocky fellow with a wide set grin on his aged face sitting at the oars of the boat. "See yer still alive, Cap'n."

I flash him a smile. "Wishing I'd perished?"

He shakes his head playfully. "Ah, never. And look, ya've brought a friend."

On cue, Raven clamps her hand around my arm that's keeping her still and pulls my fingers upwards. Pain shoots through my hand. Involuntarily, I grunt. I release my hold on her, but don't dare drop my dagger. Instead, I brandish it in front of me, daring Raven to fight. All she has is a defiant fire in her deep brown eyes. But I've got her cornered.

"Hmm. More prize than friend. This one is going to solve all of our problems."

"Great. Get 'er in the boat," Penn says, as he rows to the edge of the dock.

Raven doesn't budge. Neither do I. The standstill could last for eons. My patience is thin enough. I prod her with the tip of my blade. She turns her gaze to her town, searching for her brother no doubt, or perhaps an escape route. Thankfully, she's discouraged enough to obey me.

Once Raven is seated in the center of the dinghy, I hop in after her. I can sense the calculation in her mind, see the gears turning behind her eyes.

"You know as well as I that the seas are dangerous. Would you really risk greeting what's beneath the waves?" I challenge, hoping it will keep her from trying to jump. Or worse, tip the boat. Granted, this close to shore there's probably nothing dangerous, but losing her would be just as bad.

Raven glares at me, keeping her mouth clamped shut. I can't begin to understand what's going through her mind, but her silence is no solace. One like her is not so easily subdued. She's planning something. Whatever it is, I'll be ready to stop her. I will not let my crew down. Not again.

When she closes her eyes, it's far from comforting. Her magic is subtle, an element not easily detected; the mind, perhaps, though I pray not. I'd rather she control flame. Destruction is easy to sense. Whatever she has, it's mostly imperceptible, relies more on surprise than strength. Dangerous because it's underestimated.

She remains still until we reach my ship, easing my anxious

thoughts. I shake out my fingers. Everything will be fine. A rope ladder flies down the side of the hull, dangling a foot above us.

"You first," I say to Raven, who snaps her eyes open. The tranquility in her glare unnerves me. No one in her place should be so calm.

Without a word, she reaches for the bottom rung and begins to climb. Not only is she nimble, but she's strong, fearless. In another time, she would have made a good addition to my crew. Perhaps good enough to rival even myself. A notion that doesn't bode well for me or my crew if Raven ever manages to escape.

Exchanging a suspicious glance with Penn, I slip my dagger into its sheath and heave myself onto the swaying ladder. Near the top, she stops.

"Move it," I order. "Or I'll make you."

She hangs her head, shuddering breaths shaking her body. I bite my lip, almost, *almost*, reconsidering. But finally, she jumps over the railing and lands on the wooden deck. Shouts echo from up above. Before my crew attacks her, I swing my legs over the metal railing. The angry shouts turn to whoops of greeting.

"Whoo!" I call, pumping my fists in the air, elation swelling in my chest, in the air around us. I'm home, safe, and so incredibly close to freedom. "Your captain has returned!"

"Welcome back, Rélia. Where's the gold?" Ori, the boatswain, pipes up from the midst of the crowd. Others murmur in agreement.

I grin, turning my attention to Raven, who is stock still. Beneath the stern observation in her wildly flickering eyes is a spark of fear. Fists are curled at her side. Pity strikes my heart at her terror. But it's too late to change my mind now.

"I haven't got the gold," I reply, holding my hands up at the groans and annoyed mutterings that follow. "Quiet. I brought something so much better. This woman—" I hop down to the deck and put my hand on Raven's shoulder. "This woman is the key to our freedom, mountains of gold, anything our hearts desire. She's the key to *everything*!"

4

Raven

Cheers erupt from the crowd of leather clad men and women. Rélia's hand is tight on my shoulder and her eyes alight with victory. The brown skinned man who rowed us here—Penn, she called him—clambers over the railing and pulls up the rope ladder with him. Now that there's no one in the water to stop me, I can finally set my plan into motion.

"Cap'n!" Penn shouts. Both of us turn in his direction. In his hand, he holds a stunning cutlass. I close my eyes and will my Sight to aid me, even if it will drain me. Clear as day, I see him throw the sword to Rélia, see it sailing straight into her palm. When I open my eyes again, it has yet to happen. "Welcome back."

Just as I saw, Penn tosses the sword, the blade cutting through the air with a strangely melodic sound. Before Rélia can catch it, I elbow her in the throat, launch myself forwards, and catch the sword by the hilt. Sparing no hesitation, I reach for the dagger in Rélia's sword-belt while she's winded. It's not the energizing welcome of my staff, but it's better than nothing.

I point the blades at her throat. A pirate at my mercy! Intoxicating triumph pulses through me as Papa's face flashes across my mind, twisted in terror, bloodied, clawing at the heavy black chains wrapped around his neck. His strangled screams for me to run echo in my mind. The sickening sneer of victory on the face of the *Divider's* captain lights a vengeful fire in my core. This isn't him. It isn't revenge. But it's one step closer. Kill her, kill everyone on this ship, and I'm one step closer to ridding the world of their kind.

Like King Macos seeks to do to the Nightbloods, a voice says in the back of my mind. *Purge the pirates and you're no better than him.*

I try to ignore it, despite the fact that it's right. Honor is not nearly as important as avenging my papa. I don't care. I've been training for years, building my skill, fighting for this moment. Seething with anger, I drive the sword further towards Rélia, stopping until the blade is a hairsbreadth from pricking her. Behind me, the crew surges forward.

"Today, you die," I growl.

Unperturbed by the sword at her throat, Rélia throws her head back and laughs. My blood boils, yet my stance falters. Only madmen laugh in the face of death.

"*This* was your big plan?" she says, once she's caught her breath. "To point a blade at me? I can't believe I was actually beginning to fear you. Love, you're alone on a ship full of enemies. You haven't got a chance."

Everyone around me laughs. I scoff. This is entertainment to them. Fine. I'll give them a show.

"You couldn't kill me if you tried," I sneer, playing on her pirate nature. How could one back down from a challenge? If she takes me up on it, I will win.

She raises an eyebrow, as if impressed. "Alright. Let's see what you've got. Tell you what, if you win, you're free to go. You have my word."

Something tells me she's lying, but when I win, I'll hold her to it. Or I'll kill her. Maybe both. All I know is she's too cocky. That will be her downfall.

I toss her the sword. Smirking, Rélia drops the scabbard holding my staff on the deck in front of me. Not once taking my eyes off of her, I slide my staff free. "Ready to lose?"

Rélia grins, and it almost seems genuine. "If you are."

Without another warning, she swings her sword at me. I parry the blow. Adrenaline explodes in my veins, and I push back against her blade. I take a step back to aim and swing the weighted end of the staff at her head. She ducks. I grunt as I swing the staff back around, blocking another of her blows. Sparks fly as our weapons clash, steel against nearly impenetrable wood.

The infuriating smile on her face, the ease with which she fights fuels my rage. How can this pirate be winning? I've been sparring every day for the last six years of my life! And she's *beating* me?

I send another blow aimed at her head, but she catches the staff between her sword and her free hand. I plant my other hand on the outside of hers, twisting against her wrist until she's forced to let go. Rélia's smile grows, and she kicks at my knees before I have the chance to react. Unable to catch my balance, I drop to my knees.

Rélia jumps as I swing the staff at her feet. She lands hard on top of it. Desperately, I try to pull it from underneath her boot. Heart hammering, I slowly raise my hands in a show of surrender. She begins to lower her sword, and when she does, I scoop the remaining nachnuii from the pouch at my side and toss it at her face. Coughing, she steps away, nearly dropping her weapon.

"Finally!" Rélia takes a shuddering breath and rubs at her reddened eyes. "You're playing dirty."

Blows growing more vicious, she swings at me before I can get to my feet. Blocking as best as I can, I scramble back on my haunches until she kicks the staff from my grip. It clatters to the deck just out of reach. I dive for it but catch her boot in my face instead. Pain throbs in my cheek.

Rélia pins me down, blade at my throat. Sweat drips from her hairline, but other than that it's like she hasn't been doing anything at all. Even the bruise on her throat is faint. How can that be possible? Unless...

"You fought well," she pants, severing my speculation, "but you're too predictable. Any one of my crewmates would have defeated you. Ten seconds into the battle and I already had your fighting style pegged. Your repetition will always be your downfall."

"And your arrogance will be yours," I spit.

I lift my hands up and wrap them around her sword, one on the hilt, the other directly on the blade. Stinging rages across my palm as the edge cuts deep into my skin. Blood flows down my wrist, hot and thick. Rélia's eyes widen. I push with all my might, gritting my teeth against the intense pain in my hand.

When the blade is far enough away from my throat that it won't get slashed, I knee Rélia in the stomach and roll out from under her. Scooping up my staff, I swing the weighted end towards her head. She rolls out of the way. My staff cracks hard on the deck, leaving a gorge of splinters.

Black from my wound discolors the fine wood of my staff as I grip tighter to it. Seething, I whirl around and slash the staff at her again. She barely manages to raise her sword to parry. I keep going, swinging until I knock the sword from her grip. Fear flickers in her eyes and my confidence soars. Lust for vengeance courses through me like a fiery poison, filling me with an unfamiliar sort of fury. In the next moment, I will have a taste of what it's like to avenge my papa, avenge all those whose lives were ruined by pirates.

I aim the bladed end of the staff at Rélia's throat, raise it high, and—

Drop it. I can't do it. Why can't I do it? Why can't I kill her?

A tear slips down my face, mimicking one of Rélia's. I've never killed. And now, staring down at her, locking gazes, I wonder if I ever will be able to. Rélia is a woman who feels fear as viscerally as I do. Human, like me. It isn't her fault Papa is dead. None of these people are the Dividers.

"Can I go now?" I whisper, throat tight.

For a moment, I think Rélia will say yes. All of this will be in the past and I will return home to Tezin and Mama. But then she rises to her full height, intimidating even if she's a full head shorter than me. Her eyes turn to stone.

"Penn, Drew!" she shouts, her voice shaking. "Lock her up."

"No!" I scream as two men grab my arms. I fight for my staff, but Rélia's already picked it up, turning it over in her hands. "No! You promised! You gave your word you'd let me go! I won! Hey I WON!"

Rélia doesn't so much as flinch at my words. Instead, she turns away from me, slipping my staff into its scabbard and hooking it around her shoulder. Claiming my weapon as her own. Maybe not killing her was wrong. Weakness. And I am *not* weak.

Surging with strength, I elbow the one on my left—Drew—and he grunts, loosening his grip just enough for me to break free. I kick him in the groin then jab the heel of my palm under Penn's nose. He cries out, but isn't distracted for long. Legs pounding, I run for the edge of the ship, readying myself to launch over and greet the cold waves, but Penn hooks his arms around my middle, drawing me back from the railing.

I thrash in his grip as he lifts me off the ground. I pound on his arms. I do anything I can, but he doesn't release me. Not until we've descended two flights of stairs and he sets me down on the grimy floor. Rusty bars that make up a door clang shut before I can get to my feet. I grip onto the bars, shaking them, the rattling filling the empty darkness.

"Hey!" I scream, voice growing hoarse. "Let me out!"

Only Penn's receding footsteps reply. I let out another rageful scream and kick the door. Slowly, I release my grip on the bars. I bite back tears as I grip my right wrist, staring at the deep cut in my palm. It burns like hell. Oh gods, it burns. At the very least, the bleeding has slowed, although I'm not sure how much that matters considering how much I lost. Already dizziness sends the world spinning. If I don't escape now, blood loss will get the better of me. I won't let that happen. I won't let this filthy pirate win.

Grunting, I tear off a piece of my shirt and wrap it around my palm. It stings, but I push through it. Retreating into my mind with a few deep breaths, separating my consciousness from my body, pain is but a distant memory even as my body is paying the price. Sweat prickles on my skin and my head starts to spin. I shake it away and pull a pin from my hair. Focusing all my efforts on the lock is more difficult than I anticipated. It's as if I'm shifting between two worlds.

"Focus, Raven," I mutter. If I want to go home, I have to get out of this damned cell. Then it's a run for it. Jump straight into the sea and swim back to the pier. No hesitation. Even if it means leaving my staff behind.

Straining with effort, I finally manage to pick the shoddy lock and push the door open. It screeches across the wooden floor. Breathing shallowly, I stumble up the stairs. Skies, it's getting harder to see. Muffled pounding fills my head. And I'm freezing. Gods, I'm freezing!

Up another flight of stairs and I'm on the main deck. I stumble out into the open air, only kerosene lamps to guide me. Panting, I barely make it another step before I collapse to the ground. Rélia's face hovers over me, doubling. Her eyebrows are furrowed, leaving a divot on her forehead.

I try to crawl away but find my limbs like lead. Before I can think of anything to do to defend myself, my mind sinks into darkness.

5

Tezin

The last few hours have been a mind-numbing blur. I'm out of tears left to cry. Everything inside of me is so empty, so numb, and yet so alight with a nauseating rage I haven't felt since Papa died. It took so long to recover from that pit of grief and darkness I fell into after that. Raven got me through most of it. And now...now she's gone.

I can't stop reliving last night. How that pirate took her, and I did nothing. I did nothing to help my little sister. And now she will pay for my cowardice with her life. If that happens, I won't be able to forgive myself. So I have to go after her. I can't—won't lose her.

Shoving the last of the bread in my pack, I lift the overstuffed bag on my shoulders and head into Mama's room. Leaving her in this state weighs heavy on my heart.

"C'mon Mama," I say, tugging her into a sitting position.

"You have to stay with Elder Agbaa. She'll keep you safe when I'm gone."

Mama's eyes shift from glassy to concerned. If I had the time, I'd rejoice about the flicker of emotion. "Hm?"

"Elder Agbaa," I repeat, smiling softly, hoping it will comfort her. "Remember? She lives a few huts down."

Mama shakes her head slowly.

I sigh. "Well you have to stay with her. I'm going after Raven. It's a long story Mama, but I promise I will bring her back. I will not fail her."

Mama doesn't respond. But for the first time since Papa died, a fighting willpower brings light to her eyes.

I pull the quilt off of her. "Come, Mama."

It's a painstakingly slow process, but I finally manage to get her legs over the edge of the bed. I lift her arm and put it around my shoulders, leading her step by step out of the room. When we reach the kitchen, a boom shakes the hut. Screams follow, piercing my ears. Acrid scents waft from the windows. Is that...smoke? Gently, I set Mama down on one of the rickety wooden chairs, trying desperately to hide the shaking of my hands.

I kiss her on the forehead. "I'll be right back, okay?"

Mama's lips twitch in a smile. I offer a feeble one in return before I slip outside my home.

Chaos greets me. The shock of it chokes me. Flames lick every roof, every lantern post, every fish barrel. Thick black smoke billows into the sky, obscuring the pink and gold rays of the rising sun. Ash floats through the air, drifting onto my hair, staining the faces of terrified children running past. I cough. My eyes sting. I've never seen a fire so monstrous, so terrible. Especially not here.

Wildly, I look around, searching for what could have possibly caused this. In the distance, out on the horizon, I catch the silhouette of the largest ship I've ever laid eyes on. And it's not the first time I've seen it.

I swallow over the lump in my throat. "Oh gods."

The Dividers. They're here. For some gods-forsaken reason, they are back here. I turn on my heel and re-enter my home. Mama is on her feet, staring at me with fire in her eyes. Maybe she knows they're here, the people that killed Papa.

I sling my overstuffed pack over my shoulder and grab Mama's hand. "We have to go. Now, before—"

Another boom rumbles across the ground. The house shudders. I stumble. Screams are silenced before they're finished. My heart hammers in my chest, pounding so hard I fear it may break my ribs. I swallow back my panic and head for the door with Mama in tow.

The curtain moves before I can reach it. I freeze. A towering man ducks through the doorframe, one massive hand planted firmly on his black hat. I remember his gruff, bearded face, his dark beady eyes, the thick scar crossing his eye. My limbs won't respond. All I can do is grip tighter to Mama's hand. My gaze strays to the bloodstained broadsword hanging at his side, surrounded by a menacing array of knives and daggers.

"You," he growls, his voice like sandpaper grating against my ears. "My scouts tell me the captain of the *Anviora* stopped by last night. Tell me where she is now."

I try to take a step back, but Mama isn't budging. When I

don't respond, the man pulls his sword from his belt and rests the tip of it on my collarbone. It's so cold against my skin it's like it's burning.

"If you value your life, you'll tell me exactly where Rélia Ryan has gone."

"I-I don't, I don't know who that is, but I was going to—"

Before I can finish, the sword is through my shoulder and out again. I cry out and press my hand to the wound. Crimson flows over my fingers in a steady stream.

"Then I have no use for you," he grunts.

The point of his blade turns to Mama.

"No," I whisper, throat growing tight. "Don't. Please, you'll..." I'm grasping at straws here. How do you beg mercy of a merciless monster? "You'll regret killing us, please you've already taken enough."

"I ain't ever regretted anything," the man replies, wrapping a calloused hand around my throat and yanking me into the air. My toes barely scrape the floor. I cough, lungs burning. Trying desperately to escape his grasp, I clamp both hands around the man's wrist, pulling. He doesn't pay me any attention.

My vision blurs as the air stops flowing. Now I can hardly feel the stab wound.

"Look at that," the man chuckles, releasing his grip on me. I crumple to a heap on the ground. "I may have some use of ya after all."

I rub my throat with my bloody fingers. He's staring intently at my shoulder. When I look at it, I understand the greedy glint in his eyes. Traces of black mingle with the crimson blood caking my shirt. It's faint, but undeniable. And completely impossible. I don't have magic. I can't be a Nightblood.

Of course, he doesn't know that. In the eyes of the pirate, all to be seen is a potential pouch of gold.

I scramble to my feet, trying not to cry from the pain. I open my mouth to tell him I won't let him take me, but the man already has his sword plunged through Mama's heart. Time stops. Shock silences the screams in my throat. I can't breathe. I can't think. I'm helpless as she falls to the ground with a thump, her eyes wide and lifeless, her gele askew, the bodice of her dress soaked with blood.

"Mama!" I cry, rushing to her side. Tears stream down my face. I press my hands to her wound, desperate to stop the bleeding even though I know she's already gone.

"Captain Navda!" A lanky man enters my home, sooty and bloody, smiling. It doesn't reach his eyes. For a moment, we hold a stare. Menacing whispers fill my mind, overshadowing pleas for help. He tilts his head, inquisitive gaze roving up and down my body. The moment passes and he turns his attention to his captain. "We are ready for departure. No one could get information from the locals."

"Obliged, Ean. On your way."

Ean nods and ducks out the door. Navda grabs me by my wounded arm, yanking me to my feet. I fight against him, eyes glued to Mama, wanting to grab her hand, glimpse life in her again. Her death was close, but not like this. Never like this.

"No!" I scream. "Mama! No!"

Feebly, I throw a punch at Navda's brutish face, but he's unfazed. I can't fight him. I can't get to Mama. I can't stop his crew as they toss a smoking pouch into my kitchen. I can't do anything as my town, my family, everything I've ever known goes up in flames.

6

Tezin

Fierce, visceral terror courses through my veins as tears carve trails down my ash-stained face. My mind reels, reliving Mama's death, fraught with panic every time I glance at my poorly wrapped wound. Black and red stain my hands, mine and Mama's blood caked beneath my fingernails. I'll never be able to scrub the image from behind my eyes.

The manacles around my wrists dig into my skin. I bite the inside of my cheek to keep from screaming when one of the Dividers pulls on the chain, snapping me from my maelstrom of thoughts. My eyes dart around so fast I can't make sense of the world around me. The crew has me surrounded. Heart hammering, head spinning, stomach twisting, I'm overwhelmed. Yesterday, Raven and I were enjoying gingersnap. Now we're both captive to pirates. Separately. And I don't know if I'll ever see her again.

It's a thought that sucks the breath from my lungs, crushes in on me, threatens to kill me.

A lump forms in my throat when they force me into a dinghy. Dividers sneer at me from every angle. The foreboding ship looming ahead sends shivers down my spine. Worst of all is the smoking, ashen remains of Ghzen. My home. That, I can't tear my eyes from. Not until the dinghy rocks against the hull of the ship *The Divider*. The letters stain the dark wood in blocky script, a word that's been burned in my mind since the day Papa died. Never in all my days did I think I'd be able to read it so close.

A rope ladder falls down the side of the ship, dropping just above the dinghy. I grab the bottom rung as one of the Dividers —the quartermaster Ean who won't stop looking at me as if I'm an ancient artifact—prods the point of his sword between my shoulder blades. Climbing with my hands chained is arduous to say the least, but the prospect of death that will greet me if I don't is enough to propel me upwards. Although what I'll find at the top probably won't be any more pleasant than death either.

I have to keep going. I have to survive to find my sister. I can't fail her. Fear will not overcome me. Even as I think that it surges through me. I breathe through the terror, blinking away tears to a blurry world. Gods I'm terrified. No matter how much I want to be strong for Raven, I can't.

I can't. I can't. I can't.

By the time I clamber onto the deck of the ship, I'm trembling, my face stained and burning with tears. Laughter bares its cruel fangs as the crewmembers of the ship mock me. I close my eyes, try to will everything away, convince myself this is nothing more than a nightmare.

A foot comes down hard on my back. I sprawl to the wooden deck, reminding me of my horrific reality. I try to stand, but someone keeps me pinned with their foot; a show of victory. That's all I am. Spoils of a raid. Nothing more.

"Got ourselves another sully-blood!" the captain bellows. "And one step closer to killing Ryan."

Sully-blood. The insult rings in my ears. I've never been called that before. Never been so degraded. *Sable. Tainted. Tarnished. A stain upon Oncarii.*

The crew cheers, a malicious rejoicing. I bite back a sob. I don't want to give them more of a reason to jeer at me.

Pain shoots through my shoulder as the captain yanks me to my feet. I cry out, eliciting another roar of appraisal from the crew. The lack of empathy in their eyes, the sheer malevolence makes my stomach churn. These are the people that killed my papa fifteen years ago. Dragged him away in chains because he was a Nightblood unfortunate enough to piss Navda off. These are the people that ran my mama through because she dared to defy them. And now I will meet the same fate. Whether or not it is today, it is inevitable.

I don't bother holding back my cries. There's no point in acting strong when they know I am not, when they see me as something more vile than the maggots in the earth. If I cry, if I fight, it won't matter. Either way it will fuel their disdain for me. Either way I will end up dead.

I don't struggle as I'm forced down into the bowels of the ship where it's cold and rank. Captain Navda pulls a set of keys from a ring on his belt and unlocks a thick wooden door. Something about its presence makes me anxious, and the newfound magic inside me thrums with opposition. As if the wood could sap the life from me with a single touch.

Navda pushes me across the threshold of the door. In the dim light of the few oil lamps, I no longer have to speculate my destination. Bars that make up cells line the room, each housing at least one disheveled prisoner. A few snarl at Navda, throw him insults and radiate rage, but most are docile, not even sparing us a glance.

At the very end of the row, we stop. Navda unlocks my shackles. I think about throwing him a punch but my shoulder sears in pain at just the thought of it. Besides, I'm no fighter. That's always been Raven. Some comfort at least. Wherever she is, she can take care of herself.

The captain unlocks the last cell, shoving me inside. Clanging rings in my bones as he slams the door shut.

"Don't worry," he purrs, sending shivers down my spine. "I'll be back for you soon, mutt. Find out what you're made of."

For a moment, he stares at me with a punitive glare, and I wish I could make myself smaller, but when he fades away, I exhale. If I can collect my thoughts, maybe I can get out. Maybe.

But even as an inkling of a plan develops in my mind, I know it's futile. These are ruthless, intelligent pirates. They take precautions.

"It's xipher wood," someone murmurs behind me, his voice smooth, velvety. "The door. That's why you feel like you've swam through Luara's rivers. Suppresses magic."

Rocks bashing against my skull would be a kinder punishment than xipher's aura. Even ingesting hemlock would be a close draw. Although I imagine xipher is nothing compared to taking a dip in the waters in the realm of the goddess of death. Of course, it's said that's where the first xipher seeds came from. It's why they're rare. And terrifying.

Near the door, someone screams in pain. I flinch and glance at the figure sitting in the corner of our shared cell.

He sighs. "Some of them haven't learned to give up yet. The rest...they're broken. All the fight beaten out of them."

"Oh." My voice is taut, and I can barely manage the response. Will that happen to me too? Will I become just a shell of a man, sitting in the depths of a terrifying ship, pleading for death to come?

The man chuckles softly, though it's only half-hearted, as if he's trying to lighten the dark mood he's just added to. "Ah, but not you. I'm sure you'll be fine."

I nod slowly, mouth dry. "Right."

"I'm Aran, by the way."

Aran scoots out of the shadows, hand extended. Hesitantly, I accept it. He smiles, somehow with enough pleasure to light up his hazel eyes. I can just barely make out an intricate swirling tattoo curling out of his hairline and across his delicate cheekbone on the left side of his face. I've never seen anything like it before.

I whisper in response, "Tezin."

"Well Tezin," Aran says, running a hand through his curly red locks. "Welcome to hell."

7

Raven

When I awaken, my head is pounding. A bandage is wound tightly around my palm. Someone rather skilled in the practice of healing must have stitched up my hand. It barely even stings anymore.

Groaning, I sit up and stretch out my stiff limbs. My bushy hair falls over my shoulders. I run my fingers through it to find it's plain. They've taken out all my beads and pins, and they replaced the lock with chains and a padlock. Insufferable as these pirates are, they're smart. I'll give them that. No matter. I'll find another way out of this infernal cell. I have to. I can't leave Tezin and Mama alone. And I'd be lying if I didn't want to escape for myself. If I don't, I'll surely end up in the service of some power-addicted noble or used as a tool to strengthen the guard. In any case, maji fetch high prices. And pirates are low enough to sell people like me.

Despite the consistent lack of success, I try shaking the bars again. They remain steadfast even though they're rusted through. I huff and kick at the door. I drop to my knees and frantically search for something, anything to pick the lock. All I find is dirt and rat feces. Until they come to unlock the door, I have no means of escape. And even then, jumping into the middle of the sea is not a plan. By now, we're probably too far from the coast to swim.

I lean against the bars and put my head in my hands. Why had the gods sent me a vision of Rélia's death? To lead me to mine? Do I trust them? Play along with their infernal plans? Maybe my first instinct was correct. It's a trick. The gods are bored, and I'm a victim of their games.

Questions and malignant thoughts toil in my mind. Before I drive myself into insanity and pull my hair out, I exhale slowly. A few hours in meditation and something will come to me. Sight will give me a plan. It has to.

I cross my legs and close my eyes in preparation for enhancing my Sight, the same as I've done every day for the last few years. Taking deep breaths, I concentrate on the steady beat of my heart, the flowing of my blood in my veins. Everything else melts away. Tranquility falls over me, flushing out my anxieties. My consciousness evanesces until all that's left is complete darkness, reposeful silence.

Water droplets echo in my mind as my spirit wanders through the tenebrosity. A flicker of light winks at me from my left—my Sight calling to me. I outstretch my arms to greet it, my fingers intertwining with the golden spindles. Clarity breathes in my lungs, pulses in harmony with my heart.

I search through the rays of gold for a vision of the future. Something near, something to help me find a way out. Nothing useful appears to me. It's all just Rélia: her wide smile lighting her eyes, her head thrown back in genuine, hearty laughter. Her white linen shirt soaked through with blood, though it's got a hue unlike anything I've ever seen before.

Gods I wish my Sight would show me something other than her. Seeing her in person is nuisance enough.

I don't understand why she's so important.

Shifting with my fingers, I sift through time, searching for something actually helpful to come to light. Still, nothing appears. I sigh, but don't leave. I like the comfort here, the warmth of my Sight. It reminds me of home.

I don't know how much time has passed when I hear the scraping of the creaky door against the wooden floor. Slowly, I blink my eyes and glance at the burly man standing on the other side—Penn, as I recall. Judging by the well-kempt cutlass at his side and the ample trust Rélia seems to have in him, I'd say he's of a rather high status. Quartermaster, probably. Strange he's here to feed me and not someone of lesser importance.

"Risky coming down here all alone," I say, brushing some dirt from my breeches. "I'm very dangerous. I could kill you without warning."

Penn shrugs. "If ya could, youda done it by now. Even then ya wouldn'. Had the Cap'n at yer mercy and ya granted it. Hardly the spirit of a killer, eh?"

True enough. I turn my head away from him, staring blankly at the opposite wall of bars. I won't entertain him with more senseless conversation. I deserve silence at the very least. Even the bilge rats have the decency to grant me that.

Penn sets down a plate with bread and an apple at the front of the cell. I barely spare it a glance despite the hunger gnawing at my stomach. I've suffered through famine before. I can do it again. I don't need their food. I need Tezin's gingersnap.

"You can leave now," I snap, hiding the sting of tears in my eyes, ignoring the dull ache for home in my chest. The last thing I want is for these fools to see me cry.

Without another word, Penn pulls the door shut, snaps the padlock closed and retreats up the steps. Once again, I am alone with my thoughts. And the rats. A particularly pudgy one with fur white as snow scampers up to the food. It scurries across the rim of the plate, sniffing. Apparently satisfied, it turns to look at me with its small black eyes, tilting his head as if asking for permission.

"What?" I grunt, glaring at it. "You can have it. Might as well not let it go to waste."

It squeaks and nibbles on the roll of bread. I watch for a moment, then withdraw back into my mind. Though it brings me peace as always, nothing of interest manifests. Finally, when my energy is burnt out, I return to the harsh reality of my cell. Exhaustion weighs my eyelids down. I shift my legs, lying on the floor. I hug my arms around my body, trying to keep warm.

Just as I'm about to fall asleep, something small and furry skitters up to me. I snap my eyes open and find the same white rat curling up under my chin. I'm grateful for the warmth, however faint. Gently, I stroke its pale fur with my finger. It's almost enough to remind me of home, sleeping outside with the brown field mice. Not quite as friendly as this guy but just as cute.

"You know they say white rats are messengers of the gods," I murmur, scratching it behind the ears. "Are you here to tell me they're going to help?"

Its whiskers shift. I'm not sure if that's a yes or no.

I sigh. "You got a name?" The rat remains still. "I'll take that as a no. How about Pidge? Like that?"

It chitters again. I let my eyes flutter closed. "When I get out of here, I'll take you with. You can meet Mama. And my brother Tezin. You'll love him."

If I get home. I know Tezin would tell me to have more hope, but it's getting harder and harder with every passing second. Soon there will be none left.

•••••

For the next couple days, the routine is the same. Penn comes to collect the remnants of whatever Pidge doesn't eat, leaving behind a platter I don't touch, save for a few sips of water to keep me alive. I spend the majority of my free time searching through my Sight for help and talking to Pidge who, of course, never responds. By the third day, the hunger pains gnaw at my stomach with a dull aching, driving me near to insanity. I breathe through it. Soon, somehow, this will be over. Whether that ends with me home or me dead, it will end.

Penn's familiar footsteps echo through the brig and I groan. I don't want to hear another of his insufferable jokes. They've been killing me faster than starvation.

"Can't you take a hint?" I say. "I don't want your food."

Penn snorts. "Ya, so I've noticed. Cap'n don't appreciate it. She wants ta see ya."

I narrow my eyes. "Tell her to choke on her invitation."

The door to the cell scrapes open. Penn steps inside. "Ya, that's not gonna take. Up ya get."

I roll my eyes. "Make me."

Without another warning, Penn stoops down, latches his rough hand around my arm and yanks me to my feet. I swing a kick at the back of his knees. He stumbles. With my free hand, I ram the base of my palm under his nose, but he catches my wrist before I can connect with his face. I try to yank free to no avail.

Penn keeps his grip tight, unrelenting. "Good effort. But'chya can't stop this. Not unless you want it to end with yer head off yer shoulders."

"Oh, so your captain executes people like the king," I mutter.

Penn chuckles. "Not the same. She ain't all bad. None of us are. You'll see."

I huff and bite my tongue. Sure, some pirates are more benevolent than others, but a lesser evil is still evil.

Penn leads me across the main deck where everyone is hard at work swabbing the deck or hauling rope. Others nurse large mugs of ale, chatting and smiling. Above them, Motley deftly climbs up to the crow's nest. Fresh sea breezes tug at my hair. I take a deep breath. It's refreshing from the stale, putrid air in the brig. I never thought I would be so happy under the gentle warmth of the sun.

All that fades when Penn opens the door to a lavish cabin on the back end of the ship and shoves me inside. When the door closes behind me, silence falls.

This cabin is certainly the most ostentatious portion of the ship, what with the gilded window sills, lavish red curtains sheltering a nook, and obscene paintings hanging here and there. To my left is a niche, nestled in which is a cluttered bookshelf. In front of me sits a weathered wooden table, Rélia's feet propped atop it. Behind her, tall double-paned windows shed sunlight into the room. Again, I'm captivated by the way it glints in her hair, how it almost looks spun of gold. Today, her hair is down, cascading over her shoulders. Some strands are braided together, and they're much lighter than the rest of her hair. White almost. Curious.

She gestures to the chair at the opposite end of the table. Set in front of it is a plate filled with much more than I've ever been served: grapes, rolls of bread, even some meat though I don't recognize the kind. My mouth waters. I cross my arms in a desperate attempt to hide the gurgling in my stomach.

Rélia leans her head back and groans. "What's it gonna take for you to just sit down with me?"

A sharp, bitter laugh escapes my lips. "For starters, get me the hell off this ship."

"No. Sit." Rélia lifts her feet off the table and raises a challenging eyebrow.

I don't move. Not once breaking eye contact, she pulls a dagger from her boot and stabs it into the table. I roll my eyes. Overdramatic. Moving like lead, I sit, teetering on the edge of the chair. Better to endure small talk than have a blade through my eye. Marginally.

Rélia smiles. I fold my hands in my lap, waiting for her to talk.

"I hear you haven't been eating," she says, lifting her cup and sipping. My eyes stray to my own tin cup, filled with red liquid I can only assume is wine. I haven't had the pleasure of tasting it.

I push the desire from my mind. "Hm. Perceptive."

Rélia takes another sip and smacks her lips. She stares at me inquisitively for a moment too long. I clench my hands tighter. Why does it feel like she's stripping down my defenses, laying my soul bare just to see what makes me tick? "You should eat. It's good, promise. Captain's finest."

"I'd rather chew off my own foot."

Rélia throws her head back, laughing. It's a hearty, full sound. Familiar. It strikes me that it's the same enchanting laugh I heard in my vision of her. "Oh you *do* make things fun, don't you? Try some of the wine, at least. Unless you'd rather head back to the brig with your rat friend."

"His name is Pidge," I snap.

"Right," Rélia says, raising an eyebrow. "Pidge."

Silence settles over us as we stare each other down. Pain radiates in my palms—my nails dig crescents into my calloused skin. After three days of sailing the Hebringg, I have no idea where we are, but if I follow the coast south it shouldn't be a problem. If I'm going to find a way out, I suppose I must first dine with the sordid filth.

Trying to keep my composure, I bring the cup to my lips. At the sweet, enriching flavor, my poise wavers. I let the wine linger on my tongue, savoring the taste.

I lick my lips. "Where'd you get something so classy?"

Rélia eyes me curiously. "Amazing what little you know

about nobility. If you think this is class, you've seen nothing. It's refreshing, really."

I pop a grape in my mouth, relishing in the burst of juice. "Don't patronize me. Robbed the king himself, did you? I don't see how else you could have wine like this. Let alone such a fancy ship."

Rélia's face darkens. Warning bells ring in my mind. *Don't push. A knife will end up through your neck.*

"Something like that," Rélia replies, voice flat. Her eyes glaze over, fixating on the empty space over my shoulder. With one gulp she finishes her wine and smirks at me, suave as if nothing happened. "Good. You're eating now. That's all I wanted."

I swallow my bite of bread, somehow among the best and sweetest I've ever tasted, even though it's not fresh from the oven, not expertly made by Tezin's hand. I'd almost think it's straight from the king's table were it not stale. "Really? I'm your prisoner. Why not just let me suffer? Eases your conscience to feed me?"

"No—"

I snort. "Right, I forgot people of your sort don't have consciences."

Rélia huffs. "You talk about me and my crew, my *family*, the same way everyone in the kingdom speaks about you and the rest of the maji. You're too pretentious to realize you're no better than the rest of us."

I clasp my hands together, fighting back the simmering rage. "Is this why you called me up here? To lecture me before you pawn me off and ruin my life?"

"We're not all bad, Raven. In fact on this ship, we are kinder than most. I don't want the worst for you, it's just, well, you're collateral damage. I'm only doing what's best for my people," she explains, softening her voice. It almost makes her sound sincere. "If it's not you, it's going to be someone else with your blood."

"Why?"

Rélia pulls the dagger from the table and dances it over her fingers in an enchanting, graceful flutter. "Unfortunately maji fetch high prices, as you know. And it's the only way I and the people I care about are promised safety. Would you not do the same for your brother?"

I purse my lips. I mull over her unfair question. The gentle waves lapping at the ship eases the tension, though only marginally. Impatience rises within me. I need to escape, not entertain her with this infernal conversation.

Gaze flickering, I search for something I can use to at least knock her out. There's nothing. How the hell is there nothing? Shouldn't she have more than a dagger to defend herself with?

Her sword.

I cast a glance at her waist but find her sword belt is gone.

"You won't find anything, love," Rélia says, her lips twitching up in a smirk. Glad to see she finds this so amusing. "On this ship we are bonded by and operate through strong foundations of trust. I don't need my sword at the ready because I know my crew will not organize a mutiny. And even if there is dissent, they'll vote like civil people. I have nothing to fear."

"That's because you've only just met me."

I grip my fingers under the rim of the table and with all my strength flip it up. Plates and food spill to the floor. I leap to my feet as Rélia falls back in her chair. Her dagger slips from her hand. Both of us dive for it, our fingers wrapping around the hilt at the same time.

Rélia's touch is warm, familiar, as if I've known her touch my whole life. A pleasant tingling travels up my hand, through my veins, transgressing every earthly sensation. Rélia's eyes widen. Does she feel it too?

I shake myself free of shock, taking advantage of hers. Planting my foot on her chest, I push and yank the blade from her grasp. I aim the needle-sharp tip at her throat.

"Grant me my freedom," I growl, squaring my shoulders, "or this time I will not spare your life."

Rélia wraps her hand around one of the table legs. Rot consumes the joint at her touch. I gasp, unable to process fast enough to jump out of the way as she swings the freed table leg at my knees. I crash to the ground. She steps on my wrist, pinning me.

I grab her ankle, desperate to yank her off but she's hardly fazed. She plucks the dagger from my grip. Dismay washes over me.

"Well," she sighs, stepping off me, "this was fun. I should've invited you up here long ago."

I rise to my full height. "What, so I could kick your ass earlier?"

Rélia laughs. "Sure. That's what happened."

I glare at her. "You won't always win."

She brushes black particles from her palms: the remnants of rotted wood. "Keep believing that. Penn!"

Penn pokes his head in. "Ya, Cap'n?"

"Time for her to go."

He nods. I don't struggle as he clamps a hand on my shoulder. My eyes fixate on the crumbled wood. Now, my mind races. The way the table leg decayed with a brush of her fingers, the white in her hair that resides in no one else—Rélia is a Nightblood. It's the only explanation. And not just any maji. I think her connection to the gods runs far deeper than she lets on.

I just have to figure out why.

8

Raven

I can't stop thinking about it. About her. The wood rotting at her touch, the way my magic tingled when our fingers met. I can still feel it. Her spirit. I hate it. I hate the way I long to relive the moment we touched, the most euphoric, transcendent sensation. Now, my magic is buzzing, stirring with life.

I let out a frustrated scream and kick the wall of bars. Rattling responds, tinny and irritating. Like Rélia. Gods, she's getting in my head. How is she getting in my head?

I wrap my arms around myself, praying to the gods to get me home. I just want to go home. Or smite everyone intent on selling maji.

Injustice is spread far and wide in Oncarii, crippling everyone like a disease of which only the royals are immune. King Macos took it upon himself to eradicate magic after one out of control newly awakened Flamer accidentally burned his father to death. Even if it wasn't an accident, it was one person. One. One fault, and thousands must suffer decades later.

I sink to the ground, desperate for tranquility. Before I even have the chance to call upon my Sight, it draws me in. Light encompasses my mind when my eyes shut against my will. The comforting warmth ever-present within my veins is now a raging fire. Every way I turn, images stab at my consciousness, aggressive and demanding, but I know that's only because I'm fighting it. I've never fought my magic.

Giving in, my senses heighten. Unlike ever before, the aura of the world passes through me, the very fabric of existence tangible enough to fold, tear, mend. Every shift of the wind, every wave splashing against the hull—it's like lightning crackling across my skin. No corner of the world can escape my Sight. I need only think of my home, and I'm transported there.

But it's wrong, it's all wrong. Instead of cool sea breezes and children's laughter, the air is searing, saturated with painful cries. I think of Borziau and instantly I'm there. Chatter hums through the market, busy as always. Any place I think of my spirit follows.

I fight to stay grounded, connected to my body. Flashes of Rélia greet me when I find myself within the familiar reaches of my Sight. Her laugh as she falls to the ground, her heart-wrenching scream as tears well in her eyes, and again her shirt soaked through with blood. I force her out of my mind, finding Tezin instead. At first, I'm certain it's a vision, a foretelling of the future. But the cold, the stench, everything is too real.

My heart drops as I stare at my brother, locked behind bars in the bowels of a ship. "Tezin!" I cry, trying to catch his attention.

I step towards him, towards his cell, but my fingers pass through the bars. My breath hitches. I'm not really here.

Tezin melts into his surroundings and I fade into darkness. I take a step, the sound reverberating through the emptiness. *Inhale, exhale.* I wander through the unfamiliar void, searching for any sign of my Sight. Something powerful is here. I can feel the magic permeating the air.

Heart hammering, I turn. Hovering in the stark nothingness is a figure glowing white. I can't make out any detailed features save for their flowing white hair. It's divine. Godly, almost.

Saelvia maaĵka.

Save magic.

At the sound of the ancient Iquetí language, I freeze. It's been ages since the tongue of the gods has been so blatantly spoken. I never dared to utter it aloud.

Hearing it now makes my heart soar.

Caentathea.

The voice, the presence, it's all distantly familiar, as if it had been living within me my whole life. Like this figure standing before me is part of my spirit.

"Tae?" I murmur, hardly believing it. The god of time and sight, speaking to me. I never would have imagined.

Ket Rélia, encoņçia lae réliic.

Find the relic.

I'm compelled to agree, to take his word as gospel. But what relic? And Rélia? Not in this or any world. Even if she herself shares the blood she clearly couldn't care less about saving magic. Painting the divine language on the side of her ship is a call for trouble, a reckless disgrace of magic. Not exactly great qualities for the savior of the Nightbloods.

Saelvia maaĵka.

With that, Tae fades and I'm thrown back to my present body.

I snap my eyes open, gasping as if I haven't had air in ages. I'm back in my cell, everything solid beneath my hands. Every fiber of my being vibrates with energy, with power. I wonder if this is what it's like to feel magic breathe. Really *breathe.* Was this the life my ancestors had before Oncarii was sucked dry?

Shakily, I brush my finger under my nose. It comes away bloody. Never before have I experienced something so intense, so mind-bending.

I know Seers can peer through time, but since magic has been disappearing, I never would have believed it was possible for me to astral project across the present world. Nor did I think it was possible to experience visions so deeply I could feel the raw emotion.

It's like Rélia's touch stirred something within me. Awakened ancient roots of my magic that had been dormant, waiting to emerge.

My energy is shot. I can't find it in me to process anything I saw. Ghzen in flames. Tezin locked up. It's not real. It can't be real.

"Hey."

I startle. I hadn't realized I'd closed my eyes again until they open, and I find Rélia kneeling in front of me, her eyebrows knitted together. Gently, she cups my cheek. My senses flare. I scramble back, not ready for the intensity of my emerging magic to surface again.

Panic has never been so crippling. And in front of a pirate no less. Embarrassing.

"Are you okay?" Rélia asks, her voice calm and steady. "You were convulsing."

I take a few deep breaths and nod slowly, though it makes my head swim. More blood trickles from my nose.

From a pocket hidden in her billowing wool coat, she pulls a white cloth. Rélia moves to wipe the blood, but I hold up a hand.

"Don't. Don't touch me."

Rélia sighs. "Love, you're bleeding."

"I know," I snap, miraculously finding energy in her irritating presence. "I'm well aware."

She tosses me the cloth. "Clean yourself then."

Hesitantly, I pick it up, staunching the blood flow. I narrow my eyes at Rélia who's studying me intently. "What?"

"You look drained."

I open up my mouth to contest, even though it's true, but the words won't come, and she rolls her eyes anyway.

"I don't care to hear your opposition. You don't need to explain why, but you *are* exhausted. You need a break. And I can help with that."

I drop the blackened cloth to the floor. "Why?"

"Because I don't hate you as you hate me." Rélia grabs my hand and guides me to my feet. I grimace, expecting my magic to rush back, full thrust, but it's just a tingling warmth, a fluttering in my stomach.

I exhale slowly. "I do. Hate you, that is. But I have a right to."

"Yeah, yeah. I know. You do, and I understand. I'm not trying to change your mind. Just try not to think about yesterday. Or tomorrow. Or any moment but now." Rélia doesn't seem to be talking to me, but rather to herself. Maybe guilt is crushing her. Good. I hope in the coming days it will suffocate her. Karma will strike, eventually. Hopefully I will be there when it happens.

For now, I will entertain whatever it is she has planned. I let her lead me to the main deck where the sun peeks out of the clouds, and the crew is drinking. Rélia snags a mug of amber liquid from an incredibly inebriated man, and hands it to me. It hasn't even been touched, which begs the question how many times was it refilled?

Against my better judgment, I take a sip. Far from the tangy, warm flavor of wine, rum brings a new sort of life to my taste-buds. Strong, sweet, burning. I cough, but lick my lips, eager for more. I chug half the mug before Rélia stops me.

"You'll pass out if you keep that up, lightweight," she warns, a smirk curling across her lips. "The rum's more potent than you think. Try to enjoy it."

I follow her to the middle of the deck, sitting when she directs me to as much as it pains me. Patience is a virtue. I will play nice for now.

Taking another sip of rum, I wait for something to happen. By the time my blood begins to buzz with the effects, the rest of the crew has congregated around me, smiling, clearly anticipating something exciting. Rélia paces in front of us, squaring her shoulders, hand resting on the hilt of her sword. Clad in her tricorn hat and long woolen coat, she could have been mistaken for a fearsome pirate. The twinkle of mischief in her eyes belies her stern expression.

"So," she says, voice strong and commanding, eyeing her crew sharply. "I hear there's been a crime aboard our ship." Rélia paces back and forth in front of us before jabbing a dagger at one man I recognize as Drew. "Vin Drew! You've been accused of stealing and espionage!"

Drew holds his hands up, feigning shock. "What? Outrageous!"

Rélia grabs his hand and pulls him towards the main mast. Held at sword point, he begs for mercy.

"You shall receive what you ask if the jury finds you innocent," Rélia promises. "Our first witness is the accuser herself, none other than our trusted sail-master. Mina! What have you to say?"

A pretty, golden-skinned girl with almond shaped eyes and mussed brown hair steps forward. She sniffles, putting on a rather convincing display of heartbroken deception. When she speaks, it's a heavy, overly accented drawl common in Qada, the capital. Making fun of the king. I can get behind that, at least. "Madam, it is true! That rat bastard Drew stole my engagement ring I received from my darling Kurtis. He's stationed in the sea chasing down those scoundrel pirates, gods bless him. OH, how can I go ON without it?" She bursts into tears, burying her face into Rélia's shoulder.

I choke on my rum. Laughter builds in my chest at the display. Why is my body so insistent on betraying me?

Penn chuckles beside me. "Ridiculous, ya?"

"Is this...a mock trial?" I ask.

Penn nods. "Gets slow. Need somethin' ta entertain ourselves. So we pretend we a navy ship. And make fun of 'em. Besides. Cap'n? Loves theater."

I snort. "I'll bet she extensively studied melodrama."

Penn chuckles again, turning his attention to the absurd play. I, however, do not care to encourage such frivolity. While they cycle through more witnesses to the supposed crime, each testimony more baffling than the last, inciting raucous bouts of laughter, I keep my eyes glued to the darkening sky. The air grows heavier, filled with the promise of rain.

"I sentence you to death, pirate spy!" Rélia proclaims after half an hour of trial, suppressing a smile and failing miserably. Joy glints in her eyes.

Drew falls to his knees, letting loose the most over-dramatic scream I've ever heard. It turns to fits of giggles.

Violent waves rock the ship. Lightning flashes in the dense clouds. Thunder rumbles. Laughter dies abruptly, like a cord was cut, silencing them. Everyone races to their stations without a word from Rélia. In the midst of the frenzy, no one pays me any mind.

Rain cools my face. It starts with a sprinkle but pours harder by the minute. I stand still on the deck, searching for a way to use the storm to my advantage. Karma will come, and it will come today. I will be sure of it. I prayed for a chance, and this is it.

Rélia will get what she deserves.

9

Rélia

I can barely see through the torrents of rain. Wind whips at my hair. How strong is it now? Forty knots? Fifty? Strong enough to tear our sails or roll our ship.

Drew stands at the helm, desperately trying to maneuver the crashing waves. Half the crew frantically reef the sails. The others tie down ropes and shelter supplies in the hold.

I rush for the foremast, fighting to maintain my balance. By the time I reach it, I'm completely soaked through. Grabbing tight to the slippery coil of rope, I hoist the storm jib. Once secured, I order everyone who can to get below-decks.

Halfway to my cabin, I run into Raven who hasn't moved. Without another thought, I hook my arm through hers, dragging her towards my quarters.

Raven slips from my grip. I turn to look at her, shielding my eyes from the pelting rain. She's just standing there, glaring.

"What are you doing?" I shout, voice barely audible against the roar of the storm. "If you stay out here, you'll die!"

No response. I step towards her. Lightning strikes. Steel glints in the brief flash of light. Gasping, I glance down at my waist to find she's pulled my sword from its sheath. How could I not have noticed?

I lock eyes with Raven. Despite that I can barely see through the rain, her eyes are enigmatic. Striking. Darker than the night sky, devouring light in their intensity, like the whole universe lives within them. Staring so deeply, it's like our souls touch and I finally know what it means to stargaze.

I've never been so drawn to someone. Especially since we touched hands. My magic soared unlike it ever had before, every part of me vibrating in harmony with the world. I know she felt it too. For some reason our fates are tied together. A cosmic joke, probably. Or the gods are having fun screwing with my life.

"Raven...wait," I say, holding up my hands in surrender.

As soon as the words leave my mouth, she swings the sword at me. It's almost amusing how clumsy it is in her hands. I imagine her staff is the only thing she can keep under control—and admirably so—while everything else she wields is fueled by some deep anger. I recognize the pain, the need for vengeance. It takes root in all of us sooner or later.

I side step, and the blade catches air. Again, she strikes, but this time it clashes with the dagger that I pull from a smaller sheath on my sword belt. Confidence flows through me. I push on her sword, grabbing the hilt with my free hand. Ignoring the tingling on my skin when our fingers touch, I yank the sword from her grip. Now I have two blades leveled at her.

Wind blows stronger across the deck. I stagger. "If you don't get into the cabin, I'll make you."

Raven balls her hands into fists, still as a rock. I can't believe she still won't listen even after I've disarmed her. Then again, she did relent easily, and she doesn't seem the type. She wanted me to beat her. A fact I pick up on a moment too late.

Golden light wisps around her fingers, glows in a ring around her eyes. Magic buzzes in the air, alive in a way that reminds me of the vitality prominent in the hidden safe-havens of Qada. Every breath I take is crisp, warm, filled with clarity. Deep within my core, my own magic thrums with energy. I try to call it forth, to infect Raven with a sickness that will hinder her, but I can't move. Even the particles around me freeze. There's no wind, no sound, nothing.

She's stopped time.

At least that answers what I've been wondering. She's a Seer.

Jolts of vivacity rush through me, like I've been swimming and find myself inexplicably standing on the beach, completely dry. I fall to my knees. My fingers close around air. Strange prickling sensations spiderweb up my side. I gasp, breathing as if I haven't in years. I wonder if the rest of the world feels as strange as I do, if they picked up on the fact that their lives halted for a moment. Or more.

A pang in my ribs draws my mind from speculation. Protruding from my side is my own dagger. Looking at it exacerbates the pain. Burning spreads across my skin. Energy saps from my muscles. I take another breath, rattling my lungs. On unsteady legs, I slowly rise.

Both Raven and I struggle to stay upright. Sweat glistens on her forehead, and she's leaning on my sword for balance. Gritting my teeth, I pull the dagger out. Immediately, I press my palm over the wound to staunch the heavy flow of blood. I can't let her see that my blood isn't normal, that I'm not normal.

Already, my wound is meticulously stitching together, working from the inside out. I hate when my body heals. It's more painful than getting stabbed in the first place. Searing pain pulses from the wound. I bite back a scream. I refuse to appear weak in front of her, though I fear I am losing that battle. Closing my eyes helps to push through the agony of healing, but not the crippling nausea.

Another gust of wind rocks the ship. Both of us stumble. I grasp the rail at the edge of the deck for balance. Bile fills my mouth.

"I will not," Raven says, her voice weary but filled with conviction, "let you turn me into nothing."

I hold up my free hand in a placating gesture, blinking away tears. Thankfully, the rain hides them. "I'm just trying to save my family!"

Raven steps towards me until our faces are a hairsbreadth away. Fire ignites in her eyes, a striking resemblance to burning coals. Nearly tangible rage emanates from her. "You are the very bane of my existence. You are a heartless hell-sent. A traitor to your blood."

I open my mouth, rebukes on my tongue to prove I'm not what she says, but instead a scream tears from my throat. Weakness overcomes me. I collapse, heels of my hands pressing into my eyes. Gods I hate healing.

Raven kicks me in the face, knocking me to my back. She

looms above me, sword poised and ready. Last time she granted mercy. She isn't a killer. This time is no different. I'll be sure of that. Not only to save my own ass but to spare her conscience.

Ignoring my anguish, I sweep my foot under hers and roll out of the way as the sword clatters to the deck. Waves crash against the ship. It lurches. My sword slides down the deck. I scramble after it. When my fingers wrap around the hilt, a sense of relief washes over me. Strength surges through my veins, and the pain of my skin stitching together dulls.

With a grunt, I leap to my feet, whirling on Raven. She's scooped up my dagger, but it's hardly formidable in her shaking hands. Blade at the ready, I kick the dagger from her hand and grab hold of her shoulder. Her gaze rolls over the wound in my side, which is just a thin line now. Water washes the blood away. Soon it will be as if nothing happened at all.

I force Raven forwards, towards the door to the brig. For a moment, she tenses, fights back, but then she collapses, unconscious. Despite the fury burning in my chest—she almost succeeded in killing me—pity strikes my heart. She fought so hard. All she wants is to go home. Someday, I wish to grant her that much after all this. But I have to put myself first. I have to.

I have to.

Returning my sword to its sheath, I lift Raven in my arms. With her eyes closed, her face is set in tranquility.

Down another flight of stairs, past the hammocks my crew is readying to sleep in, I finally reach the brig. I open the cell and gently set Raven on the ground. A white rat scampers to her, sitting on its haunches, staring at me with its beady eyes. I try to ignore the fact that it's practically staring into my soul.

I unwind the coils of my braids and shake out my wet hair. Something nags at me as I turn to leave. True, I'm going to trade her freedom for mine. But she deserves some semblance of peace before that happens. I kneel beside her and put my hand on her forehead. It's burning.

Breathing deeply, I call upon my magic. It tingles in my fingers. An aura of silver light emanates around my hand.

"*Deçanôa*," I whisper. *Rest.*

Her spirit shifts, writhing beneath my fingers. Steadying my breath, I take in her stress, her rage, everything that is weighing her down, latching it to my mind. I will hold it until I cannot any longer. Drained, I stand. The steady rise and fall of her chest is the last peace she may feel for some time.

Tonight, she'll dream. Tomorrow, she'll wake to a nightmare.

10

Tezin

"Here."

Aran hands me half of his loaf of bread. It's not quite as hard as a rock yet. I shake my head, picking at my own. I wonder if I could use it as a hammer to break out of the cell. "No, I can't."

He rolls his eyes. "Gods. You're going to starve if you don't take it. Navda gives me real food every day anyway. I'm his favorite."

Aran spits the last word, face twisting in disgust. I try not to think about what that means. Though I fear I'll understand in the coming days. Navda uses maji for petty crimes and fruitless work. But some are forced to do much worse.

Reluctantly, I accept the bread. He's persistent, and I'm not exactly upset about it. The bread isn't good, not in the slightest, but it satiates the hunger pains. Jealous glares peer at me from every cell. I shrink into the shadows. The scorn doesn't last long; they all resume their hollow, gaunt stares at the filthy floor.

Sniffles suffuse the silence. Squinting, I make out a girl sitting with her knees drawn up to her chest in the cell across from mine. Muted red hair falls over her face when she looks up at me. I'm taken aback at her youthful face. By my guess, she can't be more than fifteen.

"That's Marie," Aran says, nodding to her. "She's been here longer than any of us."

"What? That can't, well that's! But she's just a kid!" I splutter, throwing her another wary glance. She's whispering to something clutched between her spindly fingers.

Aran shrugs. "She's also a Nightblood. Not safe for any of us."

"I know." I swallow over a lump in my throat. "Do you umm...what can you do? You know, like with your magic. If you don't mind me asking. If uh, if you do totally fine, I'm just trying to well, I dunno—"

"Tezin, stop." Aran holds up a hand.

I clamp my mouth shut.

Heat rises in my face as he says, "Gods you talk a lot." I start to apologize, but he shakes his head, lips curled in amusement. "No, it's refreshing. Here, I can show you."

Closing his eyes, he mutters something beneath his breath. I can't imagine how strenuous it must be to call upon his gift when impeded by xipher wood. Just as I tell him to stop, to not hurt himself, I sense it. Around us, the air warms. It swirls around me, carrying the scent of summer. I linger in the fragrance of lilies and daffodils, of sour-berries and pineapple. I can almost believe I'm sitting on the beach under the sun.

And then it's gone. Disheveled and clearly exhausted from the small feat, Aran slumps against the wall. Yet he, too, is smiling.

"You're a Galer," I say. "No wonder Navda likes you."

"My magic, you mean. One flick of my wrist, I can send us shooting across the sea at seventy knots. Another, and I can suck the breath from his enemies." Aran's face falls. His lip quivers. "It's horrible."

Silence descends. Part of me itches to comfort him, but I don't know how to without it sounding like insincere pity.

"I guess that means Marie is a Tamer," I say, nodding to a mouse scampering from her cell towards the door, moving with a sort of purpose.

Aran nods. "Yep. Been trying to contact someone called Monty. Shockingly, she's received nothing."

From across the aisle, she shoots him a glare. She rises to her full height, which granted isn't much, but the belligerence in her sharp eyes makes her taller. Maroon and blue crisscross in intricate swirling patterns on her grimy billowing pants, not unlike the scarlet and black of Aran's. Considering that and the equally vibrant shawl wrapped around her brown linen shirt, my guess is she's from the Savach desert.

Marie grips the bars of her cell and sneers at Aran. "Just because you've decided to let your fear torture you doesn't mean I'm hopeless."

Her voice is smooth, velvety, resonant, and yet strangely high. Between the similarity of their voices and clothes and the not-so-subtle animosity between them, I figure they've been acquainted long before the hell of these cells.

Aran scoffs. "I'm not afraid."

"Really? Because when they came for you what did you do? You ran. Instead of fighting," Marie said, overflowing with disdain.

"Yeah, and look where that got you. I certainly evaded capture longer than you did."

Her bright blue eyes freeze over like ice, and I turn away from her cutting glare. "You're a coward."

"No, I'm a mechanical engineer." Aran brushes his finger across a golden bar piercing lanced through his right ear. It's shaped like an arrow, the head protruding from one end of his ear and the fletching out the back. Schemes flash behind his eyes, but whatever he's contemplating he seems to decide against it and lowers his hand.

Both hurl insults at each other in Ucano, the pidgin language of the Savach desert. Before they can keep up with their swelling argument, the horribly familiar jangling of keys on the other side of the door interrupts them. Marie clamps her mouth shut and drops to the floor. An uncomfortable hush falls over the room.

"When they take you," Aran hisses, "don't work too hard or they'll see your skill and make you do things you'll regret. But if you wanna avoid lashings don't make it shoddy."

A lump rises in my throat. *When not if.* "So what am I supposed to do?"

"Small gray area."

The door swings open. I tense. Beneath my breath I mutter a prayer, hoping the gods are still listening. Unfortunately, my woes fall upon deaf ears. Thick black boots halt in front of my cell. Panic writhes in my lungs, stealing my breath. I squeeze my eyes shut. Though it's horrible, cowardly, I hope they take Aran.

Rough hands clamp around my wounded shoulder and yank me to my feet. I lock eyes with Aran, begging for help. He holds my gaze, shifts forward ever so slightly, but freezes.

Heart racing, I flinch at the captain's nails digging into my shoulder. When he whispers in my ear, it's raspy, hot, makes my skin crawl.

"Time to see what you're made of mutt."

Navda shoves me forward. When we pass the threshold of the xipher door, my magic shifts with unease, hums with revulsion. I try to keep from collapsing into hysterics as I take the stairs up two at a time. On the deck, all the crew turn their eyes to me. Sneers curl on their lips. I brace myself for the cruelty to come.

Insults and mockery ring in my ears as I'm forced to the middle of the deck. But as I muster courage, glare out at them defiantly, I see trepidation in their mirthless smiles. Even as they scorn me, they lack the sincerity.

Voices stab at my mind as I pass through the crowd. Most of them are desperate pleas. Pity for me. Rage. Fear. Some are muttering; some are screaming. Every pair of eyes I meet, a new voice joins the fray. My breaths quicken. I slam my hands over my ears. The chorus refuses to be shut out. Gods, what is happening to me?

Navda kicks me in the back, and I spill to the floor, knocking over a bucket of dirty water. It soaks the sleeves of my shirt. I scramble to turn it upright, before more water is lost. A mop clatters beside me. So I get to swab the deck. At least the voices are gone. But a splitting headache lingers.

Aran's warning reverberates in my mind as I hesitantly pick

up the mop. I rise to my feet, but again Navda strikes me down. Dull pain aches in my ribs. Groaning, I blink away a few tears.

"Pff," Navda guffaws, planting a boot on my cheek. "Perhaps the most pathetic sully-blood to board the ship. Fight back."

I roll out from under his foot and scramble backwards. Teary eyed, I stare up at him, silently begging for mercy. Though from the lack of anything remotely human in his lifeless eyes, I doubt he's got the capacity to grant such a thing. As I hold his gaze, my blood runs cold. Everything numbs. Malicious whispers drown out everything else in my mind. Trapped beneath that shroud of malevolence is a sob, solitary and choking. Mournful beyond anything I've ever known.

Navda raises his foot to kick me again.

"Stop!" The word rolls off my tongue with a strange, almost sentient force.

He obeys. Eyebrows drawing together, he tilts his head as if considering why his limbs refuse to respond. In an instant, he scowls and bares his teeth. My eyes widen. Had I...*made* him stop? Armed with a bout of courage and an inexplicable consciousness to my words, I rise my feet, not once breaking eye contact with the captain.

"Get away from me," I say, the words thick in my mouth, enchanting. Even as my voice rings with power, energy saps from my body. My magic swells, a cool, tranquil strength encompassing my mind. Is this how Raven always feels? No wonder she's spent all that time harnessing her magic.

Nostrils flaring, Navda slowly puts his foot down and takes a step back. Whispers echo around me as the crew watches. Some are astounded, others alarmed, but most cheer me on. I glance at Ean to find him smirking.

"Sit down," I order, pulsating with power. Brimming with bravery, a series of commands pass my lips. Navda sits down, he puts his hands together, he orders one of his crewmates to tie his wrists. If I can keep this up, I can get everyone free. That's all I can think about. Freedom.

Thunder cracks in the distance. For a brief moment, I tear my eyes away from Navda to the darkening sky. Clouds steadily approach, blotting out the sun. As I watch them roll across the sky, my nerve slips away. Terror creeps back in. When I open my mouth, my voice is trembling and void of magic. Deep in my core, coldness spreads, like I've used up my reserve of magic. My knees buckle.

Navda rises to his feet, shoving away the reluctant crew mate who had approached him with a coil of rope. When he steps towards me, my heart practically beats out of my chest. I try to concentrate on that surge of power I'd had a moment ago, but I can't reach anything. Maybe it's my fear getting in the way. Maybe it was a one-time shot.

"You insolent, wretched sully-blood!" Navda roars, spittle flying.

I wipe it from my cheek with shaking hands. He slaps me so hard across the face I spin and sprawl to the deck. Stinging rages across my skin. Another onslaught of tears threatens to fall.

"Thought because you're a Psychic you can try that shit with me? I ain't gonna be beaten by the likes of you."

I make a break for the side of the ship. Whatever is beneath the waves is dangerous, but I'd rather face them than Navda's wrath. Before I can leap over the edge, arms wrap around me.

"No!" I cry, gripping the rail, fighting to no avail.

The crewmate throws me across the deck. Another picks me up and latches my arms around the main mast. Rope coils around my wrists so tight it burns.

"No," I breathe, hysteria clouding my mind. "No no no no!"

Navda rips open the back of my shirt with a dagger. "Maybe this'll help teach you a lesson. But I hafta say, I really hope it don't. The stronger the spirit, the harder it is to break. And when it finally does...that victory has the sweetest taste."

I squeeze my eyes shut. My throat is tight and voice barely audible when I reply, "I have no strength." The truth of the words crushes me.

There's a tense moment of silence that lasts forever. I wait with bated breath for what comes next, but nothing could have prepared me for the pain I endure. A whip cracks on my back. Searing pain erupts. Over and over, it snaps. Screams tear from my throat until it's so raw it goes numb. Blood coats my back, hot and sticky, dripping to the deck in pools of crimson and black.

I can't tell when it has stopped. Sweat and tears mingle on my face. The lashes across my skin still throb with indescribable agony. Ean unties my wrists. I slump to the ground. My vision blurs and weariness weighs me down. I'm thankful for the swooping exhaustion; I can barely even acknowledge my pain.

Ean's clouded face hovers above mine for a split second. I'm certain I'm hallucinating when he smiles and puts a finger to his lips, but something about it convinces me it's real.

Navda crouches beside me, taking Ean's place. "You may lack strength in spirit, but not in magic. I'm *very* excited to have a Psychic on my leash."

Feebly, I shake my head. This can't be real.

My head spins when Navda yanks me to my feet. One more strangled cry escapes my lips before I succumb to the darkness.

11

Tezin

I wish for the painless void of unconsciousness. Dull pain aches in my back with every shift of my body as I strain to sit up. Nausea overwhelms me. I clutch at my stomach and close my eyes until it passes.

A shawl slides off my shoulders. I catch it before it hits the ground. It's soft, finely woven material. Intricate shapes are stitched against the black background with scarlet thread, clearly detailing a story I cannot understand. Even so, I'm mesmerized by its beauty. I trace a peculiar circle crowned with squares.

"It's a cog," Aran says, startling me. "I got that sewn on when I got an apprenticeship with the best mechanic in Ucann."

"This tells your whole life story, right?" I ask, turning to him. "Isn't it like the most important thing in your culture? Why would you give it to me?"

"You were shivering. What would you have done?"

"Let you shiver," Marie mutters.

Aran rolls his eyes. "No one's talking to you. Tezin, what did you do up there? I told you not to make it shoddy work. No one's been whipped as bad as you. Nor gained such favor from the quartermaster."

I bite my lip to stop it from trembling. "Well I discovered my connection. Took it a little too far."

"Wait, you *just* discovered your connection?" Aran asks, astounded. "You don't look like you're thirteen."

"Look, I...I don't know how to explain it. My sister is a Nightblood. One day she gets kidnapped by pirates, and the next Navda arrives looking for those pirates, kills my mama, and I discover I have magic in my blood."

There's a bout of silence. Heat rises in my cheeks. I choke out an apology over the lump in my throat.

"Hell of an origin story," Aran says, cracking a smile. I furrow my eyebrows. I know he's trying to make me feel better, but it doesn't work. "No wonder you've gained such favor with the quartermaster. He came down here to allay your lashings with some salve. Never done that for anyone before."

I picture Ean's face in my mind, his consistent infatuation with whatever I do. Maybe I can use that to help us get out.

Aran must see the optimism in my face because he sighs. "Hey, look, I'm not going to give you false hope. Getting out of here, it's probably not in the foreseeable future even if you've curried Ean's favor. But I'm willing to try to help you get back to your sister. I'd give anything to see mine again."

"You have a sister?"

"Well if you shared your traumatic backstory, I guess I'm

obligated to share mine. I had three. They all died or went missing."

"Not all of them," Marie fumes.

Aran shoots her a glare. "You're not my sister."

She scoffs. "Only in a kind timeline."

Once again, she dissolves into Ucano mutterings. Aran turns his attention back to me, though it seems more to spite her than actual interest in my presence. I hand him his shawl, opting for silence rather than curious questions about their familial feud.

"No, you keep it. It's not much but it might protect you from infection seeing as you don't have much of a shirt left." Aran wraps the shawl around my shoulders.

I stare wide-eyed at him. "You'd really trust a stranger with your shawl?"

He shrugs. "We were strangers, but it's hard to remain so down here."

Despite the dire situation, the unlikelihood that I'll ever escape, I smile softly. At the very least, I'm not alone. I'll never be alone.

I open my mouth to thank him, but he interrupts me before I can get a word in. "Don't say anything. That was about as sappy as I'm gonna get. Just...I'll have your back, alright?"

Marie snorts. "Yeah, I wouldn't hold him to that."

"Will you shut up?" Aran snaps, clenching his hands into fists. Around us the air warms. Dusts swirls at my feet. "Gods. You've always been so entitled, throwing temper tantrums by running away, trying to find the Lost Cities."

"They were not temper tantrums!" Marie spits. "I was trying to help people. Share knowledge, our knowledge!"

Aran scoffs. "You mean my knowledge."

They're both on their feet now. Wind ruffles my hair, blows across my face. At first, it's a comforting breeze, but it grows wilder by the second. A sheen of sweat glistens on Aran's face.

"I have a cog on my shawl too, Aran!" Marie shouts. "I am just as good a mechanic!"

Aran laughs dryly. "Please. Mother just called in a few favors, so you'd be out of her hair and under control. You didn't create the best streamlined irrigation system in Oncarii. I did that. I passed the apprenticeship. I got the mark!" He aggressively gestures to the swirling tattoo on his face. "Not you!"

Wind is whistling now. I stagger to my feet, bracing myself on the bars against the force of the gusts. Neither of them seem to notice, but everyone else does. I'm not sure if it's fear or hope but there is finally a spark of *something* in the eyes of the surrounding maji. Aran's fury is practically overriding the unbearable aura of the xipher door. Even I feel more powerful.

Getting out of here might not be so impossible after all.

I can barely hear the two shouting over the roar of the wind. Wood creaks and bars rattle. He's going to tear the ship apart.

"Hey!" I shout, praying my voice isn't lost in the wind. "Hey, stop!"

The ship begins to tilt. Pounding thumps on the other side of the door. I can't make out what the pirate is saying but I don't care. One problem at a time.

Steadying myself, I take in everyone's sheer terror and relish in the confidence pulsing through me once again. Power overtakes me, becomes me, fills my every nerve. Holding onto that feeling, I grab Aran's arm and spin him around to face me. We lock eyes. Mustering every ounce of power tingling across my skin, I throw it into my words.

"Stop."

Immediately the wind hushes. The ship rights itself. Even the man pounding on the door halts. Complete, utter silence falls.

Aran collapses in my arms. Sweat plasters his hair to his forehead. His breathing is shallow and his limbs shaking. Gently, I lay him on the floor. As the power evanesces, panic takes root. He's burnt himself out, the fool.

After an interminable moment of quiet, Marie pipes up, her voice soft, "Is…is he okay?"

I put a hand on his forehead, finding his skin practically burning to the touch. I don't understand much of Psychic magic, but I'm hoping I can sense his mind. Letting my magic take the reins, I reach out to him. Whispers echo in my mind. Faint, indiscernible, but there.

"He's in pain and his mind is subdued but I think he'll be alright. If he hasn't burnt out his core."

Marie sinks to the floor. Relief flashes across her face for a moment before melting to the familiar stone-cold expression she's so fond of. "He's such a drama queen."

"He almost died because you two can't talk without fighting!" I snap. "My sister and I have never been like that. Frankly, I don't care what happened, but I don't want either of you getting hurt. So stop it."

She purses her lips and turns away from me.

The door flings open. Navda storms in, his footsteps nearly cracking the floor. Ean follows close behind, expression schooled into neutrality. No one cowers. Instead, they all turn their intrigued gazes towards my cell, awaiting for something to unfold. My impromptu death, perhaps.

The captain halts in front of my cell, eyes like burning coals. Instinctively, I shelter Aran from his view. I force myself to wear a cool exterior, despite the roiling terror. For once I will swallow my fear. I will not be bullied into submission.

"What the hell did he do?" Navda growls.

I rise to my feet. Crossing my arms grants me a faux sense of confidence. "Nothing. I made him do it. I wanted to test my power. Turns out I can make anyone do my bidding."

Navda narrows his eyes. I hold his stare, but after a moment begin to waver.

"You're lying."

My heart stops, breaking the dam on my fear. I glance at Ean, finding little comfort in his gaze. "N-no."

"You're making attachments. Good," Navda muses, the triumph in his voice sending my stomach somersaulting. "He does that again, I'm going to kill him and the girl. You step out of line, same thing. I'll be needing your services when we reach Tashul. Refuse, they die."

With that, he turns on his heel and strides out the door. Ean lingers. I try not to cry in front of him, but the onslaught of tears is getting harder to hold back. The stone blocking the emotion from his eyes falls away. His thoughts whisper in my ears with a cool, scratchy voice, one more prominent than most.

Don't give up.

He presses his hand to the bars, then follows his captain out the door.

Shakily, I slide to the ground, vision blurring.

12

Raven

Strange. Rest has never been so rejuvenating. Worries don't weigh me down. Even the air drifts lazily, like it too has had a burden lifted. I yawn and stretch my stiff limbs. It takes me a long time to shake the sleep from my mind and check back into reality. When I take in my surroundings, everything from the day before rushes back. I clutch at my head, groaning through the dull ache.

It passes and I'm left astounded. Yesterday, I stopped time. I can hardly believe it. Seers in the old ages could perform such feats, when maji were revered and their powers meticulously tuned. But me? I never would have imagined.

Then again, I thought the same of astral projection. What the hell did Rélia do to me?

Gods, the way it felt though. Power flowing through me like it *was* me. Breathing the stillness of the world like breathing peace itself. I'd never felt so amazing, so important, so far from the worthless sully-blood everyone in the kingdom sees me as. I almost killed Rélia.

But she's a Healer.

Alight with fury, I kick the bars, shake them, punch them. I scream. None of it helps. There's nothing I can do to save myself. Stopping time again is out of the question; I haven't got the energy reserve for such a feat. Rélia won't give me an opportunity to escape. I can't save myself.

Footsteps pull me from my simmering rage. I clench my jaw as Rélia comes into view. I narrow my eyes. She's completely healed. Not even a limp. Avoiding eye contact with me, she unlocks the cell.

"I'm sorry about this," she says as she unclips a pair of manacles from her belt. And not just any manacles—I recognize the sinister glint of odrite metal. Not poisonous like xipher wood, but it'll beat back my magic and give me hell if I try to use it.

I glare at her, painfully aware of my magic pulsing in my hands. They're glowing gold again. Heat scalds my veins. The more I feed into my anger, the stronger it grows. Rélia's eyes widen and immediately she grabs hold of my hand. Her nose twitches, the only sign she senses the twin spark in her magic that lights in mine.

Cold cuffs clamp on my wrists. The spark dies and with it all sense of magic. My core is nauseatingly empty. It's like all my magic froze. I gasp at the unfamiliar sensation.

"So now you're going to chain me like an animal?" I spit as she forces me out of the cell. "You're despicable."

She sighs. "Yeah, yeah. I've heard it all before. I'm sorry. I truly am."

"You're full of shit."

"You'll never understand why I have to do this."

She puts her hand on my shoulder to guide me up the stairs. I elbow her in the ribs. "Right. Because it only takes a monster to know one."

Rélia scoffs. "Believe your prejudice. Not worth the argument."

I open my mouth, ready to push her more, but my words die on my lips when we step onto the deck. I've never been outside Ghzen or Borziau which makes Tashul—the port city favoring slavers in the name of "serving the king"—all the more terrifying.

Mountains loom in the distance, dark points piercing the gray sky. Towers rise out of the rocky terrain, crafted from ghostly white stone shot through with tendrils of red. Hyenas, the sacred animal the royals stole from my kind and twisted into a symbol of malice, are stamped on every building. As if anyone couldn't already tell from the excess of guards and lackluster aura that this port belongs to the king.

Beside me, Rélia tenses. Muscles shudder in her jaw, and her nose twitches ever so slightly. Her eyes are clouded with apprehension. I hope her fear consumes her.

Penn begrudgingly readies us a rowboat, a sour expression puckering his lips. Rélia gives him a pleading look, one that's deep with concern and icy with command. Extending her hand insistently, he sighs and clasps her forearm.

"Onwards and forwards," he mutters.

She nods, a small smile quirking the corners of her mouth. "Forever free."

Slowly, they release their grip, and the boat launches into the water. I try to enjoy my time here on the open water before I walk into hell, but Tashul looms before us like a sick gray cloud. I consider the fact that being alone with Rélia will make it easier to escape, but as soon as my feet touch the cobblestone street, I shudder with despair. Escape will have to wait. For a long time.

"Everything is so lifeless here," Rélia says, walking so close to me that the heat emanating from her is like an incorporeal hug. It's comforting, relieving. All Healers have a sort of nurturing warmth about them. From anyone else I'd relish in it.

Slave traders shuffle past us, leading their maltreated maji towards the Penitentiary. Shackled in rows, they lumber through the streets, heads down. Slavers bark at them. They obey without hesitation. One boy falls, crying with exhaustion. He's stepped on. Left alone. Kicked, trampled.

Bitterness fills my mouth. "Because there isn't any hope. That's what these people do. They carve away at your mind, your soul, everything. Until you're a hopeless nothing willing to do anything just for the empty promise of death."

Rélia falters. I raise an eyebrow in contempt as she says, "That's..."

"Oh drop the act. You knew exactly what you were leading me into."

"I was going to say that was poetic," Rélia snaps, shoving me forwards. "And it's not an act."

I snort. "Right."

She doesn't respond. Part of me is disappointed. I can't run, I can't fight the marshal army prowling this whole city. But I can battle with my words and wit. She won't even permit me that.

We stop in front of a check-in stall, a rickety brown sign carved with the letters *REGISTRY* hanging above it. It's not so different from the banking post in Borziau, save for the imposing iron bars preventing entry. And escape guards stand on either side, guns in hand, swords at their belts. Both Rélia and I tense, but she's better at hiding her apprehension. I'd find that shocking, considering the magic in her veins, but it's a pirate's job to lie, I suppose.

The guard sitting in the stall narrows his eyes. At first, I think his suspicion is directed at me, but Rélia holds his stare with a belligerent glower. She rolls her shoulders back and straightens her spine.

"Name?" The guard says.

"Rélia Ryan," she replies, her voice cool, collected, commanding. Regal, almost. Like she's commanding a battalion. "I need to meet with Admiral Girardin Talley. Immediately."

The guard snorts. "We don't take requests. Entrance two will take the..." His eyes trail up and down my body, sending shivers of disgust curdling through me. "They'll take that off your hands. For a good price."

"She. Not that," Rélia growls. "If you feel you must escort us, fine. But I have to see Admiral Talley and no one else."

The surrounding guards raise the barrels of their guns ever so slightly. A warning. Uneasiness sets in my stomach, sitting there like a nauseating rock.

"Your lackeys don't scare me. Get me to Admiral Talley. He'll want to see me." Rélia reaches into her pocket and slams something on his desk. It's a gold band, thin, etched with the symbol of a hyena adorned with rose vines. The royal crest. Why would she have a signet ring with the royal crest?

His eyes grow so big they could be used as dessert saucers. "Yes, he certainly will. I'm sure you know where to go."

"Yes," Rélia says, voice dripping with disdain. "I do."

The guards step aside and open the gate. I resist Rélia's pull, but only for a moment. Guns already send my nerves rocketing sky-high so when the guard to my right aims his weapon at me, I drop all urges to fight.

"Why do you carry the royal crest with you?" I ask, not caring to keep my voice low. Whatever secrets she's hiding aren't my problem. Maybe they'll get her locked up beside me. *That's* what would be poetic.

She keeps quiet, but her pace quickens. I yank my arm free, whirling on her. "Answer me!"

Rélia's eyes burn with challenge. "I lifted it off a royal. Comes in handy."

Her voice is too clipped for that to be the truth. Grabbing her wrist with ferocity, I raise my voice. "Bullshit. Who are you?"

A few guards swivel their heads in our direction. I take pride in the panic that flashes across her face.

"Keep it down," she hisses. "Or we'll both end up in a worse position."

I scoff, incredulous. "Are you kidding me? *Worse position?* You might as well be walking me straight into Luara's realm."

Rélia clamps her hand down on my shoulder and steers me under a stone arch adorned with menacing rust-red spikes. "Yes.

This is gonna be hell for you. But I guarantee it's nowhere near the land of tortured souls."

"Speaking as if you've been."

Her nails dig into my skin. I wince. Some darker story lingers behind that tension in her fingers. Maybe there is a real reason why we're connected, why I keep getting visions of her. Before her, I always trusted the gods, even if they're fading. Should I still have faith? After all this?

"You know that day you were hung?" I say, keeping my gaze trained forwards, as I march towards my impending doom. "I only saved you because I had a vision of your death that tortured me for months. *Months.* I was convinced the gods had some grand purpose for saving you."

"And now?" Rélia asks, a slight tremor in her voice as if she doesn't really want to hear the answer. "You would doubt your gods?"

I've never been surer about doubt in my life. Sharpening my gaze, I spit, "Yes."

We stop in front of a polished oak door without a line of maji to be sold off. This is where my freedom truly comes to an end.

"Well, then, maybe you should've killed me when you had the chance." She pulls the door open to darkness.

I shake my head. "No. I should've let you hang."

She turns to me. In the dim glimmer of the sconces on the wall, I catch a flicker of hurt in her eyes.

"This is where we will part ways. I know you won't believe me," Rélia whispers as heavy footsteps march down the hall, "but I hope you find your way back to freedom. Soon."

The sincerity in her voice strikes me like a knife to the heart.

A well-built young man rounds the corner. Keys jangle on a ring looped through his belt, almost hidden by his elegant mauve overcoat. His light brown hair is cut short at his ears. When his gaze falls upon us, his dark blue eyes twinkle with a sadistic sort of delight. I steel myself against his roaming glances. I refuse to be intimidated. Rélia has a harder time maintaining her composure.

"Ah, Miss Ryan," Talley says with the long, rough drawl of the capital. "I was wondering when you'd come out of hiding."

Rélia snarls. "*Captain* Ryan. And I wasn't hiding. I was biding my time. That's over now. I got what you asked for. Now you're going to give me my freedom."

Talley strolls towards us, hands clasped behind his back. Though he evaluates us both, he's clearly more transfixed on her than me. "Always so sure. If I believe this woman you've brought me is enough, I'll lift the kill order."

Kill order? I guess that explains the general trying to hang her. But what has she done to incur the wrath of all the higher-ups in the royal army? I mean she gets on my nerves, sure. Is that all it takes to get a *kill order*?

Rélia glares at him. "And I'll owe you nothing. I haven't in years."

His regal stance wavers. A frown ticks at his lips. "What is she?"

"Seer. A really powerful one."

Talley clucks his tongue not once averting his gaze. "Interesting. You've seen it first hand?"

A beat of silence hangs heavy over the dark room. All I can hear is the erratic pounding of my heart in tune with Rélia's. I'm not Psychic, but I swear I can hear her thoughts. Or one, rather. Loud and clear.

She stopped time. She stopped time. She stopped time.

Barely audible, I whisper, "Don't."

"She stopped time." She says it all in one breath, rushed, as if she'd been holding it in, unsure of whether to let it out.

My heart stops and takes with it my nerve. I won't be lucky enough to do petty grueling work for lowlife slavers. No, I'm going straight to Qada to serve the king and his army. I'll be a weapon in a war against my kind. Escape won't ever be an option.

Oh gods. Escape *won't* be an option.

"Well," Talley appraises. "That is quite what I was looking for. For once, you've managed to do well. Hand her over, and you'll get your freedom and your price. I'll even top it off with an extra four hundred pieces."

"How generous," Rélia says. Though her words have a bite, her voice is defeated, awash with guilty relief.

He puts a hand on her face. There's a genuine tenderness behind the gesture, which he clearly doesn't care to hide. Although the revulsion in Rélia's face leads me to believe it's one sided. Talley leans into her, whispers something in her ear, and drops a bulging leather pouch in her pocket.

"Alright sweetheart," Talley says, turning to me. "Time to go."

Cold, calloused hands clamp down on my arm. He yanks me away from Rélia. Strange how I miss being near her. As loathe I am to admit it, I prefer her presence to serving this man and his king. Even my magic, though suppressed, reaches for her.

Rélia's lips are pursed. One hand she keeps steady on the

pouch, the other clenched in a fist at her side. Our gazes cross and for a moment I think I've stopped time again. It's just her and me in a still world.

But then she turns away. I fight against Talley's hold on me.

"Rélia please!" I shout, detesting the pleading in my voice. Will I always remain like this? Constantly begging for help?

She stops, stiffens. But she doesn't turn around.

"You said you were different!" I scream, wanting nothing more than to make her hurt, to make her suffer an inkling of the berating and mockery that will torture me for the rest of my life. "I am called sully-blood, but it's really you who is a stain on Oncarii! I don't know why the gods brought me to you! You're worthless."

Rélia raises a hand to her face, lingering for a moment. And then she's gone. It takes everything in me not to break down in tears.

13

Rélia

You can run from everything, but I will always be here, waiting for you. Never forget you and I will change the world.

Talley's words echo in my mind. Mingling with Raven's insults, my spirit weeps, begging to shatter. Taking deep breaths, I steel myself against the voices taunting me in my mind. I've been through too much to let today hinder me. Talley thinks he can control me. Always has. *We will change the world.* A bullshit mantra he repeated to me when we were naïve kids.

Like that'll happen. When I get my way, he'll burn in every hell in turn for the rest of time. It's the least he deserves after his betrayal.

That's in the past. Selling Raven off is in the past. Finally, *finally*, I can look forward. I turn the leather pouch between my fingers. We'll be safe. Free. Happy. It's been long, too long, since

I've been this close to everything I've wanted. If I can just get off this damn port, everything will be fine.

As I near the pier, a rat scampers across my feet. Without another thought, I watch it run. But a few steps later, it returns and sits on its haunches in front of me. I furrow my eyebrows, matching its stare. Why does it look so familiar?

"Pidge?" I ask. The rat blinks. I roll my eyes. "Gods. I'm talking to a rat who followed me off my ship. I sound insane."

"Sure do," a voice rings out behind me.

I startle. Turning, I find myself face to face with a grinning Penn. "Flaming hells. You scared the shit out of me. I told you to stay on the ship."

He shrugs. "Eh, forgive my worry, Cap'n. I know who ya are. Figure you'll do somethin' stupid."

My foot taps a quick rhythm. Shoving the pouch in his face, I snap, "What, something like this? Shove a fork up your ass. I did everything fine. And you'll do well not to talk back to me, got it?"

Penn frowns. "Cap'n, ya doin' alright?"

"I'm fine!" I shout, drawing a few glances. I lower my voice and grab his elbow. "We're going back to the ship."

He digs his heels into the ground. "Nah, we're not."

I jut my chin out and cross my arms. "Come again?"

Penn puts his hands on my shoulders and gives me a friendly squeeze. "Cap'n, I've known ya for years. I know ya wanna get the navy off our tail. But I also know ya don' get like this often. Ya care about Raven. Yer not gonna leave her in there."

My stony exterior slips. A lump rises in my throat. I swallow it back. I refuse to cry about this. I barely know the girl. "I have to, Penn. One sacrifice. And we can be free."

I barely finish my sentence before I find myself surrounded by a cluster of white rats, Pidge leading the charge. My eyes widen as they collectively take a step towards me.

"I don't think the gods are gonna let ya leave her."

I cross my arms. "Please, white rats are just messengers."

I shift my weight between my feet as the rats stare, unrelenting as if chipping down all my mental defenses. Penn nudges me. I throw up my hands, and the rats scamper away.

"Fine! Gods be damned." I sigh and rub my temples. "Yes, okay, you're right. I don't want to leave Raven in there with Talley of all people. But what am I supposed to do? It's not like I can just—"

Oh. Wait. Yes, I can.

"I see a plan tickin' in yer eyes," Penn says with a mischievous grin.

I pull out the gold ring and dance it over my fingers. The cool metal has a resolve to it. Never comforting, but I carry it like it is anyway. Someday, maybe it will be. Eons down the road. "Penn, I think it's time for my past to come out and play."

I flash him a smirk and slip the ring over my middle finger. Pulling my hair tight, stripping my coat and jerkin, I can only pray I'm presentable enough for this to work. Gears turn in my mind, fitting puzzle pieces together with every step I take. I haven't been this reckless in a while, but gods it feels good. Adrenaline courses through my veins, mingling with a regal confidence I was taught to command in childhood. I haven't pulled out these skills since the day I fled my home. I hated it then.

I hate it now. But it might just save a life. Someone the gods clearly care about.

I curl my hands into fists to steady their shaking, burying my anger. I can be bitter later. For now, I feed that resentment into my assertive expression, square my shoulders, hold my head high, and stride towards the Penitentiary. Sneaking back into Talley's quarters will be too suspicious. But if I pose as a buyer, and a filthy rich one at that, I might have a chance.

"Er, Cap'n?" Penn implores. "What's the plan?"

I crack my knuckles. "I'm going to command my way in."

"Ya, that's not really a plan."

"Whatever. We're winging it."

Penn protests, "But—"

I turn over my shoulder and roll my eyes at him. "Too late now. Follow my lead."

I strut up to the main cast iron gate entrance, far from the convenient slaver registry posts, Penn close in tow. Two prison guards glower at me from their stations on either side of the gate. I move to pass through, but the one on the right stops me, gun drawn.

"Put that away," I order, my voice cold and commanding. A part of me that I shoved deep down inside stirs, taking me back to Qada, to my life before I found purpose. As much as I hate to, I channel every horrible memory, every awful lesson, every tragic waking moment of my life within those stone walls. "I'm here to have a word with the Admiral. A lucrative proposition."

"Credentials," the guard orders. "Need to see 'em or we're going to have a problem."

I glare at him, putting as much cold ire into my gaze as I can.

"You want credentials? Here." I shove my ring in his face. "Let me pass or I'll contact my father and have you both beheaded."

For a terrible, silent, eerily still moment, I think perhaps my sister's looks have strayed far from my own by now, or it's gotten out that I'm a runaway and not a studious shut-in. But with a panicked exhale, he withers under my gaze, melts like putty at my ring.

"Yes, of course Highness. No offense intended."

I take a step forward, Penn close behind, but the guard makes a sound in protest. "Er, you can pass of course, but your—"

I whirl on him, keeping my voice cool and steady but dripping with poison. Gods. Is this what I would have become? "My attendant?" I can practically feel Penn rolling his eyes at me. He should count himself lucky I only had him carry my jacket. "He's to be with me at all times. Defy me again and I will not contact my father. I will run you straight through where you stand."

Hesitantly, he nods. "Of course."

Narrowing my eyes, I let Penn pass in front of me, following only when he's been cleared. Fear radiates from the guards as they return to their stations. Good to know the Nazario title will always come in handy.

Darkness descends when we enter the Penitentiary, only a few dim sconces to guide the way. Our footsteps reverberate through the halls, seemingly the only sound in existence. Unease falls over me. I shake it from my mind. One misstep and both Penn and I will end up behind bars. Well, he will. I won't be so lucky.

"You feelin' alright, Cap'n?"

I nod, pushing through my nausea. "Fine. I'm fine."

He purses his lips and doesn't press, though I'm sure he doesn't believe me.

"Got a plan now?" Penn asks, avoiding eye contact with the sullen prisoners and raucous slavers.

One of the patrolling guards shoots us a suspicious glance but I return it with a stony glare. I keep my voice low. "Well by now, Talley will be in his private quarters, doing gods know what with Raven. He runs this place so his private quarters are well protected from people like us and families with vendettas. Not that they'd get that far anyway. Point is, it's on the other side of the Penitentiary. For now, we blend in fine. Once we near that territory, it's gonna look real suspicious."

"So we gotta be smart about this."

I shrug. "Or, I abuse my power until these pricks figure out what I'm doing, wing it, save Raven, and run like hell."

"Sure, seems sound."

I flash him a smirk as we round a corner to yet another hall of cells, though many of these remain empty. Getting closer. "Whoever got anywhere by being sound?"

"Ya make a good point, Cap'n," Penn replies.

"I always do."

Another turn, and we finally make some good progress. A staircase spirals up into darkness. I race up the steps. Anxiety gnaws at my mind; we're close and our encounters with guards remain scarce. Some would say something's not right, but perhaps the gods are doing me a favor. Making my job easier.

Panting, I halt at the top. A heavy wooden door stands tall, locked tight. Behind it lie Talley's extensive quarters. Only problem: revulsion thrums in my veins at the aura the door gives off. Xipher. I should have expected as much.

I take a deep breath and step towards it, but Penn grabs my shoulder. "Cap'n. Ya know that door'll hurt ya."

"Please. Nothing I can't handle. I'm not your everyday Nightblood, remember?" I chuckle. It's dry and halfhearted. Gods this is going to suck.

Ignoring my instincts screaming at me to run from the wood, I press my hands to it. Searing pain shoots across my palms. My hands begin to steam. Gritting my teeth, I bear the agony and instead focus on the comfort of my magic. Around my hands, the wood begins to rot. Biting back a scream, I beckon my magic. A surge rushes to my fingers. Within seconds, the entire door crumbles.

I blink away tears, cradling my hands. They're red and blistering but not split open. Already, they're beginning to heal. Thank the gods. I'm not ready to deal with xipher poisoning. I have enough problems as it is.

Motioning for Penn to follow, I cross over the threshold of the rubble. Here, the floors are carpeted, the lighting softer but brighter. Almost welcoming. As if that isn't unnerving enough, the deafening silence sends shivers down my spine. I can hear my blood pumping and our soft footsteps, but nothing else.

"Er, Cap'n?" Penn whispers. "Doesn't it bother ya that there aren't any guards?"

It does. But that will only deepen his worry lines. "One problem at a time."

We halt in front of a heavy ornate door at the end of the hall. Gold lines the frame and makes up the unnecessarily large ring handles. Talley always was one to flaunt his wealth. He's really settled into his own surrounded by nobles of distasteful caliber. Expecting it to be locked, I pull on one of the handles, testing the door. Strangely, it glides open.

"It's not locked."

"Yes, thank you Penn," I hiss, fighting back my rising terror. Gods this is a monumentally bad idea. I guess that's my forte. And he knew I'd come. "Which means he's expecting me. Stay here. Just in case, okay?"

Knowing better than to dispute me, he nods, if a bit reluctantly. Alone, I tiptoe into Talley's lavish quarters. Centered in the main room is a round table covered with a silk cloth, atop which sits a plate of half-eaten food. Whether he abandoned it to take a piss or to tamper with sinful poisons in his laboratory, I'm not sure, but my luck seems to be holding out. For now.

Keeping my footsteps as quiet as I can, I prowl around the extent of his quarters until I finally come across a locked door tucked away in a nearly invisible nook. Sure, the padlock is made of odrite but that doesn't mean it can't be picked. I slip off my boot and dig in the inside fold where I'd sewn a pocket. Two delicate silver instruments fall into my palm. Sparing no hesitation, I pull my boot back on and make quick work of the lock.

After a minute of intense concentration, the lock falls into my hand. Cheering silently, I push the door open. Shadows spill over my feet. Kerosene lamps burn low in the chilly room lined with metal rings, a set of manacles dangling from each. Only one of them is actually filled. Dismay washes over me when I find that the prisoner isn't Raven, but instead a scrawny kid with olive skin and jet black hair leaning against the wall. His eyes seem to stare right through me.

"Oh, please not again. We just went through our daily give and take," he says, holding his hands in front of his face as if to shield from an attack.

I purse my lips. Time is slipping away from me, but I can't in good conscience leave him here. "Hey, kid, I'm not gonna hurt you," I say, kneeling in front of him. I glance over my shoulder, paranoid at every shift of the world. Talley is due to show up any moment now. "The name's Rélia. I'm gonna get you out of here. Okay? And then I have to find my...friend."

All he does is offer me his wrists. A symbol inked into his skin catches me off guard: two lines curving around each other, the bottom end stretching the length of his forearm. The mark of the rebels. An emblem Shaia Rydar adopted to represent "transformation." She always thought she was so clever. Bet she still does now that her insurgency is growing. You'd think the queen of the rebels would pick something more discreet to imprint upon her pledges.

"Are you going to help?" he asks.

I snap back to reality, setting to work on the cuffs. Thank the gods Talley never thinks to take proper care of his equipment, or the manacles wouldn't be so rusted I could practically pull them open.

With one hand free, the kid perks up. His pale almond eyes roll towards me, unfocused. "I'm Monty."

"Well Monty, what makes you so special that Talley keeps you locked up in here?"

Besides being an operative of the rebellion, anyway.

He shrugs. "I'm a Welder. I suppose we're hard to come by."

I suck in a surprised breath. "A Welder? Gods. No wonder."

I've met many maji in my time, but never one who could manipulate the earth itself.

Halfway through unlocking the other manacle on Monty's wrist, a scuffle in the adjacent room catches my attention. My stomach drops as a plethora of horrible scenarios flood my mind, each worse than the last. And all totally probable.

"Here," I say, pressing the lock picks into his free palm. "Finish it yourself."

Swallowing back my fear, I step towards the door, hand on the hilt of my dagger. Not quite the same as my sword but if you're not a registered guard they allow nothing bigger. I whip out my weapon as soon as I cross the threshold.

Near the entrance to the quarters, Penn is on his knees, two guards planting their hands on his shoulders, pinning him in place. Talley sits at the table, relaxing into his hands. Raven sits across from him, staring at her lap, her face blank.

"You took longer than I thought," Talley remarks.

I cross my arms. "Sorry to disappoint."

At the sound of my voice, Raven lifts her head. Our gazes cross. Magic floods my veins when I see the terror in her eyes. It takes everything in me not to surge towards her and kill Talley in the process. For once I have to think this through, or I'll lose. And I *never* lose.

Eyes flitting about, I sweep my surroundings, desperately trying to make a plan. Guards block the door. Some have their guns drawn, aimed at Penn. Windows might work if I'm okay with breaking both my ankles jumping out. There's nothing. No escape. Not unless I use my magic, but I'm sure Penn will have a bullet between his eyes if I try.

For the first time in a long time, I am completely, utterly powerless.

"You were right," Talley says. "This Seer girl is rather powerful. Having her could turn the tide against the rebels. King Macos could eradicate all of them. Ensure the extinction of magic."

"I'm aware."

Talley smiles. The warm familiarity of it sends tears pricking at my eyes. "Which is why you came back for her. You were always one to defy the king, make his rule difficult."

"Because he doesn't deserve the throne," I fume, trying to reign in my anger. It doesn't work. "And neither do you."

His face darkens. "Don't presume my intentions. Wouldn't want anything to happen to your friends would you?"

A baffled laugh escapes my lips, shrill and dry. "Always with the threats. You don't scare me, Talley. Surely you haven't forgotten who I am."

Silver light wisps around my curled fists, feeding on my growing rage. Trying to keep my magic under control is useless. Unease saturates the room. Some of the guards take cautious steps back, but another presses the barrel of his gun into Penn's temple.

Talley steps to me, close enough that the minty rank of his breath envelops my nose. He raises a hand, but I steel my gaze.

"I wouldn't touch me if I were you."

He freezes but doesn't drop his hand. My heart rattles against my ribcage as if desperate to get free. Bile creeps up my throat. Standing so close to him, I'm a terrified teenager again, trapped by his ruthlessness, disparaged by his duplicity. In the blink of an eye, my magic drops away, drowned out by fear, leaving me defenseless. Pity spreads across Talley's chiseled face. Lightly, he traces my cheek with his finger. Shivers of revulsion drown me.

He sighs. "I wish you wouldn't be so adverse. We were friends once. We can be again."

Rumbling rocks the room, shaking the candles on the table, showering us with dust. Fissures crawl over the ceiling. Beneath us, the building creaks in protest. The guards release Penn, nervously glancing around. Even Talley seems anxious.

I look over my shoulder. Monty stands in the doorway, raised hands encased by swirling emerald light. A joyous cry spills from my mouth.

"Hell yeah, kid!" I shout, reveling in the panic that spreads through the room. With Talley and the guards distracted by the growing chaos, I race to Raven. As soon as I touch her, she lurches to her feet, vigor blazing in her eyes in unison with the burst of energy in my heart. "I'm getting you out of here. Can you walk?"

She nods. Sluggishly, she takes a step. I catch her when she stumbles. I sling her arm over my shoulders and head for the exit. Talley and his soldiers are already gone, so we're more or less safe. Given the fact the roof doesn't collapse on us within the next minute.

When I'm almost to the door, I turn around to find Monty still standing in the room. "Hey, can't you see we're moving? Let's go!"

He turns in my direction. "That's the thing. I can't see. Pretty much blind. Please help."

Raven slumps against me. I turn to Penn. Without any words passing between us, he lifts Raven in his arms and ducks out of the room. I make my way to Monty and loop my arm through his.

"Great!" he says, gripping tight to my arm. "Now let's get out of here fast. This place is gonna come down."

Racing for the exit, I chuckle in disbelief. "How the hell do you manage such a thing?"

"Whole place is made of stone. Stone is a natural part of the earth. Hence I can communicate with it."

I tug him along, making sure not to lose hold as I shove my way through a crowd of panicked guards and slavers until we finally burst outside. Behind us, all of Talley's quarters crumble, taking with it a third of the Penitentiary.

I whistle. "Damn. I should've befriended a Welder sooner."

Monty grins. "Sure. If we're friends, mind if I grab some water?"

"Yeah kid. Water, bed, whatever you need."

He sways. "Great. Because I feel..."

Sighing, I heave him over my shoulders, heading towards the harbor. Maji really need to learn their limits.

14

Tezin

I trudge onto the docks of Tashul following Navda's footsteps. Shivering, I hold my arms against my body, missing the warmth of Aran's shawl. My thoughts wander to him and Marie, still trapped on the ship. They were the only two maji who didn't trade bars for fetters. Navda wants to control me and he's using them to do it. I bite my lip to keep it from trembling.

Even here, surrounded by the will-less, mindless lackeys of the king, Navda is feared. Guards shift uneasily as he passes. Slavers scurry, practically tripping over themselves to avoid crossing his path. Is even the king himself afraid of a violent pirate? It's not like they're scarce. No, there's something more to this tangible fear Navda radiates.

"Hey, mutt, no lagging," Navda barks over his shoulder. "Unless you prefer to see your friends mutilated."

I race to catch up, falling in stride beside Ean. I keep my gaze trained forwards, avoiding eye contact as much as possible. I don't need to hear what goes on in the minds of dutiful servants to a tyrant's rule.

The only guards that don't clear a path for him are those that stand on either side of the massive gate to the Penitentiary. Distaste sours their faces. They level their guns at Navda, but the apprehensive shift of their feet gives me little hope they'll follow through.

Navda barks a laugh. "I've a proposition for your Admiral. All of these in exchange for a meeting with a certain customer of his." He waves his hand at the seven maji chained in front of him.

The guards share a wary glance. The one on the left clears his throat. "Er, sorry. We can't let you through. Admiral Talley gave specific orders not to let you pass."

Navda shoves me forward. "I think I can persuade you otherwise."

I swallow, trying to steady my voice, shaking before I've even opened my mouth. Even under the threat of harming Aran and Marie, I can't push past my fear. Staring at the guards, I can hear their thoughts, hear how they're mocking me, how terrified they are of Navda. But for the life of me, I can't weave magic into my words. I'm like a floundering fish, my mouth opening and closing with nothing coming out.

Behind me, Navda growls in warning. I splutter, desperately trying to form words. Both guards aren't hiding their disdain anymore. Their thoughts show on their faces, in the laughter in their eyes. For the sake of my friends, I choke past my dismay and search for my magic. Faint tingling spreads across my body, but it fizzles away in seconds. Empty. Is my magic reserve empty? Is that even possible? Why won't my magic work? What's wrong with me?

In the corner of my eye, I see Ean take a step towards me, sympathy hidden beneath his professional exterior. I glimpse a spark of black between his fingers, nearly imperceptible.

The ground shakes. I stumble. Panic spreads like wildfire as the back half of the Penitentiary collapses in on itself, sending up a cloud of dust. Shouts fill the air. Guards and slavers alike trample over each other, desperate to reach safety.

Navda straightens, as if he's spotted something more intriguing than a falling building. He grabs the back of my shirt, dragging me along behind him. I glance over my shoulder. Confused hope sparks like wildfire around the fettered maji Navda has left behind. Ean gives me a brief nod, a twinkle of chaos in his eyes, before dropping a key on the ground. In the commotion, the maji take the chance to free themselves and run for it. At least some of them will find liberation. But what is so important that Navda is careless enough to leave his merchandise behind? For that matter, why would his quartermaster *help* them get away?

Wildly, I search the crowd for a sign of what's going on. Every pair of eyes I meet, curiosity and hysteria encompass my mind. It pulsates in the air around me, pumps in my veins, fills my lungs, becomes me. And I can't make it stop. Not until I lock eyes with someone familiar.

Her thoughts wash over me, drowning out every other voice. Desperation overtakes me. Without thinking, I race forward, shoving my way through the crowd. No one and nothing else matters. My sister is here. Raven is here, and—and she's hurt.

Her thoughts are diluted, tired. This never would've happened if I'd been able to protect her! She would be okay. I would be okay. Everything would be okay.

Fraught with distress, I burst free from the crowd. My heart seizes as I catch Raven leaning heavily on a brawny man. Though she's limp, she's alive. She's alive! I run towards her, but someone grabs my wounded shoulder before I can get far. A cry escapes my lips. Every moment I stand here, Raven gets farther away.

No. I won't let her out of my sight. I can't let her down again. Tears well in my eyes as I fight to reach her.

"Stop moving, boy!" Navda bellows. "You don't need your fingers to use your magic. The real prize is here. She's here. I can feel it."

I follow his gaze to a familiar woman with coiffed golden braids and a kid slung over her shoulder. It's the pirate who kidnapped Raven. What the hell is she doing? I thought she'd have sold off my sister and disappeared by now.

For the briefest moment, I meet her gaze. All her thoughts barrel through my mind, stronger than anyone else's. There's something distinct, something powerful about her essence that intrigues my magic as her thoughts intertwine with my own. I try to focus on her stream of consciousness. Separating it from my own is difficult. I latch onto her voice, using all my concentration to hold tight.

...couldn't be, could it? Shit shit shit. Gods, Talley is really gonna be on my ass now. Father too when word of this inevitably gets back to him.

She glances at me and Navda. Her train of thought whirs

with panic, hitting me like a boulder with so much force I nearly topple over. Refocusing, I lock in on her again.

No! Oh my gods this is so much worse than I thought. Holy hell. Navda's here. And who was that? Raven's brother? Sure looked like him. Is that good or bad? Who cares. She should be with him shouldn't she? Oh gods I really don't know what I'm doing, do I? I just made everything a hell of a lot worse for...

I lose the connection abruptly. Furrowing my eyebrows, I try to reconnect but I'm scraping against a wall, like she's sensed me poking around and shut me out.

Navda drags me forward, clearly hell-bent on getting to her. He was looking for her that day too, that day he killed Mama. Whoever this pirate captain is, she's clearly worth enough to Navda that he'd lose his livelihood, burn the whole world to get to her. What's so special about her?

Picking up my pace, I follow after Navda as he chases the woman down. Now that she's aware we're on her tail, she expertly disappears into the crowd. I can't even catch a whiff of her thoughts. She's good. And I'm glad she's escaping. Better for Raven to be with her than at Navda's mercy. And I must ensure her safety with a brash decision.

I hook my foot around Navda's ankle and dig my heel into the ground. A baffled grunt bellows from his chest as he tumbles to the ground. Frantically, I glance around, catching a glimpse of the man with my sister hopping onto a longboat with the blonde pirate captain. They'll be okay. This will all be worth it. What will inevitably happen to me, to Aran and Marie, it will be worth it. It's bittersweet comfort.

When Navda rises, my confidence dissipates. I try to hold

onto that fleeting feeling and step in front of him. Time to act like even more of an idiot.

"S-sorry, Captain Navda sir, I didn't—"

Navda wraps his meaty hand around my throat and lifts me up. I cough, splutter, struggle to take a breath. Despite the pain wracking my chest, I still manage surprise when I see tears glistening in his eyes. His voice shakes with a desolate sort of rage when he growls at me, "You insolent filth! She got away. And it's your fault. Oh, you'll answer for that."

He drops me to the ground and pushes me forward. I barely have time to catch my breath. I'm torn. Sure, I protected my sister. But now two innocent maji, friends, will pay for my impertinence. Any choice I make I will always incur someone's wrath.

15

Raven

Slipping in and out of consciousness, visions grasp at my mind. I can't make sense of most of it. I try to latch on when an image flashes behind my eyes, hold onto it, delve into it, but I'm too exhausted. I can only watch passively as my magic tries to speak to me.

There's a woman. Tall, elegant. Mousy brown hair cut short. She's cloaked by darkness. I try to wander the vision, find the exit, but nothing works. Even if I was fully functional, I don't think I could move. Something is strange about her surroundings; it's like there's a boundary of wards. If I try to get closer to her, searing pain shoots through my mind. If I try to escape, my muscles seize. Does she know I'm here?

The next vision to pass through is that of an island. Seeing it unfurls a deep longing in my soul. I know this place. I don't recognize it, but I know it. Some deep part of me knows this lush land is home. Caentathea. The birthplace of magic. I try to hold onto the image of it, but it slips away.

I catch a glimpse of a shattered golden scepter. Broken crown. Bloodied swords. I don't know what any of it means. I've never experienced visions so plenty, so fast. It's almost as if the gods are in a frenzy.

My eyes snap open. I heave a few breaths, wiping my sweaty palms on the bed sheet beneath me. I shake away the remnants of the visions. Groaning, I rub my temples. Seeing can really be a pain.

As the pounding in my head fades, I take in my surroundings. I'm lying on a well-dressed bed, warm cotton sheets over my legs. Wooden walls circle me. Hiding the nook is a thick red curtain.

Wait. I know that curtain.

Groggy, I stumble off the bed. Nausea washes over me. My head swims. I steady myself against the wall. When the spots leave my eyes, I push aside the curtain and stagger into the main cabin. Rélia sits at her desk, idly spinning a dagger on its tip. When she catches sight of me, she perks up.

"Hey, you're up. How're you feeling?"

"How do you think?" I search the room, scanning for anything I can use to fight her with. A spark of hope ignites in my chest when I see my staff set on a stand like a prize. If I can just get to it, I'll regain my strength. Kill her. End this once and for all. Then maybe I can decipher the mess of visions swimming in my Sight.

She approaches me, stopping close enough that I could touch her. Maybe strangle her.

A small, reassuring smile flits across her lips. "What did he do to you?"

The memories of the day before flood back, burning away all other thoughts. I gasp. The admiral did the unthinkable. Drained my magic. But I saw his blood, red as the sun in the eve. He's not a Nightblood, not a Healer or a Reaper or a Psychic—any of which could manipulate me. Yet somehow, he was able to penetrate my mind, force me to use my Sight, force me to lose it. Just one prick of a needle, and it was all gone.

I feel violated. Sick to my stomach. How could someone be so vile, so cruel? So powerful? Rarely do Psychics even have the charm of control. No red-bloods should have been able to intercept my connection. Especially not with a simple needle.

Weak in the knees, I almost fall to the floor. Rélia catches me, cradling me close to her chest. Genuine concern radiates from her. Part of me wants to fight her off. After all, she's the reason I'm in this mess. But I welcome her warm touch, the comfort her magic gives mine. I just want to be held.

"He...he got in my head," I whisper between sobs, choking on my own words. "He made me stop time. Again and again. Until I couldn't anymore. Even after that. He pushed me past my breaking point. He gave me something. I...there was a moment. Just one, where my magic disappeared. Completely gone. It was the worst thing I ever experienced and I...I—"

Rélia caresses my hair. It's such a gentle, tender gesture. One I would never expect from a ruthless pirate. "I know exactly how deep his poisonous hooks can sink. I know how painful it can be. And I'm sorry this happened to you."

I push away from her. Cold seeps into my bones the further

from her I get. "You're sorry? You did this to me. You are the reason my life is a living hell."

Rélia sits back on her haunches. She sighs. "I know. No amount of apologies in the world can make up for that. Trust me. I get it."

My gaze flickers to my staff. I scramble off the ground, fighting the urge to vomit. As soon as my hand closes around the familiar shaft, energy flows into my veins. All sense of sickness dissipates. I take a rejuvenating breath.

I level the bladed end at Rélia. She doesn't so much as flinch.

"Listen, you don't have to stay on the ship," she says, holding her hands up in a plea for mercy. "I can take you home if you want, leave you alone forever. Or you can stay. You'll be treated with the respect you deserve. Just until we figure out what the gods want with us. Together."

"To save magic."

She scrunches her nose. "What? How are we supposed to do that? I get we're a power-duo but—"

I exclaim, "Stop saying we! I don't want to be a we! The gods are driving me mad with the visions they're sending me and you're not helping!"

"Visions? Of what?"

I shrug. "I wish I knew. Caentathea. A woman practiced in wards against Sight. Your various golden objects. Don't know what they're trying to tell me."

Something clicks behind Rélia's eyes. "That woman. Short brown hair? Cold, manic look in her eyes? Dark living space?"

I lower my weapon, curious. "Yeah, exactly. How do you know that?"

She rolls her eyes. "That's Shaia Rydar. Leader of the Resistance."

My eyes widen. "Hold on, you know her name?"

"Oh, trust me, I know *much* more about her than that." Rélia smirks suggestively.

Heat rises in my face. She's slept with the queen of the rebels? Her? Sure, she's got an alluring charm about her, but enough to entice such a legend? I highly doubt it.

She snorts. "Believe me, don't believe me. It's the truth. And as one who has had an unfortunate amount of connection with the gods, I'm pretty sure they're telling you to find her. In the capital, of course. That's the last place I've known her to operate out of."

I mull over her words for a moment. She's right. My Sight never betrays me. It's never led me astray even when I've doubted it. For whatever reason, I have to see Shaia. But that also means my vision of Tezin was real. "My brother is a captive too. I saw that in my vision a while ago."

Rélia tucks her hands in the pockets of her woolen overcoat. "I'm not much good for rescue missions, but it's the least I owe you to try."

I collapse into the chair tucked at her desk. Wherever Tezin is, he's in danger. I don't know if I can get to him. Shame settles over me as I consider leaving him to fend for himself. I can't ignore the gods. Once magic is restored, then I can go after him.

Locking away my guilt, I turn to Rélia once more. "No. No, I'm sure he can take care of himself. We should head towards Qada."

A teasing glint lights her face. "Aw. You said we."

I glare at her. "But first, you are going to tell me everything about you. Everything. Starting with why the hell you have a royal signet ring."

II

CONTENTIOUS UNDERTAKINGS

16

Rélia

"Well," I say, shifting uncomfortably. My skin prickles. I itch to claw away my rising anxiety at the thought of reliving the most horrendous years of my life. But Raven needs to trust me. Opening my soul to her is the first step. I guess. "It's a long story."

Raven crosses her arms over her waist, one hand ever-present on her staff. "We have a few days until we reach Qada. Feel free to use it all."

I scrunch my nose, still hesitant to divulge my story. "You won't like what I hear."

She shrugs. "I already don't like you."

"I have ways of changing that," I tease, winking. "One night with me could change your world."

Her glare hardens. "Story. Now."

"You're no fun. Fine. Have it your way." I pull my signet ring out of my pocket and lay it on the table. "Let's start the day I got this."

•••••

I raced through the palace corridors, laughing so hard my stomach ached. In my wake, I left a trail of fallen suits of armor and shattered flower vases. The skirt of my floral silk dress sailed behind me as I rounded a corner. Footsteps and giggles echoed ahead of me. I caught a glimpse of my youngest brother bolting into the ballroom.

Panting, I stopped just inside the enormous ornately gilded mahogany doors. Tapestries woven of vibrant colors hung on every wall, depicting the story of Oncarii back to the beginning. Well, what I thought was the beginning. All maji history had been erased before the time of the throne. And twisted thereafter. But back then when I looked at those tapestries...I was proud of all my ancestors had accomplished.

•••••

"Can you get to the point?" Raven huffs.

I cross my arms. "Sure if you don't interrupt me. Stories take time, love. You said to use all the time we have."

She rolls her eyes and motions for me to continue.

•••••

So, as I was saying, I was in the ballroom. Lavish curtains hung over the ceiling-high arched windows, one of which I saw moving. I pretended not to know where my brother was hiding. Silencing my footfalls, I pattered around the room until I reached the billowing curtain and yanked it away.

"Gotcha!" I hollered, lifting my brother up in my arms before he could scamper away. "Now I get your dessert, Diego!"

Diego broke down in a fit of giggles as he tried to break free. "No! No, you always get my dessert!"

"Because I always catch you," I replied, tickling him.

In the split second I paused to catch my breath, he jumped out of my grip and tackled me. Both of us tumbled to the ground, laughing. That euphoria shattered when our sister interrupted.

"You're going to be late!" she yelled from the threshold of the ballroom.

I sat up, tossing my hair over my shoulder. With her hands on her hips, a frown turning down her lips, and her perfect blonde hair curled around her face, she looked every bit my lesser, evil half. She glared at us with piercing blue eyes. Like knives. Itty bitty butter knives. She always thought she was so intimidating. Jimena was a pain in my ass. Nothing more.

I sighed and helped Diego to his feet. "Gods why do you even care? You're automatically second in line, aren't you? Would you rather I duck out?"

"No idiot. Diego, Teo, and I would have to fight for the right to ascend. Do you not pay attention to any of our customs?"

I shrugged. "They're about as dry as you are."

Jimena turned her nose up, ignoring my comment. "Today, Father will pick his successor. Since I'm the only one here who respects our traditions like the Heir Nomination, he'll have no choice but to appoint me."

I rolled my eyes. "Yeah, whatever. We're coming."

She scoffed and turned on her heel.

I sauntered after my sister, Diego bouncing with energy beside me. At eight he was hardly old enough to understand the ceremony. Just old enough to be picked as successor though Diego barely understood that he was royalty.

He raced ahead of me, leaving me to be the last in the throne room. Often, that was where you could find Father. As always, he sat in his gilded throne, one he'd had specially designed when he ascended. A gold ceremonial crown nestled in his graying locks, every spire adorned with a string of rubies. Dressed in fine black silks and wearing a tight-lipped frown, he looked every bit the fearsome king I knew him to be.

Per custom, I knelt beside my siblings, bowing my head. In the corner of my eye, I caught Jimena smiling. I refrained from rolling my eyes or anything so disrespectful. It wasn't worth the reprimanding. After the ceremony, she'd get the title of heir, build her ego even more, and I could go about my business as a privileged teenager. At least Timoteo, my other brother, gave me a reassuring glance. Always using those pale brown doe eyes to mediate between me and Jimena.

Father rose. Simultaneously, all of us raised our heads. I forced myself to meet the king's cold stare. Today would be the last day he could intimidate me. It would be the last time I had to look into those eyes, bow my head, and let him terrorize me into subservience, let him strip away everything that made me who I was. Finally, I would be free.

Drawing on countless hours of courtly training, I kept my features level. I fought every primal urge to run out of the room and never look back. I wouldn't give anyone more of a reason to think I would make a terrible queen. Truthfully, I believed that. Apparently, my father did not.

After droning on about the weight of the crown, the duties

that await each of us, chosen or not, the honor of being a ruling monarch—for an hour at least—he finally pulled the signet ring from his finger: an heirloom that had been passed down since the first king had it forged. He paced in front of us. Just like him, drawing out an already agonizingly long ceremony to prolong our torture.

"Everything you've been taught has led you to this moment," he said, voice rough like sandpaper. Funny how I used to think his voice was the most soothing sound in the world. "As my last years draw near, I must bestow the responsibility of the throne upon the most suitable heir."

He stopped in front of me. My heart hammered in my chest. Not me. There was no way in all the layers of hell he was going to pick me.

"Darling Rélia. Rise."

Breathing through my shock, I gracefully stood. Respectfully, I curtsied. I kept my eyes glued to the floor, trying to keep from spiraling. This couldn't be happening. Yeah, sure, I was the oldest. But that didn't qualify me to lead the country. Besides, I wasn't sure I had ever impressed him, not like Jimena. Every cold, punitive leer, every harsh reprimanding, everything he ever said or did to me pushed us further apart.

He placed a hand on my cheek, tilting my face up. His hands were warm, soft. Comforting. My father's touch was foreign. Like it didn't belong to him. I couldn't help my smile. After everything I'd done, I still had a place in the world. That one touch convinced me I was valuable.

If Father thought I was worthy of being his heir, then I must have been. No one could tell me otherwise. I could prepare for my coronation. Everything would become official. There would be no challengers, no royal combats for the throne. First Rélia the Crown Princess. Then Rélia the Sovereign Queen.

He lifted my left hand. Though his face remained stern, a kindness broke through the stone in his eyes. Pride. "In all my years, I have never known a woman so strong, so willful, so full of potential. Watching you grow over the years, molding into the perfect daughter, my heart has never been warmer. There is no one I'd rather bestow upon the honor of being my heir."

Jimena's jaw ticked, the only sign of her rage boiling over. Justifiable anger in every way, even I had to admit that. Pretty much none of what he was saying held truth. But, like a good little princess, she stayed in her place. As I stayed in mine.

"Will you accept the honor, and begin preparation to become the next sovereign of Oncarii?"

Everyone stared at me earnestly. Silence beat down on me. All I could hear was the blood pounding in my ears. Breathing became trying. The walls of the throne room began to close in, every extravagant tapestry wrapping around me, strangling me.

This wasn't what I wanted. Following in my father's footsteps was the last thing I wanted. But I hardly had a choice.

Diego broke protocol and turned to me. He smiled, and I was at ease.

I took a deep breath. My voice was strained, barely audible. "I accept."

He slipped the golden ring over my finger, beaming with pride. It was heavy on my hand. With it came the promise of burdens, the weight of my title, a life of stuffy bureaucrats and misery.

Next day, I ran. Didn't look back.

•••••

"Wait, you ran?" Raven says, astounded. "After becoming heir to the throne, a fortune, power, you just ran away from it?"

I shrug. "Yeah. I know my father well enough to know that moment before he gave me the ring was a calculated moment of weakness. He was manipulating me. Wanted to twist me into something horrible. And I didn't want to see myself turn into a worse version of Jimena."

Raven taps her fingers on the desk as my words sink into the empty space between us. "So aren't you still technically heir to the throne? Since you didn't *officially* abdicate, I mean. One of your siblings would be able to step up as regent but you're the rightful heir, aren't you? You could just take it back."

I snort and flash a smile, trying to hide my distress. "Well look who's been reading up on their royal decorum. No. I'm the designated heir, but I'm not Crown Princess. If I don't show up for the coronation ceremony by the time my sister's of age to assume the throne, which is in a few months if memory serves, I'll be forced into abdication. Father can't pick another heir because I still have the ring, not that the public would know that. They all think I'm a recluse. So if my father doesn't want Jimena to lead, his hands are tied. Either she will get the throne, or my brothers will fight her for it. I'd be allowed to challenge as well, but uh, I'd rather not die for a crown."

"So do the ceremony."

"Brilliant. Wish I'd thought of that." I shake my head, skin crawling at the idea of breathing capital air again. "I can't go back there. Not now, not ever. I won't set foot in Qada. You're gonna have to talk to Shaia yourself."

Raven frowns. "What? You can't abandon me like that."

"Oh, so now I'm abandoning you? That's something friends do, and we are far from that. You've made that abundantly clear," I say, growing increasingly annoyed.

Sure, I made a huge mistake taking her from her home, nearly sentencing her to a short, painful life. Raven has every right to hate me. But I can't help my bitterness. For years it's been sitting in the pit of my stomach, festering, getting harder to swallow back with every passing day. Now it bleeds out with every breath I take. "I'll take you wherever you need to go. Help you in any way I can. But I will not go back to Qada."

Raven's glare hardens. Before she can get in another word, somehow convince me with that cold allure of hers to enter the viper's den with her, I stand. Outside my cabin, music drifts through the air. The hum of violin and banjo strings mingle together, entwined in an upbeat, jaunty tune.

"The crew beckons," I say, nodding towards the door. "C'mon love. Let's have some fun for once in your life."

She narrows her eyes. At first I think she might fight me, stubborn as she is. But I'm pleasantly surprised to see her shove past me and out the door.

"Great!" I call after her. "You know, this is one step closer to us being friends!"

Shockingly, she doesn't respond.

17

Raven

Reassured by the familiarity of my staff on my back, I lean against the railing, watching the crew in full swing, dancing to the jovial music. They all move in time with one another. It's almost graceful, though it becomes less so the more the rum is passed around.

Something deep inside me yearns to join in. I can't remember the last time I danced. I haven't had much reason to, not since Papa died, not since anyone caught celebrating Remembrance Day was to be arrested. Papa told me stories of the celebration when he was a child. Once a year, the world was alight with color and vivacity. Music played in every town. Nightbloods danced, feasted on crab delicacies, rejoiced in their magic.

Now, we all hide in the safety of our homes, burning sea-salt incense, surrounded by flickering candles. It's a private tribute to Isolde, the first Nightblood to set foot on the earth. Many are like my papa. They see more appeal in the grandeur of a party. But I've always enjoyed the quiet accolade. I can celebrate without the risk of being discovered. It brings me closer to her, to the origin of what I am.

I wonder if she's watching now from beside the gods.

"Whatcha thinkin' about?" Rélia's voice startles me so much I jump.

I shrug, turning to the sea. There's nothing but gentle blue waves as far as the eye can see. "Remembrance Day is today."

Rélia leans over the railing, staring out at the horizon. I glance at her. Tranquility placates her face. It's hard to grasp. Princess, heir to the throne, all this power at her fingertips and instead she chooses to captain a pirate ship, play at being a rebel. "Ah, you celebrate then?"

"In a way."

Rélia gently wraps her fingers around my wrist and tugs. I reach up, my staff already half out of its scabbard. Smiling, she rolls her eyes.

"Relax, love. Relish in some freedom. You'll have *two whole days* after tonight before we reach the hellhole we call capital to wallow in your morose thoughts. Dance?"

Something in her eyes makes me want to give in. Give in to her gentle touch, to her invitation for the dance floor. Fighting the insistent fluttering in my stomach is no use. Slowly, I release my grip on my staff. I don't make a move for her hand. Everything about this makes me want to disappear. And it's not solely because I dislike her, I realize.

I don't remember how to dance.

My stomach knots. My mouth goes dry. "No...no. I don't dance."

Rélia chuckles and holds out her hand. "C'mon. It'll be fun. No judgment if you've got two left feet."

Again, I find her twinkling eyes and impish smile irresistible. Which in turn makes my stomach roil. Another reason to hate her. She has some sort of enchanting power over me.

I purse my lips, staring her down. Her sprightly energy doesn't fade. Childlike joy trickles through me. I set my staff and scabbard against the railing. Taking her hand reluctantly, I say, "Okay fine. One dance. That's it."

"One dance is all it takes to get you hooked."

She pulls me closer to the rest of the crew. Laughter grows louder. I try to ignore the pounding of my heart. I can handle my own in a fight. Hell, I can stop time. I can certainly find my way around a simple dance.

Rélia takes both of my hands in hers, palms up, mine down. After a moment of nodding along to the music, she takes a step backwards, tugging on my hands. Trying to copy her moves, I also step backwards, nearly toppling someone else.

"No, no," she laughs, pulling me back to her. "Follow my lead. If I go back, you go forwards. Mirror me, don't copy me. Make sense?"

"Yes, I'm not a child," I snap.

"Didn't say you were. Let's try again. Relax."

I focus on her movements, allowing myself to let go a little, relinquish control. With fluid movements, she guides me across the deck. For just a moment, I'm unburdened. Everything lifts from my shoulders. All the worry, trepidation, simmering anger dissipates. My mind is blissfully blank. Rélia is all I can focus on. Moving in sync with her, becoming one with the music, it's all that matters. Around me, the sea melts into the horizon, faces blur, the rest of the world fades into nothingness.

Elation swells in my chest. A smile stretches across my face as Rélia spins me and pulls me back into her. One thing she was right about. It's only taken me one dance to fall in love with the music.

I don't notice when the tune halts. I'm still in ecstasy. Only when I stumble over Rélia's feet do I realize all the eyes still on me. She tries to catch me before I fall, but I only end up taking her down with me. I land on top of her, knocking our heads together. Embarrassment creeps up my face.

Rélia grins at me. Part of me finds the teasing glint in her eyes irritating. Another deeper part enjoys it. "Well this is nice."

My voice catches as I stare at her, tremendously aware of how close our faces are.

"You gonna get up or should I carve out some time to lay on the ground for a while?" she asks, brushing stray hairs from her eyes.

I clear my throat and clamber off of her. Regaining my composure, I narrow my eyes at the crew. They're still laughing at me. That's what I get for letting my guard down. I'm not one of them. I know that. They'll always remind me of it. Using Rélia's vessel to follow the will of the gods is the only reason I'm here. Soon, this torture will be over.

I turn my back on the crew, only to find another inebriated crewmate glaring at me. I recognize him as Ori, the boatswain.

He sways with every gentle shift of the breeze. I steel my gaze, trying to intimidate him into leaving me alone. It doesn't work.

"Why're you still here?" he grumbles.

I itch for my weapon, my back bare without its comfort. I keep my mouth shut. I will not indulge a drunken pirate. I try to shove past him, but he blocks my path.

"Y'know you aren't the first maji Cap'n has taken pity on. You won't be the last. You're just another distraction in her conquest. You don't belong here."

I know that. But for some reason, it's like a slap in the face. Bristling, I rise to my full height. To my surprise, Rélia steps in-between us, glowering at Ori.

"Watch yourself, Orion," she warns, yanking his tin cup of rum from him. "Raven is as much a part of this crew as any of us."

He scoffs, staggering slightly. "Bullshit."

"Tread carefully, or she will be the next boatswain," Rélia says, downing the rest of Ori's rum.

I lower my voice. "Oh, um, I don't actually know what that is."

Rélia rolls her eyes. "Not helping. Ori, I'll give you a pass this once because you're drunk and I'm in a good mood. But one more word against her, from *any* of you, and you will find yourself dangerously close to being keelhauled. Understood?"

Ori sways, huffing. Everyone else remains silent in her outburst.

Rélia reels on her crew, fire and daggers in her eyes. Cold ire lines her voice when she repeats herself. "Understood?"

They all murmur in agreement. An awkward silence ensues

until the musicians resume their tune. Ori heads downstairs at Rélia's behest to sleep off his intoxication.

She gives my shoulder an apologetic squeeze. "Sorry about that. He'll warm up to you. They all will. Everyone was a newcomer once. Sometimes they get a little aggressive with the hazing."

I tilt my head. Why does she care what her family thinks of me? "So...I'm a part of your crew now. That's what you think?"

"Offer is on the table if you want."

I scoff, amazed at how enticed I am. To be a pirate means a life of adventure. Freedom to practice my magic in the open waters. Taste what true power really is.

Rélia is far kinder a woman than I ever believed a pirate could be. Everyone here is so unburdened, so just, and quite frankly, they can be rather fun. Piracy is a sort of blessing—the ne'er do wells and do-gooders bonding over a love of the sea, watching out for each other, living how they want, free from the scorn of the king.

But I can't forget that pirates took my papa from me. His spirit would never rest if he knew I wanted to be one.

"No. It's like you said. We're not friends. I only need you for your ship. After we do what the gods want, we're done with each other." I say, crossing my arms.

Rélia keeps her features cool but the disappointment in her eyes betrays her. "Cold and to the point. Got it."

Ignoring the guilt seeping into my bones, I stride to the railing of the boat, pulling my scabbard over my shoulder. Holding it close like a doll I can't let go of, I watch waves lap against the hull as the strum of strings drifts across the wind.

18

Tezin

I tug at the manacles clamped around my wrists. The chains loop through a metal rung bolted to the wood, steadfast. Everything I try fails. Kicking, pulling, twisting—none of it works. I've tried to reach my magic, but every time I attempt, a wave of intense pounding fills my head. Makes it hard to think.

Dejection washes over me. I run my hands through my hair, grimacing at the metallic jangling. How am I going to make it? How the *hell* am I going to make it? Navda made his threat clear. Punishment is coming, far worse than the lashings I got. The only comfort I have being locked in Navda's cabin is that it's ten-fold nicer than the brig. If I can get past the crushing loneliness.

I lie down. Waves gently rock the boat, luring me into a false sense of security. It's been an eternity since I last saw someone. Or had something to eat. I should enjoy the silence, the boredom. But I can't. Too much hangs over me, a maelstrom of distress constantly swirling above my head.

I'm not sure if it's a relief when the cabin door opens. Heavy footsteps follow.

Slowly, I sit up. Panic creeps through me, threatening to take control, but I force myself to swallow it back. I have to be strong. Just for today. I think I can manage that.

I look up at the face of the man who killed my parents, who will eventually kill me. I'm not sure man is the right term. Demon, maybe. Monster. Something far more twisted than a dark-hearted man.

He sizes me up. An amused smile cracks his scarred face. "Playing the hero today, eh? Good. It'll be more fun for me."

I don't dignify his taunting with a response. Silence will be my only friend.

He pulls open a door at the back of the cabin, which a normal person would use to shelve clothes. Instead, it opens into a frightening array of weapons. Some I've never seen the likes of before. I turn away from the sight. Focusing on the blue sky of the cabin window is distracting enough. Calming, almost.

Navda hums as he peruses his selection of torture devices. My stomach churns at his blasé. "Ah, this should be a nice start."

In his hand he holds a curved silver blade. Impossibly thin. Turn it one way and it disappears into thin air. Nothing is so utterly sharp as the point of the dagger. The golden cross-guard winds around the base of the blade in intricate swirling patterns until it disappears into the fuller.

"No design quite like it," Navda muses, crouching in front of me. He tilts the blade sideways, showcasing the shallow fuller in the center. Clear fluid runs straight through it to the tip, from which it drips to the ground in slow, heavy drops. I try to tell myself it's just water, but that's hardly the style of a pirate. "Only dagger in Oncarii that produces its own poison. Dutiful work of a Welder and a Healer. I spent many long years trying to find it. I save it for special occasions. I think this will suffice."

Instinctively, I lean away from the dagger.

Navda wraps a hand around my arm, pulling me towards him. Struggling is no use. I can only watch in horror as the point of the dagger draws a line of blood across my collarbone. It stings, though not quite as terribly as I expected.

A cool numbness follows, turning my blood to ice. I inhale sharply. Navda releases his hold on me with a satisfied grin. Already, the poison creeps through me, slow and deliberate, as if it's taking the time to freeze each individual cell.

"It begins with an attack on your blood," Navda says, sauntering in a circle around me. "Painful, but not deadly. Then comes the nausea, the breathlessness, the confusion. You'll be trapped in a circle o' agony and delirium till your mind descends into hysteria. And the best part 'bout it's it can be used again and again 'cause it ain't ever lethal."

Navda's toothy grin looms over me as I fall on my back, trying to fight the effects of the poison. "At least, not in the first dose."

Every breath I take is taxing, like the air thickened into molasses. I gasp, desperately trying to escape the burning in my lungs. As soon as I replenish with a breath, a wave of nausea drowns me. The world spins. Everything is muffled.

My nails dig into the wooden floor as intense prickling

pain sears through me. Each wave comes stronger than the last. Agony overwhelms me. Every time I think I'll get a break from it, visions torture my mind. All my worst fears manifest in the air around me. Death greets me every way I look. Blood stains the walls, the floor, my hands.

I close my eyes, hoping for escape, but the visions only exacerbate. Tears threaten to fall. Try as I might to fight them, they slip down my cheeks in steady streams. Colors blur. The walls of the cabin melt into the floor. I can barely make out Navda's sadistic smile hovering above me.

He leans down, grabs my chin. My skin burns in the wake of his touch. "This dagger has been called many names."

With the little strength I have left in my body, I yank myself free of his grip. Vomit creeps up my throat. A mangled scream erupts from my chest.

"But my personal favorite," Navda continues, watching my suffering triumphantly. I can barely understand his voice beyond the blood pumping wildly in my ears. "Well, I call it Entropy."

I give into the anguish, unable to hold back anymore. What little I have in my stomach spills to the floor. Everything blends into nothing. I can't escape the strangeness of this pain, a perversion of what agony was meant to be. Even when my mind and body go numb, it's still there, prickling my skin. I turn my muddled gaze out the window, losing myself in the serenity outside the ship. How can the sun shine so bright, the waves be so gentle, when I am crossing between a painful reality and a silent afterlife?

I almost don't notice when it stops. There's a dull ache in my bones. Putrid scents waft under my nose. Sweat and tears cake my face. But everything is quiet. Blissfully silent. Pink and orange sunset hues illuminate the cabin with a comforting glow. Candles flicker contentedly in their sconces.

Taking a deep breath is cleansing. Shakily, I sit up. I relish in the utter lack of anything. I don't even care that I'm starving. The emptiness inside me is welcoming.

"I thought you'd never wake up."

I startle. Aran's sitting in the corner of the cabin, knees drawn up to his chest.

"Had me worried for a second there," he says, smiling softly. "Navda definitely didn't go easy on you."

Remnants of pain flicker through me. I clear my hoarse throat. "No, he did not. Sorry, why are you here?"

Aran tilts his head, grinning. "What, sick of my face already? Can't say it's a record."

I stretch out my aching limbs. "Seriously, Aran."

Somberness casts a shadow over his face. "Probably not for a nice chat."

My lip trembles. I know what's coming. Navda warned me what would happen if I stepped out of line. The consequences were clear. Now as they stare me square in the face, guilt crushes me, steals my breath.

"I'm sorry," I whisper, trying to keep my voice steady. "This is all my fault."

Aran shakes his head. "What are you talking about?"

I clench my hands into fists, beating back the fear, containing the self-loathing that rears its ugly head. "I did this. I screwed Navda. Now you're going to pay for it."

"Like you haven't had your fair share already." Aran moves

from his spot in the corner to sit beside me. I flinch when he puts an arm around my shoulders. "You have not had enough life experience if you're going to blame yourself for everything that Navda does to you, to me, or otherwise. It is only Navda to blame."

I lean my head on his shoulder, grateful for his support. To distract my mind, I fiddle with one of the tassels hanging from Aran's shawl. The material is softer than the coarse thread of the shawl itself.

We stay like this, in a state of bliss, until the sun slips below the horizon, leaving the stars to wink at us from the sky. Now, the sconces are our only source of light. In the dim hue, Aran's hair glints like burning embers. His touch is nearly as warm. Or perhaps that's the gentle gusts of warm wind wrapping around us. I glance at him to find he's smiling.

"It's so much easier up here," he murmurs, twisting his fingers to harness the breeze. "Freer."

"I like seeing you like this."

"Yeah, well. Don't get used to it."

I turn my gaze to the stars twinkling outside the window. Just barely, I catch a glimpse of a vaguely tome shaped constellation representing the goddess Mihsoi. My patron saint if I'm a Psychic. I wonder if it's a sign. Out of all the clusters of stars to show themselves to me, it can hardly be a coincidence that hers would appear. And the gods aren't known to be subtle.

I shake my head clear of thoughts. Whatever the gods want doesn't matter. All that matters is this peace, right here.

But peace can only last so long. All life, all tranquility drains from the air when the door swings open and Navda steps in, Ean at his heels. Aran tightens his grip on my shoulder.

Navda drops his sword on his cluttered desk, running a hand over his face. Leaning against his desk, he crosses his arms, as if deep in thought. Once more, I'm struck by the weariness of his thoughts, the misery in his mind. Ean exhales, a sound barely audible, and hardly out of the ordinary. But with that sound, Navda flips a switch, sneers at us.

I cast my gaze to the ground, melting under his punitive glare, though my mind runs rampant with questions. To enter Navda's mind is the only way to answer them. And I have no idea where to begin.

Aran steels beside me. I pray he doesn't say anything, that he doesn't make this worse on himself. Thankfully he remains silent. Navda grabs his arm, pulling him away from me. He struggles, gets in a solid kick to his groin, but the whole spectacle only seems to amuse him.

Navda punches Aran so hard he sprawls to the floor. Blood trickles from his mouth. On his haunches, he scrambles backwards. Miraculously, he remains stoic. If he's terrified, I can't tell.

Navda peruses his collection of weapons and selects a serrated dagger. Useless in battle. Perfect for making a point.

My heart pounds in my ears. I can't look.

Searching for some semblance of comfort, I find myself locking eyes with Ean. He's leaning against the wall of the cabin, watching with a slight pucker of his lips like this is leaving a sour taste in his mouth that he rather enjoys. Hushed words snake through my mind. Nearly sentient malice smothers all my thoughts. I can't hear anything coherent beneath it.

Abruptly, it stops. Ean doesn't relent in his inquisitive, green-eyed stare. I can't hear anything in his mind, even as I try to prod deeper. He smirks.

Navda's lips curl in a snarl. "Watch this, boy. Or I'll go until he's dead."

I know that's a lie; he wouldn't dare kill his Galer. Still, I force myself to turn. Fighting back tears, I watch as Navda draws the blade across Aran's arm. To elicit more cries, he digs his thumb into the wound. I taste bile. Time stops. Navda cycles through canes, knives, old -fashioned punching. After a while, Aran stops screaming. Even the captain himself grows less enthusiastic with every blow. Lighter strikes, even. Like he's putting on a show he wants no part in.

My eyes go out of focus. All I can see is the pool of black beneath my friend.

Finally, it stops. Aran lies still. My stomach turns. How the hell is he going to recover?

"This is what happens when you interfere with my plans," Navda says, voice flat and weary. I bite my lip to keep it from trembling. "Now, use that filth of yours and get in Captain Ryan's head. Find out where she's gone."

Exhaustion lines his words. Part of me doubts he wants to continue with this, but I'd rather not test that theory.

I swallow over the lump in my throat as my gaze strays to Aran's limp body. I can't let him die. As much as it pains me to do so, to give Navda the tool to get closer to my sister, I don't have a choice. Or at least, the less horrendous choice.

Closing my eyes, I try to draw on the connection I had with the pirate. It was brief, but powerful. Deep inside my core, spindles of warmth curl up to meet my desperation. I strain to hold onto that lick of power, but something pushes back, as if trying to box up my magic. Sweat breaks out on my forehead. I focus every thought I have on Rélia, trying to delve into her mind from afar. Blurry images flicker in and out of my mind, accompanied by a cacophony of incomprehensible voices. Again, the weight of the force presses on my chest. My connection wavers. All I can make sense of in the host of images is a palace. Which can only mean one thing.

Exhaling slowly, I open my eyes. The force eases as I relent on my magic. "Qada."

"Not so hard, was it?" Navda grunts. He rubs his face as if trying to wash the memory of tonight away. "Ean, clean them up and return them to the cells. I'll make orders to set course for the capital."

He gives his captain a single nod. After Navda is gone, he crouches in front of me, pulling a key from a ring at his side. I can't tear my eyes from Aran even as one of the manacles falls from my wrist.

"He'll be alright," Ean says. "Captain wouldn't let our Galer go to waste."

I flit my eyes to him. "To waste. Like he's a basket of lard."

He flinches. "Right. I apologize for speaking in such a manner. Your friend is mighty important is all I'm saying."

Ean unlocks the other manacle. I rub my wrist, groaning at the dark bruises forming a ring. He holds out a hand. Hesitantly, I take it. Chills run up my arm, sending my hair standing on end.

Sorrow overwhelms my senses. Tendrils of black twine over our joined hands. Startled, I yank my hand away. Slowly, the cold melancholy dissipates from my being.

"What just happened?" I breathe, turning my hand over as if it could reveal secrets. It does not.

Ean shakes the intangible black residue from his hand, ignoring my question. "Take the Galer, make sure he gets lots of rest. I'll get what I can to help for now."

I shoot him a sidelong glance. "Thanks."

Ean heaves Aran up, who groans slightly. I duck under his arm, shouldering the majority of his weight.

"Don't worry, Aran," I whisper in his ear. "I'm here. I'm right here."

19

Raven

On the horizon, the spires of the royal palace pierce the brightening sky. Golden rays of the rising sun glint on the brilliant white stone. Foreigners might think it welcoming. Seeing it for the first time in my life, the birthplace of every prejudice against me, fills me with unease. It brings back memories I'd rather not face. Old, deep ones. Fresh, bleeding ones.

I close my eyes and Talley's face is there, looming over me. Taunting me. In his hands, he holds a syringe filled with gray-tinged liquid. My lips trembles as it did then.

"Do you know what this is?" he asked, smiling at me. It was a beautiful smile, one that was nearly disarming. It was seductive. Terrifying.

There was a pause. I was already so tired. I'd pushed my limits to show him what I could do, to save my life. My spirit was unbearably weary.

Faintly, I shook my head.

"They call it aphonixa. Rare, if you don't know how to get it." His smile grew. "Luckily, I do."

Talley crouched behind me and grabbed my hair. I bit back a cry. He pulled my head to the side, exposing the crook of my neck. I struggled in vain to escape his grip. I barely noticed when the needle pricked my skin, but the aphonixa, that *I felt.*

It coursed through my veins, slow and cool. Nausea washed over me. The room spun. I shivered. I tried to breathe through the drug as it muddled my mind. Exhaustion rooted me to my chair. Fighting to stay awake, I reached for my magic. For a brief moment, power surged through me.

The drug met my magic with a stoppage I could feel in my gut. Warmth tingling across my skin vanished. I searched my mind, my core, but no golden light shone. I couldn't hear the comfortable hum of my Sight, couldn't feel it.

It was gone. I'd never understood how empty someone could be until my magic was ripped away. I yearned for the clear bleakness of the odrite cuffs. Not this swallowing void of nothing. I screamed.

"Magic is just biology," Talley murmured in my ear. "And when I figure out how to manipulate it, I can finally fix the world."

I exhale shakily. Salty wind whips across my face. I take a deep, refreshing breath. Talley and his drug are in the past. What matters now is the task at hand: Shaia Rydar.

"Thinking hard?" A melodious voice rings out beside me. "Daydreaming? Worrying? Or just staring into the sea?"

I startle and turn to find the kid that saved us leaning against the railing. "Oh!" I regain my composure. "Sorry, who are you?"

"Monty. Don't you remember?"

"Right. You helped us escape."

"Least I could do!"

I offer him a small smile, but he doesn't react.

Monty grins after a moment. "If you're making some sort of appreciative face, you should know I'm blind. Intuitive as hell, but everything before my eyes? Pretty much dark."

I glance at his arm. A familiar mark is imprinted there, the same I caught a glimpse of tattooed on the sage woman. Curious.

"So, Monty the Intuitive, why come talk to me?" I ask, turning my attention back to the approaching coastline. Buildings rise out of the ground, some stretching almost as tall as the palace itself. There's too many for me to count. My heart pounds harder. How am I supposed to find the rebellion's base of operations in such a vast, chaotic city?

"Everyone needs someone to talk to. Whether they know it or not."

"So is this for me or for you?"

Monty shrugs. "Both, I guess. I was in Tashul for so long. That cell was all I knew for the last half year. You understand what it's like to have your connection interrupted. Imagine getting dangerously close to being cut off."

If Rélia hadn't come back for me, would that have been my fate? Losing my magic forever?

Monty sighs. "I can't wait to go home."

"Qada is your home?" For some reason, I can't envision him growing up there. I've gathered nothing but gentleness from him.

"Of sorts. The people I love are there. Isn't that what makes a place a home?"

Everything I love came from the same place. All my memories, life, love, is rooted in Ghzen. I'm not sure I can call anywhere else home.

Rélia interrupts the contemplative silence following Monty's remark. "Ten minutes until we're anchoring down away from prying eyes. The boat's gotta launch before then. You two ready?"

I sigh, adjusting the strap of my staff's harness. "As I can be."

"Good enough. Penn will be waiting for you in the dinghy the whole time," Rélia explains, leading us across the deck to the port side, where an unassuming boat rocks gently, suspended in air by coils of rope. Inside, Penn sits at the oars, ready for launch.

Monty runs his fingers across the rail, seems to memorize the shape of the dinghy against the ship, then nimbly leaps inside with a surprising amount of grace. Again, Rélia stretches her hand to Penn. Sharing an imploring stare, they hold tight to each other's forearms and mutter that same mantra when Rélia departed the ship for Tashul.

"Onwards and forwards."

"Forever free."

Gnawing at my lip, I set my sights on the city of Qada, closer than ever now. If I make any slip ups there, I'll end up dead. Or worse. Gripping my harness strap calms my nerves. I can handle my own.

As I turn to get into the boat, Rélia grabs my arm, stopping me. Hesitantly, I face her. Before I can ask what she's doing, she throws her arms around me, hugging me tight. I tense. Tingles of warmth race up and down my skin, basking in the comfort of her body pressed against mine.

"Stay safe," she murmurs.

She clings to me for a moment longer. When she pulls away, I catch a glimpse of genuine concern in her eyes. There's more and more of that for me lately. Why is she so insistent on being my friend?

Then again, a deep foreign part of me yearns to care about her too. I crush the feeling.

I clear my throat and nod at her before stepping into the boat. I keep my back to her as the boat slowly lowers. I can't bear the look in her eyes, like I'll never come back. Sure, Qada is the belly of the beast. But I'm smart. With my staff at my back, I could get out, get back to Ghzen, to Tezin, to Mama. Leave this nightmare behind.

But I won't. I hang my head. Risking everything for a sacred, divine mission to save magic is more important than anything waiting for me at home. I already got a taste of what life would be like without magic. I never want that yawning void within me again.

Water splashes my face when the boat hits the cold, dark water. Rélia waves. Penn returns it. I roll my eyes, turning my attention to what lies ahead. Orange and gold paint the sky as the sun steadily rises above the palace.

With every stroke of the oars, the capital looms closer. I look over my shoulder to see Rélia's ship banking to the right, heading for the shadowy shelter of a cliff. I hope it stays hidden.

Chatter swells in the air as we approach the shore. Down the sandy beach, massive ships are docked in the harbor, blocking the rising sun. My eyes widen. There's so many vessels, all bearing the royal crest. Immediately, I'm back in Talley's dining room, his lustful eyes boring into me, my magic draining. I can't move. This is his navy. All these people, all these ships, are loyal to him.

I glance at Monty who's already on the beach, beaming wide. Fistfuls of sand rain down from his palms. Pangs of jealousy strike me. Wasn't he also captive to the admiral? How can he be so happy?

"Need a moment?" Penn asks, startling me out of my malicious thoughts.

I swallow back my apprehension and hop out of the dinghy. "No, I'm fine. Let's get this over with."

Penn grabs my arm before I can go much further. He presses a leather pouch into my palm, brimming with gold coins. "Just in case. Cap'n's dealt with the likes of Rydar before. And she often don' come free for services."

I tuck the pouch in my pocket. I can't help but wonder if I'm now carrying what I'm worth in gold. "Yeah. Okay. We'll be back soon. Don't abandon us."

"Wouldn' dream of it."

"Alright, let's go." I grab Monty's wrist, forcing him to drop the rest of the sand. He shakes his head at me. I huff. "Oh, what? We don't have time for this. Marvel about the splendor of the beach after we've saved magic."

"Sure!" Monty loops his arm through mine. "There's just as much majesty in the air as in the ground."

"Gods. You're insufferable."

Penn chuckles from the boat. I shoot him a glare. Of all the people to be stuck with, I couldn't have someone that takes this seriously? Saving magic is imperative, a divine quest. Not a joke.

Hiking up the beach proves to be quite the task. By the time we crest the top of the hill on the outskirts of the city, I'm panting. Having a kid clinging to me the entire time didn't help.

I take a deep, cleansing breath. Beneath my feet, warmth rises from the cobblestones. Delightful aromas waft under my nose. Even this early in the morning, everyone is up and working. People multiply and buildings grow in height the deeper into the city we delve. Excited babbling hums around us, vibrating in the air. Color explodes in every awning, in every twirling skirt. Lively melodies strummed by musicians in the square light the world with vibrant hues, as if the music itself is visible.

I thought Borziau was magnificent. Qada is transcendent. Something new greets me every time I turn. I can't help the smile that tugs on my lips.

"Wow," I breathe.

Monty giggles beside me. "You never thought this city could be so wonderful, huh?"

"No. I certainly did not," I reply, zeroing in on a shop selling freshly baked bread. Mouth watering, I move towards it. Sure, the gold is for negotiation, but I can't deny the painful grumbling in my stomach.

Inside the bakery, I'm overwhelmed by the amount of patrons. Some turn to us. I stiffen, but no one appears malicious. Smiles and waves greet us. I wonder if we'd have the same reception if they knew what we are.

"Monty, you got any recommendations?" I ask, surveying the

wide selection of grains. I didn't know there were so many options for bread.

He beams. "Sourdough is my favorite!"

I nod. "We'll have a loaf of that then."

The baker nods, a friendly smile crinkling the corners of his eyes. "Anything for my favorite customer. Been a while, Monty."

"Always a pleasure Becho! Hope Jac has been treating you well."

He laughs heartily. "As well as that lad can. Here. On the house for you an' your friend."

I take the warm round loaf from him, hardly believing it's in my hands. Stunned, lost in the enticing aroma of the bread, I barely notice when Monty takes the lead, moving through the bakery like he's dancing a song taught at birth. I shake my head and plop down on a bench outside the bakery.

"Well, are you going to eat it or just stare at it?"

"I'm not staring."

Monty snorts. "You are. You're real tense. I can feel it."

"I'm always tense."

I break the loaf in half, holding back a gasp of wonder when warm crumbles fall in my lap. Bread like this is a delicacy—bread that isn't hard as a rock, cold, shatters when you break it. I hand one half to Monty. Tentatively, I bring the other to my lips. Knowing I can only make it last so long, I take a prudent bite. I stifle a gleeful laugh.

Monty has already scarfed down his piece. I can't really blame him. Just this once, I indulge my impulses. In a split second, my half-loaf is gone. Only a buttery taste lingers on my lips.

"Wow. That was amazing."

"Want more?"

Yes.

"No." I stand. Once more, I link arms with him. "Unfortunately we have to find Shaia."

"I might have an inkling."

"Really? And you didn't care to share?" I eye him suspiciously. "Lead the way."

Monty beams. "Love to."

Jovially, he tugs me down the cobblestone road. I'm amazed at how well he knows the streets, how he nimbly avoids stepping in a jagged pothole by a fountain, how he dances under archways, knows exactly who to greet as we pass by shops. I chew on my lip. There has to be something beneath that cheery exterior.

Abruptly, he turns to the right. Shadows fall over us. The atmosphere shifts as if we've stepped into another realm. Leaving behind the excitement and splendor of the wealthier district, we head for the bustle and clamor of the cramped houses on the easternmost edge of the city.

I wrinkle my nose at the sour, pungent scent wafting through the cracked streets. Raucous bouts of laughter erupt from a dingy tavern to our left. What the hell am I getting myself into?

Monty pauses, cocking his head as if he's listening for something. I scan the area. While it's nowhere near the grandeur of the square, it has its own charm. Homey, genuine. If a bit filthy.

Without warning, Monty tugs me down another alley. It's even darker here and the odor of stale ale stronger. My heart hammers against my ribs so hard I fear they may crack. I'm out of my element here. I can't deny that. I don't trust Qada, and I don't trust this kid. All I trust are the gods, but even then, seeds of doubt have been sowing in my gut ever since I left home.

Monty hums to himself as his fingers glide over the slick stone walls, nails digging into the grooves. Delight brightens his face when his fingers hook in an inconspicuous niche. Faintly, I hear a click. The alley wall shifts and cracks, then swings open.

"After you," Monty says, extending a hand out.

Clenching tight to the staff over my shoulder, I step into the darkness. Behind us, the stone wall shuts, sealing us in. I take a deep breath, steadying my pulse. Shaia Rydar is a venerable leader, but I'm a warrior. True, real, powerful. Not a whisper that sends shivers down everyone's necks. Truth is more powerful than legend. I have to believe that.

Sconces flicker, lighting the walls with a dim orange hue. We turn a corner through the maze of hallways. The buzz of conversation bounces across the walls, growing louder the closer we get. Another turn, and we're in the heart of the rebellion.

I stifle a gasp. At the end of the corridor is a vast den, filled with long wooden tables piled high with loaves of bread and wreathes of lettuce rings. I've only had that once before; mammoth leaves of rich green lettuce roasted over a fire, then slathered with butter and a generous amount of spice. My mouth waters. The one thing I can concede about my home is there are only so many varieties of fish to liven my palate.

Sparks jump from the fingers of some disheveled people dressed like shadows playing snaps in a corner—a Flamer children's game to see who can create fiery images in the air the fastest. Others clad in leather command water into spiraling shapes above their palms. Near the ceiling, some float around, laughing. The weight of magic here is overwhelming, the scent of so many signatures overpowering. My own power rears up in response. So many magic signatures in one place. Is everyone here a Nightblood?

Hesitantly, I step into the cavern. A hush falls over the crowd. All eyes are on us. I crush my panic, stand tall, let challenge simmer in my eyes like burning coals. After every tale I've heard of Shaia, I'm certain strength gains her respect.

Whoops of cheer cut the tension like a knife, and I allow myself to breathe again. They're all congratulating Monty, happy to see him home. One kid about his age brightens more than the rest, the overwhelming joy aglow on his face. Freckles cluster over his golden nose. Half of his wild brown hair trails down his shoulder in tightly wound locks, while the other side is cut short and curls around his ear.

"Monty!" he cries, lunging for him.

Monty's smile stretches so wide it could split his face. "Jacopo!"

He moves to meet his friend, but I pull him back. I'm not really sure why I do it, but Monty is the only one I'm familiar with. And I hate to think it, but I might need him for insurance.

"Wait," I say, voice harsher than I intend.

Monty's smile falters. Warning lines his voice, like a thinly veiled threat. Maybe I'm right to be wary of him. "Raven, this isn't a good idea."

I push him behind me. He struggles to escape my grip, which only sends my shame skyrocketing. *Good. This isn't right.*

But I have to make sure I survive this.

A cold, silky voice rings out from the rafters of the room,

making my skin crawl. "I advise you release him before I presume you are here on uncongenial terms."

I spare a glance at the ceiling but find so sign of the woman speaking. Instead, I turn my heated gaze to her followers. "Talk to me face to face and we'll see."

Jacopo steps towards me, fingers sparking with fire. I hold up a hand, daring anyone to attack me. I'm hoping the warning is enough. If they attack, what can I do? Stop time? Sure. But then what? My magic isn't suited for battle.

I can't hear her moving, but I can feel her hovering above me, and I can see her when she drops in front of me, choppy mousey brown hair pinned away from her sharp features. It's as if silence obeys her.

Part of me wants to melt beneath her steel gray eyes. I refuse. I haven't let fear control my life in a long time. Why start now?

"So," she drawls, looking me up and down, tracing her slender fingers over the battle hatchet at her side. A long mark on her arm catches my attention: the same curling lines stretching across the forearms of everyone here. "It is you who was crawling around my home like a wraith."

My mind jumps back to the vision I had of her, the one that led me here, that she kicked me out of. So I was right. She knew my spirit was here when I'd had the vision. No point in denying it. "Yes."

Shaia purses her pale lips. "No one has been apt enough to perforate my security measures. You are rather powerful. If anything, you have enthralled my attention."

I bristle at the way she talks. Eloquent, precise, like every word is an individual challenge. Even though we're both maji, she thinks I'm beneath her. "Good. I need your help."

"I do not negotiate hostage situations." Her eyes flicker to Monty. When they fall on him, that steel in her eyes melts to warm silver. It passes so quickly I'm not sure whether the shift was imagination or reality. "If you seek a proposition, you will release him immediately and perhaps we can have a civil conversation. The alternative is rather messy. Unpleasant. For you."

Air brushes across my cheek as her hatchet sails past my head. It lodges in the wall behind me with a dull *thunk*. Challenge glimmers in her eyes. It's as if she wants me to test her. No doubt that wall could have been my skull if that's what she desired, and she'd do it without blinking.

Threats. Shocking it's her preferred language. As much as I hate to be bullied into subordination, this is not my turf. Perhaps it's best to do things on her terms if I want her help. Though it strikes me that I don't know what exactly it is I want from her.

Trust the gods, Raven. Less and less a comforting mantra with every passing day.

I release my hold on Monty. Like nothing ever happened, he breaks into a dazzling smile and walks around me. Shaia nods at him, lips quirking.

"Monty, your cane has been awaiting your return," Shaia says, her voice honeyed and warm like a spoken embrace.

Jacopo pulls a retractable pole from a loop in his belt and flicks it out until it's nearly as long as my staff. Monty takes it in his hands, lovingly running his fingers over the lustrous bronze shaft. He swings it around. I can tell by the way it cuts through the air it's heavily weighted. Both a seeing cane and a weapon. Classy.

Apparently satisfied with the way his cane moves, he leans on it. "Marie?"

Another crack in Shaia's cool exterior. "Nothing."

Monty's face falls. Jacopo slings an arm around his shoulder, presses a kiss to his temple, and leads him away. Everyone else seems to take that as their cue to resume their activities, leaving me to Shaia's mercy. She saunters around me, scrutinizing me with narrowed eyes. In one swift, distinguished move, she's freed the hatchet from the wall and slipped it back into her belt. Her fingers return once more to the hatchet, languidly drifting across the blade.

"Raven Zuthrié, yes?"

My shock is hard to conceal. "How did you—"

"I keep an eye on anyone worthwhile. Ally or threat. We shall see which you are."

"You have spies all the way in Ghzen?"

"Of course. It is hard to take down a kingdom brick by brick without gathering intelligence from every corner of the known world, no? Knowledge is the cornerstone of power."

Struck with a realization, my eyes widen. "The sage woman in Borziau. She knew about my magic."

Respect flickers in her eyes. As if she's impressed I made the connection. Pretentious. "My grandmother. One of my finest operatives. Only blood I have left."

"Oh. Sorry."

"Lineage does not constitute family. Come," Shaia replies, leading me out of the den into an adjacent room. It's darker.

Quieter. All that fills the dusty space is a chair, a worn desk piled high with documents, a hanging cot, and sputtering candles in a bronze chandelier.

Hesitantly, I settle on the edge of the chair. Shaia perches atop the desk.

"Okay, Seer. Talk."

"I need your help. I got a vision of this place, which you know. The gods led me here because I believe you have an idea of what I should do."

Shaia raises a thin, prim eyebrow. "Vagueness is the enemy of progress."

Heat rises in my face. Condescension is as irritating as threats. "I'm here to save magic."

"Hm." An interminable moment of silence passes as she seems to mull that over. "Interesting. Appears the gods have been listening after all."

"What do you mean? You pray?"

"Everyone prays. I knew there was a reason I've been watching you. You might be just what the insurgency needs to succeed," Shaia muses. "I cannot easily purge the kingdom of indecency, not with magic so weak. To kill the king without interference, I need the connection restored. And that is what you plan to do?"

"Yes. So what is it you know that I don't?"

Shaia's lips quirk. "More than your mind can wrap around, darling." I scoff. She ignores me. "But the answer you are searching for lies with the pirates. The only way to save magic is to awaken the power in Isolde's staff, lay it with her in Caentathea, and perform a ritual to solidify the tether."

Isolde's staff. Relic of the first maji. No telling how much power courses through such a weapon. I thought it had been lost to the ages.

Shaia continues, "I would have done it myself by now, but blood tethers tend not to agree with Reapers. Or anyone, really, and I'm not inclined to sacrifice more of my people for a futile mission. Even if it would further my cause."

"Blood tethers?" I ask, stomach turning over.

"An archaic magic. Dangerous. Unpredictable. And the only way to secure the connection between the divine and mortal planes." Shaia gracefully, soundlessly, leaps off the desk and grips the rusting chandelier hanging above our heads.

Fascinated, I watch as she pulls herself to the top of it, one hand gripping the chain, feet resting on the curling rungs of the chandelier. With her free hand, she unscrews a candle from its holder. Swiftly, she wedges the candle against the chain links, sawing at the wax until the candle crumbles. A slender silver instrument delicately falls into her palm. Like it's nothing, she flips, landing softly on the desk.

I take the blade she hands to me. No longer than my little finger, it's weightless in my hand. Runes are carved along the blade. I don't recognize any of them.

"Take that, offer your blood and that of a compatriot when you are ready for the ritual. And only then. It will bind your connections together, one the anchor, the other the conductor, allowing you to tether the staff to the final resting place of Isolde. If you wait too long, the tether your connections form may find something else to latch onto."

"Meaning?"

"You mess with blood magic, you may land deep within the realm of Luara."

Death.

I clear my throat, trying to brush past my rising terror. I've never heard of blood magic. Touching that is risky. A twisted lure down a dark path. "Appears as if you have all the tools and your only reservations are about blood magic."

"Darling, if I had all the tools, I'd find someone expendable to perform the ritual. Unfortunately, I have never been able to get my hands on the staff."

"How do you know all this?" I ask, skeptical.

Shaia smirks. "Secrets are the currency of Oncarii. I am wealthy."

Moving past her cryptic words, I instead prod for more answers. "So I get Isolde's staff, bring it to her tomb, and perform a blood ritual?"

"Look at you, a fast learner indeed."

I huff. "I don't suppose you know where to find this staff?"

"As I said before, with the pirates. Captain Ryan will understand."

I suppose I shouldn't be surprised she knew I've been traveling with Rélia, but my skin crawls all the same.

Once more, Shaia vaults off the desk, over my head, and scales the brick wall like a spider. I lose her in the shadows of the ceiling. When she returns, there's a scroll in her hand. "The ritual. I presume you read Iquetí?"

I nod.

"Good. Then all that remains is if you are up to the task."

"I wouldn't be here if I wasn't."

Shaia presents the scroll to me. I take the yellowing, scratchy paper in hand, but she doesn't let go. Sighing, I give her the pouch of coins Penn gave me. Gold received for my services as a slave traded to restore magic to its fullest. I suppose some poetry did come out of Tashul after all.

"I assume you want this?"

"I desire to see the persecuted free and the king's head on a spike, but this will suffice. For now." Flaunting a condescending smirk, she releases her hold on the scroll. I carefully tuck it away inside my coat. "It took me several years to gather these instruments. Do not make me regret giving them to you rather than my own people."

"Well, like you said, you'd rather not risk their lives. I want nothing more than to feel magic breathe again, so what do you care if I die as long as you get what you want?"

"Well put. You should be getting back to your ship. I doubt it will stay hidden long."

I follow her back to the den, where no one spares us a second glance. At the exit, she pauses, scanning the crowd.

"I will send someone to accompany you to Caentathea. Make sure the work is done and my utensils returned to me if not."

"Thought you said you wouldn't risk your own?"

Shaia shakes her head ruefully. "And I do not trust you."

Monty approaches, shoulders relaxed, fingers wrapped lovingly around his cane. "I'll go."

"I thought perhaps I'd send Jacopo," she replies.

"Jac can barely tell the difference between left and right. I love him but he is not ready for this. You know that better than I do."

Jac sticks his tongue out at Monty without breaking concentration from his game of dice.

Monty looks at Shaia with a sunny grin.

After a moment, she nods coolly. "Very well. Come back safe." Shaia turns to me. "Best you be off."

Monty darts ahead of me, his cane knocking against the stone walls. Before I can take a step, Shaia calls out to me from a rafter she hadn't been on a moment ago. "Do give Captain Ryan my regards. It would do us both some good for her to return for another tryst."

Bowing my head, I ignore the burning in my cheeks. In my coat, the blood dagger and the scroll are impossibly heavy. But perhaps that's just the daunting task of saving magic finally weighing me down.

20

Rélia

One, two, three, four.

Music plays in my head, the classical piano notes a rhythmic, jovial tune. It's the last good memory I have of my sister—Jimena playing the instrument as if it was a part of her, something that had been wired in her brain from the moment of birth, me leaning against the slick ivory piano, singing a song our music teacher insisted we memorize to impress suitors in the future. Both of us tired of it. Rather than worry about our future partners, we belted out drinking songs at the top of our lungs, danced around the ballroom like the improper heathens we so desperately wished to be.

Everything about that moment was perfect. All a rosy glow, giggles filling the air, not a care in the world. My heart aches to relive that.

I wonder if it was a slow, jagged death when she killed the

only kindness in her heart or if she granted herself the mercy of a clean cut. I peer at the clear blue waves lapping against the hull of the ship. They don't have answers for me.

Turning my head to the cloudless sky, I close my eyes. Sunlight warms my face. Another hour and it'll be noon. Raven's been gone much longer than I anticipated. Everything I've used to try to distract myself from the worry has failed. It gnaws at me, deep and slow. I want to believe her search for Shaia is going without a hitch, but Qada is filled to the brim with secrets and ruthlessness.

Part of me wishes I'd gone with her, but my skin crawls at the thought. Even hidden beneath a cliff where I can't see the city, just the knowledge of being so close is nauseating. I take a deep breath, trying to keep the world from spinning. When I close my eyes, a memory arises. I can't hide from it, no matter how hard I've tried.

•••••

Sixteen. Just a few weeks before I was chosen as heir. Rain came in downpours, the heaviest we'd ever had in Qada, so much so it flooded the streets. Revving with more energy than I'd had in months, I danced through the empty cobblestone streets. I was soaked through, and I loved it. In the Lost Cities, the cluster of towns south of the Savach Desert, I'd heard tales of rain festivals. Everyone dressed in shimmering pastel colors, kept vibrant gardens, decorated and danced with their umbrellas. I wasn't sure if it was true, but I longed for it to be. I longed for my city to do the same.

I passed by the lower district, the place I'd met Shaia. Glimpses of our first encounter flashed in a grim alley. I saw her drop from the tallest building, somersaulting and righting herself in front of me. I was crying, broken-hearted, grieving the loss of the Jimena I knew in childhood. I'd known who Shaia was. I had feared her. Father had told us horror stories of the rebels, those who wanted nothing more than to wash their hands in my blood. But all she did was dry my tears and help me to my feet.

When I was with her, I never felt more alive. We met each other there, in that dank nook every week. Laughing. Talking. I gave her what gold I could spare to cultivate her cause. Technically it was treason, but for the first time in my life, I'd had a reason not to care.

One night, that last rainy night I wandered the streets, was the last night I held love for Qada.

Shaia's brazen smile brightened her eyes as I rounded the corner into our rendezvous spot. Before she launched into her spiel of questions, pestering me for information, I had her pinned against the wall. Her sleek eyebrow rose, and her eyes flickered to my lips. A silent invitation. I didn't wait another second. I couldn't. The moment I'd met her, a fire had ignited in me that I could barely contain. With my lips locked on hers, the fire erupted, searing the air around us, turning the rain to steam.

It all happened so fast. Our clothes fell away. Our limbs tangled. I laughed. Between us was an explosion of ecstasy. When it was over, a realization struck me, cleared my mind, my life.

"I want to run," I said, pulling my soaked clothes over my head. "Fake my death. Let my sister be queen. I want to be a part of your insurgency."

Shaia ran a hand through my hair. My scalp tingled at her

delicate, deliberate touch. "Darling, you were not bred for that. You are better an asset in the palace."

Her words stung, and I was unable to mask the hurt on my face. But her expression was cool as ever. "I mean that little to you?"

"You mean the world to us."

"Sure, to your cause. But to you, nothing?" I studied her carefully. Stone. I choked back tears. I thanked the gods it was still raining. "Don't you enjoy my company?"

"Of course," Shaia said. "I care for you, *princhasa.* Enough to put us both in peril."

I loved when she spoke Iquetí, especially when she used that name for me. Priestess. Not a princess, but someone much more powerful, valuable, revered. "I should distance myself, then. If you are in danger."

Her lips pursed. "Perhaps."

Footsteps at the mouth of the alley pulled my attention from her. Even through the gray blur of the downpour, in the darkness of night, I couldn't miss who it was. I scrambled to my feet, glancing over my shoulder. Shaia was gone. Melted into the shadows. For all I knew, she was hovering a hair above me, but I'd never be able to tell. More likely, she was rooftops away.

"Shaia?" I whispered, desperately searching the alley. Nothing. I was alone.

"You really shouldn't be running off in the middle of the night." Talley's voice echoed down the alley as he strode towards me, hands in the pockets of his commodore coat, suave, smug as ever. "I'm tired of chasing you down for your father."

"No, you're not," I said, crossing my arms. I glanced around the alley. Even if I was good at scaling, the walls were too slick to try. No avoiding this conversation. "It makes you feel important. Because that's all you've cared about lately. Being important."

He stopped within arm's reach, mimicking my stance. Residual instinct from our childhood days: we'd picked up so much from each other that he was almost my mirror. "You know that's not true. I'm only trying to help you. And consorting with ruffians is not in good taste for the future queen."

I scoffed. "I may not be queen. No one has been chosen as heir."

Talley's face softened. "True. But I can't imagine any of your siblings will measure up against you. The whole kingdom knows, and that makes you a target for people like Shaia Rydar. I'm protecting you."

My eyes widened. "How do you know I was here with her?" He remained silent. My heart pounded in my ears. "Girardin. Tell me."

"You have to know I only did what I did to keep you and your legacy safe."

It struck me then, as a distant explosion rocked the city. For weeks, he'd been letting me slip out of the palace to meet Shaia, to follow her whereabouts. Maybe once he would have helped me sneak away, before he became part of the navy, before he stopped being my friend. I should have known.

Tears stung my eyes. Only when she was with me did she ever dare to let down her guard. And it had outed her base of operations.

"You just killed them," I whispered, throat tight. "You just killed so many people."

"Rélia."

"Don't!" I snarled, spit flying. He didn't bother to wipe it from his cheek. My blood boiled as I stared at the face of the man who had once been the only thing that mattered to me. "You're dead to me."

Talley took a step back, shock painting his features. Words tumbled out of his mouth, but I didn't care to hear them. Deep inside, my magic roiled, curling towards my fingers. One strong, concentrated touch and I could turn his wrist to saggy, flaking decay. I raised my hand, ready to do the unthinkable. But the familiar pain in his eyes stopped me. It was the same pain I'd seen when I held him after his grandmother passed, after he'd taken beatings from the guards to stop me from getting in trouble with my father.

For as much as I hated him, I couldn't hurt him. World blurring with hot tears, chest aching with a broken heart, I shoved past Talley into the bleak night.

•••••

I take a deep breath. My knuckles are white around the rail of the deck. Another breath and I relax. Mina shoots me a questioning glance. I smile and mock-salute to hide the quick swipe of tears trailing down my face. She shakes her head and returns to joking with the others.

Another minute passes, and it drags so much it's like half the day has gone. Turning away from the rail, I take up pacing the deck. Part of me is scolding. I could be completely free, not worrying about Talley, nor the king, nor ever being in Qada again, if only I hadn't gone back for Raven. I push the thought away. Can't change what's been done.

On the horizon, the silhouette of a massive ship steadily sails towards us. Slowly, my crew takes notice. Nervous energy rises in the air. I pace faster, practically jogging now. Dividers. How the hell did they find me? Until Raven and Penn are back, we can't leave. But gods, they're cutting it close.

In the distance, I catch sight of a dinghy heading for us. Relief washes over me. The itch that's been irritating me the past few hours, the itch to sail as far from here as possible, worsens. I grab the rope ladder and toss it over the side. Mina and Ori work to raise the anchor.

Come on, come on. I hope through sheer force of will that Penn rows faster. Everyone else on the ship is just as antsy to get away. The nerves are tangible.

Finally, the dinghy knocks against the hull of the ship. Inside, I see Penn, Raven, and Monty; the latter I'm guessing Shaia sent back to keep us honest. I snort. Trusting has never been a strength of hers. Not that I blame her. She has not known the world to be kind.

I help Penn over the ladder, then Monty. Last is Raven. She's worrying at her lip, her eyebrows knit together, and her mouth pursed. I reach out to take her hand.

That's when the first bullet strikes the rail beside me.

21

Tezin

I scrub the same spot on the deck for the hundredth time with a shabby sponge. It's grueling, repetitive work. Every time I clean it, another crew member dumps his piss bucket there or accidentally spills ale, though accident is hardly the proper term. Irritating as it is, I don't have the energy to do anything but turn and clean it again. Demeaning, but preferable to sitting in Navda's cabin or the cold cells.

At least out here the sun shines against the calm sea. It's a warm, gentle caress on my face. Like a reassurance that everything will turn out alright. If I focus hard enough, the wood of the ship can become the docks of Ghzen, and I can pretend I'm scrubbing fish scales away. It's just a normal chore and I'll return to a normal day at home.

Marie slams her mop on the deck, aggressively sliding the filthy water around, pulling me back to reality. Her coils of red hair pulled back with a grimy white bandana are as stunning as her brother's under the light of the mid-morning sun. The sleeve of her left arm slips up, revealing a mark; two curling lines stretching towards her elbow. She tugs her sleeve down when she catches me looking.

"Take it easy," I say, glancing at the crew members idly standing by. Subtly isn't a proficient skill on this ship. Their eyes constantly flit to her, always ready for an opening to make their advances. "Don't irritate them."

Marie glares at me. "I'm not afraid of them."

"Maybe you should be," Aran replies, sitting atop an empty crate. Bruises still discolor his face, and he winces with every step, but for the most part, he's healed. With a large task ahead of him, Navda needed him rested enough to function properly. Lots of quiet and curative tonic. Aran hasn't got any work to do, not until the *Anviora* is in sight.

Her grip tightens around the handle of her mop. "Talk to me again, I'll take this broom and shove it—"

I clear my throat. "Why doesn't Navda just keep you in the cells until we reach Qada?"

Aran crosses his arms. "Nice, thanks."

Marie snorts and swabs the deck with a little less fury.

I mentally scold myself. "No, not what I meant. Just like, er, aren't you a bit dangerous walking around free up here?"

He explains, "Longer I'm away from the xipher door, the faster I recover from its oppression, the stronger my magic is. Besides, Navda's ruthless. What makes you think I'll do anything to defy him while you're here?"

"Coward."

Aran huffs. "I'm not doing this with you again, Marie."

"Whatever." Her mopping technique is more aggressive than when she began. "Don't cry to me when I've escaped, and you're still stuck here."

"I wouldn't be able to, given I'd still be a slave."

"Gods, you suck."

I turn my back on them. Tuning out their voices gives me some solace. I don't need to hear another of the same fight. They're together, at least. They should appreciate it while they can. I scrub harder on the deck, as if it will scrub away the ache in my chest for Raven.

Desperately in need of rest, I drop the sponge and sit back, leaning my head against the crate Aran's sitting on. For a moment, I close my eyes, relishing in the warmth of the sun. Aran runs his fingers through my hair, gently tugging it free of knots. I smile.

"Oi!"

A mug of ale shatters on the deck next to me. My eyes snap open. Navda looms over me, coolly irate. Something is unfamiliar about his anger. He's missing his explosiveness, his uncontrollable rage. This petrified composure is far more terrifying. In the corner of my eye, I catch Ean watching, fingers steepled, his irritated gaze threatening to swallow me whole.

Aran's hands cover my chest, as if to protect me from stray shards. I cling to his hand, steadying my heartbeat.

Navda brushes off his palms like he didn't just nearly maim my face. "Back at it sully-blood."

Seething with indignation, I reach for the sponge. To my

surprise, Aran grabs my hand. I glance between him and Marie; both have the same cold fire in their eyes, glaring at Navda.

"Guys, it's fine," I mutter. I don't particularly want to face anyone's wrath today.

"No. It's not," Aran says.

"Yeah," Marie agrees, gritting her teeth. "You've been making us clean like this all day. No need to make it harder on him. Leave him alone."

Navda grunts. "I think your show of insubordination is exactly why I need to keep it up. Learn your place, girl. Your friend certainly has."

I clench my jaw. True as it may be, I can't help the boiling rage on the brink of overflowing. Is it worth it to be under the sun if I must suffer so many insults? I breathe through the anger. It fades as I wrench free of Aran's protective grip. Fresh air and belittling is better than the cells.

Navda's boot comes down hard on my hand as I scoop up the shards. A jagged piece cuts a thin line across my palm. I hiss in pain. Gritting my teeth, I resume with my free hand. Show him I'm subservient and it'll pass. He'll get bored. I hope. Aran fingers the arrow through his ear but remains silent.

Unfortunately, Marie doesn't have the sense to keep her mouth shut. "Hey! I said to leave him alone."

The pressure lifts from my hand as Navda turns to her. Stinging prickles my palm. Looking at the wound exacerbates the pain. I cradle my injured hand to my chest, apprehensively watching Navda and Marie. She holds her head high, gripping so tight to the mop I wonder how it hasn't splintered.

She opens her mouth, though before she has the chance to

tell him off, Navda has his hand clamped around her throat and shoves her against the main mast. The mop clatters to the floor. Her toes scrape the deck. Indulging the rage burning through me, I shoot to my feet. Beside me, Aran is frozen. His eyes are wide, face red with anger, fingers still poised around the arrow in his ear. But he won't move.

Rolling up my tattered, soaked sleeves, I muster all the courage I can. It's meager. Enough to keep me from rationality. I dig my fingers into Navda's shoulder. He glares at me. Connecting once more, I delve into his mind. That cry I heard when I first entered his mind is hysterical now. Whispered commands echo in my ears. Orders to scare me, to threaten Marie.

"Drop her," I command, my voice thick with sentience.

Marie falls to the deck, gasping. In a split second, the wisp of power lining my words is gone. I grasp at the fading tendrils of magic but scrape against an encompassing cold in my core.

Navda shakes his head as if clearing his mind from a fog. Confusion twists his features before he resumes the unfamiliar cool aggression. "Oh, everyone would like a turn? Fine. The more the merrier."

I try to reach for my magic. Nothing. I want to scream. Why don't I properly work? Is it because magic is dying that my connection is so weak? Or that I was never meant to have it at all?

Navda pulls a sharp, rusting dagger from his belt. I take a step back. In one swift motion, Marie sweeps his legs from beneath him. I sidestep. He crumples to his knees. I pull Marie behind me, but she yanks free and storms back to her mop as if nothing happened, though not for lack of a glare so scorching it could set the ship on fire.

I glance at Aran. Wringing his hands together, he shifts uncomfortably on the crate. He won't meet my eyes.

Navda rises, arms crossed, gruff as ever. Throwing out all sense of self-preservation, I stare him down, not moving a muscle. Ominous murmuring snakes through my ears, drowning out everything else. Eternity passes before the whispers hush. The captain shoves me back to my sponge, then storms to his cabin. Kneeling, I half-heartedly scrub at the deck. Ean meets my gaze, face sullen. Black tendrils recede from the whites of his eyes. Flashing a tepid smile, he takes up a bottle of rum.

Uncomfortable silence pulls taut between Aran, Marie, and me. Cleaning keeps my mind distracted, but the fact that Marie isn't slamming the mop against the deck anymore is unsettling.

By the time the sun has reached its noon apex, my limbs are aching. Together, we've managed to swab the entirety of the deck as spotless as it can get. My palm still stings, but the bleeding has ceased. I flex my hand, testing my mobility while I rest against a crate, relishing in the relaxation, however brief.

"There!" Navda's voice booms across the ship.

I peer over the rail. Spires rise from the earth, so high they could touch the clouds. We've reached Qada.

Hidden under the shade of a monstrous cliff is a familiar ship, ivory sails billowing in the wind, waves gently lapping against the dark wood of the hull. Coming along the shore is a small dinghy heading for the *Anviora*. Three figures sit inside. Despite the distance, I can't mistake Raven as one of them.

I stumble back. She's going to get on the ship. Aran is meant to destroy it. I inhale sharply, shallowly. Black spots dance in my vision. I did this. I brought Navda here, to this ship, to Raven. Once more, she will suffer from my cowardice.

Aran catches me before I hit the floor. I steady myself on his shoulder. Forcing myself to calm, I try to think. Within the next few minutes, my sister will die if I don't find a way to stop this.

"Please," I beg Aran, who has his sights set on the ship. "Don't do anything to it. My sister could die."

Vacancy drifts over his eyes, as if disconnecting his mind from what he is about to do. His voice trembles. "The last thing I want is to destroy that ship. But I have to."

Navda's crew lines against the railing, readying muskets and rifles. Gunshots echo in the open air. Instinctively, I cover my ears. I've never heard a sound so ear-splitting, so consuming. The *Anviora* furls their sails, though they've already been peppered with holes.

"Ready the cannons!" Navda bellows.

My blood runs cold. I ignore the familiar bite of tears. "You said you'd help me save her."

"If I do, then it will be me who dies, Tezin!" Aran cries. "I'm sorry, but if it's her or me, it's going to be your sister. Truly, I'm sorry. But I won't go down for someone I don't know."

Torrents of bullets whiz through the air. Gunpowder burns my nose. My heart lurches in my throat. I won't watch her die. I will *not*.

My magic rises unbidden, before I have a chance to call for it. Power tingles through me like bolts of lightning. I take a deep breath, revving with confidence, with surety and clarity. As if my purpose of existence has led me to this moment, this feeling, this overwhelming euphoria, the deception that I can do anything.

Pain is but a distant memory. Inhale, and the stinging in my palm ceases. Exhale, and the aches in my back quell like I'd never been whipped.

I can stop this. I can save Raven.

Focusing all my energy into my voice, I turn to Aran. Grabbing him by the shoulders, I force him to meet my eyes. I don't care about his fear, or the desperation for survival written across his face. I don't care about anything but the fact that soon my sister will be safe.

Words roll off my tongue of their own accord, thick, sentient, sickeningly enchanting. "Change the course of the wind. Send us far away from here, until you cannot sense their sails in the wind any longer."

Aran's eyes glaze over. His fingers turn skywards. The wind whistles so fast it knocks me off my feet. Breathing it is like inhaling air reserved only for the divine; sweet, biting, prickling my lungs.

Our sails snap, catching the air. I clutch my chest, as if the air had been ripped from me. We practically fly across the ocean. Relief cools my core as all signs of land fade into the endless expanse of water and horizon.

Aran collapses. Everything within me fades, leaving me so empty I wonder if my spirit too, was sucked away. Head spinning, I shakily sit up. Navda storms towards us, his face so deeply purple it mimics a plum. I know what's coming. For me, for Aran. For everyone.

The realization of what I must do turns my stomach over. If I am to survive, if I want to keep Raven safe, there's no way around it.

Navda has to die.

22

Raven

My hand slips through Rélia's as gunshots echo above my head. A startled scream escapes my lips. I fall a few rungs down the ladder. Rope burns my hand when I grab on tight. I clamber up the ladder and roll onto the deck.

Everyone is scrambling. The sails are furled, the rigging tied up. I stand, frozen as a torrent of bullets shower over us. Gunshots. I've never heard them before. Now it's an orchestra booming around me. My ears ring. The world spins. Am I going to die today?

"Raven!" Rélia shakes me from my daze. "Get below, now."

I take a deep breath, clearing my mind. "And do what?"

"Hide! I'll take care of this."

She turns away from me. Hastily, she ties her hair back with a vibrant bandana.

"What's your plan?"

"Keep Navda away from everyone I care about."

"That's not really a plan," I say, whipping my staff out. "Who's Navda?"

"Captain of the Dividers. Worst of the worst. And wants me super dead." Rélia rolls up her sleeves to her elbows. "Wish me luck."

My blood runs cold. The Dividers? Every muscle tenses as I face the open waters. Sitting on the waves is an enormous, menacing ship. A ship that's been seared into my memory since the day pirates killed my papa.

Revenge is so close. The thought hits me like a boulder. It burns through my veins. Nothing else matters. Not magic, not Rélia, not the bullets striking the ship. Killing Navda, getting justice, the desire of it all consumes me.

I clamp both hands on my staff, focusing all my energy on the current of the world around me. Light greets me when I close my eyes. Buzzing warmth fills me. Calling upon my magic to perform such a feat as stopping time is less arduous with my staff in my hands. Latching onto the steady hum of the world, I will it to decelerate. Little by little, everything winds down. Gunshots and the beat of the waves fade away. Bullets slow. Soon it will be only me moving in a frozen world.

A cool hand on my arm pulls me from my mind. Everything snaps back into place. I open my eyes to see Rélia holding my wrist. I yank free.

"You broke my concentration!"

Rélia's nose twitches. "What the hell are you doing? Stopping time won't do anything but exhaust you."

"I have to do something!" So close. I'm so close to avenging

Papa. "I am not going to let the man who killed my papa slip through my fingers. I have worked too hard and too long for this. You are *not* going to get in my way!"

"Yes," Rélia replies, wrapping her fingers around my staff. "I am. You can't fix this."

Magic scalds through me, searing like a wildfire. Gold wisps around my hands, rising in response to my fury. I glare at her, keenly aware of colors sharpening. That familiar burn prickles behind my eyes as my power overtakes me. Rélia holds my stare. Silver illuminates her, turns her irises to iron.

Time slows. I try to pull my staff from her grip, but she resists. Our fingers brush as we fight for control. Sparks of magic jump between us, igniting the air with power. Heat and chill surge together. White smoke curls from Rélia's fingertips. Focusing on its particles, I will the smoke to slow with the tide of Oncarii. But Rélia is moving with me, escaping the stillness of the world outside us.

The smoke twines around me, curling up my arms, clinging to my mouth and nose. Coughing, throat burning, I struggle to maintain my focus. Mucus saturates my lungs. My mind grows fuzzy, muted. I've been through this before—a debilitating cold nearly every child experiences. Irritating, but not fatal.

I push through the dizziness, through the sickness determined to placate my mind. I grip tighter to my staff. Rélia falters. It's as if she's impressed I quelled her attack. Her eyes flicker between amber and gray, and I detect a hint of fear there too. Is she scared of my power? Should I be?

My eyes widen. How much magic am I channeling right now? I've stopped time. I've kept Rélia with me. I'm roaring with vigor.

The thrum of magic rushes in my ears, drowning out all other sound. Gold hues tint the world.

I release the staff. Panting, I collapse to the deck. Rélia follows. My ears ring. Sweat drips down my face. Exhaustion overwhelms me. It hurts. My magic, still rushing with fervor, pains me as if I am burning from the inside out. I take a few gasping breaths and it dulls. Rélia staggers to her feet next to me, her eyes wild, her hands shaking. Mine are too.

A bullet strikes the deck a hair from my foot, splintering the wood. I startle. Scrambling on my hands and knees, I grab my staff and cradle it close to me, unsure of what else to do. With the assault of gunfire everywhere, I can't so much as stand without risking getting hit. Rélia was right. Stopping time only drained me. Trying again would burn me out. I scream, resisting the urge to slam my staff on the deck. Why am I so useless?

Just as I'm devising a feeble plan of action to get to the Divider's boat, to single-handedly take them down, a gust of wind blows across my face. Normally that would mean nothing. But it picks up rapidly. I glance around searching for signs of a monsoon—the skies are clear. I take a breath. Faintly, I taste a refreshing bite to the warm wind, leaving my lips tingling. My mouth parts in surprise. It's unnatural. Galer summoned. And heading straight for the Divider's ship.

"Unfurl the sails!" I shout, dashing for Rélia. Maybe we can catch the wind.

"Oh what now?" She huffs, whirling on me. "Keep distracting me and we won't—"

"We have to let the sails down!"

"Okay, do not ever interrupt me."

I refrain from driving the bladed end of my staff through her throat. "Rélia, listen to me. This wind can save us!"

She straightens, looking around as if she's sensing the shift in the air for the first time. "You're a genius!"

Jumping into action, she tugs on the ropes, letting the main sail fall free. The ship lurches. But peppered with holes, the sail cannot billow, and the wind has already passed us, carrying the Divider away.

"Damnit." Rélia plants her hands on her hips, staring at the damaged sails. "You couldn't have warned me of the wind sooner?"

I throw her a disdainful glare. "Do me a favor and drop dead."

"I can think of plenty of things I'd rather do instead." Rélia laughs and winks at me.

I turn my back on her in an effort to hide my sudden fluster. Gods she's unbelievably irritating. Who's so nonchalant after being attacked?

More than that, why do I long for that rush of adrenaline once more?

"You're insane you know," I mutter. "Laughing after near death."

She shrugs. "I prefer risk-inclined. Besides, it's nothing I've never seen before. Gotta laugh in the face of death if you're gonna get anywhere in life, right?"

I shake my head, reiterating my sentiments. "You're insane."

"Or maybe you're just boring." Rélia hands me a handkerchief. "And I mean that in the best way possible."

"Sure you do," I say, accepting the cloth. I hadn't realized how much I was sweating. "So, I got what I needed. From Shaia."

"And? More to that or am I supposed to play twenty questions?"

I roll my eyes. "We need to find Isolde's staff. She said it's with the pirates. I'm praying to the gods you know what that means."

Mischief and delight twinkle in her eyes. "It means we get to visit my favorite place in the sea. Raven, we're heading to Racha."

I purse my lips, not sure if I heard her correctly. "Wait, that's real? Racha, as in the secret island where you do all your infernal illegal exchanges."

She grins. "It's more than that. But yes. You're gonna hate it."

I blow a stray hair out of my face, skin crawling with irritation. "Oh, by the way, Shaia said you should come back for another tryst. Thought I should relay the message."

Immediately her demeanor shifts. Rélia wrings her hands together and her ears tinge red. After a few attempts at replying, I realize she's actually flustered. The ever so cocky Rélia Ryan is embarrassed at the prospect of going at it again with the leader of the rebels. It's the kind of embarrassment accompanied by distant longing. That realization sits cold and rough in my stomach.

"Sorry, did I get you all ruffled?" I tease.

Rélia smiles, her obvious fluster melting away, replaced by that familiar coy, arrogant aura. She laughs again. "Heh. I'm rubbing off on you. By the time we've saved magic, you'll be my prodigy."

"Only if there's no justice or mercy in the world," I reply sternly. But I'm grinning. And honestly, it has never felt so good to smile.

The crew emerges from belowdecks, confused muttering a cloud around them. Penn approaches us, brows knit in concern.

"What happened, Cap'n?"

"Good news, Penn. We're all alive. For now. Bad news. We need a new mainsail." Rélia sets her sights on Qada, her ease belied by the apprehension in her eyes. "Who's up for a little heist?"

23

Rélia

So far, so good.

Just thinking that is probably a jinx, like I'm tempting the gods to mess with me. I'm sure it is. I'm sure the fact that I have downed the last of my wine and am stumbling drunk through the streets with a feeble plan rolling about in my head is like I'm spitting in the face of all that's divine. Given the real chance, I might. I can picture Raven's reaction: her striking features even sharper, her full lips parted in offended surprise, her eyes pleading the gods to know she has no desire to be associated with me.

Beside me, Raven is taut, every muscle tense with focus. Her stature is reminiscent of an actual statue, the ones whose eyes seem to follow you everywhere. In the sun, though, her skin glows with an ethereal beauty unlike any statue I've seen. Her lips pucker, and she drums her fingers against her arm.

Every step I take grinds my teeth down a little further. I

can't seem to stop clenching my jaw no matter how hard I try. Even the air feels like sandpaper against my skin. Talley appears in every alley, the stink of his betrayal following us. I shake my head, desperate to clear the illusion from my mind. But it is rooted far deeper than that.

I itch to run back to the safety of my ship, scrub myself free of Qada's dirt. But I am the only one who can get us into the shipyard. Beneath my breath I mutter curses, both vulgar words and ill wishes to the divine.

"Rélia, stop." Raven nudges me.

"What? It's calming."

If possible, she tenses further. "You're going to give us away."

"Love, you're the one acting like we're already caught." I place a gentle hand behind her back, nearly touching. The desire to comfort her is overwhelming. She turns to me. My hand drops.

Raven grabs my wrist, stopping me in my tracks. "I'm being cautious. You're acting like the air is diseased."

"It very well might be." I brush off my shirt, desperate to still the beat of my heart, to disguise the flush in my skin. I glance at her fingers, still wrapped around my wrist. She lets go. Impulse whispers to me to take her hand, put it back, pull her close. Instead, I turn up the lapel of my coat and push forwards.

Eyes follow us down the streets. Whispers rise and fall around me. I know it must be my imagination, it must be. No one has seen the recluse Princess Rélia in years. But I look just the same, and perhaps that is why we cannot melt into the shadows, why my paranoia will not let me be.

Spires loom over us as we pass by the gates of the palace. Guards stand at attention at every gate, corner, probably lurking behind the walls too. Arrays of weapons adorn their belts, some of which I've never seen the likes of, though I certainly wouldn't hate to try my hand at wielding them. One guard catches me staring, his eyes narrowing. I shrink into my collar. Best not start trouble. Yet.

My anxieties ease as the palace disappears behind us. Laughter, chatter, the tinny ringing of hammer on metal drifts through the air as we reach the edge of the city. Steam and smoke burn my nose. Blistering heat sears the air—fresh stacks of coal feeding roaring fires. I'd heard of Talley's experiments with improving naval travel. But to see it before my eyes, the seamless blend of wood and steel, is enough to stop me in my tracks.

"I think I'm gonna cry," I say, as Raven throws me a questioning look.

She rolls her eyes. "It's just a fancy boat. Come on, there's Penn and Monty."

Dressed in the grubby uniform of a dock worker, Penn looks like he's been working at this his whole life. Monty, however, is far too out of place, his clothes baggy, as if he's trying to draw attention to the fact that he stole a dock worker's uniform.

I give them both a brief nod. Passing behind Penn, I hand him a small, unassuming pouch. Keeping his eyes forward, he tucks the pouch full of nachnuii powder into his breast pocket. With that, the four of us disperse in separate directions.

Blending into the shadows, I make my way towards the storage sheds. A young faced Talley beams at me from my mind's eye. Is he still so full of wonder as he was when he joined the dockworkers? I pray everything is in the same spot as it was when he first showed me around, hands calloused, face beaded with sweat and sawdust.

Lingering beside the well-kept shed, I pull my hat lower and turn my attention to Monty. He deftly slips through the crowd of workers, his cane sliding silently over the ground. His pockets grow heavier with the gold he slips from the drunkards on break or the dedicated shipbuilders hard at work.

"Should have just sent him to steal and bought a new sail," I mutter, leaning against the shed.

Finally, his cane knocks against someone's foot in a calculated move. Accusations ring throughout the air. Monty feigns panic. A crowd forms around him. In the corner of my eye, I catch Penn stashing small wooden boxes across the shipyard. Raven follows with flint and steel in hand, waiting for my signal.

I raise my hand. Sparks fly from Raven's hands. She's a blur as she dashes away, disappearing into the crowd. Explosions rock the shipyard: one, two, three, each moments apart. Monty is abandoned as the dockworkers rush to safety, to put out the flames, to ring bells. Beneath the noise, no one hears as I shoulder the shed door open.

Inside, it's cool, musty. Arranged in neat piles at the far end of the shed are uncut canvas covered in a layer of dust. I frown. Have sailing ships been so overshadowed already? Coal ships haven't even been out of the shipyard yet.

In the quiet of the shed, my footsteps are like gunshots. Clenching my hands into fists, I try to quiet my breaths, my body, everything. Row upon row of foresails, trysails. Finally, I reach the dwindling pile of mainsails. I run my fingers over the fabric, the finest on the sea as much as it pains me to admit it. A smile touches my lips.

"You still have expensive taste, I see."

I startle. My hand is tight around the hilt of my sword, a mirror of my clenched jaw. How the hell did he beat us here? "You won't stop me."

Talley steps into my line of vision, shoulders relaxed, free of his distinguishing overcoat. Stubble casts a shadow on his jaw. He's tired when he speaks. "I'm not going to."

I narrow my eyes. "Why not?"

"Because I know you'd put up a fight. And I don't want to hurt you, not if you don't give me reason to."

Dust showers over us as another explosion sends the world rocking. Penn's nachnuii charges are running short and so is my time.

"Then what?" I spit. "What is it you plan to do, my good admiral, with all the maji you keep behind bars, with the ones you torture?"

He's genuinely affronted. "I never tortured anyone. I regret that I must run the Penitentiary. But I am trying to help, trying to cure maji. I can only do so much at once."

"Cure maji? Magic is dying already, you idiot."

"But a little bird you once loved told me you're trying to save it." He leans against a neatly stacked pile of wooden crates brimming with rope. "So for those who wish to never fear enslavement, I will find them a cure."

Shaia. Of course she would pass him information. Not without her own agenda, but a heads up would have been nice. "How courteous. And did Monty agree to be a subject? Did your *little bird* know you had him locked up?"

Talley's eyes darken. "To help the many, there are calculated casualties."

Sorrow tugs at my heart. "What happened to you?"

He doesn't respond.

Shouts echo on the other side of the door. A series of knocks rap on the wood. Time's up.

My sword swings free of its sheath, cutting down a stack of canvas beside Talley. He leaps out of the way. I slash my sword through the canvas only to find he's gone. Stomping my foot, I huff out a sigh and shove my sword back into its sheath. Though I can't deny I'm relieved I didn't stab him. He may yet be saved.

Monty bursts through the door, Raven and Penn in tow. Each of them is beaded in sweat and smells distinctly of smoke.

"Here!" I wave them over. Penn and Raven take a corner of the canvas each, tugging it out the back door of the shed. Monty taps his cane. Earth rises to his call, rolling beneath the canvas to better support the weight.

My hand lingers on the hilt of my sword as I follow after them. Everything went off without a hitch. But Talley's words follow me like a shadow.

I will find them a cure.

And I wouldn't hate to have it.

24

Rélia

Nothing but calm blue sea surrounds us. I rest my head back on my chair, swirling my wine in my glass, grateful for smooth sailing at last. I wish Raven hadn't declined my invitation to empty the final bottle. She'd rather down the delightfully disgusting rum and listen to musicians play on deck. Can't blame her. It is far less lonely.

"Come in," I say, when there's a gentle knock at the door.

Monty pokes his head in the room. "Sorry to bother you."

I wave a hand. "You're better company than my thoughts."

"Well, that's a given," he replies. His cane slides against the floor as he moves for my desk. Following it, he walks with a graceful ease I have to commend. "You reek of loneliness."

I down the rest of my wine. "And here I thought I hid it well. Is there a reason you're here?"

"You mean other than cheering you up?"

"You sure that's what you're doing?"

He gives me a lopsided smile. "I'm trying my best. But I'm not Raven."

I relax into my chair, ignoring the fluttering in my stomach. "What's that supposed to mean?"

"Like you don't already know. I'm blind not stupid." He clears his throat, cutting through the pregnant silence growing between us. "I did have a real reason to come in here. Figured I should thank you. For saving me."

"Kid, if anything I should be thanking you. Not sure any of us would have made it out alive if you hadn't crumbled the Penitentiary."

"Ah, it was nothing. I'd been itching to do it for ages anyway. But yeah. Thanks."

Narrowing my eyes, I lean closer to him. "It's rather late for gratitude. You could've said this weeks ago and moved on. What is it you really want to say?"

"You are every bit what Shaia describes. Never should have doubted her expertise, but it's always fun to see her knowledge played out before my eyes. Well, eyes per se."

I straighten. Remnants of old memories, old feelings, flare in my chest. Denying my attachment to that part of my past only makes the ache stronger. "She talks about me?"

"Occasionally."

I sigh, letting my desire deflate. "Right. She tell you to play this game with me?"

Monty shrugs, face level. There's just the faintest quirk of his lips. "She tells me lots of things."

"Figures. She clearly hasn't changed." I pop a grape in my mouth. "Next time you see her, tell her to shove it."

Without another word, I hop out of my chair. I head for the door, ready for the astounding curative properties of fresh air. In an instant, Monty's cane is in front of me, a breath away from my knees. Forged of weighted bronze, perhaps by his own hand with his empowering Welder's touch, I'm sure it could shatter my kneecaps with one quick swipe. Why he's daring to flash less than subtle threats is beyond me.

"What are you doing?"

All essence of his cheerful demeanor evanesces like wisps above him. He tilts his head as if he too is contemplating where it's going. "Tread carefully, Captain Ryan. Shaia did a lot for me. I owe her my life, my livelihood, my happiness. I am grateful for the kindness you've shown me. I am. But she won't hesitate to bring you to your knees if you don't give her the tools she needs to overthrow the king. And I will not stop her."

I lift his cane with my foot. "She is the only person who would dare try. She'll fail. Trust me, Monty. There are things about me that not even she knows. If she wants to threaten me, I'd appreciate it if she'd do it herself instead of sending a lapdog."

Simmering with irritation, I brush past Monty. Shaia Rydar. When will my life stop revolving around her?

The answer comes clear as soon as I step onto the deck where the evening sun is shining. Raven leans against the railing, a mostly empty mug of rum in her hand, smiling so wide the corners of her eyes crinkle. Golden sun rays cast an alluring aura around her, refract across her dark eyes, turning them to rings of gold much more precious than the metal in the ground men have killed each other for. She's laughing with Ori and Penn. Already one of us. I'm sure her skin would be crawling at the thought if she had less alcohol in her system.

Our eyes meet for a moment, but it's like an eternity, a timeline where it is only the two of us and nothing else matters.

"Rélia," Raven calls, waving me over. "Question."

I glance between the three of them. Well, four, counting Pidge resting contentedly on her shoulder. "I might have an answer."

"We're uh, solving an argument. Between us." She waves her hands wildly between us. "Chances of me surviving Racha. Surviving, as if they think it'll conquer me. Wrong. I say, I'd do better than any of you. Stopping time is easier. Than sword anyway."

She sways and giggles.

"Yeah, that's enough." I wrestle the mug from her hands. Though she tries, she doesn't put up much of a fight. I glare at Penn and Ori. "Do not give her more or I'll have your ass, got it? Enough with the hazing. She's clearly not equipped for drinking games."

Raven pouts. "Rude."

"I expected better from both of you. Especially *you*, Penn." I jab a finger at his chest. He holds his hands up in defense, though glee glimmers in his eyes.

I let my glare linger for a moment, before turning my attention to Raven. Helping her down to my cabin is a painstaking process what with her attention span all over the place. Along the way, we pass Monty. His warning tugs at the back of my mind, but I ignore it. Deep in the Hebringg sea, those threats can't reach me. Even Shaia has her limits.

"You *do* have good qualities," Raven murmurs, her eyes wide as I lay her on my bed.

I shake my head. "And you really can't hold your liquor. I'm going to get water."

Raven grabs my hand, her fingers tightly winding around mine. Prickles of warmth spread across my skin at her touch. I latch onto that feeling, use it to burn away the numbing, bone-shattering cold battling for control over me. "Wait, I have to tell you something."

Sincerity breaks through that wall she never fails to build up. For once, I can see everything turning in her mind. All the broken pieces of her soul scattered behind her impenetrable barrier are lain before my eyes. I want nothing more than to mend it, to take away her pain.

I sit beside her. Warmth flows into my fingertips. Silver glints around my hands as I coax out her suffering. It comes with ease, greeting my magic with a lust for decay. It's withering to touch, a cold so freezing it's scalding. Stifling a gasp, I press my free hand to her heart. It's pounding, pumping her trauma through her veins at a rate I almost can't keep up with.

Grounding myself, I let my healing nature intertwine with her spirit, taking in all the sensations silhouetting her memories. They hit me like a tidal wave, threatening to take me under and drown me in her pain. Overwhelmed by the agony of her deepest, most emotionally charged moments, tears well in my eyes. How can she keep all this anger inside? How has she not collapsed under the weight of her wounds? I can barely hold on to the shredded remains of my self-worth.

Her heart rate slows to a normal pace. I pull away from

her. Exhaustion sweeps through me as the remnants of her pain flicker to my core. When I'm too weary to hold onto it anymore, it will return to her. For now, she can be happy.

I fetch her a glass of warm water which she downs in one swallow. Making sure she's comfortable, cuddled close to Pidge, I turn to leave.

"I still have to tell you something."

I hover at the threshold of my bedchamber, pulse quickening. What is it I think she's going to say that's making me so nervous? "Yeah?"

"I don't hate you."

The hint of a smile ghosts across my lips. I almost believe her. "Tell me when you're sober."

Raven's eyes close. Mesmerized by the steady rise and fall of her chest, the tranquility she exudes in slumber, I linger for a moment more before closing the curtain to let her rest in peace.

25

Tezin

One week. It's been one week since Aran's spoken to me. Today he hasn't so much as looked in my direction. He took the shawl back. I don't blame him, though I can't deny I miss how comforting it was to hold. Now I have nothing but the cuffs of my baggy, grimy shirt to fiddle with when my hands can't stop moving.

I've tried to apologize. My power was more intense than ever when I charmed him. I could have hurt him. I can't ever take that back. Guilt still wracks me. Apologies aren't enough. I so much as open my mouth and a vortex of wind sucks the air from my lungs.

I stare at the dark ceiling of our cell. Tonight, it's quiet. No storms. No raucous drunks. No screams of the poor new maji who fall victim to Navda's boredom. There's only the gentle rock of the ship and the skittering of rats on the floor.

I try to picture the stars. All the constellations laid out in the inky night sky, telling stories just for me and Raven while Papa roasted salmon and Mama stoked the fire. My heart aches. Seeing stars brings me back to those family bonfires, fading memories we can never rekindle. I miss the way the stars glimmer and whisper to me that everything will turn out alright because as long as Raven and I have each other there's nothing we can't overcome.

But we're far apart now. And I haven't seen the stars nor heard their murmured encouragement in weeks. Hope is more delusive with every passing night.

I close my eyes. Though my body demands rest from the day's toil, my mind is alight with purpose, fabricating schemes, tearing them apart, salvaging the beneficial, building up with those scraps, tearing it all down again. Repeat, repeat, repeat. There's something in the bare threads of these ideas spinning in my mind that I can stitch together a feasible plan to take down Navda. I have to believe that to be true before my cowardice condemns me to an empty, fruitless life in a living hell.

Pins and needles prick my temples. I groan. Has my mind ever worked so hard?

When I open my eyes again, I am no longer in my cell. Part of me thinks it is a dream. How can it not be? The stars are shining. Grass beneath my feet is soft, lush, dotted with the sweet-scented yellow wildflowers I've smelled so many times on my trips to Borziau. Owls hoot in the distance. Tranquility fills my lungs with every deep breath I take.

I turn, drinking in the rest of this landscape, only to find Raven standing in the midst of the tall swaying grasses, her eyes wide with curious wonder. Relief floods my mind. I don't stop to wonder whether all of this is an illusion, an elaborate psychological torture Navda is testing. She feels real enough when I envelop her in a tight hug.

"Tezin?" She murmurs, pulling away from me, studying my face with a tilted head. "Gods, it is you! Where are we?"

"I don't know." I pick one of the flowers. I roll the fragrant petals between my fingers, relishing in the soft reality of the bud. "I think we're dreaming."

Raven closes her eyes, tips her head to the sky, takes a deep breath. "Together?"

"We're connected. Our consciousnesses are tethered together. I can feel everything you're feeling right now."

Raven drums her fingers against her arm. "Like the pocket world for Psychics? That doesn't make sense."

"Right. Listen, I don't know how or why, but Raven, I have magic. I'm a Psychic."

Silence passes between us. Confusion clouds her already unsteady mind, echoing inside my own, like her thoughts are mine. Her fingers drum faster, and her eyebrows knit together. "Tezin, are you okay? My Sight showed me that you were in a cell, and now you're telling me you can do magic? That's impossible."

"It's not." I sigh, running my hands through my hair. "I'm not sure how to explain it to you, but you have to know I'm using it to find a way back to you. To save you."

Something glimmers in her eyes, like she's trying to hold back joy. "Worry about yourself. I'm perfectly fine. I don't need saving."

"So you escaped the pirate?" Relief cools my nerves. "Thank the gods."

Raven bites her lip. Contemplation wavers in the thick air around us. Her thoughts whisper in the golden grass, clear as if she's spoken them out loud.

"You...you want to stay with her?" I ask, incredulous. "Piracy, Raven? Really?"

Shock crosses her features, quickly replaced with cold vexation. "Get out of my head. I've had enough people rooting around in there."

"What's that supposed to mean?" I take a step towards her, but she steps out of my reach. I can't hide the hurt that tears through me. "You're not being brainwashed, are you?"

She scoffs. "Get over yourself. Are you being brainwashed?"

I swallow back my retort with a deep breath. "I just want you to be okay. Where are you?"

"We're heading to Racha. Supposedly Isolde's staff is there, and I need it. Then after that...Caentathea." Purpose glints in her dark eyes, filling them with more life than I've ever seen. She says *Caentathea* breathlessly, as if reveling in how the word tastes. "I finally understand what the gods want from me. I have to save magic."

Pride swells in my chest. Finally, she's found her place in the world. Apprehension rises to greet that lapse of joy. Is this why she's so different? Sacrificing everything about herself for the sake of magic? It's dying anyway. Oncarii wouldn't be much worse without it.

"Say something."

I cast my gaze down. "What you're doing is dangerous. Pirates are dangerous. Racha is one of the most dangerous places in the world!"

"It's not all bad," she says softly. "I have never felt so free in my life."

Anger takes root within me, a sensation so foreign and yet so deep it's like it's always been there. Malicious whispers reverberate in my mind. "Don't get lured in. They're nothing but poison."

"Rélia is different! I've learned—"

"Pirates are what destroyed our home, what got Mama killed!" I roar, unable to stop the words. The moment they pass my lips, crushing guilt drops on my chest, stopping my heart for a moment. This isn't how I wanted to tell her.

Raven's eyes widen. Her scream is so shrill it's silent.

The horizon of the dreamscape shifts. Red hues tint the sky as a sun rises, impossibly bright. Its warmth holds the same familiar aura as Raven, as if the landscape shifts in an expression of her rage. Thunderclouds roll in the distance. Lightning strikes the ground, setting the yellowing grasses ablaze. The magnitude of her pain shocks my system, sending me reeling out of my own pocket world.

I sit bolt upright. Gasping, I clutch at my head. Splitting pain wracks my mind as I try to grasp everything that just happened. I knew I could peer into the minds of others, but communicating with someone's consciousness within my own? Given how finicky my magic's been, I wouldn't have thought such a thing possible.

In any case, my mind is alight and buzzing. Ideas thrum through my body as if it's my life source. All those stray threads tie together, fitting nicely like a puzzle. Isolde's staff. That was the last piece. Confidence flows through me at a rousing immensity.

Aran is the only hitch in the plan. So long as he's avoiding me, we'll be trapped under Navda's tyranny for the rest of our miserable lives.

He's curled up in the corner, pretending to be asleep. The shallowness of his irritated breaths gives him away. I clear my throat. The air shifts, swirling in warning. I ignore it.

"You have to talk to me."

He remains motionless.

"Aran, please. I have a plan, one that will get us out of this hellhole. But I need you to do it."

Still nothing. I glance at Marie who just shrugs. Tentatively, I put my hand on Aran's shoulder. He whips around, eyes blazing.

"Get away from me," he hisses, shifting into the corner of the cell as if he's trying to become one with the wall. Unbridled fear fills his eyes. Chills run down my spine. No one has ever been afraid of me. "Your power is unnatural."

My lip trembles. "It's as natural as yours! Yes, what I did to you was wrong, but I had to do something. My sister was going to die. I'm sorry Navda hurt you, I—"

"He didn't."

Aran turns to me, his hazel eyes gaunt. Even in the dim light, I've been able to pick out the flecks of gold against the green, the amber rings around the brown of his irises. It's all gone. All the vivacity in his eyes has been sucked dry. He looks like the other maji, those who haven't got any hope left.

His voice cracks when his empty gaze rises to meet mine. "He didn't have to hurt me, Tezin. Because you already took away my will. No one has ever done that to me before. And no pain or torture would have mattered because you took my mind from me."

Cold disquiet fills our cell. His words hang over me, a cloying fog that sticks to my skin. I broke him. And the least I can do is try to fix my mistake.

Slowly, I move to take his hand. When he doesn't shy away, I cradle his freezing fingers between my palms. "I promise I will not control you again. I will spend the rest of my life trying to make amends. Right now, I need your help turning Navda's crew against him."

He laughs bitterly, pulling his hand away. "Ha. You're insane. Have you seen them? They'd die to shine his boots. You'll die trying to fight them. I'm not going down with you."

I sigh, exasperated. "You're wrong. I've heard their thoughts. With the right pressure, the right time, and the right tools, I can get his crew to break." Aran opens his mouth to contest, but I hold my hands up. "No please. Just hear me out."

When he remains silent, I continue, "My sister mentioned the staff of Isolde. I've heard legends of it. I'm sure you have too."

Aran gives a non-committal nod. "So? It's under heavy lock and key and people fight for sport to win it. No one ever has."

"But no one is me."

He scoffs. "And have you ever fought? Have any battle expertise of any kind?"

"Doesn't matter. With my magic, I can just tell people not to hurt me. I'll win the staff. With the power in such an ancient artifact, we could turn the crew against Navda."

A flicker of hope fights to break through the hollow shell

of Aran's eyes. That's all I need. A spark to ignite the fire of rebellion.

Another silence follows, warm, charged, imploring, as if the whole world waits with bated breath to hear his answer. I pray that he will believe me, regardless of how crazy it sounds.

Finally, he says, "Okay. You're insane and I doubt it'll work but say I'm on board. What do you need from me?"

A hopeful smile cracks across my face. "That arrow pierced through your ear. It's a weapon, isn't it?"

Hesitantly, he nods.

"That will finish Navda off for good. I don't know how long I can sustain power from the staff or how dangerous it is. Your arrow is a crucial contingency. Now does it only work for you or can you teach me the command?"

Aran fiddles with the arrow. After a moment of contemplation, he pulls it from his ear. Fascinated, I inspect the gold mechanism when he presses it into my palm. It's warm, humming with energy, as if anxious to be released. This strange device of Aran's creation is the final piece, the best chance I have of seeing my plan through. My only chance.

"It will work when you command it. Is that all you want?"

My shaggy hair falls into my eyes as I meet his gaze. "I want you with me. I *need* you by my side when it all goes down. You're powerful Aran. And my friend."

His lip quirks. "As long as I get to be there when vengeance is served, I can ask for nothing more."

Grinning, giddy with confidence, I whisper the command Aran tells me, relishing in the way Iquetí rolls off my tongue.

"*Inciepa.*"

III

VICIOUS MAGIC

26

Raven

"NO!"

I shoot up, hands bunching the quilt beneath me. It can't be true. Mama can't be dead. Ghzen can't be gone. It's lies. It's all lies!

Flashes of my home in ashes flare across my mind. It repeats on a loop, every detail exacerbating, clarifying, taunting me with their heart-wrenching truths. I scream as the world stops and starts around me. I fall into my Sight, unable to stop, unable to brace myself for the harsh landing in the charred remains of my hometown.

Ash rains on my face. Bones clatter and crunch beneath my feet. Smoke fills my lungs with every ragged breath I take. I fall to my knees in front of my home. There's nothing left. It's all gone. All of it, save for the tattered, burnt scraps of Mama's gele amidst cracked, brittle bones.

Tears stream down my cheeks, searing my skin to match the pain in my soul. Screams scrape against my throat until it's raw. Hands trembling, I sift through the remains, desperate to find something to prove this isn't real. There's nothing. Wracked by a sorrow so deep it cuts to my bones, carves its everlasting name there, I clutch tight to the blackened scrap of Mama's gele.

It can't be true.

"Hey, hey, Raven!" Rélia's voice pulls me back to my body. There is nothing between my fingers. The last part of Mama I had wasn't real. I let loose another scream. Tears blur Rélia's face in front of mine. "Raven, look at me."

I focus on her wide eyes, brimming with concern. She puts a hand on the side of my head. Grateful for her soothing Healer's warmth, I lean into her touch. Another sob builds in my chest. I close my eyes, lip trembling.

"What happened?" she asks, her voice soft, gentle, warm, wrapping around me like an incorporeal hug.

I take a shaky breath, unable to erase the images of my destroyed home from my mind. I open and close my mouth, like a fish out of water, before I can finally find my croaking voice. "My...my mama, she's..."

I choke on the rest of my sentence, unable to bear the bitter taste of the words. Rélia pulls me into an embrace. I wrap my arms around her, bury my face into the crook of her neck, hold tight like she's the only raft in an endless sea of sorrow desperate to drag me under the moment I lose my balance.

When we pull away, I could almost believe a decade has passed. She brushes her thumbs beneath my eyes, drying my tears. More roll down my face, silent and scorching, and those she catches too. An interminable silence falls. Grief lurks beneath it, circling, waiting for another moment to take hold, to cloud my thoughts indefinitely.

Rélia sits next to me, so close our legs are touching. Wrapping an arm around my shoulders, she pulls me into her. I let her. I don't want to fight it. Not anymore. Not when there's a numb void devouring me from inside out. I take a shuddering breath as she rests her chin on top of my head.

"I lost my mother too," she murmurs. "Not in the same way. She carried me, sang me lullabies, smiled at me one day, and the next she'd disappeared into thin air. Everyone assured me it was an illness, swift and deadly in its course. But I knew she was still alive, that she'd left, though I never knew why. I just...I never got closure. I never got to say goodbye. And it's horrible that you didn't get to either. I'm sorry."

I can barely whisper through my swollen throat. "Sorry won't bring my mama back."

"No, it won't. Nothing will." Rélia runs her fingers down my arm, leaving a trail of goosebumps that eases some of the ache beneath my skin. "I won't lie to you. The grief, it'll seem like it'll never go away. But I'm here. I'll dry your tears, hold your hand, share the burden of your pain." She pauses, gauging my reaction. "Give you my finest bourbon."

I chuckle softly, hardly aware of my own body. It's like I'm floating between realities. "Why? Why would you do that for me?"

"Because I don't want you to feel like you're alone." Her voice catches. I detect familiarity behind her words. "That is when grief will suffocate you. Coming up for air will feel like an impossible feat. And you'll lose more of yourself with every passing day, until you're so alone, not even grief can keep you company."

"Is that what happened to you?"

Silence falls as she seems to contemplate her truth. "Everyone covets the power of the crown, but they can't fathom how exhausting and lonely it is. Why do you think the freedom of the sea always called to me?"

I understand now more than ever. Tezin was right. Pirates had taken both of my parents from me, broke my family, shattered my world. But I picked up those shards and made something new. Something liberating. Maybe the sea isn't as cruel as I believed it to be. Out here I can be whoever I want to be. The waves will carry me to a new world, one filled with adventure, free of sorrow. I will never have to keep looking over my shoulder.

As the silence draws out, the grief creeps back in. Tears cascade down my cheeks. I sniffle. Sobs build. Rélia hugs me tighter as they spill out of my mouth. I cry until my eyes are dry and bleary, until my mind is empty and weary.

Rélia sings softly. It's a tune I don't recognize but immediately fall in love with. It's melodic, full, evocative. Closing my eyes, I lose myself in the haunting music. It washes over me, beating back the encompassing grief, the nauseating anger.

"I sing that song when I feel hopeless," she says.

"What does it mean?" I ask, unable to place the lilting words.

"It's an old Luomnili song about feeling adrift, watching your life pass you by without knowing where you're going, like you're stumbling through the dark without a torch." She smiles softly. I've never seen her with such a gentle expression. It makes her eyes rounder, fuller, as if she's seeing everything with a rosy glow for the first time. "But in the end, you'll find your way. No matter if it's planned calculation or blind guessing, you will make it through. However long the night, dawn will break, and you will rise."

"Well, it's beautiful. You know the language of the Lost Cities?"

"Not really. My mother spent a lot of time there. I picked up a few things."

Rélia stands and offers me her hand. Hesitantly, I take it. She leads me out of the cabin onto the quiet deck. Only Penn is awake in the darkness of early morning, tending to the wheel.

At the bow of the ship, she stops. "Are you ready for dawn to break?"

"Already?" I whisper.

"I'm right here with you, Raven."

Together we gaze at the horizon, silent. We watch as the gentle rays of the rising sun crest over the endless sea. Pink hues light the sky, flushing out the clusters of twinkling stars. With it comes a sense of reprieve.

I glance at Rélia. Her eyes are closed, head tilted back, her hair catching the golden sunlight just right. She looks as she always did in my vision. Hair spun of gold, commanding the air around her, but a childish wonder on her soft features.

I find I can't appreciate the beauty of the sunrise anymore. It's not what dulls the ache in my soul, what battles away the grief, what makes my heart beat so loud I can barely hear my own tumultuous thoughts. Blocking out the fluttering in my stomach is too difficult a feat now. I deserve to yield to the longing in my heart.

Before I can talk myself out of it, I lace my fingers with Rélia's. For a terrifying moment, I think she's going to pull away. Instead, she returns the gesture, holding tight to my hand as if she senses my apprehension. A small smile tugs at her lips. For the first time since I've met her, she looks truly at peace.

Turning back to the colorful sky, I find some semblance of that too. Enough to allow myself to breathe deeply through the heartache of my lost home. I let the serenity of the dawn carry me far from those memories. It is only me and Rélia and our sunrise.

Deep inside, the reassuring warmth of my magic rises to comfort me. It curls through my veins, reaching out to Rélia's signature. Our magic weaves together, wrapping around us, holding us close.

"Feel better?" she asks.

The sun is nearly risen now. Have we really stood here that long? I glance at our entwined hands. I guess I haven't much to complain about. "Strangely."

"That's the beauty of a sunrise." Rélia pulls her hand away, leaving me empty once more. Already, grief encroaches, ready to drown me in its depths. I square my shoulders. No. I won't let it claim me just because my life raft drifted. "Just in time too. We're about to hit the Volturi Sea."

Now it's not just the grief creeping through me. Trepidation joins the fray. I've never been so far from land. I've heard stories of what lurks in these waters. Sure, the poisonous fish and the squid with tastes for flesh are dangerous creatures off the coast of Ghzen. But here-the stories gave me nightmares as a child.

"Is it safe?" I ask, though I already know the answer.

Rélia smirks as she gathers her mussed locks and ties them back from her face. "Haven't you figured it out yet, love? Nothing is safe around me."

Maybe that's what makes her so intoxicating.

I shake the thought away. Racha isn't far. Finding the staff should be my focus. I can't afford to indulge this allure of hers that makes me yearn to be near her.

Still, I look at her, and I think maybe distractions aren't so bad.

27

Rélia

For as much as I love the open water, the Volturi Sea sure hates me. Now, I don't think it's personal. If it was, I'm sure I'd have encountered much worse in my travels. But I've had a hard-enough experience sailing here to be wary of crossing the visible line.

Volturi waters are darker, tinted purple, so entrancing it's as if sirens make up the waves. Its stark contrast to the blue of the Hebringg Sea never fails to intrigue me. The jagged white line of foam between the two waters marks the start of dangerous territory. I know what lurks down there. And I know well enough not to disturb them. I wonder if even the gods fear the creatures. I hope so. A little fear goes a long way. Maybe far enough to knock them down a peg. What I wouldn't give to see that happen. Break the divine and everything else falls with them.

Maybe then I could see my mother again.

I glance at Raven, who's humming softly to herself, twirling her staff between her hands. Why did I tell her about Mother? Rather, why couldn't the truth about Mother ease the pain of Raven's great loss instead of some tragic, picturesque version I fabricated? She disappeared from the palace without a trace, that much was true, but she never once held me. Rarely did she sing to me. Only once did she care for me when I'm sick. That in of itself was an act of kindness in her twisted mind. Mother *did* visit the Lost Cities. But she's the reason they're called that.

Oncarii is cruel, giving me a mother who could never love me. Crueler still, to give Raven a mother who loved her unconditionally but ripped her away without a chance to say goodbye.

I adjust my sword belt. Dwelling on lost mothers won't get me through today. If the wind speed remains the same, we'll reach Racha by midday. Once it's in sight, I can't risk letting my guard down for even a moment. My gaze strays to Raven. Best to get my fill of stolen glances now.

For someone who only just found out she lost her mother, Raven seems almost normal. That determination about her is stronger than ever, though every now and then her shoulders slump and the stone in her eyes crumbles. I hope her own stubbornness is enough to keep her afloat.

"Mornin' Cap'n." Penn greets me with a dazzling smile. Never one to be in low spirits, even when I know he hates Racha as much as he loves to point out when I'm wrong. "An' how are we doing this fine day?"

"Why are you talking like you know something I don't?"

Penn leans against the mast, crossing his arms. "Haven't seen ya smile like that in a while's all."

I roll up the sleeves of my white linen shirt in an effort to distract myself from the fluster fighting to take control of my fingers. "I honestly don't know what you're talking about."

"C'mon. Raven. Dawn. I've seen ya use that one before."

I move on to tightening the laces of my boots. "It was different this time. Real. And if you say one more godsdamned word about it I will cut out your tongue and trade it for a pinto bean."

Penn's grin doesn't falter. "Yer violent creativity just means I'm right."

"I'm not bluffing, Penn." I stand up straight, staring him down. "We're done talking about this. Get Monty ready. I'm gonna need him in Racha."

I turn on my heel, strutting away from him. Fuming, I set my sights on the slowly approaching land mass in the distance. Better to focus on that than Penn and his infernal insinuations. I can't discern any of the city yet, but I know what awaits. My reputation precedes me, which means I'll either have no trouble or it'll never stop. Depends how cocky Racha is feeling today.

Pacing around the deck calms my buzzing nerves. Everyone is on deck, bustling.

I pause at the side of the ship, taking a moment to stare into the water. The sun shines on the violet waves, but they swallow the light before it pierces deeper than the surface.

Deep breath in. Deep breath out. I tuck some gold in my breast pocket. The weight is reassuring. If everything goes well, I won't have to lighten it much. Morphing my anxiety into confidence, I pull a crate into the middle of the deck and hop on it.

"Listen up!" I shout. Everyone halts their work, turning to me with attentive ears. "Penn, Monty, Raven, and I have business to attend to while we're in Racha. We're leaving here with the famed staff of Isolde." Murmurs of excitement ripple through the crew. I smile.

"Drew, Ori," I continue, "you two are to go off docks, station near the pubs. Swindle as much as you can. Get me the good rum off of Captain Allors if you can. Bastard hasn't paid me back after the last game of dice we played." The two men snicker, saluting. "Parker, Talan, Veter, play the Game Houses. Steal chips if you must. No alcohol. You're there to rake us in gold. Mina, you're in charge of making sure strangers follow the rules and don't make the flawed decision to attempt to board us. The rest of you are free to do whatever you like but don't leave the docks."

I clear my throat, breaking the pause of silence as they take in my commands. "Good? Great. Hopefully we won't be here more than one night. Get ready to dock within the hour."

I hop off the crate. Chatter resumes and so does the bustle of the crew. Raven approaches me, her ever present staff tucked over her shoulder.

"Not a very rousing speech."

I chuckle. "Would you like me to try again? Give one to inspire our dark, twisted pirate hearts?"

"You know I don't think that of you."

"Anymore."

"Anymore," she agrees. "You really have a talent for leadership, don't you?"

"Fake it till you make it."

Raven tilts her head. I raise an eyebrow, waiting for her to speak her mind. I try to look past the stone in her eyes, but

I can't delve into her thoughts, can't imagine what goes on in there. Already she's lost too much, bears too much.

"You could do so much on the throne."

I roll my eyes and tuck throwing knives into the secret folds of my boots. "Not this again. I don't want to rule. I'm just not cut out for it."

"You're maji. You could mend everything your father broke. Change the world."

"Our country is broken, but it has always been so. There is not much I could do to fix it." I adjust the tightness of the vambraces on my arms as an excuse to avoid her expectant gaze. A beat of silence passes. She's still staring at me when I glance up.

Sighing, I reach into a pocket sewn inside my trousers. Silver links curl around my fingers. I haven't touched this bracelet in ages. No one has been worthy of it.

"Give me your wrist." She obliges without much hesitation. I clip the bracelet around her. Dangling from the middle is a charm with my ship's crest—a serpent curling around a sword. "Don't ever take that off."

Curiosity glints in her eyes, nearly as brilliant as the bracelet under the rays of the sun. "You should consider your birthright."

I clear my throat. "Make sure you're ready. We're about to dock."

Unable to endure more talk of the crown, I turn away from her. Another word about it and I might crack under the pressure. I almost broke the day I lost my Galer, the day I let down my entire crew. Having the wellbeing of every citizen in Oncarii resting on my shoulders would be too much for me to handle.

I've been faking strength for far too long. That responsibility would bring me to my knees.

And I kneel for no one.

•••••

Stepping onto the cracked cobblestone streets of Racha, it's like the air has changed. Not too far away is open sea, sleek galleons like mine knocking against schooners and ketches packed closely together. Out there, fresh, salty winds whisper promises of freedom and adventure. Here, the air is stifling, warns of trouble. I inhale deeply. It's an acquired taste.

Dark, scruffy buildings rise out of the dry earth, reminiscent of the lower quarter of Qada. At least here there's no sign of the crown's poisonous touch—only the grimy fingerprints of ruffians and thieves.

I know exactly where to find Isolde's staff. Anyone who frequents Racha would. Thankfully for us, the gold it draws in from pirates' infallible lust for it is worth more to the Capo than the power of the staff itself.

Beside me, Raven is tense. Every now and then, her hands move for her staff, fiddling with the strap, glances around the street, stills, and repeats. Pidge sits on her shoulder, nearly as tense as her. Why she insists on taking the rat everywhere, I'll never understand.

"Raven, relax," I say. "You're not in danger."

Her voice is so low when she speaks, I almost don't hear her. "But I'm maji. They'll be able to tell."

"You'll be fine. You're protected here, thanks to that bracelet. No one can lay claim to you because you're my servant."

Raven halts. Behind her, Monty's cane knocks against her. She yelps and stumbles. "What?"

I smirk, steadying her. "It's only a technicality. For your own good."

She runs a thumb over the bracelet. "But what if something were to happen to you?"

"Love that my tragically heroic death is where your mind first goes."

Raven huffs. "I didn't say it was tragic. Or heroic."

"I like to think it was. Legally, you'd belong to whoever took over my ship if I were to die," I reply, trying to keep a neutral face. It's a difficult feat. Especially considering how easy it is to get under her skin. "But that's neither here nor there."

"Right. Because you're not the one with something to worry about."

"Hey, in this murder fantasy of yours, I'm dead. So I beg to differ."

Raven pauses, shooting me a sidelong glance. "Then beg."

A baffled laugh breezes past my lips. Pressing my hand to my chest, I feign a heart attack. Falling to my knees in the middle of the street draws some stares, but they hardly linger. Everyone has an agenda and watching me is not on it. Yet.

She crosses her arms, glaring at me as I draw out my performance. "Are you finished?"

I hop to my feet. "Yeah."

"You're so melodramatic."

"Thanks!" I turn a corner, avoiding a puddle that smells suspiciously like urine. "But I'm kidding. The bracelet is plated with odrite. Not dangerously. Just enough to suppress your magical signature. No one can tell you're maji."

Her shoulders relax. "So where exactly are we going?"

"Heart of Racha's income: the Capo's arena. That's where we're gonna find the staff. First, I've got a stop to make." I pause in front of a pawn shop. Grime coats the windows. A cracked wooden sign juts out above the door. Painted on the sign are the split and peeling yellow words *Bertram's Trade* in Kuccesh, the language of renegades. "Penn, keep an eye on these two while I duck inside for a moment."

"We're pressed for time," Raven mutters.

Ignoring her, I open the door. Silence greets me. Candles flicker on the windowsills, in the precarious chandeliers hanging from the ceiling, even on the tables amidst the clutter of cheap trinkets. I peruse the tables, turning over brass children's toys in my fingers, wiping dust from wooden carvings. Everything here has been dropped from a stranger's life. A collection of individual memories. Untouched. Desperate for someone to relive them.

"Bertram, you really should take better care of this place," I say, well aware of the stout pot-bellied man glaring at me from behind the counter nestled at the back of the shop.

Bertram grunts, shifting his tattered cap over his bald head. His voice has the same gravelly tone as those residing in the Olash mountain range, the unforgiving gray peaks cutting through the country, stretching to Tashul. "Come less. Zen we see."

"Aw, miss me that much?" I grin, leaning my forearms on the wooden counter.

He snorts. "No. Your gold? Zat I miss. Unfortunately, it come with you."

"Shocking. So, I'm looking for a certain accessory of great value. I'm sure you have it in here somewhere." I curl my fingers around the stray hairs falling loose from my ponytail. "In fact, I've seen it before."

Bertram narrows his eyes, clearly reading between the lines. "Over my dead body. "

I lean closer to him, still smiling. "And I can certainly make that happen if that's what you'd prefer."

"Hmph."

"Aw, c'mon Bertie. I'm on a bit of a time constraint and the longer I spend here, the more agitated my compatriot is going to get. And trust me, you won't want to meet the end of her wrath." I pat my breast pocket. "Besides, I'd never make an unfair deal, would I?"

He guffaws. "HA. Joke, no? Fair ain't in your vocabulary."

My smile drops as my patience wears thin. "You're still breathing, aren't you? Now get the beads, before I start compensating for my wasted time."

Silver twines around my fingers, a silent threat. Red discolors Bertram's round face. Grumbling, he heaves himself up and waddles behind a door. A few moments later, he returns, lips curled into a scornful frown. I stretch my palms towards him. Begrudgingly, he drops golden metallic beads into my hand. Immediately, I sense their soothing power.

I roll them between my fingers, drinking in the clarity, the tranquility that seeps through my skin. Hair beads like these were once commonplace, dressed up the hair of every maji—artifacts lost to the era of thriving magic. Woven of gold, latticed in intricate designs, imbued with a comforting sort of majesty, they are almost divine. Shame artifacts never trust me. These I wouldn't mind wearing.

Satisfied, I tuck the hair beads into the secure pocket lined within my waistband that once held the bracelet. "Pleasure doing business with you, Bertie."

I toss a gold coin on the counter and turn, not sparing him another glance. Rage bleeds off him, infecting the air. Instinctively, I put my hand on the hilt of my sword. I take a cautious step, listening intently. Faintly, there's the twang of a spring. Bertram always thinks he's so clever. Without turning, I duck. A bolt flies over my head at a terrifying speed. With a crack, it lodges into the doorframe.

Chuckling, I rise to face Bertram. In his shaking hands, he holds a sleek, powerful crossbow. A cold smile splits across my face. "Try it again, I dare you."

He reaches down, taking the time to load another bolt. Poisonous anger beats in time with my heart as I wait.

"You know ze beads are worth fortune."

"Yes," I say, strutting towards him. "Many fortunes. Certainly worth more than your life, and now it seems you're willing to bargain that too."

Bertram aims the loaded crossbow at my chest. At this range, even a mundane bolt pierced through the heart could kill me. "You are demon."

"Oh no, Bertie. I'm far worse than that." *You are playing with fire, Rélia,* a voice in the back of my mind warns me. I ignore it.

Leaning forwards, I lower my voice to a frosty whisper. "Go on. Shoot me. *I dare you.*"

His finger twitches on the trigger. There it is. Hesitation reigned by fear. His face grows redder, his eye twitching; anger fighting for impulse. Power flurries through me, latching onto the threat in my words. Silver wisps in the air around my fingers. The wood begins to rot where my palms rest. Resignation turns his eyes to stone. In that moment, I know he's going to do it.

At the same time he fires the bolt, I wrap my fingers around the wooden shaft. The momentum of the bolt challenges the speed of my magic. It burns my palm as it slides through my hand. A split second before it impales my ribcage, the wood rots. The sharp head clatters to the counter. Rotten wood particles shower over it.

I reach over the counter, bunching the fabric of his shirt, drawing him close to me. Faces a hair apart, I let my impulse take over my tongue.

"Threats are a language I am proficient in. They bend to my will, kneel at my might. Let me get one thing straight. You are replaceable. I don't have patience for men like you. Test me again, and I will leave Racha wearing a necklace of your bones, got it?"

Bertram glances over my shoulder. I spare a glance. Raven stands in the doorway, staff brandished, eyes wide. Everything is so still I wonder if she's stopped time. Slowly, I release Bertram.

Forgetting my ire, I hold my hands up to Raven. "Hey..."

How do I explain this to her? How do I tell her I am everything she believed me to be? Not a dignified royal, nor a powerful Nightblood. Just a dirty pirate.

I search her eyes, heart sinking to find disappointment. I suppose I shouldn't be surprised, but it still strikes me with a deep, dull pain.

Before I can comprehend what's happening, Raven crosses the length of the store at an unnatural speed—her magic, no doubt—and tackles me to the ground. Another bolt whizzes over our heads. It would have killed me.

Raven leaps to her feet, whirls on Bertram. Staff leveled at him, she glowers. Once more, he reaches for a bolt. She slams the weighted end of her staff on the counter. It cracks. Bertram yelps, tipping over. Raven leaps over the counter, catching him by the collar before he falls. She lowers her face to his, presses the blade of her weapon to his throat. Cold determination paints her face.

"Touch her, and you have me to deal with," she warns. Slowly, he raises both hands in surrender. She releases him, letting him crash to the ground. With a powerful strike, she slams her staff on the crossbow. Splinters of fine mahogany spray across the counter. "Rélia, pay the man for whatever you wasted time to get so we can move on."

I brush some wood from my sleeves. "Really?"

If looks could kill, she would've run me through.

I roll my eyes. "Fine."

Heaving a great sigh, I empty the gold from my pocket onto his damaged counter. As soon as the coins are in his possession, Raven struts towards the door.

"Thanks," I murmur, reaching for her hand. "For defending me."

She sheathes her staff, deliberately ignoring my hand. I cross my arms, a show of what I hope is nonchalance. But I long to interlock our fingers. Everything was so perfect at dawn.

"Do not speak."

"I thought we were having a moment! You know, having each other's backs, that sorta thing."

"I do not like making threats, Rélia. I feel dirty."

Absent-mindedly, I fiddle with the hair cuffs in my pocket. "Then don't. Not for me, not for anyone. I want you to come into your own as a pirate. Live by your code. No one else's."

Raven glances at me, though it's not so heated as before. "Let's get the staff. Then we can worry about my life as a pirate."

Grinning, I hold the door open. "Deal."

28

Raven

In the heart of Racha stands an enormous arena the likes of which I have never seen before. Crafted of rough, pale red stone, it towers over every building on the island. Cracks spider-web across the massive pillars holding up the stone overhang. Several people lounge around, drinking, chatting, proudly displaying pouches of gold. Unease rockets through me. Men swelled with pride and flaunting their gold is never a good sign.

The four of us sit under the shade of the overhang, keeping as much distance from the other ruffians as we can. We've been silent for a few minutes, savoring our bites of grainy bread and roasted pumpkin seeds Rélia swindled from a distracted vendor. Food gained through questionable means is still food, I suppose.

"Mkay," Rélia says, licking her fingers. "Here's the plan. I'm gonna enter myself in the fight. Monty, you're gonna be my second."

I scoff. "What? Shouldn't that be me? I can hold my own in a fight, you know I can."

"Eager to get ourselves killed, are we?" Rélia says, raising a challenging eyebrow. "Love the enthusiasm, but the fact is you just don't know how to fight dirty. If all goes well, I won't need my second anyway. That's only if I'm gravely wounded. Or dead. Besides, I have something more fun for you to do."

I pop another seed in my mouth, relishing in the savory flavor. Pidge scampers up my arm, nestling in my bushy hair. His insistent squeaking doesn't relent until I offer him a seed of his own. "Our definitions of fun are vastly different but do tell."

"How good is your flirting?"

Heat flares in my cheeks. I try not to choke on the seeds. "That's subjective, I suppose."

Rélia wipes her fingers on her trousers, then turns her attention to her hair. Transfixed, I watch as she unpins her hair and shakes her curls loose. They bounce around her face in merry golden ringlets, accentuating the pink of her cheeks. "Right, I forgot who I was talking to. Go ahead and try on me."

I clear my throat, unable to find my voice. I can't tear my eyes away from her as she runs her fingers through her hair, braiding it once more. "Uh, your hair. It's nice."

She chuckles, one corner of her mouth turning up in a kind smirk. "Needs work. But it's fine. Your body should do more of the talking anyway."

At that, I snap out of my trance. "Wait, what am I supposed to do?"

"Here's the thing. I'm gonna be fighting in the arena for the grand prize of Isolde's staff. Catch is, no one ever wins it. The capo is too greedy to part with it. Brings in a lot of competitors, and in turn spectators who are walking bags of gold." Rélia pauses to tie off her braid, loop it upwards, and pin it to the back of her head. "Your job is to distract the capo in his box while Penn steals the staff."

I cross my arms, glowering. "Why can't you distract him, and I steal the staff while Penn fights?"

"Because you don't know your way around the arena. And the capo would recognize me. If I'm fighting, it'll draw suspicion away from Penn. You're our best bet to get him flustered. Keep his attention from straying." She shifts closer to me, putting a hand on my shoulder. "You'll be fine. Trust yourself."

Casting my gaze downwards, I purse my lips. "How do I know the capo will even be attracted to me?"

My heart pounds as she leans into me, lips brushing across my ear. In a whisper only I can hear, she says, "He has a dick." She smiles when a baffled laugh erupts from my throat. "And your beauty is enough to turn heads. But if you're that worried about it, Penn can help."

At the sound of his name, Penn turns his head in our direction, stopping short in his invigorating conversation with Monty about the best spice for potatoes. "Cap'n?"

"Pretty up Raven like she's coming from a pleasure house."

I splutter, unable to get comprehensive words out. A pleasure house! I've never even set foot in one! How am I—oh gods. I take a deep breath. "Absolutely not."

"Relax. We know you're not a hooker, though it should be noted that's an entirely reputable position," she assures. The smirk she's obviously fighting to contain does not help her sincerity. "The capo, however, cannot resist a dolled-up woman. Especially if you let him chase you."

Penn sits next to me, pulling a bottle of black liquid from the pocket of his pants. I shift, eyeing it warily. "It's alright kid. If ya really don' want this, we won' make ya."

Gently, I scoop Pidge from my head and set him on the ground. I shrug. "Whatever it takes to get the staff."

Begrudgingly, I remain still as he lines my eyes with kohl, paints my lips with red-stained beeswax. With surprising finesse, Penn brushes subtle powders over my face, accentuating my cheekbones, bronzing my skin. When he finally finishes, he gives a satisfied nod and tucks all his utensils away.

"Well?" I ask, turning to Rélia.

She studies me, nose scrunching. "Huh. Almost as pretty as me. Penn, you're a miracle worker."

I glare. "Eat another seed and choke on it."

"I'm joking. You look stunning as ever," she says, avoiding my eyes. Is that a hint of a blush on her cheeks or am I just imagining it? "I do have one more thing, though." From her pocket, she fishes out some golden beads. Beauty hardly seems adequate enough to describe them. "This is what I went to the pawn shop for."

I reach out to touch them, drawn to their faint, pulsing power. "You went through all that for me?"

She shrugs. "I wanted to give you something that felt like home. Since I sold off your silver hair pins. Sorry."

Tears prick my eyes. That dull wound I've been fighting to ignore tears open again, an onslaught of bleeding pain. Home. It's gone.

"May I braid them into your hair?" Rélia asks softly.

I nod.

Closing my eyes, I lean into her touch as she threads her fingers through my hair. The way she gently winds the strands together reminds me of the days Mama would sing to me while working sweet-smelling locra flowers into my braids. Focusing on that memory, I can almost smell the gumbo cooking in the kitchen, hear Tezin laughing as he wrestles Papa. Something about Rélia's touch brings my childhood to life.

When she finishes, I open my eyes. Rélia sits in front of me, wringing her hands. Expectancy flits in her eyes. I run my hands through my braids. Magic sparks in my veins when my fingers skim over the beads intermittently woven in my hair. It's a cool intensity, a foreign power. Focus churns through me. My magic breathes with clarity, unhindered by my own doubts.

"Are they magic?"

She nods. "They'll help you channel. Like your staff."

I glance around, looking everywhere but at her. "Do I look okay?"

She cups my face in her rough hands and forces me to meet her eyes. My skin tingles at her touch. Instinctively, I inch closer to her. Intensity builds in the space between us, warming the cool air. I yearn to kiss her. Just the thought of it feels deviant. Kissing a pirate? Tezin would blow a gasket if he knew how much I want to be with her, how much I want *her*.

Rélia moves closer, as if drawn by the same magnetic pull. A hairsbreadth apart. So close, I can smell the pumpkin on her breath, so close I can almost taste her. Is this what I want? After meeting her, I've been exposed to countless dangers. Doubted my gods. Felt freer than ever before. Do I want her?

Yes. Undeniably yes.

"Never question your beauty, love."

"Rélia," I breathe, heart pounding, desire coursing through my veins. I gaze into her eyes, delighted to find the same spark of hope burning there too. *Tell me when you're sober.* "I don't hate you."

All the nervous energy surrounding Rélia expels in an invisible eruption. A brilliant smile brightens her face. It's not backed by humor, nor mischief. No underlying snark. Simple, genuine delight. And that is the best thing I could have hoped for.

I put a hand on her face. She leans into my touch. Magic thrums from my core. Silver and gold curl between us as our power signatures surge, rising to meet each other. I close my eyes, lean forward ready to close the distance—

"A-hem."

Rélia and I snap our attention to Penn so fast our heads knock together. Sharp pain explodes in my forehead. Glaring at him, I rub my aching head.

"What?" I grunt, irritation swooping in to replace that desire steadily beating through my veins not but a moment before.

Penn nods towards the arena entrance. "Competitor entry is almost closed."

Rélia stands, brushing herself off. She shoots me a wink. "Duty calls. See you on the other side. Try not to screw anything up. Monty, let's go."

Monty hops to his feet, waving goodbye before sauntering after her. I don't take my eyes off of Rélia until she's written her name on the register and disappears down a dark hallway. Gaze lingering where she stood, the pressure of the mission crushes in on me.

Penn adjusts my attire, smoothing out my shirt, rolling the cuffs of my pants high above my boots. Supposedly it's more enticing. "Now, yer staff."

I put a protective hand on it. "What about it?"

Apology crosses Penn's face. "Ya can't have it 'round the capo. For one, yer flirting. Two, his security'll take it before ya get near him. Unless ya wanna lose it to the arena..."

Reluctantly, I put my staff in his outstretched hand. "Don't lose it."

"Wouldn' dream of such a thing."

Narrowing my eyes until he drops his smile, I finally relent my grip on the staff. I take a deep breath. I can do this without help. Gentle humming from the beads strengthens my resolve.

Unable to bring Pidge, I scratch him behind the ears and leave him on the street, hoping he'll be there when we finish this. Even if not, I know he'll find his way back to me.

Inhale. Exhale. I force myself to walk towards the arena. I'm adept at fighting. Seduction, not so much. Anxiety displaces the faux confidence that had been sluggishly creeping through me. This is riding on me. Everything is riding on me.

No pressure.

I trip over nothing. Penn catches me. I squeeze my eyes shut. Feeling the pressure. Flaming hells, I'm feeling the pressure.

Don't mess up.

29

Tezin

"Tell me the rules again."

Aran heaves a sigh. "Gods. They're so simple. Fine. This time try to make it stick. Everyone in Racha speaks in trade and threats. Try not to open your mouth. You'll probably cough and start a street riot."

"Don't speak. Got it." I glance sideways at him, smiling.

Aran chuckles. Not like he used to. Discomfort lines his half-hearted laugh. Forgiveness for controlling him is still far out of reach. I won't rest making amends until that bridge is crossed. I owe him that much.

"Good. So no talking, no rioting, definitely no boarding other ships—it gives them the right to decapitate you on sight."

"Well there goes my escape plan."

He ignores me. I guess humor isn't breaking the ice. "And try not to use your magic. Though it is illegal to kidnap maji from Racha, slavers still lurk."

This time he takes the extra measure to turn and glare at Marie. She salutes him with her middle finger.

"Noted." I risk a glance at Ean, trailing a few paces behind us. At the prospect of winning the staff, Navda's greed overruled his worry. Especially if his quartermaster doesn't let us out of his sight. "I suppose he will punish us if we step out of line?"

Aran nods. "Yeah. He's rarely as bad as Navda though. We got lucky."

I glance at Ean. Somehow, I doubt luck had anything to do with it.

Heeding Aran's words, I keep my mouth shut as we move off the docks into the belly of Racha. Sundry odors waft beneath my nose, some pleasant, most too pungent for my taste. Chaos snakes through the air, outlines everyone I walk past, ready to rear its head when it gets the chance. Shady deals are made in the darkness of the filthy alleys. Cracks stretch down every street. Raucous bouts of laughter echo from the dimly lit pubs we pass. Glass breaks in a Game House. Shouts ensue. A man is tossed out the door.

It's reminiscent of Borziau, if the market was drained of color and twisted on the wrong side of the law.

My stomach grumbles. I find the greasy aromas suddenly more enticing.

Aran smirks, sending me a sidelong glance. "Here, I know a real good pub. Well, good for Racha anyway."

"Don't mean to sound ungrateful, but are you sure?" I ask,

averting eye contact with the glowering bouncers outside the door.

"Yes."

"And what about our escort?"

"Don't worry about me," Ean says, a whisper that snakes around my ears.

Startling, I turn to see he's still trailing the same distance behind us. How the hell did he hear that?

Confusion ghosts over Aran's face. "What's wrong?"

"You didn't hear him?"

His puzzled silence is answer enough. I shake my head. It must be the unfamiliar atmosphere messing with my head. "Never mind. How do you know so much about this place?"

Something in him softens, as if reliving a past pleasant life. "Ran with a good crew for a while. Tragedy struck, as it always does."

As much as I want to push, I force myself to hold my tongue. Better not to risk rocking our half-sunken boat. Silence hovers over us until finally we reach the pub, though the name I can't understand.

Marie huffs. "I hate this place. People here are not the most pleasant sort."

"Well you have something in common with them then," Aran snaps.

I groan. "Do you ever take a day off?"

Both of them flash irritated glares my way. I hold up my hands in defense. Pursing my lips, I enter the pub after them. Tankards of mead sit on every table, some overflowing, others empty. Grease stains the floor. Rancid scents waft from the kitchen. I fight the urge to plug my nose. How is it that Aran seems so in his element here?

Marie makes a disgusted sound as we plop down in a sticky booth. Ean takes a seat at the bar away from us. When he catches me staring, he smirks and raises a glass. Ignoring him, I turn my attention back to Marie whose eyes stray around the dim pub. Anyone that makes the mistake of smiling at her receives a sneer. A young, handsome man staggers to our table, eyeing her up and down. Before he opens his mouth, she gives him a stern, blunt "no." He sets his sights on me. Immediately my face heats.

"You, lad? I can buy you a round, show you a good time." He leans closer to me. My heart stops. I've never enraptured the attention of a man, much less one so attractive.

"Sorry, he's taken," Aran says, sliding an arm over my shoulders. He grins cheekily. "But we will take that round."

The man laughs, clapping his hand on Aran's shoulder. "Missed having you around, Noem. Bring more men like your boy toy, eh? Then we'll see about that round."

"Bring me a waiter, and perhaps."

He wanders off, chuckling.

"Thanks."

"Anytime." He nudges my shoulder. Butterflies flutter in my stomach. I glance at him, then Marie. She rolls her eyes.

Surveying the patrons, I notice how many wave at us, smiling jovially. "They know you? Well?"

Aran sighs. He flags down a waiter, grabs a round of mead, then turns to me. "Piracy has been my life for a long time, Tezin. Used to frequent Racha with my old crew. Before my captain was tricked, nearly killed by Navda. I tried to protect her. Paid the price for it."

Bitterness lines his words. Yearning belies his spite. It's as if he's conflicted about whether to hate her or miss her. Maybe both. I stare into the depths of my drink, wishing it would swallow me whole, take me to a better world. One where my life doesn't suddenly revolve around pirates.

My knuckles whiten around my mug of untouched mead. Nausea creeps through me. What would Papa say if he saw me in Racha? How would Mama react if she knew how deeply connected I am to these two? Raven would tell me to follow my heart. But where the hell is it leading me? Aran? The sea? Fixing my magic? Caentathea? Home? Where *is* home? Why is everything so godsdamn confusing?

"Whoa, easy bud," Aran says, gently prying my fingers from the glass mug. "Squeeze any harder and you're gonna break it."

"What, pirate's life isn't for you?" Marie muses, sipping her drink. Disgust crosses her face. Still, she goes for another taste.

"No," I snap.

I shift my attention to the ground, startled to find a white rat sitting by my foot, staring at me. It's pudgy and somehow well-groomed. Intelligence flickers in its beady eyes, as if it holds secrets of the universe I couldn't possibly understand.

In the corner of my eye, I see Ean stiffen. Following his irate gaze, I find him zeroed in on the rat. Interesting. White rats are said to deliver messages between the divine and mortal realms. Understandably intimidating. But why is such a powerful quartermaster uneased by a rat?

I clear my throat. "Hey Marie, can't you communicate with animals?"

"Duh. Why?"

I nod towards the rat. "It's staring at me."

Marie perks up. Eyes bright, she crouches and ushers the rat into her cupped palms. Slow, quiet moments pass as she listens to its faint squeaks. Joy enlivens her face. Since I've known her, I've never seen such hope in her eyes, nor such color in her cheeks.

"It's...Monty!" she exclaims, beaming wide. "It's Monty, he's here!"

Aran's eyebrows shoot up. "Really? Huh. Who is he anyway?"

She turns her gaze to both of us. Nothing other than love could describe the depth of the exaltation in her eyes. "Someone very important to me. And our cause."

"Your cause?" I inquire.

"In Qada," she explains absently, focusing her attention on the rat. Her eyes flit to me again. Hard to miss the perturbation drifting there. "Tezin..."

"Yes?" I try to steady the hammering of my heart. Any more distress and it's going to explode.

"So weird." She clears her throat, shifting the rat to her shoulder where it sits expectantly. "Normally creatures connect to Tamers. We're the easiest to communicate with. Warmer energies for animals to approach. But this guy," she pauses to lovingly scratch his head. "He has imprinted on your sister."

"Meaning?"

"She's got a little guardian angel." Marie's lips turn up in a lopsided goofy grin similar to Aran's. Her voice rises an octave as she bestows plenty of scritches to the rat, accompanied by compliments on his cuteness. "Y'know. Because white rats are kinda like angels. This one's been keeping an eye on her." She leans in as the rat wriggles his whiskers. "Oh. He says Mihsoi is keeping an eye on *you*, Tezin."

Unease slithers through me. "Perhaps you should tell him to ask her why my magic is broken."

The rat squeaks, scampering into her coat pocket. "Oh great, you offended him."

I run a hand through my hair, combing out the tangles. Time ticks by slowly as Aran downs two tankards of mead before I make it through half of mine. Part of me wants that infamous warm buzz, for it to take me away from my worries. Tempting as it is, the genesis of my plan must take place in Racha.

Am I ready to do it? Skinning fish nearly made me vomit and I did that for a living. Fighting for sport, I might never eat again. Winning? Harder still. But if I can get the staff before Raven, I can save her from herself. I can mend my magic. Finally, the world will be freed of Navda's reign of terror.

Aran taps me on the shoulder. I'm not ready for the earth-shuddering belch that erupts from his mouth. Someone claps a few booths away. He grins wider than I've ever seen. Pride twinkles in his eyes.

"Oh...my gods." I cover my mouth, a futile attempt to block the acrid scent wafting towards me.

Marie scoffs. "Please. That was nothing."

Like brother, like sister, a nearly sentient burp erupts from the bowels of her stomach.

I pinch my nose. "Charming."

The two share a hearty grin. Laughter explodes between them. It slowly dies as they realize they're having fun with each other. Even as their smiles fade, the atmosphere is lighter. That unease churning in my stomach finally settles. I can do it. I can fight. For Aran and Marie, I can do it. They deserve a real home. One where they can mend their relationship, one where they don't have to look over their shoulders every moment.

Steeling myself against the encompassing bitter taste to come, I grab my tankard and chug. I cough and splutter, but don't stop. Half dribbles down my chin. By the time I'm done, I'm churning with liquid courage. Terrible as it tastes, I relish in the warm rush it bestows.

"That's my man!" Aran praises, raising my hand like I just won a tournament.

Relishing in the attention, I pump my other fist up. Heat rises in my face as Aran interlocks his fingers with mine. My gaze lingers on our joined hands.

"Flaming hells," Marie mutters, rolling her eyes.

Part of me, the part choked by embarrassment, wants to break away. But the fact that he *wants* to hold my hand after what I did to him is as sincere as forgiveness. Holding tight to him, I grin at the raucous, applauding onlookers. Some follow suit, earning resounding cheers from their friends. Only one man isn't amused. Envy ices Ean's glare. Tendrils of black ghost over the whites of his eyes. Shaking off the chill settling over me, I focus on Aran's warm hand in mine.

"Tezin," Marie says, "don't you have somewhere to be? Competitor entry closes soon."

Reluctantly, I break away from Aran. "Right. How do I enter?"

"Just tell the gatekeeper," Aran replies, concern flickering across his face. "You'll have to write your name on the register so they know which ship to deliver the news of death, should it occur. If you're late, and you might be, just tell them you're executing Navda's will. Even if they doubt you, they won't question it; too scared."

"Sounds reliable." I sigh. "Thank you, for being on board."

"Anything to see Navda eat shit," Marie says. "I'd give my left middle finger to never swab his deck again."

"Why that specific finger?" I ask.

"So I can leave it on his desk."

Aran chuckles. "Not if I do first. You should get going, Tezin."

I worry at my lip, looking between the two of them. "Just don't get into too much trouble, okay?"

All of us slide out of the booth. Anxiety weighs my heart down. If this goes wrong, I might die in the arena. I'll never see them again. Desperately hoping that isn't the case, I pull them into a tight hug.

Aran whispers, "Don't die."

"I'll try my best," I murmur, pulling away. "Stay safe."

Holding onto the muted confidence wheedling through my veins, I head for the exit. A hand closes around my elbow, yanking me to a stop.

"You'll bring the staff home to us," Ean says. It's not a question.

Staring into his malevolent eyes, overwhelmed by the malicious whispers in my mind, I struggle to find my voice. I swallow over the lump in my throat. Does he know my true plans for the staff? That I wouldn't ever hand it over to Navda?

Amused, he says, "Don't worry. I want you in that arena as much as Navda, but for very different reasons. Win. Get the staff. You're not the only one who wants to be free."

So I was right. The crew isn't as loyal as it preaches. Downplaying my relief, I tug my arm from his grip. Giving him nothing more than a non-committal nod, I turn on my heel and stride out of the pub.

Wandering the streets is far less enjoyable without my friends by my side. All I can think about is the arena. If I win, this might actually work. With Ean on my side, turning the crew will be easier than I thought.

My pace quickens as I spot the sun lowering. Almost supper time. I'm late.

I race to the entrance of the arena, hardly having time to take in its rustic majesty. Panting, I stumble to a halt in front of the burly man guarding the entrance.

"Wait! I want to enter!"

He raises an eyebrow. "A little late, kid."

I pause, hoping Aran is right. Trying to appear as formidable as possible, I cross my arms. "Direct orders from Captain Navda."

Shifting uncomfortably, he hands me a piece of lead. I scrawl my name on the register.

"No second?" he asks when I return the lead.

My heart skips a beat. What the hell is a second? Hesitantly, I shake my head, hoping that won't destroy my chances at fighting.

He nods me through. "Alright. Go ahead. I pray you survive."

Calming the panic in my veins, I step into the dark, musty hallway.

30

Tezin

I strap rusting iron vambraces over my forearms and slip-on fraying leather gloves. I've never worn armor before. I'm not really sure this counts. But the rules dictate all competitors must be provided some form of protection. Makes the fight last longer, if nothing else.

Darkness hangs heavy around me. Anxiety gnaws at my stomach. I might be more comfortable if I wasn't waiting alone, if I had any idea what the people I'm going to fight look like. Instead, one of the capo's guards led me through the musty maze of tunnels beneath the stands until he left me alone at a dead end. A steel gate muffles the raucous crowd eagerly awaiting for the battles to begin. Behind me, another gate cuts off my escape. No turning back.

Flexing my fingers, I try to strategize my victory. My mind is moving too fast for me to keep up. So much is riding on this. Will I kill? At the thought, my stomach turns over. Only if necessary. Gods, how much of my soul will be left when I'm finally free of this pirate business?

A voice booms across the arena, though I can barely hear it. Screeching, the steel gate in front of me slowly cranks open. Light from the setting sun pours into the tiny room.

Breathing deep and slow, I steady the hammering of my heart. Thunderous applause erupts when I cross the threshold into the massive arena. Blood pumps in my ears, drowning out all other sounds. Blinking, my vision slowly adjusts to the light.

I inhale sharply at the packed stands. People surround me on every side. Filling the benches, clad in every variety of colors, adults and elders, even children, sit there cheering.

Jutting out from the middle of the arena is a highly decorated balcony. Judging by the distance, I'd say it's the best seat to catch all the action and avoid all collateral damage. Squinting, I make out a well-built middle-aged man. Surrounding him is a detail of stoic guards. Most curiously, there's a woman sitting in his lap.

Gates screech open all across the arena. There must be at least thirty other competitors waiting restlessly at their stations. In the center of the sand covered arena is a long rack of weapons. Sharp, blunt, tall, short. My breath catches. Will I meet my end on one of those?

Standing on a dais protruding from the left side of the arena is a man in red-dyed leather, a metal cylinder in his hands that amplifies his voice.

"Competitors," the man announces. "There are no rules in the sand. Magic, your weapons, our weapons, anything is fair game. Should you have a registered second, they may take your place only when you fall. Winner gets claim on the famed staff of Isolde." The smug pause that follows solidifies the unease in my gut. Why does that feel like a lie? "Be the last!"

With that, a brass bell chimes. Everyone takes off. For a moment, I'm rooted to my spot, taking in the chaos. The battle for weapons is vicious. Immediately one man is struck down. Crimson stains the sand. Another man bolts from a gate, assumedly the fallen man's second.

Adrenaline courses through me in lethal amounts. Finally, I jump into action. All other competitors have raced away from the center, locked in other battles. For now, no one pays me any mind, a luxury that won't last long. Making the most of my precious seconds of freedom, I grab the first weapon I can find: a thick wooden cudgel wrapped in sharp twine.

It's heavier than I thought it would be. Nothing about it sits right in my hands. I almost drop it, searching for something else, when I catch someone bolting towards me out of the corner of my eye.

Acting completely on instinct, I heave the cudgel up to meet the flash of silver swinging towards my head. The lanky man takes another swing towards my leg. Dancing out of the way, I just barely avoid a deep gash.

Before he can launch another attack, I strike him upside the head. His freckled face twists in pain. The sword slips from his grip. He takes one stumbling step, then another, before collapsing to the ground. Blood pools around his head, turning his blonde hair red. For a sickening moment, he looks starkly like Aran.

Deafening cheers erupt. Buzzing fills my ears. All sounds

drown away until I can hear only my panting breaths. Vomit creeps up my throat. Tears blur my vision. I just killed that man.

Hands shaking, I grip tighter to the cudgel. I swallow back the bitterness in my mouth. Already, half the competitors have fallen. The stench of blood overwhelms me as I pass fresh corpses. I try to keep my focus on those still alive.

Get the staff, save everyone. The mantra repeats over and over in my mind, numbing the guilt and horror wrapping tight around my throat.

From my left, a burly man charges. I can't react fast enough to avoid the cut of his dagger. Crying out, I retaliate in an effort to avoid the burning in my thigh. He catches my cudgel with his meaty hand, yanks it from my grip. A wave of magic roils from my core, bolstered by my panic.

"Give it back," I hiss, sentient words hanging thick in the air between us.

Confusion crosses his face as he puts the weapon in my hands. I don't wait for him to return to his senses. With two powerful blows to the back, the head, he pitches forward into the sand. Nausea threatens to overtake me. I force it away.

Blood streams down my leg, hot and sticky, a helix of red and black. I can't feel the pain. Only the adrenaline in my veins.

A spry woman leaps at me, garrote in her hands. I raise the cudgel, ready to strike. Swiftly, she wraps the sharp wire around my weapon, twists, and pulls it from my hands. Before I can make a move for it, she jumps from the ground, expertly plants her hands on my hips, and vaults onto my shoulders. I stumble. She wraps the garrote around my throat.

Gasping for air, I try to throw her off. Her thighs clench tight around me. Burning rages across my skin as the wire cuts a thin line across my throat. Black spots dance in my eyes. I drop to my knees. Her balance falters. Desperation grants me another dose of strength. I grab her wrists and flip her over my head. Pressure relents, allowing me a gulp of air.

I scramble through the sand on my hands and knees until my fingers close around the cudgel. We jump to our feet at the same time. Sweat drips from my hairline. Lust for victory flashes in her eyes.

She charges. This time, I'm ready for her.

I catch her garrote with my weapon, using the force to pull her close to me. She wiggles free of my grip empty handed. Her garrote is still caught in the wire wrapped around my cudgel. Fear replaces her desire to win. My stomach drops. I can't strike her, not when I can almost taste her dread.

In the end, it doesn't matter. A middle-aged man stabs her from behind with the most menacing curved sword I've ever seen. Before her body even hits the ground, he sets his sights on me. I can barely register his brutish movements as he lunges towards me. I parry the strike and the next. My muscles burn as I keep the cudgel level with my head, blocking his every powerful blow.

Splinters crack across the cudgel. My eyes widen. I trip over the woman's body, landing flat on my back. Just in time, I deflect another blow. The cudgel nearly breaks in half. I roll out of the way as he stabs the point of his sword into the sand where my head had been a moment ago. Taking advantage of his transient distraction, I slam the cudgel into his leg. Blood splatters. The wood snaps. He snarls.

I kick his sword hand. It falls to the ground. Pulsing with unending energy, I grab a fistful of his hair, ramming his head into the sand. I pull a dagger dripping with resin from the man's sword belt before he recovers. His fingers curl around the hilt of his sword. Before I can think too hard about it, I plunge his own dagger into his throat. Gurgling screams ooze from the wound. More blood. It's blinding. I'm caked in it. The sand is discolored. Maybe it's becoming a river of crimson. I'm not sure I can tell the difference.

Waves of dizziness wash over me. I struggle to stay upright. Have to...I have to finish this. There aren't many competitors left.

Resin slowly rolls down the blade in my hand, dripping from the tip in thick, sticky globs. Something is familiar about its repulsive energy. Could it be xipher sap?

Soft footsteps pad behind me. Strange how accustomed my ears have become to the song of battle. Exhaustion weighs heavy on me. I'm not ready for another death to tarnish my soul. But I turn. I brandish the dagger in front of me.

The woman's eyes widen. "You! What the hell are you doing here?"

It's the pirate captain, Rélia Ryan, the one who kidnapped my sister, the one who started this. Everything about her—her stance, the frenzied energy flowing off of her—I know she's ready for another man to dare to challenge her.

But something in her eyes tells me her concerns are elsewhere. She's not fighting to win. She's tired.

"Where's my sister?" Not the most opportune time for conversation, but I can't help myself. Last time I spoke with Raven, something had shifted in her. Piracy is luring her in, as it is trying to do with me. If Rélia is here in the arena, I don't doubt Raven is nearby.

She glances towards the balcony. "Doing her part to get the staff."

My blood runs cold. The woman sitting up there. Gods, what is she doing? "Not if I have anything to say about it."

Her eyes dance around, but no one is approaching us. We're safe for the next minute. A wry smile cracks across her dirt and blood-streaked face. "Good thing the arena isn't for talking."

Rélia steps forward but hesitates. Slowly, the point of her sword lowers. Why would she have reservations about killing me?

Her gaze strays to the balcony again. It's clear now where her mind really is. Heart too, I imagine. It's the same look that lit up Marie when she heard about Monty.

"You won't kill me," I murmur. "You won't do that to Raven."

She purses her lips. "You're right. You've just made this a whole hell of a lot harder."

Our time is up. The remaining competitors surround us. We whirl around, back-to-back. For now, we're on the same side. Both of us are fighting for the sake of Raven. One of us has to win. She just doesn't know it's going to be me.

I kick back the lithe man bolting towards me, machete in hand. Hardly fazed, he side steps, swings around, charges again. I parry his blow with my stolen dagger, but he's clearly more skilled with a blade than I have any hope to be. I can't stop him as he recovers, then slashes at my arm. Sparks fly as the vambrace protects me. Rage fills the man's eyes. He slashes higher. Tears well in my eyes. Pain screams in my arm. The dagger slips from my fingers.

I drop to the ground. Rélia spins. She feints to the right. Before my attacker can defend himself, she cuts him down in a flurry of dirty blows from slim throwing knives tucked in her boot. I jump to my feet, ready for the man's second as he comes barreling from the edge of the arena. In his hand he holds a bow and arrow. He draws the string taut. Grabbing the arm of a woman advancing from my left, I hold her tight in front of me as a shield. Arrows pierce through her chest. I drop her to the ground.

The archer fires another arrow. I duck. It whistles over my head. He maintains distance. Easy. Archers don't like close range. Once he's out he'll be vulnerable. Hoping the gods haven't yet marked me for death, I bolt away from the safety of Rélia's dirty fighting. As I expected, the archer keeps his sights trained on me. For now, I maintain my distance. Let him sit in his false security. One arrow fires, then another. Both strike the ground near my feet.

Only a few arrows left.

Running directly towards him throws off his balance. Panic flares across the young archer's face, filling me with confidence. His aim worsens. Stumbling back, he tries to keep firing, while also putting more space between us. The last arrow from his quiver strays widely to the right.

I tackle him. Between us, the bow snaps. Pinning him down, I grab the broken bow, ready to jab it into his gut. Fire ignites in his palms. He clamps one flaming hand around my wrist.

Screaming, I clamber off of him, yanking my hand free.

Blisters in the shape of a handprint sear my skin. Fighting through the pain, I square off against him. My magic withers as I reach for it. Fueled by roiling rage, excruciating pain, I latch onto it, forcing it into my veins. Today, it *will* obey me no matter what. Pulsing with power, I grab his shoulders, stare into his eyes and let my words come to life.

"Burn the sand."

Without hesitation, he reaches down. Infernos curl off his arms, struggling to light the sand. I step back as intense heat yields a thin layer of glass.

"Stop," I command.

Panting, he slumps to the glassy ground. I stomp on it. Shards explode. I pick one up, move to jab it in his eye. Quick death. No more suffering.

When he stops writhing, I rise. Rélia has fallen several more. Two straggling competitors stick to the edges of the arena, prowling, waiting for an opportune moment. I return to the captain's side, drenched in sweat.

"How do we get out of this?" she mutters. "I'm not leaving without the staff, but no one leaves unless they're crippled or dead." Smirking, she looks me up and down. "Would you rather lose a hand or not walk for a few months?"

Irritation flares. I will not let her ruin this for me. If I wound her, I will win the staff. Maybe I'll even free Raven of her wiles. The dagger I dropped is still by the body of the man who struck my arm. Rélia notices my gaze fixated on it. We lock eyes. I can't hide my intentions.

She can't stop me.

I race her for the dagger. A split second before she can stop me from picking it up, the cool hilt slides into my palm. I drop to one knee. She tries to stop herself from colliding with me. Dagger extended, I close my eyes.

Her breath catches. She drops her sword.

I crack my eyes open. The dagger is impaled in her side.

"Why?" she wheezes, eyes still trained on me as if not daring to look at her wound.

Tears trickle down my face. Sorrow and shame overwhelm me. "If I can get the staff, I can save everyone. I can ensure a better world, a healed world. You just won't be there to see it. I'm sorry."

I pull the dagger from her side. Gasping, she presses a hand to her wound. Seeing the blood rapidly soak her shirt twists my stomach even more. Though it's strange—her blood isn't black as I expected. Nor is it red, not entirely. Scarlet, with an ivory hue. Like nothing I've ever seen, nor even heard of.

Slowly, she turns in the direction of the balcony. She takes one step, then collapses. She clenches fistfuls of sand as if that will assuage her shallow breaths.

Soon, she will be dead.

Half of me is frozen with heart-wrenching guilt. The other half is relieved to see her suffering. I try to block it all out.

The ground shakes. Cracks spindle across the arena floor, sucking sand down. I focus on the black-haired kid striding across the arena, polished bronze cane guiding his path. Silence falls. A Welder. I've never seen one in person. The hush of the crowd tells me one has never fought before.

One of the competitors that had been hugging the wall bolts

for him. Ditching the dagger for Rélia's sword, I take stock of the Welder, assessing his skill.

He stops, tilting his head as if waiting for his opponent to strike. Rays of the setting sun catch on the cane, reddening it as if it's painted with blood. With a well-placed blow, the kid strikes the competitor in the knees. I can almost hear his bones shattering from this far away. The man's screams ring high above the swelling roar of the crowd. Nerves fraying, I slowly step away from Rélia, who's still breathing shallowly on the ground. Despite his small stature, unassuming appearance, it's clear this kid can navigate his way around a battle. Not many can casually strike someone down without so much as breaking a sweat.

The final competitor seems to take it as a challenge. Strong gusts of wind blow across the arena, kicking up sand in its wake. Raging around cane-kid is a golden tornado of sand. I recognize the tingling in the air that comes with a Galer's will. It's not the same as Aran's. Colder. Sharper.

After a moment, the tornado dies down. Cane-kid is crouched on the ground, head down, cane balanced in his hands. He's completely still. A trick. Never trust an unmoving man in a fight. The Galer advances, wavering slightly, yet still confident in stride.

Heart hammering, I watch as the cane strikes out, connecting with the Galer's shin. He goes down, fingers curling into fists. Cane-kid clutches his chest as if the air ceased flowing in his lungs. It doesn't hinder him for long. One well-placed blow with the cane silences the Galer's scream before it's finished.

It's the two of us now.

He's the only one standing in my way of the staff. And he's just a kid. I can defeat him. Right?

That seems less and less likely as he advances. Now that I'm so close, the pressure of winning crushes me. The sword grows heavy in my hands. Struggling to keep the blade level, I use it to keep distance between me and the clearly devastating cane.

"Don't come closer," I warn, rolling my shoulders back, clenching my jaw.

Up close, his youth is striking. Younger than anyone else I struck down. Despite everything I saw him do, the small smile tugging at his lips makes him appear nothing less than innocent. "What, you wouldn't hit a blind kid, would you?"

"I won't take joy in it. Believe me when I say that."

He sighs. Fondness passes over his face as he tilts his head. My stomach clenches when he shifts the cane to lean on it. "Neither will I, friend. I hate this place, you know?"

The sun's slipped below the horizon now. I'm not sure how much time I have left until Navda comes looking for me, expecting the staff. I swing at his leg. Tinny ringing resounds as he parries the blow. I go high, but he still seems to sense where I'm aiming, and deflects.

He swings at my shoulder. I drop to the ground, narrowly avoiding the loss of my arm. "Marie only likes that she can be brutally honest without consequence here. Jac would love it, though. He's missing a few gears, but we love his curious wonder."

I pause, risen only halfway. "Marie? Marie Noem?"

Now he's the shocked one. "You know her?"

"Monty?" I venture.

His eyebrows knit together, confirming my suspicion. This is the Monty that makes Marie's eyes light up. Damn. I have to be strategic. Hoping it won't exhaust me too much, I reach for my magic. Again, I scrape against a cold emptiness. Faint tendrils of my magic spindle through my core. Hardly enough, but I have to make it work. Even momentary control will give me an advantage.

Before I can open my mouth, bells ring across the arena. The crowd quiets, heads swiveling, murmuring curiously. I glance at the balcony to find it empty, save for a few frantic guards.

"Spectators, remain seated. There's an issue with the staff," the announcer shouts from the dais. "Competitors, off the arena!"

Again, I glance at the balcony. Gods, what did Raven do?

"NOW!"

Chaos erupts as the panicked crowd scrambles to escape the guards blocking exits. More menacing guards pour from the competitor gates, picking up bodies, ushering us out.

Everything is falling apart. I'll just have to make do without the staff. Somehow. I'll find another way to defeat Navda. For now, all I can do is run.

31

Raven

Holding my head high, I stroll up the stairs at a leisurely pace. Thinking sexy thoughts as Penn suggested I do does not seem to be helping my innate lack of seductiveness. Having him with me is some comfort, at least. For now. Shadows wrap around me. Strangely, they give me comfort in the absence of weaponry at my back.

At the next landing, I halt. Stairs spiral up into the darkness. Somewhere in the rafters, the staff is locked away, kept under heavy lock and key. Supposedly.

Kind lines crinkle around Penn's eyes. "Ya got this, Raven."

Offering him a faltering smile, I nod. "Yeah. Thanks."

Penn extends his arm to me. Unsure what it means, I just stare. Chuckling, he lifts my arm and brings it to meet his. Hesitantly, I clasp my hand around his forearm.

"Onwards and forwards," he says.

That mantra...why is he sharing it with me? He encourages me with a nod. I whisper the responding words. "Forever free."

Penn grins. "You got it."

"Forever free." It rolls off my tongue as if I've said it my entire life.

Beaming with pride, he salutes me. Then he's gone. I listen to his nearly silent footsteps ascending into the dark. Soon, that fades. Anxiety gnaws at my chest. This is it.

"Um, could you move? I have business." A light bell-like voice rings out behind me.

Startling, I find a lean woman at least two heads shorter than me standing on the threshold of the landing. Judging by her revealing black dress, her sleek feather boa to match the deep accentuated kohl around her eyes, it's clear she's here for the capo. A real pleasure house girl. Flanking her are two guards glaring daggers.

Panic claws through me. I didn't plan for this. Doubt Rélia did either. I try to keep my eyes trained on her, so the guards don't catch me estimating their skill. "As do I."

She turns her nose up at me. Great. A pretentious consort. "I have been with the capo for several matches. He only gets the best of the best, from the House of the Red Orchid, not some—"

I roll my eyes. Time is of the essence. Deep breath in, power flows through the beads in my hair, focus turns my skin cold. Deep breath out, magic glides in my veins like it's my blood. Throwing one hand out, time ceases. Already, my energy reserve saps away. I pray I won't be too exhausted to mindlessly flirt.

While time is frozen, I take the sword from the guard on the left and use the pommel to knock her comrade unconscious before hitting the first one. Time snaps back. Both guards collapse. The woman gasps. Before she can scream for help, I grab the ends of her boa, wrap it tight around her throat, and pull. She claws at the boa. I turn my head to the dark ceiling, so I don't have to watch as she slowly stops fighting.

"I'm sorry," I whisper.

She stills. Gently, I lay her on the ground. Peeking around the corner, I find a dim, empty hallway. Where the hell am I supposed to hide them? Down the stairs, I remember passing a broom closet. I groan. Hastily, I drag them all down to where the closet sits unperturbed. As much as I wish to make them more comfortable, time is precious. I shove them in the closet unceremoniously, slam the door shut, and tie the woman's boa around the knob and a rung of the stairwell railing.

I race back up the stairs and take a left down a maze of halls. Rounding a final corner, I'm met with a door guarded by two armed soldiers. On the other side lies entry to the balcony reserved for the capo—best seat to enjoy the fights. Plastering a coy smile on my face, I grab a stray hair free of my braids and twirl it around my finger.

My gait is slow. Stiff. I try to relax but only end up tenser than before. Heart pounding, I drop my voice, thickening it like honey, praying it's as enticing as I want it to be. "Greetings. I have been sent for the capo."

The guards exchange a confused look, eyebrows raising in unison. Doubt crosses their faces.

I'm overthinking this. No one talks like that. I close my eyes for a moment, trying my best to channel Rélia's unerring charm. The golden beads settle the nausea twisting in my stomach. It's like Rélia is with me, guiding me through my movements. If she believes I can do this, then maybe I can.

Batting my eyelashes, I step up to one of the guards. I draw a finger down his chest, brush my lips against his ear. My voice is soft, breathy, barely audible. "Do you know how many nerve endings act for pleasure?" I pause for a moment, let the question sink in. "Every single one, if you know how to make it happen. Lucky for you, I do."

Moving fluidly, as if dancing through water, I circle behind the second guard, running my hands across her shoulders, down her arms. She shivers. Confidence flows through me. Rélia would be proud.

"If you allow me the honor of the capo, I'll allow you the honor of me." I draw the first guard closer, skimming my fingers across the two of them. "Whatever you desire, I can deliver."

They shudder. Another moment passes and they finally open the door, allowing me entry. As soon as it closes, I allow myself to breathe. Already, I've almost messed up. I shake out my hands, expelling excess energy. What did I even say out there? For the life of me, I can't remember.

"Can I help you?"

I stifle a scream. Recovering quickly, I bat my eyelashes at the squat man standing before me. "The Capo requires company for the fight, no?"

He looks me up and down, unconvinced. "You ain't from the Red Orchid. Don't recall any other such appointments. Scram before I compensate for my wasted time by taking a limb."

Drastic. I bite my lip to keep it from trembling. What now?

A sultry voice rings out, "Now that's hardly a way to talk to a beautiful creature who made her way up here just to kindly bless me with her presence."

Emerging from the shadows of the hallway is a tall, stocky man hitting middle age. Scruff adorns his rugged face, where it lacks on his head. Lust glints in his dark, bloodshot eyes. Two curved blades with curling cross guards hang menacingly at his side.

The Capo.

I force myself to smile. It's half-hearted. Hardly sincere. I wouldn't believe I had flirty, innocuous intentions if I were him. Fortunately, he doesn't seem to have the same mindset. The Capo takes my hand, gently kissing the back of it, then holds out a toned arm to me. Discomfort knots my stomach.

Surprisingly chivalrous for a man of his reputation, he guides me down the sconce-lit hallway to a set of double doors. Chatter from an eager crowd seeps through. I'm about to watch Rélia fight for sport. Possibly to...no I can't think of that. We're going to be fine. Positive thoughts, positive energy, positive outcome. I hope.

"I have not seen you 'round these parts before," the Capo says with a shrewd smile. "And I'm familiar with all the fine ladies and gents of the pleasure houses."

Heat rises in my cheeks when my voice comes out as a squeak. "I'm new, sir."

He chuckles softly. "Relax, angel. I don't care."

Grooves indent his skin; my nails dig in a little too tight. He doesn't seem to mind. The capo pulls open one of the doors. Light from the setting sun blinds me momentarily before illuminating the rustic, charming private balcony with an ample view of the arena.

"Tell me angel, what's your name?"

As if I would tell him that. "Angel works fine, Capo sir. If you don't mind the privacy."

"Only if you don't mind reserving formalities for the subordinate. You are far more divine than that," he says, smiling. "Call me Gustus."

He doesn't seem as bad as Rélia made him out to be. Either he's deceptive or she's irritating enough to garner the wrath of every person in power. Both, likely. If anything, I'm a bit more at ease. Gustus hasn't given any indication he's bothered by my lack of flirtation. Rélia did say he likes the chase.

Gustus steps down the polished stone steps to the edge of the balcony. I release my hold on him, instead holding tight to the brass railing. Leaning over, I take in the sight of the arena. Weapons are racked in the center. An announcer on a well-kempt dais near the sandy floor is adjusting his leather jacket. Tilting my head towards the sky, I close my eyes. Gentle, salty wind tugs at my hair. Warm, orange sun rays caress my cheek. I can almost tell myself I'm standing on the docks of Ghzen.

"You like the scent of battle?" Gustus asks.

I open my eyes to find him looking at me with a gaze that makes my skin crawl. Right. The battle. "Sure."

Folding his hands together, he leans against the railing next to me. "It's alright, angel. It used to make me squeamish too."

"Bet that went away when your pockets got heavier," I mutter. As soon as the bitter words leave my mouth, panic rips through me. I clear my throat. "Sorry, I shouldn't speak out of turn."

He puts a finger to my lips. I try not to shrink away. "Never fear for speaking your mind. I am the Capo of Racha. Not the King of Oncarii."

Below, the announcer informs us the fight will begin in but a minute. Gustus leads me to an iron throne near the edge of the balcony. He takes a seat, motioning for me to follow. Hesitantly, I sit on his lap.

Guards circle the throne, standing stoically in their mauve leather uniforms, hands on the hilts of their serrated machetes. I try not to let my gaze linger on the blades. Should this go south, I might meet my end on one of those. I fiddle with the buttons of my shirt to distract my mind.

"If you'd like help undressing, just ask," Gustus grunts, smirking. "I'd be more than happy to bask in the blessing of a natural woman."

Embarrassment strikes. My fingers halt. Abhorred, I grind my teeth. Pursing my lips, I give him a cold, miffed glare. "No, Gustus. Another lewd comment and I'll cover myself more."

He chuckles, drawing me closer. "Feisty. I like that."

Fighting the urge to break away, I lean into him, kicking one leg up on the armrest, leaving the other curled between his legs. I rest my head on his shoulder. Gustus wraps an arm around me. Gently, he draws his fingers down the length of my arm until he twines his fingers with mine. Revulsion twists through me. I long for the comfort of Rélia's touch.

As if the universe read my mind, the announcer heralds the start of the fight. Gates open in a cacophony of horrendous screeching. Keeping a stoic face, I watch as Rélia emerges from a gate directly opposite to the balcony. Monty lingers in the shadows. My gaze strays to a gate near hers. Standing there is...no. Tezin? It can't be. Deep down, I know it is. His hair is longer, wilder, and there's something distinctly different about him, but it is undeniably my brother.

"Nervous, angel? Don't worry. No blood will mar your pretty face up here."

My smile lasts for but a moment. "That's...that's good."

Pretending like avoiding blood splatter is all I care about only worsens my nausea. Maybe this flirting tactic will serve as a distraction for me too. Focusing my attention away from the arena, I channel the art of seduction I picked up in the last ten minutes.

I lower my voice, brushing my lips against his ear. "Gustus."

"Yes, angel?" he hums, holding his hand out to a guard near him. She gives him a polished black pipe, then lights it for him with controlled flames from her fingertips.

"Isn't that illegal?" I ask, momentarily forgetting that I'm supposed to be leading him on.

He cocks an eyebrow. "Only for outsiders. My guards are trusted."

Gustus takes a long drag from the pipe. Smoke rings circle me when he exhales. I cough. He smiles.

I bat my eyelashes. "Of course. Excuse my curiosity. I'm only amazed at the power you hold."

Refraining from rolling my eyes at my own words, I draw a finger down his face, pulling his gaze from the arena to me. I bite my lip. He cocks an eyebrow and turns his attention away from me, though I can tell he's feeling rather victorious.

Time ticks by slowly. Watching two people I care about battle sends my heart somersaulting. Every clash of swords, every fallen body is agony. It could be either one of them.

A hush falls over the crowd, shattering the suffocation of battle. My heart leaps in my throat as I stare at the bloody scene lain beneath me. Tezin is still alive, thank the gods. How he managed to kill so many people, I don't know. I try not to think about it.

Cracks spindle across the arena floor. Sand spills into the abyss. Monty strides from a shadowed gateway, cane sliding across the ground.

But if Monty...if Monty is fighting...

My stomach drops. I refuse to acknowledge the dread coiling through me even as I scan the arena for Rélia. Cold shocks my system. She's lying on the ground near my brother. Her hands clutch at her side. Even from this far away I can't miss the blood. *Her* blood. Her strangely colored blood.

I saw this.

She's not healing. Why isn't she healing? My head spins. Pressing a hand to my chest, I try to make myself breathe. Air feels like fire, scorching my lungs. Tears well in my eyes.

She can't be dead. She can't be dead. SHE CAN'T BE DEAD.

"Are you alright, angel?"

At the sound of Gustus's voice, I snap back to my body. Every part of me crawls with hysteria, with despair. I turn to look at him and all goes numb, as if I've never felt anything at all. I can get the staff. I can save Rélia. "Fine."

The door to the balcony bursts open. Several guards stream towards the capo. I curse under my breath. Behind them, a disheveled pleasure house girl glares haughty daggers at me. They got out much sooner than I anticipated.

"There, sirs," she says, pointing an accusatory finger at me. "She's the one that tried to kill me."

"Angel?" Gustus pins a suspicious gaze on me. I leap off of him. No way I'm talking myself out of this.

"I didn't try to kill her," I mutter, my fingers tingling with magic. "She's probably just not used to anyone disliking her."

Ignoring the risk, I channel as much power as I can. It rages through me with a burning pleasure rooted in a deep-set anger. It's the same intensity that arose when I tried to kill Rélia, when I first stopped time. At the thought of her, my power grows like never before. The odrite bracelet sears my skin but the pain is faint. It snaps and falls to the floor. I throw my arms out. Golden light explodes from my hands, striking those around me. Everyone freezes in place, surrounded by pale yellow auras.

My eyes widen. Hesitantly, I step past the capo's detail. They don't make a move towards me. Curious. Touching the light surrounding them, I find it familiar in warmth. Deep down, my magic thrums.

Keeping my power focused on suspending them in time, I slowly make my way towards the door. Once through to the other side, the tether thins. I grit my teeth, clench my fists, and push on. Penn better hurry the hell up. I will not fail Rélia. I will not let her bleed to death in that damn arena.

Halfway up the next flight of stairs, I drop to my knees. My energy wavers. Gripping the railing, I let out a guttural scream. Anger surges through me. Magic flurries at my fingertips. I find the strength to race to the top landing. There's no sign of Penn.

"Hey," I hiss, trying to catch my breath. Shadows dance in the sconce-light, setting my nerves on edge. I can't deal with more armed guards. "Penn! Where are you?"

Alarm bells sound. I startle. The tether to those frozen on the balcony snaps so abruptly it's almost audible. I pitch forwards as my magic floods back into my veins.

"Run!" Penn shouts, hooking his arm through mine as I stagger to my feet.

Footsteps pound in the corridors behind us. I take the steps down two at a time. I barrel past the capo's detail as they storm off the balcony. Behind me, Penn is caught in their blockade.

"Catch!"

A long wooden staff sails through the air. A guard reaches up to grab it.

Panic takes hold. Curling my fingers into a fist, I focus on Rélia, on my connection with her, on my fear for her. Just for a moment, I freeze the guards in their place. With my free hand, I catch the staff.

I gasp. Ancient power runs through the dark, knotted wooden staff. Indistinct whispers murmur in the air around me. Half-truths and fragments of secrets no one should know ring in my ears.

White light shines between my fingers where I grip the staff. Familiar power thrums through me, power I've never tasted before but feels like it's always been meant for me. Forgetting my surroundings, I channel that intense, cool magic. Hints of every maji element tingle in my fingertips. My Sight soars, as if trying to show me images before my eyes, not just in my mind.

"Raven come on!" Penn is ahead of me now.

More guards swell to their frozen comrades. I snap back to reality, taking off through the halls. Doors slam shut around me. They're trying to cut us off. I will myself to run faster. Lungs burning, I skid around a corner, nearly slamming into the wall. Barely, I catch a glimpse of Penn as he darts down an adjacent corridor.

Guards spill from a side door, barring my escape. Turning on my heel, I try to backtrack only to find myself surrounded. Swords gleam in the dim flickering light. Heart pounding, I search for an escape route. Nothing.

Brandishing the staff in front of me, I try to think my way out of this. If I had enough time, I could ask my Sight for help. Even with ample time I'm not sure my body can take the exhaustion of using magic.

"Isolde," I plead, my voice but a whisper. "Help me."

All sound drowns away. A deep, resonant humming fills the silence. The staff shudders. White light brightens along the knots in the wood, extinguishing the darkness of the halls. Clarity flows through me with a cool intensity reminiscent of the goblet I drank from in Borziau. I close my eyes, breathing deep and slow, letting the invigorating power pulse in my veins.

For the first time in a long time, I'm whole. Like this magic is a part of me I never knew I was missing. All my panic drains, displaced by a comfortable confidence. My eyes snap open. The white light is subdued, awaiting my command.

Just as the guards swarm me, I slam the base of the staff into the stone floor. Fissures spider-web across the stone. An explosion of hazy white light throws everyone back. Not a single man rises to attack.

Silence ensues. Only my footsteps echo through the hallways as I sprint for the exit. Finally, I burst into the dull luminosity of twilight. Clamor fills the shadowed streets. Sticking close to the wall, I search for any sign of the crew. Every pair of eyes that strays in my direction makes my heart pound harder. Soon everyone in Racha will know I carry the most valuable object in the world.

A hand wraps tight around my wrist, yanking me into an alley behind the arena. Thankfully, Penn's kind face greets me. Both of us crouch low behind a stack of crates brimming with sand.

"Can you make it stop glowing?" he asks.

Panting, I wipe sweat from my brow. Ivory hues faintly gleam beneath the dark wood. "I don't know."

"Let me hold it."

At first, the notion of handing it over is repulsive. Give away all that power? I shake my head clear of those poisonous thoughts. Trembling, I drop the staff into Penn's hands. Immediately, it goes dark. Something halts inside me. Queasiness threatens to upend my last meal. Despite the weight lifted from my shoulders while apart from the staff, part of me misses the security of unending power.

It's not like the comfort of Rélia at my side.

My chest tightens. "Rélia! Where is she? Where's Monty?"

"Right here," Monty wheezes, rounding the corner. Beside him, a sentient bed of earth carries Rélia. "Thank you, so much, for being so far away. Tactful."

I barely hear what he says. All my attention is focused on Rélia's nearly lifeless body. It takes everything in me not to cry. Her chest is still rising. Shallowly, but rising. That's what matters. If there's breath in her body, then she can get up. And if she can get up, she can fight. She can survive.

Lip trembling, I kneel beside her. Blood soaks her shirt. Sweat rolls down the side of her face. Gently, I stroke her reddened cheek. Her skin is burning up. Thinking of nothing else but her, I lift her in my arms, hold her tight.

She shivers violently. Setting my jaw, I turn to Penn. Speechless, he takes a step back. Seeing the lack of self-assurance in his face ages him beyond comprehension. "Take us back to the docks."

"I can try," he says slowly, as if unsure what words hold meaning. "But…I…"

"I don't care!" I shout, unable to cage the anger that's been bubbling in my core. It is all I am. I hand Rélia off to Penn, taking back the staff. Mournfully, he stares down at his captain. I grip tight to the staff. My hand nearly goes numb.

Coward. Already grieving her. I refuse.

Harnessing the power of Isolde's staff hardly feels substantial. Rage overpowers my every sense, every thought. Stepping out of the alley, I turn the glowing weapon on the streets before us. "Stay close."

I'll get her home. No matter the cost.

32

Raven

Fury burns through me as I storm through Racha. This city of pirates will yield to me, or I will bring it down in its entirety. Rélia's violent coughing spurs me forward. Everyone knows where I am. Everyone knows what I have, what I control. All eyes turn to me on every street I race down.

Two ballsy men advance, pistols raised. I swing the staff in their direction, barely glancing at them. Powerful gusts of wind pick them off their feet, slamming them into a Game House. Startled shouts echo from inside.

Screams tear from my lungs as pirates, guards, all manner of thugs and ruffians, swarm towards me. One jab to the right, and a building crumbles. Another, and a fire rages from a pub. Head held high, I stride through the chaos. No one else dares challenge me. They're smart enough to want for their lives.

Hope surges when the docks come into view. Fueled by that

relief, I run through the haze of smoke curling in the air. Already, it's a thick wall. I can barely sense the sea air when I near the ship. I step aside, allowing Penn and Monty to board the ship first. My gaze lingers on Rélia. My stomach drops when she coughs, splattering blood on Penn's shirt.

I turn the staff on the burning, tumultuous city. Silhouettes emerge from the smog. Vibrations shake the staff. Focusing on the glint of swords, the cool, metallic comfort of Welder magic rises at my fingertips, begging to reclaim its metal. Sparks fly as swords drive straight down into the stone road.

I've bought us time. Just enough.

Pulsing with power, I race up the gangplank to the deck of the *Anviora*. Everyone is in a confused frenzy. Questions of their captain's state buzz in the air. I search for Mina. She stands in the midst of the deck, dark hair loose, eyes wide.

I grab her arm, shaking her from her stupor. "Mina! Has everyone returned to the ship?"

"Yes."

"Good."

No time to lose. At the bow of the ship, I angle the staff towards the sea. Its energy is cold, restless, smooth. Ever-shifting, it's hard to grasp. Gritting my teeth, I will the staff to connect with the water. Its power grows inside me, roiling with dissent. My head pounds as I struggle to maintain control. Escape consumes my thoughts. Envisioning the ship in the middle of the sea, I channel the fluidity of the waves. They break against the hull, rocking the ship side to side. Water magic, this magic I have no right to control, resists my will.

Releasing one hand from the staff, I curl my fingers, searching for that mischievous energy in the fabric of the world. I brush against it. It's elusive, and I almost miss it. Now, it writhes against my skin. I tighten my grip. I yank. The ship lurches forward at an impossible speed.

When finally there is nothing but the star-speckled sky reflected on endless black waves, I drop the staff. Silence. Exhaustion weighs me down. Blood pumps in my ears, exacerbating the agonizing pounding in my head. I've never been so drained in my life. It takes everything in me to step towards Rélia's cabin. Momentarily forgetting the staff, I stumble across the deck, ignoring everyone else's distress.

I throw the door to her cabin open. Rélia lies moaning in her bedchamber, Penn attentive at her side. Heart-wrenching fear overwhelms any sense of rationality. I can only focus on how sickly she looks as I slowly approach the bed.

I kneel by her side, opposite Penn. Coughs wrack her chest. Her face is pale and splotchy, her forehead dripping with sweat. Beneath her half-closed eyelids, her eyes shift rapidly. A strained scream tears from her mouth.

"What's happening to her?" I whisper. I bite my lip, trying to keep it from trembling.

Penn's stare is gaunt. "Blood rot. Xipher poisonin'. Whatever ya wanna call it. Cap'n is in...indescribable pain."

"But..." My voice cracks. I take a deep breath, composing myself. "Why isn't she healing?"

"She is. But that's what blood rot does. It feeds offa magic. The more her body tries ta heal, the more she'll deteriorate."

I put my hand on hers. There's no spark between our magics.

I tell myself it's only because I've exhausted my reserve. "She'll have no magic?"

Penn sighs, voice low as if speaking the words will make them true. "First she has to survive. Then…I dunno."

Rélia coughs again, staining the bedclothes. Feverish murmurs pass her lips. She clutches at the duvet, kicking, screaming.

"Hallucinations," Penn says flatly. "I'm gonna make ginger-mint tea to help ease the pain and slow the effects on the blood."

"Yarrow," I choke out, clearing my throat of the lump sitting there. "It'll help her fever if you have it."

Penn gives me a single nod before ducking out of the room. My knee bounces as I tuck Rélia's hair behind her ear. I'm not going to let her fall victim to this. Blocking out her pained groans, I try to think. A feeble idea springs to mind, born of desperation. Doubtful it'll work, but I haven't any idea what else to do.

Gently, I pull up her shirt, exposing the deep reddened gash still oozing with silvery blood. Pressing my palms around her tender wound, I draw upon the willing fragments of my already fatigued reservoir. The beads in my hair give me a fresh, invigorating boost, leaving the tips of my fingers tingling. Golden wisps of time magic brush over her wound, leaving it shimmering. Optimistic relief edges through me. Until the blood rot has run its course, her wound will remain frozen in time. Maybe that will preserve her magic.

I run my thumb over her hand. There it is. Faint. Weary. But there is a spark reassuring me she'll fight. She'll survive.

Cool relief tugs at my heart when Penn returns, steaming mug in hand. I take it from him, inhaling the sweet, refreshing scent. Throwing a sorrowful glance at Rélia, he once more leaves us alone, drawing the curtain closed.

"You're going to be okay Rélia," I murmur, lips grazing against her clammy palm. "I promise. I'm not going to let you die."

"As...as long as...as long as you don't make me drink that bastard tea. I hate mint," Rélia croaks, slowly turning on her side to face me. A weak yet merry smile cracks across her sickly face.

No longer can I hold back tears. The roll down my face, hot, heavy, full of hope.

"Crying over me?" She laughs softly, a laugh that turns to fits of coughing. Less blood. Good sign. "Wait for the funeral, love."

I help her into a sitting position. As soon as I'm sure she's stable enough to hold herself up, I wrap her fingers around the warm mug. "Just for that, I'll force this tea down your throat if you don't drink all of it."

She scrunches her nose. "Ugh. If you insist."

"I do." Taking a seat next to her on the bed, I help her drink. Her face twists in disgust. I tilt the mug back to her lips, forcing more down before she can spit it out. Half of it is gone before I finally let her rest. "There. Better, right?"

Rélia snuggles closer to me. My heart stops for a moment. Tentative, I wrap my arm around her shoulders, hugging her tight. Smiling, I relish in the comfort of her warmth. Focusing on the ease of her breathing, the beat of her heart in time with mine, I finally feel like I am where I'm supposed to be.

"Everything feels right," I murmur, hardly aware of the words breezing past my lips.

"Hm?"

I run my fingers through her hair, unraveling the tangled knots. "Nothing. Just drink. And rest."

Rélia slurps her tea. "You're not in charge."

"You're in no condition to argue."

She finishes the tea, then tosses the mug to the end of the bed. Her eyes droop as she twines her fingers with mine. "Fine. As long as you stay with me."

Brushing my lips across her forehead in a faint kiss, my stomach finally settles. Ghzen is in ashes. My roots have burned. But she is my home. "I wouldn't dream of leaving."

•••••

I can't be sure how much time has passed when the rocking of the ship wakes me. Rélia and I are tangled together, her head nestled into my chest. I take a moment to relish how perfectly she fits into my arms before the ship lurches again. Rélia stirs. Half-asleep, she mumbles incoherently.

Sliding out of bed, I gently rest Rélia's head on the pillow. Unfortunately, the tea must have worn of its sleeping aid because she sits up as soon as I head for the curtain.

"What's going on?" she mumbles, yawning.

"I don't know. Stay here."

Rélia rolls off the bed, clutching at her middle. She holds up a finger before I can object. "I'm fine. I just need a minute."

I cross my arms. "Stay. Here."

Taking deep, shuddering breaths, she pulls herself back onto the bed. "I'll stay."

Something slams against the side of the ship. I stumble as the room teeters sideways. Unease rockets through me. Another deafening thump rocks the ship to the other side. Staggering, I finally make my way to the main deck.

Chaos.

Night swallows the world, nearly snuffing out the oil lamps swaying wildly from their hooks. Thick clouds hang heavy over us, pouring with rain. Barely, I can make out Penn frantically barking orders from the ship's wheel. Everyone is scrambling to tie down rigging. I race through the mayhem to Penn.

"Hey!" I shout, voice nearly lost to the whipping wind. "What's happening?"

Terror lines Penn's shaking voice. "Mermaids!"

I gasp. I've never encountered such creatures before, though I've heard tales. No one's seen them and lived to tell about it, not for years. Hesitantly, I peer over the side of the ship. My heart leaps into my throat. Beautiful blue scaly tails with an eerie violet iridescence surround the ship on every side. They're larger than I imagined. Larger than the ship itself.

Transfixed with fear, I'm powerless as one rams their tail against the ship. This time, I hear the crack in the wood. If they keep going, we'll sink.

Gears already turning, I yell, "Where's the staff?"

Penn nods to his weapons belt, where it's wrapped in dirty cloth next to my own staff. Tearing it free of fabric, I harness the jolt of power bursting through me. Blinding white light emanates between my hands, catching the attention of the mermaids. Another slam nearly tilts the ship over. The staff slips from my grip, rolling down the deck. Screaming, I fall after it.

"I think yer makin' them angrier!" Penn shouts.

I hook my ankle around the main mast, swinging myself the

other way as the ship rights. On all fours, I scramble across the water-soaked deck. Just as my fingertips brush the staff, the ship tilts. It rolls off the rail and into the stormy sea.

"NO!"

Everything falls out beneath me. My fingernails scrape against the wood, desperately clawing for purchase. I grab hold of the rail just before the water claims me. Gasping, I try not to think about the fact that there's nothing beneath my feet but air and deep, dangerous water.

"No, no," I cry, trying to pull myself over. My fingers ache as I clasp the railing with a vice grip. As the ship rights, the slick railing proves too hard to hold onto.

Warm hands wrap tight around my wrists. It's Rélia. Tremors shake her. Holding me up is too much.

One of my hands slips from her grip. The other is not far behind. Our eyes meet. It feels like goodbye.

Rélia reaches down to grab my other hand. Beads of sweat roll down her face. She can barely stand. She has to let go or she'll go down with me.

"RAVEN!"

Her outstretched fingers are all I see as I plummet.

Rushing air swallows my scream. Exhilaration sweeps through me. Cold shocks my system as I plunge into the dark waters. Adrenaline takes over my limbs. Frantically, I propel myself towards the surface. I gasp for air when my head breaks the waves. Distressed shouts rise over the swell of the crashing waves and howling wind. I try to scream for help, but another wave drags me under.

Tumbling through the numb, dark, never-ending sea, I can't

discern which way is up. Every stroke of my arms only seems to send me deeper.

A melodic humming rings in my ears. *The staff!* Wildly, I spin around. Nothing. Closing my eyes, I try to keep my panic at bay. Focusing on its call, I let my magic rise in response. There! I can sense its presence falling deeper. Holding tight to the connection, I plunge down, until the humming is deafening. White glows around my hands. Not too far below me, the staff pulses with the same dim hue. Despite my lungs crying for air, I swim for it. As soon as it's in my hands, light explodes.

All my breath escapes in a single, soundless scream. Illuminated by the staff is the giant face of a mermaid in front of me. Luminescent blue scales cover the sides of its face, cover its thick body, make up its tail that's so large the end is consumed by the depths of the sea. Each of its piercing yellow eyes are bigger than I am. Two rows of teeth sharp as swords gleam in the white light when it opens its mouth.

Three more surround me. My blood runs cold. I can sense their anger. They link hands. Around me, the water boils. Are they trying to kill me?

My chest is burning now. Black spots dance in my eyes. Breaking free of my shock, I plead the staff to take me up. I shoot through the water, cresting the surface in a matter of seconds. Taking deep gulps of air, I search for the ship. I can barely see it in the torrent of rain pelting against the turbulent sea.

Before I can command my staff to take me to the *Anviora*, scaly, webbed fingers wrap around my ankle, dragging me under. Hot pain flashes up my leg. The staff's light illuminates a talon-like fingernail digging into my calf. For lack of a better idea, I ram the staff into their hand. A deep, strangely alluring scream erupts from the mouth of the mermaid nearest me, rippling the water, sending me reeling.

Another mermaid tries to rip the staff from me. It should be nothing at all to the mammoth creature, but the staff resists, clinging to me as if I am its safety and not the other way around. Light pulses around us. A tingling sensation engulfs my mouth and nose. Galer magic, gifting me breath. Inhaling deeply, resolve ignites my anger.

I'm breathing. Time to start fighting.

I spin the staff around, calling out to the sea. Its energy is as elusive as ever, but I'm ready for it this time. Envisioning a whirlpool, I swing the staff in circles above my head. Just as I imagine, the water churns, keeping the mermaids at bay.

Lighthearted energy curls from the staff. I breathe it in. It coats my tongue. Sweet, unlike anything I've ever tasted. Tamer magic. My last chance at communicating.

"Please!" I cry, focusing on channeling three elements at once, trying not to collapse under the pressure. "I'm not here to hurt you! I'm trying to save magic!"

The mermaids pause. They converse in hushed, melodious whispers. Words aren't exactly what passes their gargantuan mouths. More like breathy tunes, lilting and clicking in unique patterns. I can't hear clearly, but I can understand. Doubt floats between us. There isn't enough time to forge trust. I hope they'll believe me.

I focus on water magic, releasing the weight of controlling the other two elements. Drawing from desperation, I reign in its carefree nature. I shoot upwards, barely avoiding the deadly swipe of a tail.

Breaking the surface, I take deep gulps of air. Lanterns flood the *Anviora* with flickering orange light in the distance, blown out of the storm's path. Riding the waves as if I am one, I reach the ship in the blink of an eye. With the help of the wind, I spill onto the deck of the ship. All is silent. No sea creatures have followed.

Immediately, Rélia is at my side. She gathers me into a tight embrace. I drop the staff, wrapping my arms tight around her. Relief overwhelms me. When we pull away, she's smiling brilliantly.

"What happened?" She nods to the blood pooling around my leg.

I chuckle, unable to hold back a grin of my own, even as hot pain throbs from the deep gash. "I faced down mermaids. For you. Well, for the staff, actually. But it sounds more heroic to say it was for you."

Rélia hugs me again. "Whatever you did it for, I'm glad you're alive."

"Me too."

We stare into each other's eyes for a moment longer than we should. I lean closer, yearning to kiss her. I don't care that everyone's watching, or that we're both drenched and exhausted. All I want is her.

The staff's humming interrupts. Both of us reach for it. When I touch it, that power surges again. Rélia yelps. Sparks fly. She snaps her hand away, cradling it close. Burn marks discolor her palm. Stranger still, streaks of white drain some of the gold from her curls.

"Weird," I mutter. "That hasn't happened to anyone else."

Penn appears behind us, scooping up the staff. It remains dormant.

"See!" I take Rélia's scorched hand in mine. "Why is it trying to hurt you?"

Rélia twirls white strands around her finger. She sighs. "I have an idea."

"Well?"

She stares at the horizon. Her gaze lingers there for an eternity before she turns to me. "There's a reason why my father was so insistent on me being queen when my sister was obviously the smarter choice, why there's a kill order on me, why no one will ever just let me be free!"

I squeeze her hand. "It's okay, Rélia. No judgment."

"My mother is Ylaa."

I jerk away from her. "Ylaa? As in the goddess? The goddess Ylaa. Of health and disease. That goddess. Is your mama?"

"Yes, we're on the same page."

I glance at Penn who's wrapping up the staff once more. Without looking, he nods. I gape at her. "You're a demigod? But that's unheard of! Impossible!"

Rélia shrugs. "Living proof that it isn't. Trust me. It's not all intrigue and adventure. Not the good kind anyway. I can channel more power than I should. I guess that's why the staff doesn't particularly like me. Artifacts were created to help mortals get by without the help of the divine. Plus, Isolde was never on good terms with the gods. Though who is, right?"

I roll my eyes. "Not the point."

"You're right. I'm a powerful demigod, not to mention the king's bastard, which makes me a threat to the monarch's integrity and everyone loyal to it." She presses the heels of her palms into her eyes. Her voice shakes. "I'm sorry I didn't tell you sooner. And now I've dragged you into this. I just—"

Enveloping her in a tight hug, I cut her off. "I almost lost you." Pulling away, I cup her face in my hands. "Thank you for telling me. Now, let's go put this staff in its rightful place before one of your many headhunters catches up to us."

Rélia wipes her eyes. "Mina, chart a course for Caentathea. I think it's time we fulfilled our destinies."

"Not before yer patched up," Penn interjects, nodding at our rather concerning wounds. "Then ya can be as reckless as ya like."

He winks, a twinkle in his eye.

I shake my head. "No. You absolutely *cannot*. But he's right. My leg is killing me. Literally, soon."

Rélia's laughter fills the air as we stagger into her cabin.

IV

LAND FORGOTTEN

33

Tezin

Standing at the bow of the *Divider*, I gently touch the tender skin around the new golden accessory in my ear. Returning to the ship without the staff leaves my heart heavy and hopeless. Aran's arrow is little comfort. It's not exactly precise in aim. If I can't subdue Navda with the power of the staff, killing him will be impossible. Especially since Ean has been more hostile than usual. He was my key to turning the crew. No staff, no crew, no plan.

I sigh, staring up at the night sky. I'm not sure where we are. None of the star clusters are familiar. The lodestar at the height of Mihsoi's constellation is brighter than it's ever been. I assume we're rounding the northern side of Oncarii, past the capital now. Soon the Hebringg Sea will become the Navat Ocean. The ocean without an end.

Stars blur together. My eyes go out of focus. I close them

and find myself retreating into my pocket-world, searching for solace. Since I was last here, it's changed. It's not a pile of embers and ash anymore. Pine trees surround me, rising from the rocky soil, stretching towards the clear night sky. Curling across the rich earth are rose vines, the flowers blooming full and deep in color. Shooting stars streak above my head in a never-ending cascade. The breeze is warm. Familiar to Aran. I smile.

"Well, you should know you didn't succeed in killing me."

I startle. Turning, I find Rélia perched atop a boulder in the center of the forest. There's no sign of her battle wounds. Externally, she seems fine. Her composed veil faintly disguises the turmoil simmering beneath her skin. Raven's anger was a scorching presence, so hot if I focused on it for too long, I might have burned like the pocket-world we'd shared. But Rélia, her center is a cold, confining pool of self-loathing. Lurking not far beneath that is the biting taste of fear.

Sporting a smirk, she glances around. "Nice place. Looks like Al-Surid. Ever been?"

"To the monster infested forest? No." I cross my arms. "What are you doing here?"

"You tell me. One minute I'm having a lovely moment with your sister, the next I'm in your fantasy."

I scoff. "This is not my *fantasy*. It's a pocket-world. I'm a Psychic."

Rélia hops off the boulder. Hands in her pockets, she saunters around me. "So why am I here, oh powerful Psychic?"

No excuse comes to mind. Words bitter in my mouth, I reply, "I don't know."

Rélia twirls a strand of her hair around her finger, staring up at the sky. "Hm. And why is that? Shouldn't you have more control over your power?"

I glare at her, finding myself wishing she'd perished on the arena floor. Mortified at my own thoughts, I exhale, relaxing my stance. Being in her presence doesn't make it easy. "It's not my own fault. I only just found out about my magic a few weeks ago."

She pauses in step. "Really? Does your magic fade in and out?"

"Yes," I reply. "Why?"

She snorts, resuming her mindless pacing. "Sounds like you're a Hallow. I knew one once. She did anything *not* to be one."

"What are you saying?"

"You're a Psychic?" I nod, and she continues, "Yeah, you're Mihsoi's bitch. Your magic is powerful. But you're tied to her, must do her bidding when she calls on you. You can *try* to practice without her help, but the truth is you're not likely to do magic unless she wants it to happen."

"What?" The world shakes. Fir needles shower me. "Why is it always strongest when I'm trying to help you or Raven?"

"I can't pretend to know the divine agenda."

Her nose twitches. She averts her guilt-ridden gaze from me. She knows something. I doubt she'll tell me. Prodding in her mind probably wouldn't help either. Somehow, she can bar her thoughts.

I huff. One problem at a time. "How do I get independence over my magic?"

Rélia snorts. "With great difficulty. If you really wanna get total control of your magic, you're gonna have to find Shaia

Rydar. She's the only Hallow I know that severed her connection. How, is the question though."

"Great. Another thing to add to my impossible agenda." I rub my temples, trying to soothe my looming headache. "Listen. You obviously care for my sister."

Rélia stops in front of me. A sincere smile lights her face. "Incredibly so." She scrunches her nose. "You, not so much."

"Mutual," I snap. "Since we both want the best for her, granted I think we both know that would be to get her as far away from you as possible, I feel I should warn you the Dividers are out to kill you."

"Yeah, what's new." Cold breezes shake the trees. Rélia's suave demeanor melts away. Her self-doubt surges, chilling the world. Snow flutters around us. Our breaths plume in the air. "We'll help you escape. After all this is over. For her, I will not let you die."

"You might get that chance sooner than you think."

Before she can reply, I'm pulled back to reality by the cold bite of a singular metal cuff around my wrist. Odrite.

"Enough of that," Navda says, standing beside me. Weariness lines his voice. For the first time since I've been on this ship, I catch a glimmer of humanity in his black eyes. He's exhausted. Of what? Making our lives hell? "Can't have you giving up our position. Your information will allow us to catch them by surprise. Without that element, we will taste defeat."

With that, he leaves me to join his crew for the night's last round of ale. Hard to catch, but faintly I catch the quirk of his lips.

Lurking behind the rowdy crew is Ean, sullenly nursing his

drink. Our eyes meet, and he scowls. I turn away before that numbing cold snuffs out my thoughts again.

Aran and Marie join me, both with cuffs of their own. The ship glides soundlessly through the dark water. Tranquility surrounds us.

"How much longer?" Aran asks after a long, comfortable silence.

My skin crawls, and I don't have to turn to know why; Ean's eyes are practically burning holes in my back. Ever the watchful hawk. I bite my lip, trying to ignore the unease creeping through my veins. Instinctively, my hand flutters to the arrow in my ear. Having something of Aran's so close is enough to beat back my ever-present fear.

I chew on my lip, trying to calculate the distance. "Eight days. We'll hit Caentathea. My sister will arrive on Rélia Ryan's ship. Then we'll be free. Somehow. I'm not walking off that island a slave."

Aran raises an eyebrow. "Rélia Ryan?" A somber smile tugs at his lips. "Your sister was never in much danger with her."

Studying his reminiscent glow, it dawns on me. "You were part of the *Anviora* crew?"

"Well, the name constantly changes. We were the *Eretea* when I was one of them. *Everlasting* in Iquetí. I suppose she felt the need to change the image of her crew after she lost me."

"Right, because you were so important," Marie mutters.

Aran sighs. "We were a family. You would have loved it, Marie. Freedom unlike anything else. Helping people. Bringing swift justice but living by our own tenets. Answering to no one." He stares placidly at the clouds puffing across the stars. "The

Dividers got the drop on us. Tore apart the crew. Destroyed the ship. Nearly broke Rélia's will. Navda was going to kill her, not because she was competition, not because she was a threat, but because he wanted to get back at the gods, but for what I don't know. And I couldn't let that happen."

Silence falls. I shift uncomfortably. Living in Ghzen all my life, I never knew of the battle on the seas, how many people it hurt. All I knew was that pirates tried to destroy my family. I suppose not everything is as black and white as I believed. Aran used to be a pirate. He loved it. Part of me twists with disgust. Drowning that out is soothing warmth sweeping through me. No one has ever brought me solace like he has.

I'm beginning to understand Raven.

Finally I speak, voice low, heavy with the weight of Aran's confession. "You sacrificed yourself. Damned yourself to misery. Very noble."

He shrugs. "Onwards and forwards, we would always say. I moved on. So it seems did she. I'm not so noble anymore. I'm not sure I ever was. I only ever cared about myself. For a while, she changed that for me. But I...I, uh." He clears his throat. Red blooms in his bruised cheeks. "I'm sorry."

Marie and I glance at each other. Apologies can mean so much. In those two words is a tapestry of choices woven by a lifetime of regret.

"You are a noble man, Aran," I murmur, sliding my hand into his. "More so than I could ever hope to be."

He squeezes my hand.

Marie adjusts the bloodstained bandana in her hair. She

shuffles her feet. Then she, too, interlaces her fingers with Aran's. "We lost a lot. But not everything."

Aran looks between us. A genuine, fond smile brings the light back to his eyes. Navda hasn't broken him beyond repair. He wouldn't break any of us. "No. Not everything."

34

Rélia

Waking up next to Raven is bliss. She's insisted on sleeping in the chair near my bed, tending to me as I recover from blood rot over the last few days. I still ache. Undoubtedly, that was the worst bout of blood rot I've ever experienced. Xipher poisoning directly to the bloodstream. Harsh. Effective. If it weren't for the great reserve of my magic and Raven's quick thinking, I might have died.

Nursing my stab wound has been the worst of the lasting effects. Recovery has been slow. Every time my magic tries to help, the pain intensifies. Every step is dull agony. I lift up my shirt. A red line stretches across my belly, crisscrossed by crude stitches. Tears prick my eyes. Healing the old-fashioned way, I'll actually have a scar. My stomach churns. I've never had a life-long mark from battle.

Sniffling, I hastily wipe my tears before they fall. I stretch out my stiff limbs. Raven is still asleep, head hanging over the back of the chair, drool dripping from her open mouth. Relaxation exudes from her. Every breath I take near her is soothing.

Flashes of her screaming and commanding the staff race through my mind. Though I was barely conscious, consumed by excruciating pain, the intensity with which she governed the magic wasn't hard to miss. Everything about her is so overwhelming.

I crouch beside her, gently brushing stray hairs from her face. Slowly, she stirs. Part of me feels guilty for waking her. Raven deserves all the rest she can get. "Morning."

Yawning, she rubs the sleep from her eyes. She leans closer to me, wincing as she puts weight on her injured leg. "Good morning. How close are we?"

"Is there ever anything else on your mind other than this mission?" I tease. "Not enjoying the domestic bliss of the last few days?"

Raven slides off her chair, joining me on the floor. "On the contrary."

Sitting so close to her, in the serenity of the morning, the ship gently rocking on the waves, I'm entirely at peace. Drawn to her, moving as if in slow motion, I find my face a hair away from hers. For weeks, I've been denying the ache in my chest every time I look at her. Does she feel the same?

I scoot away. Raven deserves the world. I can't give it to her. I haven't been able to give it to anyone since Shaia. I'll have to let that fire that burns for Raven simmer to embers.

Raven tilts her head. I offer her a smile, opening my mouth to tell her we'll hit Caentathea tonight. Before I get that chance, she pulls me back to her by the collar of my nightshirt. I find my gaze flitting from her lips to her eyes, where there burns a passion fiery enough to rival my own.

"Trust me," she murmurs. "There is one thing I can't get out of my mind."

I can hardly hear her over the fluttering of my heart. Since when was the bastard thing so loud? "Can I guess what it is?"

"Kissing you," she replies, her voice but a whisper, as if she's terrified I haven't been fighting the same desire.

"Then by all means."

An interminable moment passes as we stare into each other's eyes. Between us the air burns with desire. Even in the dim light of the room, Raven's eyes seem to glow. Golden irises nurtured by an unwavering resilience, a devoted faith to seeing the best in the worst.

In me.

Our lips meet. It's far from perfect. It's awkward. Quick. Her breath reeks. But gods, if I don't want to do it again and again until she's stolen all the breath from my lungs. Warmth buzzes through me. Overwhelms me. Distracts me from my pain, my worries, from the horror of the world, the gravity of the mission awaiting us.

Together, we smile. Elation lifts my heart.

I cup her face with my hands. Her fingers tangle through my hair. Eyes fluttering closed, I breathe in her every breath between our hungry kisses. Her lips are softer and smoother than the finest wines in Oncarii. Out of every pair of lips I've ever met, hers are by far the most divine. My magic quivers with ecstasy. With her in my arms, power is like a trivial opulence.

When I open my eyes, we're standing. Raven backs me against the cool, wooden wall. I wrap my arms around her neck. Her hands skim across my hips. Every touch is invigorating. Raven's lips are intoxicating.

Finally, I grant my lungs the reprieve they demand. Panting, revving with pleasure, I throw my head back, taking deep breaths. Grinning like an idiot, I meet Raven's eyes. They're brilliant. Matched only in beauty by her equally idiotic smile.

"Wow," I say, giggling. Gods, when have I ever *giggled*? "Who knew?"

"Oh shut up. I haven't had a lot of practice."

"No, you misunderstand." I put a finger under her chin, tilting her head up. Holding her attention, I switch our positions. Bracing myself against the wall I cage her in between my arms, not once looking away from her. "You're a fantastic kisser."

She beams even wider. Once more she kisses me. Long, slow, deep. Passion twining with comfort. A cool fire controlled between our lips.

"Cap'n we—" Penn shoves aside the curtain sheltering my bedchamber. Raven and I snap away from each other. She smooths down the creases of her clothes. Penn wiggles his eyebrows suggestively. "Oh, *Cap'n*."

I glare at him. "Stuff it. What's so important you have to barge in here? You know I hate being interrupted."

Penn's teasing aura fades. "We have a problem."

Problem is understating it. Morning has sprung. Clear skies and a brightly shining sun belie the danger in the water. Steadily approaching from the west is an all too familiar three mast frigate, bearing the king's crest. My blood runs cold. Raven tightens her grip on my hand.

"Shit." I can't tear my eyes away from the billowing sails. "Well, we have time to think of something. Talley's not gonna risk hurting me, so we won't have to worry about gunfire or cannons."

Monty strides to the edge of the ship, tilting his head to the sky. "Please tell me we're not talking about the admiral obsessed with Rélia."

"I'd give up alcohol for that to be a true statement, Monty." I turn to Raven, gently squeezing her hand. "The staff. It's the only way to get him off our tail."

Raven shakes her head, eyes darting anywhere but my face. "Are you sure there's nothing else? I'm not sure how many times I can use that power before I...succumb to it."

Ominous. I bite my lip. Trying to control my nervous energy, I pace in front of them. Every glance at the admiral's ship makes my stomach drop lower. Is it getting closer already? No...no that's just in my head. But it will be a reality if I don't come up with something soon. The staff is the only way through this. If she won't use it, then there's only one other choice.

"I'll use it."

"No! It hurt you. There's no telling what'll happen if you try to channel its power."

"You're right. But someone has to, and if you're not comfortable, then by no means will you wield it." I nod to Penn. "Please fetch it for me."

Penn purses his lips and gives me a curt nod. Before Raven can form coherent words from her dissenting spluttering, he reappears, cloth-wrapped staff in hand. My hands shake as Penn slowly presents the staff to me.

"Stop!" Raven clamps a hand on Penn's wrist. "Maybe Monty should use it."

I scrunch my nose, thinking it over. "I suppose that could work."

Granted, my trust in him remains less than plentiful.

"Anything to help!"

Sighing, I nod. Penn hands him the staff. We all wait, staring as he unfolds the cloth, gently holding the staff in favor of his cane. Nothing happens. He turns it, swishes it. Nothing.

Monty shrugs. "I can sense the arcane power. But it's like it doesn't want to communicate with me."

The *Royal Avarice* has nearly caught up to us. My heart drops. They have the advantage of the wind's direction. They'll be upon us within the hour. Exhaling, I hold my hand out to Monty.

"Only one thing to do then." I flash my friends—whose abundant concern is painfully clear—a smile. "Don't worry, loves. I'm not your everyday maji, remember?"

Denying my apprehension is next to impossible. Artifacts demand trust. Unfortunately, my mother gave me a divine status that makes trust hard to obtain. I hope this is different.

Sparks fly when my hands wrap around the staff. I yelp, dropping it. Catching it with my foot, I toss it back to my hand. Again, it burns, vibrates in protest. Immeasurable power courses through the wood, fighting against me with a painful bite. Ignoring the intense searing pain encompassing my palms, I focus on the power of a Galer's wind. I think of Aran, the only

Galer I'd ever seen command air, of the joy he radiated when he worked his magic.

Cool rage rises to meet my determination. He was lost to the cruelest pirates on account of my hubris. I won't let the same happen to anyone else. Especially not Raven.

Power stutters through me. My magic tries to tangle with it, but even the slightest contact with the staff's power sends excruciating shocks through my system. Sweat trickles down my back. Already, I'm exhausted. Nausea flips my stomach over. This is how the xipher poisoning began. I hope it can't relapse.

"Rélia!" Raven's voice is warbled, muted like she's underwater. "You have to stop!"

My blood crackles like lightning. Moving takes every bit of concentration I can muster. I glance at my hands, horrified to see my veins glowing white. Not just there either—the power crawls up my face, down my legs, burning me from the inside out.

Dizziness washes over me. I can't focus on the power. I can't even remember which magic I was trying to channel in the first place. The unbearable magnitude of every discipline of magic rages in every fiber of my being. Even my own Healer's magic is revolting, churning through me, bearing every disease known to the world. I fight to control it.

The glow of my veins is blinding. Unable to even think about controlling the staff anymore, I drop it. Stumbling, I reach for the railing. At my scalding touch, the metal melts. Flames erupt from my fingers, catching to the wood. Wind howls around us, tearing our sails clean off the masts. Every breath is like my lungs are filling with dirt. Coughing, I try to scream.

Blinking away tears, I collapse to my knees. Everything halts around me. It's like when I was pulled into Raven's magic ages ago, connected to her, frozen in time with her. This time, I am alone in a still world, torn apart by magic. It lasts but a moment.

Ethereal voices whisper in my ears. Ghostly figures dart around me. They wisp over my head, pass through me, sending jolts of cold to my bones. Reaper magic. I was always curious about the connection Shaia had, the one she broke. Experiencing a glimpse of it, I can imagine why she hated it.

Everything is white. Blood drips from my nose. It's bitter on my tongue, warm on my hand. But I can't see it.

Curling my fingernails into the deck of the ship, I scream. Colors blur around me, seeping into the blankness that has overcome my vision. The world beats in time with my heart. White light explodes. All power writhing within me expels. I fall to my side. Panting, I try to focus on one of Raven's many concerned faces hovering over me. My skin is hot, but relief cools my core. Tentatively, my magic snakes through me, replenishing my energy reserve. Penn and Raven hook their arms beneath mine, helping me to my feet.

For a moment, all is still.

A creak sends my stomach plummeting. Everyone on the ship freezes. I raise a shaky finger to my lips. Maybe if everyone remains silent and still, we can avoid the catastrophe I just caused.

Beneath my feet, the scorched wood splinters. A deafening crack splits the ship down the middle. Teetering towards us is the main mast. I jump out of the way. It crashes down, crushing the roof of my cabin. Water floods into the hull. I watch, devastated, as the prow of my ship breaks off into the dark waters of the Navat Ocean.

Screams pull me from my melancholy. Mina and Ori fall through a jagged gap in the wood. Others of the crew shout, jumping before the stern capsizes over them. Wood I'd accidentally charred crumbles, giving way beneath my feet. I scramble for a hold to no avail. I take a deep breath as I hurtle towards the water.

Ignoring the agonizing frigidity of the ocean, I swim for the surface. Gasping for air, I tread water, searching for everyone else. All are accounted for, except Monty and Raven. Heart pounding, I frantically scan the wreckage. They're not here. Not in the water.

I turn my gaze to the remainder of my ship, still collapsing. At the highest point, they stand, swaying near the edge. "JUMP! YOU HAVE TO JUMP!"

Monty is frozen. Even from this far away there's a noticeable hitch in his breath. Shaia's spy is afraid of heights. Ironic. Tragically so. And if he takes Raven down with him—

Shaking my head free of those thoughts, I swim for a piece of what used to be my stern, resting on it. Penn joins me.

"I don't know what to do!" I cry, kicking closer to the ship, as if that will help. "If they don't come down *now*, they'll get trapped under the ship!"

He shakes his head, distraught. "Nothin' we can do. S'up to them."

Dread seeps in my bones, colder than the water soaking my clothes. "No, no. I can't just sit here and do nothing." Hysteria claws at my throat. I can't stop my voice from wavering. "I'm not going to watch her die, I'm not going to, I'm not gonna lose her like, like—"

Penn puts a hand over mine. "Ya won' lose her."

As soon as the words leave his mouth, the ship lets out a thunderous groan.

Gnawing on my lip, I force myself to look up. Raven and Monty hold hands, edging near the burned, splintered, hardly-even-there railing. Monty slips. They both crash to the deck. Water churns as it consumes the ship. I barely catch their silhouettes plummeting. I can't hear their splash. What's left of my ship crumples over them.

"No!" I scream, pushing off the wood, swimming through the floating wreckage. I splash around, desperate to find where they fell, where Raven fell. Nothing. They should've popped up by now. Why haven't they come up for air?

A maelstrom of horrendous outcomes poisons my mind. Drowned. Struck by debris. Dead in any manner, each theory worse than the last, dissolving into unrealistic fabrications of a hysterical imagination.

I'm going to lose her. And it's all my fault.

"Here! I'm here." Raven emerges from the water, Monty's arms slung over her neck. "We're both right here."

I allow myself the indulgence of tears. "Take longer next time. See if you kill me with worry."

I push a large plank in her direction. She heaves Monty onto it, then tosses his cane and Isolde's staff after him. "Had to make sure we didn't lose the essentials."

"Sure," I mutter. "It destroys my ship and everything in it, but the stick is fine."

Penn paddles over to us. I join him on his plank. "Hate to break up the moment, but uh, 'nother problem. They're goin' to catch up to us. Real quick."

I scrunch my nose, trying desperately to think of a way to escape. Swimming is out of the question. We're a day of sailing from the coast of Caentathea. None of us are Tiders, so controlling the ocean isn't likely. I'm not apt to use the staff again any time soon.

Staring at Talley's ship, trying to convince myself he won't reach us in half an hour, I catch a glimpse of a gargantuan blue fin breaching the calm ocean water. My heart pounds. I exchange a glance with Raven. That's not...is it?

A moment later, the head of a mermaid rises from the wreckage, wood, cannon fodder, wine cups caught in its tousled green hair. It stares at Raven, at the staff. Shrill notes fill the air when it opens its mouth.

"What's it doing?" I murmur, barely audible, terrified of offending it.

Raven slowly reaches for the staff. "I'll find out."

"Are you sure?" I ask, unable to tear my eyes away from the two other mermaids that rise to join their friend. "Like you said, the temptation of power is a lot and neither of us want you to surrender to it."

She smiles faintly. "I'll be okay."

I watch warily as the staff hums to life beneath her touch. All three mermaids lean closer to her. In an effort to block out the cacophony of their melodic, ear-splitting voices, I cover my ears.

"They want to help," Raven says. "If magic dies, they can

no longer sustain themselves. It's why they were so protective before. They're willing to take us to Caentathea."

Worrying at my lip, I stare at the *Royal Avarice*. It's closer than ever. Better to risk the dangers of sea creatures than Talley's poisonous grip.

"Okay. Take us away loves." I give a single nod to the mermaid in the middle.

They duck under the water. All is silent, until I rise, cupped in slimy blue hands. I link arms with Penn and Raven, and she with Monty. My skin crawls as the water trickles from its webbed fingers, leaving us sliding against the scales. A sensation unlike any other. Wind whips through my hair as the mermaids take off through the ocean, holding their hands above the surface for our sake.

I hold tight to my comrades, hoping we will not be thrown asunder, scattered across the ocean.

My stomach lurches as we stop abruptly. We hurtle into the water, about a half hour's swim from shore. The mermaids smile at us, bearing their jagged yellow teeth, before retreating back into the depths.

I gape at the island before our eyes. Hints of green linger in the tall brown stalks of grass. Hills roll over the land, a homely brown color, spotted with gray boulders.

Caentathea. I thought it'd be prettier.

A journey that should have taken us several hours, we crossed in a matter of minutes.

I beam at Raven. "Well. I reckon we start swimming if we're to fix magic by noon."

35

Raven

It's not as beautiful as I imagined it would be. In my Sight, I only caught a glimpse, but I swore Caentathea was greener. Perhaps that was just the manifestation of my desires. I suppose if magic is dying, its heart would slow as well.

I rake my hand through the dry, cracked dirt. Faint traces of stable Welder magic hum from the earth, but it's barely discernible. Sticking my hand in my pocket, I run my thumb over the flat edge of the blood dagger. It leaves my skin tingling, malicious and greedy. Dangerous indeed.

Words tumble through my mind over and over. Shaia will certainly be irritated when she comes to collect her tools to find the parchment has been swallowed by the sea. Hopefully the loss of my own staff soothes her.

I repeat the enchantment, terrified I'll forget a word. Energy buzzes through my veins. This is it. Tonight, everything I've been waiting for will come to pass.

I stumble over a sharp rock poking out from the barren ground. Rélia catches me. Her hand lingers on my back, steady and comforting.

"Careful love. Wouldn't want to hurt your leg any worse. Step out of your mind. I trust you know the ritual like the back of your hand."

I drum my fingers on Isolde's staff, longing for the comforting presence of my own. Unending power so close at my fingertips sends nausea rocketing through me. Guilt wracks my being. If I'd just faced the virulent magic again, Rélia's ship wouldn't have been destroyed. We wouldn't have lost so much.

"There's just so much that could go wrong." I sigh, kicking a rock. It skitters down the hill, rolling through the dry soil, taking with it my confidence. I pause in step, frozen, throat tight. "I'm scared."

Rélia laces her fingers with mine. "There's strength in fear. If you don't let it control you, it's only telling you something momentous is to happen. Today, we're saving magic. I'd say that's rather admirable, wouldn't you?"

I smile. "You always know just what to say."

"Only to those who matter. And I've never met someone who matters more than you." She tugs me forward, cresting the top of the hill. "Gods."

Sprawled before us is the entirety of the island. Ruins of a red-stone temple have been nearly devoured by ravenous yellow vines, curling across the ground, rising in spite of the wilted greenery everywhere else. Sickly blossoms cry for aid, twisting from the sea-soaked boulders lining the rocky beach. Every inch of Caentathea is disheartened. All shores of the island are visible to the naked eye; a distance that would take several hours to cross but looks as if I could make it in one.

Isolde's staff is quiet. Perhaps it too is grieving the once-revered island, home to worshiping maji, sanctuary to those crippled by fear. I exhale slowly. No. I refuse to let this be its fate. Caentathea will have all that and more once again.

Holding tight to Rélia's hand, I carefully make my way down the hill. Pebbles and dust stir in our wake. Ignoring the panic prolific in my mind is difficult when there is only desolate silence to replace it. I take a deep breath of stale air.

"Something's off," I murmur, when we halt at the base of the hill, a stretch of barren forest before us.

Rélia scrunches her nose. I expect her to say something snarky. In fact, I hope she does. Finding it's all in my head would ease my spirit. Unfortunately, she echoes my sentiments. "I feel it too."

Our crew circles up behind us. All of them are silent. Not even Penn has anything to say. His hand is ever-present on the hilt of his blade. Not a good sign.

"Monty?" I whisper, hoping he'll refute the looming danger in the air.

"We're not alone."

My skin crawls. Instinctively, I whip out the staff, brandishing it before me. Power tingles at my fingertips. Energy surges in my veins. Every sense intensifies. Once more, that addictive desire to hold onto this magic forever seizes control of my mind. I fight to keep it at bay.

Holding my breath, I listen intently to the still world. I sense the shift in the air a split moment before it rages. Latching onto Galer magic like I've practiced it all my life, I swipe the staff upwards. Howling wind curves over us, blocking the concentrated blast of air that would have incapacitated us all.

Everything dies away. Nothing emerges from the shelter of the trees, nor creeps up behind us. Heart pounding, I wildly glance around. My hair stands up. Someone's lurking.

Penn gasps, dropping to his knees. Immediately, Rélia is at his side, frantically trying to console him as he clutches at his throat. His eyes widen. Already, life drains from him.

I swing the staff at nothing. Jet streams of fire streak towards a particularly close-knit cluster of trees, the roots of which twist out of the soil, twine together. Gusts of wind quench the flame.

Everyone who managed to save their weapons from the sea draw them, turning back-to-back, rallying for a fight. A torturous silence hangs heavy over us, broken only by desperate, stifled moans as Penn fights for air.

Then Rélia goes down too.

My vision tunnels. Magic thrums in my fingers, desperate to fuel my sparking rage. Hearing Rélia gurgling, unable to breathe, brings tears to my eyes.

"Okay!" I scream, stepping protectively in front of her. "Okay, come out! I surrender!"

Figures step out from the grove of gnarled trees, swords at the ready, faces like stone. One lanky kid in particular stands out, not just because of his fiery red hair. It's the apology in his face, the way he keeps his gaze glued to the ground. His hands are outstretched, curled into fists. Slowly, he uncurls the fingers of his left hand. Penn gasps.

I glance at Rélia. Purple and red splotches discolor her face. Terror drains the color from her eyes. "Release her too! Please!"

The Galer purses his lips, refusing my command.

A gravelly voice grates against my ears, one that tears open a wound carved when I was small. "Drop the staff."

Stepping out from the shadows is Navda, Captain of the Dividers, the man that killed my papa. Driven by a choking desire for revenge, I take a step forward. White light sparks from the staff.

"You might kill me," he says, shoving a familiar figure to the ground not far from me; my brother, hands cuffed behind him. "But your magic won't be fast enough to save this dirty rat. And 'specially not your girl."

Slowly, I lower the staff to the ground. Grass sprouts where it touches the dirt.

I raise my hands, begging for the Galer to let Rélia go. Finally, he releases his hand. Rélia inhales deeply, coughing. I crouch beside her, brushing stray hairs from her face, kissing her forehead. She smiles, though her bluish lips are trembling.

"Don't worry," I whisper. "I'll protect you."

The Galer turns to Navda, keeping his eyes lowered. "Please, let her go."

Navda waves his hand. A man dressed in finer linen than the others—quartermaster, I presume—heaves a red-haired girl up by her ponytail. He shoves her towards the Galer who catches her with ease, holds her tight.

"Aran, I'm sorry you had to do that," she says, voice strained.

I barely register their reunion. All my attention is focused on Tezin. Black curls fall into his aged eyes. A golden arrow is pierced through his ear. Thin white scars crisscross his collarbone. Dirt besmirches his face. Tears well in my eyes. I don't know what's become of him. But I want to hug him. Make gingersnap with him. Be at home, comfortable, happy, together.

Will we ever be there again? Or are those just rosy memories trapped in amber?

"M-Marie?" Monty murmurs.

The girl turns, eyes wide. Despite the tension, she breaks into a relieved smile. "Monty!"

I recognize the desperation to run to each other, to risk harm to be in each other's arms. Love. Not breaking eye contact from my brother's disheveled state, I put a hand on Monty's shoulder before he can take another step toward enemy lines. Beneath us, the ground is like glass. Move incorrectly, it'll shatter. We'll all be impaled.

A streak of white leaping from Marie's shirt pocket catches my attention. Smiling faintly, I bend down, opening my palms for the rat to climb into.

"Been a while, Pidge. Good to see you." I nuzzle my cheek against his fur, then set him on my shoulder.

He chitters. His beady eyes are steadily focused on Navda's quartermaster who shifts as if he wants to make a run for it.

"Now." Navda clears his throat. "How to continue?"

Beside me, Rélia shakily rises to her feet. I slide my hand into hers, grateful for her strength, hoping I'm offering her the same. Ever so slightly, I move for the staff. Now that Rélia is fine, I can use it quick enough to end this. All of this.

Navda prowls in front of his crew. "I see what you desire, girl. You can't win. Never could. This boy—" He nods to Tezin, still under the watchful eye of the quartermaster. "—he means something to ya. So if you're willing to let him suffer, ya might finish your task. Or you can hand over the staff and you'll all live."

I purse my lips, clutching tighter to Rélia. No. Under no circumstance am I going to let my brother suffer. Hesitantly, I take a step forward. Risking a glance at Tezin, I find that the quartermaster has slipped him a key. I suppress a smile. There's a way for us to come out of this.

Trying to calm my buzzing nerves, I pick up Isolde's staff. Throwing it in a smooth arc, I pray nothing ill will happen. Navda can't use the staff. He isn't a maji, not as far as I'm aware. I hold my breath, waiting for the worst as he catches it in both hands. Relief washes over me when it remains dormant.

Quiet contemplation smooths Navda's rough features. Slowly, he turns the staff over in his hands, as if gently considering the purity and nostalgia of a fond memory.

Pidge's paws tighten on my shoulder, a silent warning I don't have to be a Tamer to understand. My stomach drops. Horrified, unable to move, I watch as Navda's face twists in anger. A feeble crack resonates through the silent world as he breaks the staff over his knee. White light, power, the very fabric of magic itself wisps into the air, disappears into the ether.

Heavy numbness crushes my chest. No tears come to my call. There's only a raging emptiness. That feeling carves a hollow hole within me, echoes in the mournful features of Monty and Rélia, of the two red-heads. Even Navda's quartermaster. Tezin,

I may have saved. But I just condemned us all to an eternity without magic.

I can't bother to scream or cry. Not even my anger can spurn me forwards. The man that took my parents took the only thing that can save my magic; the last part of me that matters. He's taken everything. Revenge begs to take over me. But I can't bring myself to care anymore. Nothing I do can change the fate of magic. I can't win.

I let down all Nightbloods.

Monty slams his cane into the earth. Dirt fractures, cracks snaking to the feet of the Dividers. Silence wraps thick around everyone, ready for a fight. Everybody's faces are stone, their eyes flickering, their knuckles white around their weapons.

Monty's nostrils flare. He drives his cane deeper into the ground, with a force that sends me to my knees. The cracks widen to a crevice, taking down one Divider after another.

Tension snaps.

Battle cries fill the air. Swords clash. The ground rumbles. Fighting rages all around me.

I can't find the strength to stand.

36

Tezin

Blocking out the storm of battle, I focus on unlocking my cuffs. Despite Ean's seething disappointment when I returned without Isolde's staff, at least he's still committed to overthrowing his captain. He stands behind me, arms crossed, sheltering my hard-working fingers from the rest of the crew. Especially Navda, though he seems all too obsessed with the staff to pay attention to me.

Fumbling with the key, I curse myself for not having steady nerves. I no longer have a plan. But this is my chance. I can't mess it up.

"Why are you so okay with this anyway?" I mutter, unsure whether Ean is actually listening. "Me killing Navda?"

A moment passes as I sidestep an attack and whirl behind Ean. Black twines around his hands, choking the life from my attacker. He shakes his hand out then replies, "You'll find out soon enough."

The key slips from my fingers. "What's that supposed to mean?"

Warning flashes across his face, accompanied by that terrible chill and black spindles in his eyes. I stumble back, tripping to the ground. Transfixed, I finally fall deep into his gaze. Darkness swallows me.

Images of a castle writhing with sentient darkness whistle past me. Shivering, I duck as shadows bear down on me from every angle. A forest of xipher trees rises up from the endless expanse of nothing. All the trees quiver with excitement, thirsty for the magic running through my veins. I turn, and a tall, slender figure with a halo of glowing white hair waits patiently before me, her fingers tapping on the arm of a stone throne.

Everything stenches of death.

I gasp, pulling free of Ean's mind. He takes a step back, eyebrows quirking.

"What are you?" I scrabble through the dirt to find the key. When my fingers close around it, it's like a reassurance I'm still on the physical plane. "Why are all your memories, all your thoughts, central to Luara's realm?"

His voice is cool, flat. "I think you already know."

My hands shake. I wish they would work faster.

Finally, the lock clicks. Wrenching myself free of the cuffs, I scramble away from Ean. I still have a mission to complete. And the farther from him, the better.

I focus on Navda and scream, "*Inciepa*!"

The golden arrow in my ear whirrs to life, Aran's ingenious

machinery leaping at the command. It streaks towards Navda, moving so fast it's a blur. No one bats an eye. Swords clash, blood sprays. No one has time to notice.

Navda cries out as the arrow strikes clean through his throat.

The final step of the plan is nearly through—killing him for good. Aran's arrow is meant for a swift death, a piercing through the eye. But suffering was demanded. And so I shall be its perpetrator.

I dodge two men locked in battle, narrowly avoiding the loss of my arm. Cold determination prompts me forward. For the first time since commanding Aran, I grasp the full lengths of my magic. There is no divine intervention, no resistance to my call. It rises from my core, feeds my anger, tingles in my veins. Churning with power, I stand over Navda. Blood spurts from his wound, pools from his mouth. He gurgles, choking on it.

Everything he's done to me, to my friends, since I first saw him the day he killed Papa; it all flashes through my mind, a torrent of painful memories. Shaking, I pull his sword from its scabbard. I level the point at his chest.

"You took everything from me," I murmur, voice taut, barely audible.

Blood bubbles between his lips. His eyes dart to Ean.

Trembling with rage, I continue, "Death is too good for you. But your reign of terror must be ended. This is the only way I know how."

Grinding my teeth, I plunge the sword through his chest, straight to his heart, its final beat faint against the blade.

Navda coughs, splutters. He tries to say something, but the last of his words die on his lips.

Something deeply human flickers in his eyes, more so than I've ever seen in him. Not fear, as I expected. Acceptance. Relief. Gratitude. That cold, malicious whispering in his mind disperses, leaving an empty, echoing sob. Navda breaks into a smile, teeth wet and red. And then life is stripped from him.

There's a near tangible shift in the world. My breath hitches. Head pounding, I double over. The sword slips from my hand, falling silently to the ground. A disembodied force chokes me. Scorching tears burn my cheeks. My ears ring. Every sense magnifies tenfold, crashing in on one another. I can feel every brush of the air against my skin, hear the unsteady beat of every heart around me.

Abruptly, it stops.

Turning over my shoulder, desperate for comfort in Aran, I find instead Ean, staring at me across the battlefield, lips curled in a victorious smirk. Cold, unnatural, *inhuman*, I finally begin to understand him, and Navda too. Ean has always been a shadow in Navda's cruelty. And I'm beginning to wonder if that is a coincidence.

Ean is not a maji, nor a man.

He is something far worse.

37

Rélia

I can't tear my eyes from the broken staff. Even as senseless battle thunders around me, it's the only thing I can focus on. Raven is stoic beside me, eyes wide, jaw slack.

After everything we've been through, this can't be where it ends. Hope drains from Raven, seeping across the ground in a nearly visible vapor.

I can't let her lose that. So much has been ripped from her. If she loses this too, loses all her hope, I know all too well the self-destructive spiral she's sure to fall down.

Don't worry. I'll protect you.

Raven's voice echoes in my mind. Strength drains away my exhaustion. Hearing those words from her lips was more sublime than kissing them. Nothing else matters except her, helping her, protecting her in return. Faint, feeble whispers hum in my ears.

It's the staff. Weak, broken, but there's still magic. If I can mend it, I can fix this.

A flash of silver curves towards me. In a split second, I tear my sword from its sheath. Tinny ringing peals through the chorus of shouts, of clashing weapons. I kick my attacker in the shin. Momentarily distracted, I take the opening to swipe the sword from his grip. I slice him across the inner leg. He cries out, clutching at the wound as blood soaks the ground.

Ignoring screams of pain and the cold pity in my heart, I fall to my knees beside the staff. Tezin stands nearby, still hovering over Navda's corpse. First revenge kill. I can imagine how heavy his heart is, despite the relief. Vengeance is a tricky, poisonous lure.

I reach for the broken halves of Isolde's staff. Indignant white puffs of pure magic coil up to my fingers, sparking in protest. I snap my hands away cursing at the painful tingling.

"I'm going to help you," I mutter to the staff, trying to sound less bitter than I am. "But you have to let me."

Sparing a moment to let my words sink in, I slowly cup my hands beneath the staff. Thankfully, there are no sparks, nor burning, nor angry surges of power. Just a quiet, desperate humming. Gently, I press the halves together, lining up the broken ends as well as I can. Closing my eyes, I focus on the warm, consoling energy of healing magic.

Beneath my palms, the wood shivers, weaving together as the staff mends. Power rises in response, revitalized. I urge my magic to work harder. It weaves with the white tendrils of pure magic, nourishing it, twining the wood to the power, sealing the splintered seam.

I sense his presence before he attacks. My eyes snap open. I roll to the side, dodging the deadly point of a sword. Navda's quartermaster looms above me. My eyes dart to the staff. We both lunge for it at the same time. The stench of malice chokes me.

"What are you doing?" I pant, wrestling for control.

He yanks harder. My right hand slips. Black smoke envelops us. I gasp. "Taking control, cousin."

So he knows what I am. He can smell my divinity the same I smell his demonism. "Ugh, don't remind me."

He grins, and it's blinding in the encompassing darkness of his magic—chaos magic. It's a familiar smile, one that sows doubt, instills fear. A smile born and bred in the underworld. "You're family, born of resentment and ungrateful gods, same as I. Let me take this, let me set this world right."

"You want anarchy," I snarl. "I want peace."

"You wouldn't know what to do with peace."

I inhale sharply, taken aback by the truth of his words. He wrenches the staff from my grip. Magic floods my senses as it pours from the staff, from his being; curling waves of madness and disarray searching for satiation. My fingers itch to grab my sword, run it through those who would oppose me. I take a deep breath, focusing on the dirt beneath my boots, the air outside of this darkness. I will not allow this magic to take away my control.

Gritting my teeth, I launch towards the demon, tackling him at the knees. Like a fog, the darkness disperses. I plant my feet on his chest. With all the force I can muster, I yank the staff from his grip. It responds to my touch with a gentle kinship.

Blinding white light flashes across the land. Power tingles in my every nerve. It's heavy in the air. Lungs shuddering with the magnitude of sweet, addictive magic in every breath, I turn to the demon.

He's gone.

My fingers tighten around the staff. A problem for another day.

"Stop!" I cry, holding the staff high above my head. Silence descends. Energy thrums through my being, feeding into the staff, lighting my veins, igniting depths of my power even I never thought I could achieve.

Everyone turns, staring at me. Crimson and black pool into the dry earth, which laps it up like it's water. There are only a few bodies, and none of my own. The rest are heaving breaths, caked in sweat and blood, but alive. I thrust the staff into the dirt. "There will be no more fighting. Not until we are at sea. We are all pirates. The navy is on their way, and they will come for each of us, no matter our own grievances and enemies."

Uneasy glances are my only response. But no one raises a weapon.

"Raven," I say softly. "Come here."

She rises, joining me with a hand on the staff. Jolts of warm energy shock my system. Silver and gold twist together around our joined hands.

"Nothing stopping us now," she murmurs.

I grin. "My crew, follow us to the shore. Dividers..." I narrow my eyes. "Well, you'll do as your new captain commands."

They all turn to Tezin. He freezes. Eyes wide, he glances over the crowd of pirates waiting for him to speak.

"I, um." It's a squeaking whisper. He clears his throat. "Stay near the caves. Should the need arise, you will come to our aid. We will fight off the navy as one crew today."

Grumbling, they oblige. Weapons sheath. Slowly, my crew follows suit. Good. Temporary truce.

"What the hell?" Tezin rasps, dropping to his knees. "Captain?"

I tilt my head. "You didn't know? You killed the last captain, thereby replacing him. In all manners. Including the tether to the ship. And the gods. It's the curse of the Dividers."

Raven runs a thumb over my cheek, then kisses me sweetly. "We don't have a lot of time, but I need to talk him through this."

I nod, and she crouches to comfort him. For a moment, I drink in the reunion between brother and sister, the tearful rejoicing between Monty and his red-haired friend Marie. Nothing is secure. But the elation is too great to not revel in our small victory.

"Captain Ryan."

I spin around. Standing before me is a freckled face I never thought I'd see again. "Aran!" I tackle him in a hug. He grunts, then slowly returns the gesture.

"Been a while," he says, when we pull away. "I see you're still *you* as ever."

"I'll take that as a compliment," I reply, grinning. "I—" My smile drops. Flashes of Navda attacking my ship race through my mind. Screams echo in my ears. Aran's bloodstained face is the last to cross, his sacrifice saving me from certain death. "I can't believe what you did for me. That was stupid. I'm sorry for everything you went through. Forgiveness is what I'm asking, I won't deny that. But I won't expect it. I failed you as your captain."

Intrigue fills his worn eyes. "Since when have you apologized? I would've done anything for you. We all would've. You gave us everything."

I hook my arm through his. "I suppose you're right. But now I've got more than ever to lose. I'm not sure I want so many people to lay down their lives for me."

Aran nudges me. "Hey, we don't do it for fun. We do it because we believe in you."

My gaze falls on Raven, holding her brother tight. Our eyes lock for a moment. "Maybe I *am* meant for more."

"Hm?"

"Nothing. Just...I've begun to believe in myself more. All thanks to her." I smile at Raven. "I don't believe in benevolent gods, but if they brought her to me, then surely there's at least one that's got good intentions."

"Oh you *love* her, huh?" Aran teases, though there's sincerity in his voice. He's staring at Tezin with a recognizable longing. "I spent weeks with her brother at sea. Those two. There's something intoxicating about them."

"You have no idea." My lips tingle, yearning for more than the memory of her kisses, both passionate and delicate. Clearing my throat, I give Aran a final, amicable squeeze on the shoulder. "As lovely as it is to see you, Talley is on his way here. If we don't reach Isolde's tomb by nightfall, we're going to have more problems."

He gives me a faint smile. We approach Raven and Tezin, helping them to their feet. Tezin shakes, unsteady.

"Is he alright?" I whisper to Raven.

Her lips are a thin line, matching the concerned furrow of her brows. "I don't know." She sighs. "I'll find a way to help him. After all this is done."

I press my forehead to hers. "And I'll be with you every step of the way. Come, love. No time to waste now."

Sorrow weighs heavy on my heart by the time we reach the cove bearing entrance to the cave system. Every step on this godsforsaken island fills me with a sour, imminent dread. Having my crew at my back and Raven at my side brings me an equaling comfort.

I hold tight to Raven's hand, staring into the encompassing darkness of the tunnel sprawled before us. Water laps gently at my boots. Twilight falls heavy around us, ready to swallow us if the caves do not.

"Okay, everyone. Stay here. You're the first line of defense if anything happens. The only line, really," I say. "But don't do anything stupid. I'm not losing any lives tonight. Penn, please keep an eye on everyone."

Penn sidles up next to me. "Alright, Cap'n. We'll watch yer back."

Raven gives me a gentle squeeze. "It's time."

Together, we step into the mouth of the cave.

38

Tezin

I rake my hands through my hair, nearly pulling it out with worry. How can this be happening? How can I be the captain of the godsdamn *Dividers*? Is that what Ean wanted so bad? Did he know I'd be tied to the ship, tied to him? A demon, no less. I didn't think they were more than cautionary tales. Now I know they are magic at its worst; living, breathing bodies of dark, chaotic magic.

I glance at the cave. Saving magic…what if it demands Raven's life in recompense? Nourishment? For fun? Whatever the reason, it doesn't matter. Magic is sentient and that means it's dangerous.

I sit on a stone shelf jutting out from the face of the rock wall. My feet dangle over the warm, shallow water. Sniffling, I put my head in my hands.

"Hey." Aran sits next to me, nudging me with his shoulder. "Raven will be okay."

Wiping my eyes with the heel of my palms, I turn my gaze to the dark horizon. For a long moment, we sit together in silence.

Finally, I barely manage a whisper. "I miss my mama. Even with her last breath, battling a muddled mind, she fought. She'd know what to do. I can't ever match that, Aran. Raven's always been strong-willed, just like our parents. I never inherited that."

Aran puts a hand on my shoulder. "Maybe not in the same way. But I've seen you in action. You are far from weak. You fight to protect people. That's as good as intrinsic strength."

I put a hand over Aran's and rest my head against his. Comfort settles the nauseating anguish in my stomach. The call of the *Divider* is ever present deep within, begging me to return. All the whispers in my mind grow more malicious by the second, threatening me with my darkest fears, enticing me with my deepest desires. I focus on Aran. Everything else drains away, if only for a moment.

Rélia's quartermaster seems to be the only one as worried as me. Arms crossed, he paces back and forth in front of the cave entrance. The rest of the crew has busied themselves with splashing each other, sparring, or staring into the star-freckled sky. Marie and Monty stand together, hand in hand, whispering and giggling.

Guarded voices brush against my ears. Low and commanding, they send my hairs standing on end. Eyeing the land above us, the open sea before us, with suspicion, I sit up straighter. I'm not looking anyone in the eyes, but I'm hearing thoughts. Silver lining to being tied to the *Divider*. Power is something I'll never be short on.

"Something's wrong," I murmur.

Suffocating silence falls over the lagoon. Everyone halts, as if warning sparks in the air.

Dozens of men and women silently round the front of the cove, soaking wet, all dressed in purple and white sailing uniforms. Instinctively, I push Aran further back on the ledge, keeping one arm in front of him. The navy. They're here.

Tinny ringing of sword-on-sword cuts through the tentative peace. Rélia's crew springs into action, attacking and defending with skilled, ruthless precision. Admirable as their fighting is, they're outnumbered three to one.

Aran yells, "Look out!"

I whip around. A sword slices through the air, heading straight for my throat. Aran throws his hand out, catching the blade with a powerful gust of wind. With the sailor off-guard, I aim a kick straight to his groin. Howling in pain, he pitches sideways off the ledge.

Aran falls at my feet. His face is red, his arms shaking. "The air here won't communicate with me. I've never felt so...rejected by my connection."

The heart is slowing.

"I know the feeling." Gently, I help him up. He sways, knees buckling.

Another sailor darts up the ledge. I grab a sharp rock near my foot. She swings her sword left, then right, trying to fake me out. Her thoughts give away her every move before she makes it. I sidestep her, hook my foot around her ankle, then bash the rock against her head. Blood streams down her face. Her eyes squint as if not sure how I beat her. She collapses.

Frantically, I glance around. My heart sinks. All of Rélia's crew are pinned, fighting losing battles. A few have surrendered. More will follow. We'll be at the mercy of the royal navy, a forbearance I doubt extends far for pirates and maji.

I reach into my mind, searching for the tether to the *Divider*. It greets me with curious energy to match my hesitation; a new limb feeling me out as I question whether to trust it. A strange sensation pricks my every nerve. Holding tight to the tether envelopes me in a kind, warm embrace, far more comforting than any communication I had with my own magic.

Releasing my inhibitions, I let the tether guide me to my core. With the helping hand, connecting to my magic has never been easier. It seems to view the tether as a mediator, easing its stubbornness. Power flares through me, as if I am breathing it.

The only person on the *Divider*; my crew now, I suppose, that I know well is Ean. As much as it pains me to call him for help, I won't let Rélia's crew die. Not if they mean so much to Raven. I focus on the cool contempt I have for Ean, on all of his promises of help that covered subterfuge, secrets, and lies. Clear as day, his surroundings appear in my mind's eye. His bitter thoughts resonate in my ears.

Help.

It's the only word I can say before my connection cuts. His lingering emotions brush through my mind. Reassurance. Hopefully that means he's coming with the cavalry. If not, I'll have to find some other way to help Raven. Warn her. Even if it means abandoning everyone here.

Scuffles cease. Splashes echo around the cove; swords dropping from pirate hands, irate surrender on their faces. A smug chuckle fills the tense quiet that follows. Admiral Talley strides through the defeated pirates, hands clasped behind his back. Somehow, amidst the chaos of battle, his purple overcoat is pristine, his every hair perfectly in place.

Even before all this began, I knew I had no compassion for the admiral. He's always been as bad as the pirates. He's just better at fooling a nation.

Talley whistles, circling Rélia's quartermaster in particular. Bristling, he crosses his arms, staring back at the admiral with a withering glare. "Disappointing. Miss Ryan sure spoke highly of her dastardly crew. I suppose I shouldn't be surprised you were felled so easily. She doesn't belong out here. Not with the likes of you."

"Don' disrespec' my cap'n," he flares. "There'll be nothin' left of ya when I'm finished."

Talley's eyes narrow, scrutinizing, but not exactly angered. It's more like he's amused, assessing how much of a threat he is, and ultimately deciding he's not. "Adorable. I do love the fighting spirit so profound in pirates these days. Makes winning all the more thrilling."

"Pretentious prick," Aran mutters under his breath.

My lips quirk ever so slightly. "He'll get what's coming to him. One way or another."

He leans closer to me, saving no distance between our cheeks. "Is that a plan I hear?"

"Partly." I glance up at the ridge above the cove. Satisfaction tugs my lips up in a smirk. No sailor, not even the admiral, has the good sense to look up. I can always count on arrogance to be blinding. "As soon as I'm gone, and the admiral follows me, because he *will* follow me, signal the Dividers. They'll defend you while I try to warn my sister. Remember the gray area."

"Always."

Trying to maintain some composure, I quietly leap off the ledge, sharp rock in hand. Sneaking through the water is nearly impossible. Each step is like a roaring river. Muscles tense, I grip tight to the rock. One sailor breaks rank, charging at me with his sword raised. I duck. Before he can swing at me again, I catch his sword hand at the wrist. Even as I twist beyond what should be incredibly painful, the sailor maintains his grip on the sword and tosses it to his other hand.

The point of the blade cuts across my cheek. Hissing in pain, I slam the jagged edge of the rock against his throat. Blood sprays, splattering my face. Crimson floats through the water as the sailor falls with a heavy splash.

Now I've got the admiral's attention. He turns to me with punitive eyes, cold and gray. "Now, who do we have here?"

I clench tighter to the rock. "Someone you don't want to mess with. Remember Captain Navda?"

The admiral chuckles. "Ah. The feared pirate scourge. Am I to presume that he is no longer with us?"

"I took his place."

"In that case." The admiral dips into a sweeping bow. Mocking lines his leer when he looks at me again. "A formal introduction is obligatory. Admiral Girardin Talley at your service."

"Tezin," I spit, refraining from glancing up. Surprise is all we have now. "And today, you'll have no victories."

I chuck the rock at his head. He ducks, but not quick enough. Crying out, he holds tender the side of his face. I take off into the cave. I have to separate the admiral from his navy.

Victory pounds in sync with my heart when I hear his footsteps chasing me.

39

Raven

Water sloshes over my soaking boots as we make our way through the dark caves. I shiver. Longing for a torch, I try to make out anything within arm's reach, but I can't even see my own hand. I clutch tighter to Rélia. Our sodden footsteps reverberate across the damp walls, the only sounds in the infinite darkness.

Everything is silent in my mind. All I can focus on is the mission ahead. Even as thoughts fraught with worry for my brother pass by, they fade into the intense quietude. I drum the fingers of my free hand against Isolde's staff. Soon, I'll be free of it. Oncarii will be replenished. It will breathe again, and so will I.

Water thins as we trek up a flight of eroding stone stairs. Cool air brushes across my face. Our footsteps echo into what must be a large cavern. Heart quickening, I pull the staff out. Holding it tight with both hands, I can barely contain the overwhelming power crackling through it. Never before has it been so intense.

I focus on the smoky, burning touch of Flamer magic. Answering my call, flames engulf the head of the staff. In the dim, flickering light, I catch sight of two enormous pillars, a stone trough between them, stretching the expanse of the cavern. Acrid liquid sloshes in the trough. Hoping it's still viable, I gently touch the staff to the liquid.

Fire erupts. Hungrily burning, it races through the entire cavern, following the path of oil feeding it. Contained to the stone trenches, the fire lights up the enormous cavern. Stalactites glistening with water protrude down from the ceiling—the only evidence that there is one at all, not just a devouring darkness. Pillars of smooth, magnificent red stone line the cavern. In the center, cracked stairs lead up to a dais, upon which rests a weathered stone casket.

My heart stops.

Isolde's tomb.

We're finally here.

Carefully, I climb up the worn stairs to the dais. Images are etched across the top and sides, depicting the story of Isolde's life. Her birth, her rise to power, her fall. Entranced, I trace every carving, drinking in the history. A nook on the lid has gathered a fine layer of dust and cobweb. Perfectly shaped to her staff.

Resolution settles over me. Finally, the mother of all maji will know peace in her everlasting rest.

Exhaling slowly, I pull out the blood dagger. "Okay, Rélia. Ready?"

She nods. "Just tell me what to do."

"Give me your hand. We have to bind our signatures together to create the tether."

Gently wrapping my fingers around her wrist, I press the point of the blood dagger to the center of her palm. Reciting the Iquetí ritual, I draw the rune for bonding across her skin. Blood coats the dagger, lights half of its runes with a faint black hue.

Bracing myself for sharp pain, I move my own hand, holding it beside hers. Growing louder with my chanting, I carve the rune for magic into my palm. Stinging rages across my skin. I force myself to push through the pain. It is nothing compared to the renourishment of magic.

The runes on the hilt glow, nearly blinding. It grows heavier in my free hand, weighed down with the promise and power of both mine and Rélia's blood. Continuing my chant, I grip her bloody hand in mine, merging the runes. Invigorating energy surges through me, crackling through my veins like lightning, burning with pain and pleasure. I falter in my speech, overwhelmed by the sensation.

Silver and gold twine together around our joined hands, our magics bonding together. Every memory I've ever had of her, from the first vision to the fear, the pain, growing desire, all of it runs through my mind. My heart swells, choked with emotion when her memories collide with mine.

Both of us are crying. I hold onto that deep bond between us, the one cutting new veins, pumping between our hearts. Our signatures bind together around our hands, tightening into a pulsing knot, alight with power. Free hand shaking, I bring the tip of the blood dagger to the center of the knot.

Black light drips down the handle, the blade, twisting around our power signatures. As it hungrily sweeps through our magic, heat rises in my core, practically boiling my blood. Sweat rolls down my face. It stains Rélia's collar. Her face contorts in pain. My legs tremble. I fight to stay upright.

The moment all magic drains from the blood dagger, I drop it. I can barely hear the clatter as it strikes the damp floor. Grabbing the staff, I tilt our hands towards the top of it. An explosion of silver and gold erupts the moment the staff joins our magic. Unable to bear the scalding pain tearing through me, I release Rélia's hand, falling to the floor with a scream.

She collapses beside me, groaning. "Gods burning in every torturous hell for eternity. That was the *worst* thing I've experienced. And I once drank a barrel of Penn's horrendous moonshine to prove a point."

Wiping sweat from my brow, I grin. "I'm glad that didn't take too much out of you."

"Gonna take a lot more than an ancient blood ritual to take the fight out of me." Rélia wraps her arms around me. "I'm glad we're okay. Did it work?"

Regretfully leaving the safety of her embrace, I turn to the staff. Black and white light chase each other around the staff, crackling with energy.

"We made the tether," I say, relief washing over me. "Now we bind the staff to the stone. You anchor me. I'll be the conductor. If you break concentration, I won't have enough power to do it." Noticing the flicker of fear in her eyes, I squeeze her shoulder. "No pressure."

"Heh. No pressure." She holds her hand out to me. "Don't worry, Raven. I won't let you down."

"One more chant and we've saved—"

"Raven!" Tezin's distraught call cuts me off. I snap my

attention to the mouth of the cavern. Drenched in water, face and hands streaked with blood, my brother races towards me. In a split second, I'm on my feet, halfway across the cavern.

Before I reach him, the point of a sword stops him in his tracks. It's in and out before I can comprehend what's happening. My breath catches. Tezin's face twists in pain. The sword missed his heart. But the wound is gaping. He collapses.

"No," I breathe. Rationale thrown out the window, I catch my brother before he hits the ground. "No, no, no!"

Teary eyed, I glance at Rélia. We have to finish the ritual. But I can't leave him.

"I admire the tenacity," says a chilling, sultry voice. Talley wipes the blood from his sword on the floor; an ear-splitting sound that sets my teeth grinding. "But I do not let attacks on my men go unanswered."

Gently, I lay Tezin on the ground. He clutches at the wound in his chest. I try not to sob.

Talley levels the sword at me. "On your knees."

Anger rises in my core. I will not allow us to be his victims, not anymore. Churning with power, I raise my hand, ready to stop time.

"Not this time," Talley chides, bringing the point dangerously close to my throat. Seething, I slowly let my magic fade. He grabs a fistful of my hair, yanking me towards him. He sheathes his sword. I slam my head into his face, but he doesn't relent. Only the prick of a needle in my neck stops me from struggling more. "You remember aphonixa. This dose is much more concentrated than the last."

I can read between the lines; if that toxin enters my

bloodstream, it will eat away at my remaining magic, destroying it. Forever. My heart sinks. We don't have much time. The tether needs to be bound. Even from so far away, its restlessness is stifling.

"Good girl," he says. "Rélia, please. We need to talk."

She doesn't move. She barely even takes a breath.

"Unless you'd like to see her lose her magic." Talley brushes my hair away from my neck. He presses the point of the needle deeper into my skin. I cry out. "Or worse."

Rélia's terrified gaze slowly shifts towards me. I try to be encouraging. No look I give her seems to matter. There's a war in her mind and the casualties are spilling out, rooting her to the spot.

Talley's fingers twitch. Panic rises in my throat. I swallow it. Rélia has risked her life for our mission, saved me from myself. It's time I do the same for her. "Let me go, Talley. Before this gets unpleasant for you."

He chuckles. Chills snake down my spine. "You're not exactly in the position to make bargains."

I clench my fingers into fists. Gold twines through my fingers. Talley grabs one wrist, twisting my arm up behind my back. Biting the inside of my cheek, I keep quiet, refusing to give him the satisfaction of more of my pain.

"Interesting," he muses, slowly releasing the pressure on my arm. I let it drop to my side. "You'd risk your life for her. A royal you know nothing about."

"I know I care for her." I hiss. "And that's all that matters."

Something about my words clearly strikes a chord with him.

Irritation displaces his suave demeanor. "Do you know all her secrets? The origin of her power, the destiny that awaits her?"

"You mean, do I know she's a demigod? Yeah, I know. You have nothing on me. On *us*."

Talley yanks my hair. The force of the movement drags the needle across my skin, leaving a thin, deep wound. Blood trickles down my collarbone, staining my shirt. "I will show you your place."

"Please," Rélia begs. "Girardin, please. Don't hurt her."

"Begging is in poor taste for the future of Oncarii." Though I can't see his face, I can feel the callous grin creeping up it. "But you should learn the weight of difficult decisions as reigning monarch. I'll give you a choice. Outside, my navy is awaiting the command for a slaughter. So which shall it be? Your girlfriend? Or your crew?"

Rage sparks in her eyes, even as tears carve trails down her weary face. Fingers curled into fists, she takes one taut, hesitant step down the stairs. Her gaze flickers to Tezin. He is pale, and wheezing. But there is a knowing glint in his eyes even as he breaches the line between life and death.

His crew. The navy doesn't stand a chance.

Sentient fury gives me strength. It burns through me unlike anything before. Incomparable to my Sight, to Isolde's staff, even to the scorching inferno of blood magic, it *burns*. Rélia will not make a choice. This world will not take anything more from her. From us.

"Hey asshole," I seethe, voice dripping with heat. "I *am* her crew."

I reach up, clamping one hand over Talley's before he can

inject the aphonixa. Steeling myself against the pain, I yank the needle out of my neck.

I kick backwards, connecting with his groin. He falls to his knees. For good measure, I grab a fistful of his hair, ramming his nose into my knee. Blood erupts, staining my pants.

Talley leaps up with a surprising amount of agility, tackling me. Stars dance in my eyes as my head slams against the ground. The syringe skids across the floor.

Forcing my knee into Talley's chest, I gather just enough room under him to crawl towards the syringe. He clamps a hand around my ankle, dragging me back. One kick, another. Each he dodges. He pins my wrists to the ground. Struggling, I try to kick him, try to reach for the syringe. It's all futile.

Tezin staggers to his feet, inching towards me. I shake my head. He is too weak.

"GO!" I scream, headbutting Talley in his moment of distraction. Tezin lingers for a moment. Then with chattering teeth and ragged breaths, he stumbles into the tunnels.

Splitting pain tears through my head, but I force myself to scramble for the syringe. My fingers brush it. Talley yanks my legs. The syringe spins away from me. Veins bulge in his bruising forehead. Pure loathing raves in his eyes. His knees dig into my arms. His hands wrap tight around my throat. Lungs on fire, I writhe beneath him. No air comes to relieve the pain.

On the dais, the staff trembles. Its desperation is palpable. A thin crack in the staff sends a beam of light to the top of the cavern. A thundering crack echoes. Time is running out. The staff will kill us all to find a tether.

Spots dance in my eyes. My fingers tingle. My mind grows

fuzzy. Strength saps from my spirit. Not even my magic rises to help.

"Enough."

Talley's hands loosen. I gasp.

Rélia stands over us, brimming with power. Eyes glowing white, she levels a cool gaze at Talley. "Leave her."

"By the gods," he murmurs. "It's all true."

I wrench one hand free and jam my thumb into his eye. He screams. Rélia kicks the syringe to me. With as much force as I can muster, I jab the needle into his neck. Victory churns through me, fuel to my numbing rage. "You lose."

Poisonous satisfaction overtakes me as the aphonixa enters his bloodstream. He cries out. Red tints his face. He coughs. Crimson splatters across the floor. He glowers at me, wiping away the profuse amount of sweat dripping into his eyes.

Revulsion coils through me when he clamps a hand on my wrist. A barely noticeable flicker of power sparks between us. For a moment, it looks as if he'll say something, but he clutches at his stomach and stumbles out of the cavern.

Rélia envelops me in her shaking arms.

"I…I…" Her voice catches. "Raven."

I stroke her hair. "Hey, it's okay. I'm here now. Part of your crew. Nothing will hurt you without facing my wrath."

She chuckles, the sound melodic in my ears, hot against my neck. "So you're staying."

"Can't imagine it any other way." I pull away, taking a moment to soak in her beauty.

A sharp pain in my palm jerks me back to reality. Rélia

clutches at her bleeding hand. Cold crawls between us, dimming the fire in the trenches. My stomach drops. The tether.

40

Tezin

By the time I make it out of the tunnels, my crew and Rélia's are locked in combat with the navy. Crimson water splashes against the dark rocks, glitters in the moonlight. Several of my crew have fallen. The unfamiliar shackle to the *Divider* surges through me, spurning me forwards.

I stumble over the body of a navy man, sword lodged in his back. I grit my teeth; I can feel the sword still in my chest, a mind-numbing pain that saps the strength from my body. The world is spinning. Trying to stay the flow of blood oozing between my fingers, I lean against a large rock. I'm shivering now, and the world is beginning to gray. Is this what death is like?

Strong arms catch me before I fall. Ean holds me close to his chest, his presence oddly comforting. Maybe I just don't want to die alone.

"You're damn right you need help," he grunts. "What were you thinking?"

"Why do you care?" I mumble. Black spots dance in my eyes. I can't make out Ean's face above me.

He huffs. "Because I have plans for you and I. And they don't include you dying."

I can't find the strength to respond. How ironic, that Talley will soon be tied to the *Divider*. I almost want to die just to spite him.

"This hasn't been done in centuries, but I know enough to try."

Black spindles snake across his eyes. Like before, when he was fighting with Rélia, a vortex of darkness surrounds us. Ean thrusts his hands into the swirling cloud. Threads of darkness follow his fingers, like he is weaving the night itself. It settles over my skin like a writhing film, a chaotic magic resisting control. Ean directs it to the wound in my chest.

I gasp, sitting bolt upright. Vivacity pumps in my veins, and I am stronger than I've ever felt in my life. My heart beats wildly in my chest. I place my hand over it, to steady it. There's nothing there. I tear open my shirt, astounded to find there is no wound, no blood, nothing to suggest I'd been stabbed, save for a faint pulsing darkness right above my heart.

The vortex disperses, and the sound of battle seeps back in. I leap to my feet, scooping up a stray sword from the water. Holding it feels so natural, like an extension of my strength.

"Whoa," I breathe, glancing at Ean. "Thank you, for whatever you did."

Ean nods, a glimmer of a smile in his eyes.

Gusts of wind churn through the cove, twisting into a funnel.

Several navy men scream. Abruptly, the wind dies. They plummet. The resounding cracks of bones on stone freeze everyone in their tracks. For a moment, it's like time is frozen.

One navy man screams in rage, charging Aran. I snap into action, parrying the blow. He conjures a strong gale, knocking the man off his feet. I shove the blade through his throat.

"I could've handled that myself," Aran says, flexing his fingers. "Whatever your sister is doing, it's working."

Another round of steel charges us. Aran and I work in sync, air and sword humming together to cut down the navy. Killing gets easier with each body that splashes into the water. Every spray of blood energizes me.

Marie screams. I nod at Aran, and he dashes to aid her.

Ean approaches again, this time wielding a terrifying pair of sais. His moves are swift, easy, like it's second nature. Maybe it is. "You're feeling it, aren't you?"

"I am," I reply, without hesitation. The taste of chaos. As much as I don't want to give him the satisfaction, I am stronger than I have ever been. "Captain of the Dividers. This is what you wanted for me. Why?"

Together, we cut a navy man in half. I can't help a grin. They are only getting what they deserve.

"You have potential. And I will be here to guide you."

Admiral Talley stumbles out of the tunnel, clutching at his neck, face red. "Fall back!"

Immediately the meager remains of his navy take off. Cheers echo. Panting I hold my hand out to Ean. At least he helped us survive. Perhaps there's something to that.

"This is the beginning of a wonderful companionship," he says, shaking my hand.

Energy buzzes through me, sending me to intoxicating heights of elation. "Maybe."

Rocks plink into the cove. Beneath us, the ground shakes. Even from this far away, I can taste the magnitude of the power emanating from the staff. It'll take down the whole island if they don't finish.

Come on, Raven, I plead, collapsing into the water. Exhaustion creeps in. *You can do it.*

41

Raven

"We have to finish this! Now!" I grab the staff in one hand, Rélia's wounded palm in the other. "Focus on your magic, on the earth, on me. Stay grounded but feed me your power as carefully as you can."

Resolve turns her face to stone. Tightening her grip on my hand, she closes her eyes. Silver light spirals up and down her body, encasing her. I call forth my Sight. Golden light ignites my mind, curls out of my lips, across my skin, a faint warm touch as delicate as a lover's breath.

Slowly, Rélia's power signature travels up my hand, curling between each of our joined fingers, twisting around my own magic. Strength funnels through me at an immeasurable capacity. Numbing cold and raging heat battle for dominance as magic thrums through me. Thinking of nothing but Rélia, the sovereignty of our magics unification, I channel all the power towards the staff.

Even as vigor buzzes within me, my legs grow weaker. Gritting my teeth, roiling with unimaginable power, I lay the staff in the groove atop Isolde's casket. Lights of every color erupt beneath it, twining around it, through it. Fibers of the staff's wood begin to turn to stone.

Slowly, but surely, it knits to the casket, becoming one being.

Despite the aches in my limbs, the overwhelming exhaustion weighing me down, I can't help but smile. Already, the air blows lighter, sweeter. Magic is mending. Oncarii is healing.

Another bout of searing pain tears through me. Blood streams from my nose, hot and sticky. Screams echo through the cavern—both Rélia and I praying for relief.

"*Enlacze!*" I cry, pushing every bit of my energy, every aspect of my being into the world. Over and over, I repeat the Iquetí word for bond, the final part of the ritual.

I watch, struggling to maintain the stream of magic, as the head of the staff finally turns to stone. Brilliant white light explodes, filling the entirety of the cavern, blinding me. I collapse. Weariness sweeps through, replacing my strength. Black spots dance in my eyes. My ears ring.

All is silent.

Panting, caked in sweat and blood, I pull myself to my knees. Praying I didn't let go too early, hoping this wasn't all for naught, I brush my fingers over the top of the casket. Life tingles beneath my fingers. Magic hums in the stone. It lives all around me.

I laugh. It worked. Never again will we be without our divine connections.

"Rélia, we did it!" I exclaim, voice hoarse, scraping against my dry, burning throat. Bursting with pride, with relief, I turn to face her.

She's motionless.

Dread displaces the joy coursing through me but a moment before. Ignoring the shaking of my arms, the fatigue in my legs, I crawl to her side. I try to keep my distress under control. Her heart is still beating. Her chest is still rising. Gently, I lift her head into my lap. All her hair is white now. As if she is a goddess.

I plant a kiss on her sweaty forehead. "Come on, Rél. Time to wake up."

Nothing.

My voice shakes. "Wake up. Time to see the good you've done in the world. You're amazing, and you deserve the praise of saving magic. I couldn't have done it without you."

Still, she doesn't wake.

"Wake up, damnit!"

An interminable moment passes. Finally, she stirs. Her eyes snap open. For just a moment, her irises are as white as her hair, but fade to the kind amber color I know.

"Please, shower me with more compliments," she says, struggling to sit up. "Tell me all about how great I am."

"And let it go to your head? Not a chance." I pull her close to me, wrapping my arms around her in a tight embrace.

Rélia kisses me, then offers me her hand. "Let's go see the bounty of our work, shall we?"

Beaming, I take her hand, rising to my feet. "More than that, let's go see our crew."

Genuine joy radiates from her. "Yeah, my love. Our crew."

42

Tezin

The change in the world has not gone unnoticed. Everything is different. Not just in the splendor of the flowery fields, or the clear ocean waves. It's as if every step I take, I can hear the earth's gratitude, feel Oncarii sigh in content. So much destruction. Death. Agony. But for the first time in a long time, peace settles onto me. Even amidst the charred remains of my home.

Dejected, I shift through the cold ashes where my home used to stand. Virtually nothing is left. Only the stone oven stands tall, if a bit lonely. I run my fingers over the rounded top, remembering fondly the last time I used it. Gingersnap always brought Raven and I closer—our whole town really. Every time we had a dispute, or someone was terribly sad, I'd make as much as I could. Simple joy in the face of hurt feelings made it worth the work.

Raven lingers at the edge of our home's remains. I'm not sure how long she's been standing there, silently staring. I follow her gaze to the ash that used to be Mama's room. She picks up a strip of once-red fabric now caked in soot. Tears well in her eyes.

"Mama would be so proud," she says softly, the words crackling as if she had to force them over a lump in her throat. "I think she would be, Tezin. Even if we're pirates now."

She smiles. It's melancholy but not bitter. Her eyes soften. I carefully step through the cinder, coming to a stop in front of her. Bearing a kind smile of my own, I wrap my hands around hers where she grasps the strip of Mama's gele.

"You did a lot of good." An insistent tug in my chest is a painful reminder of my duty to my ship. "I'll find a way to do good too. Maybe I can make the fear of the Dividers a good thing. Serve justice where it's called for."

"If anyone can do it, it's you." Raven closes her eyes, tilting her head to the sky. Silence wraps around us like a blanket. It seems to last forever. When she speaks again, it's barely audible. "Do we have any candles?"

Forlorn, I shake my head. "No."

She sniffles, dropping to her knees. "We can't even properly honor her." Mistiness glistens in her eyes when she turns to me. "What if she doesn't meet Papa in the afterlife because we couldn't guide her? What if no one does that for us and we're lost forever?"

Her words grow more rushed, choked, the inflections warning of sobs to follow. Heart sinking at her despair more than my own, I take a seat beside her, pulling her close to me. "Neither of us are going to die anytime soon. And Mama can find her own way."

Another stronger pull at my chest sends jolts of pain through my bones. I grit my teeth, fighting its call for a few more precious moments with my sister.

"I wish we could make gingersnap," she murmurs. "Fill the town with the scent, eat some to remember our childhood. Just relive it for a little while."

"If we close our eyes and dream hard enough, it might become a reality."

Raven sighs. "I've never had your imagination. Besides, maybe the gods are doing their best to honor Mama for us. We did save magic, after all."

She nods at the horizon where the most beautiful sunset I've ever seen paints the sky. Red and orange rim the golden sun sinking into the dark waves. Purple and pink hues blend together, stretching into the sky like long, slender fingers waving goodbye to the earth for another night.

"Sorry to interrupt," a quiet voice rings out behind us.

Our friends stand in a half circle, somber but in the most hopeful of ways. Pidge skitters from Marie to Raven, who gratefully catches him in her hands and scratches him behind his ears. I turn to Aran, finding him smiling softly at me. Such a tender gesture almost takes away the pain of grief in its entirety. Almost.

Rélia steps forward, hand in hand with Monty. I eye him warily, not keen to be near him after experiencing his skills first-hand in the arena. Neither of them I'm particularly fond of, but Raven gently touches my arm, giving me the only confirmation I need to let them pass by us. Faint scents of soil and stone, of snow and rose waft beneath my nose; traces of their magical signatures following them.

In the center of our charred home, where the worn kitchen table used to stand, they kneel together. Rélia brushes away the charcoal, digging a small hole into the soil beneath. She drops a brown seed into the hole and covers it again. Monty takes her hand and places their joined palms atop the fresh ground. Silver and emerald colors curl around their fingers, wisp into the ground. A green sprout rises. Branches grow, leaves pop up, blossoms unfurl until a magnificent tree stands sturdy and tall, sheltering us.

Healer and Welder magic working together to create something beautiful. I only ever saw the adverse.

"A new beginning," Rélia says, when she and Monty finish their work. "To honor your mother and your town. *Enlacze fut'gio kāmeros, delae çincys lévangerôs.* In fire we burn, from the ashes we rise."

"And together we start anew," Monty finishes, beaming. He runs his fingers across the bark of the tree he helped raise from the ground.

Raven sniffles. My vision blurs with tears. I hold Raven tight. Warmth surrounds us as our friends gather us into the most welcoming, supportive embrace I've ever experienced. Someday, Ghzen will return stronger than ever. For now, I am happy to witness the start of its rebirth surrounded by more people than I ever imagined my heart could hold.

I turn my head to the star-speckled sky. Mihsoi's constellation is bright over my head, only partly obscured by the leaves of the fresh tree. It's not supposed to be in this part of the sky. I stand, unable to bear the pressure in my chest. Tonight, I'll give in to the ship's demands.

I have work to do.

43

Raven

Midday sun beats down on the bustling city of Qada. Already I'm sweating, though not nearly as much as Rélia. Pallor drains the color from her perspiring face. Her white hair is tucked up in elaborate coifs beneath a maroon headscarf. Gently, I tuck a stray lock under it.

"You don't have to do this if you don't want to," I say, turning her gaze from the city of her nightmares to me.

She lets out a shaky breath. "No, I have to face my fears. Besides, I'm not going to let you do this next step alone."

Unable to deny my sweeping relief, I squeeze her hand. "Good. I'll be right here with you. Always."

Rélia kisses me sweetly. Her lips taste of salt and rum; the latter of which she takes another swig of when we pull away. Liquid courage. I suppose she'll need an ocean's worth. Resolve hardens her soft features. She tucks the flask back into the folds of her jacket, then smooths down the creases in her shirt.

Presenting my hand to her, I escort her from the outskirts of the city straight into the thick of it. Like the last time I was here, delectable scents make my mouth water. My stomach growls, yearning for another loaf of crumbling, buttery sourdough. I force it away, instead focusing on the slight change in the atmosphere.

It's been a few days since magic has been restored. Our triumph has not gone unnoticed. Though sellers shout their wares, there's a slight tremor in their voices as if terrified a Flamer with renewed energy will burn down their stall. Royal guards are more on edge than ever, eyes flitting over every person that walks the streets, hands ever vigilant on their swords.

Some are happier, though. Refreshed. There's a clear jubilance in the air, one that hues the sky yellow with glee. As we make our way to the lower district, that joy is nearly tangible. Street rats pilfer with constant smiles on their faces. Mercenaries' pockets grow heavier. For all the ruffians and thugs, all the maji that have been turned away by the crown, the sun is shining a little brighter.

I catch whiffs of magical energies when I pass the nooks and crannies of the filthy backstreets between equally unkempt pubs. I hope these stray maji keep their magic under wraps. From what I understand, it's unlikely for the guard to patrol down here. But for the spoils of maji practicing against the law? I'm sure they would brave the sludge. Fear is a potent force, especially in the hands of someone with power.

Recalling Monty's instructions, I duck down a dim alley,

quiet and secluded. I run my fingers across the cracked, damp stone, searching for the hidden groove. When finally I find it, I dig my fingernails in. A quiet click, mechanical whirring, and the stone door slides open. Chatter grows louder as we saunter down the sconce-lit hallway.

Warm air puffs across my face when we enter the den. It's as lively as the last time I was here. More so. Magic signatures are stronger than I've ever experienced; condensed and powerful. Beautiful displays of Flamer and Galer magic fill the empty space above our heads; dragons formed of sparks soaring from the ceiling, swooping over the crowd of maji heartily enjoying lettuce wreaths. They whoop and cheer.

I beam.

"Whoa," Rélia breathes, speaking for the first time since entering the city. "I haven't been here. Suppose the queen of the rebels couldn't trust the enemy with her home. Smart. Though I am disappointed I almost never got to appreciate this wonder."

"If it consoles you, the last time we looked upon each other, I hadn't yet discovered this safe haven." Shaia drops down from the rafters, startling me. I'll never be used to her ghost-like movements. "I would have shown you every nook. What fun we would have had."

Jealousy pricks at my heart. I narrow my eyes. Amusement crosses Shaia's face.

"Lengthy in speech as always," Rélia muses, smirking. "Did not miss that."

"And your brashness was a comfortable absence as well." Shaia grins, a look I've never seen her wear. It's almost unsettling on her stony face. "But I will confess it is welcome on this day of celebration."

I clear my throat, handing the blood dagger to her. "Came to return this to you."

She quirks an eyebrow. "No scroll?"

"Uh, it was lost. Sorry."

Irritation flickers across her face. With a sigh, she accepts the dagger. "I suppose the journey was not without risks. Thank you, in any case, for returning my property. I have something that belongs to you as well."

In one swift move, she leaps up the chandelier, using it to launch herself up to the rafters. I try to follow her in the darkness of the ceiling. She drops down behind me. I yelp, eliciting a laugh from both her and Rélia. Crossing my arms, I turn to fire a few choice words at her. All vexation dissipates when I see what she holds.

My jaw drops. "I thought it was lost to the sea! How...how did you—"

"A good spy never reveals her secrets." Shaia presents my staff to me. Overwhelmed with relief and gratitude, I can barely raise my shaking hands. She rolls her eyes, though it doesn't seem entirely ill-natured. "Take it, Zuthrié. If you're finished basking in my incredulity, that is."

Unable to find it in me to glare at her, I gently take my staff from her. The blade is dull, and the wood chipped, but it's here. Grinning, I turn to Rélia. She's bursting with pride. For the first time in my entire life, everything is completely, utterly perfect.

"So what next?" Rélia murmurs, not once taking her eyes off

of me. "You did the impossible. You saved magic. You got me back to Qada."

I take her hand in mine, turning my attention to Shaia. "I think it's time the crown was put on the right head. Shaia, if you'll have us, we'd love to partake in your insurgency."

Though she maintains a professional expression and a regal posture, glee glints in her eyes. "Having the pirates who replenished the energy of my people under my roof could prove quite fun indeed."

"Right." A burst of impulsive confidence overtakes me. I have more power now than I ever did in my life. More love, more adventure. More than I ever could have dreamed of. And I want to make sure everyone in this room gets that wondrous, heady feeling too.

Unceremoniously, I jump onto a mostly empty table, careful to avoid tipping any plates or knocking any dice to the floor. I pound my staff once, twice, on the rough wood. Everyone turns their gazes to me, surprise, intrigue, apprehension painted in their faces. Expectant silence falls.

"For far too long," I say, voice reverberating across the room, fluttering the flames, "we have been in hiding. Maji everywhere persecuted, enslaved, killed for something we are born with. At the beginning of this country we flourished! We were revered, respected! Magic was everywhere and it was beautiful. I wanted that again. I wanted the comfort of magic ever-present in my core and in the world around us. I did everything I could to solidify the connection. You can feel it. I know you can."

I pause as the rebels' attention becomes eager, washing out confusion. Rélia gives me a thumbs up while Shaia stands silently, leaning against a wall, lips barely turned up in an impressed smile.

Feeding off the rising energy in the room, I continue, voice stronger, "I am done being spat on. I am done living in fear. I am done with this king and his gods-forsaken laws!" I survey the crowd, raising my staff above my head, overflowing with conviction, amplifying my words over the tide of cheers. "We are *not* sully-bloods. We are Nightbloods! And it's time we take our kingdom back!"

Pronunciation Guide

ANVIORA: an-VEE-or-AH

APHONIXA: a-phone-EEX-ah

BORZIAU: bore-z-EYE

CAENTATHEA: s-eye-ANT-uh-THEY-ah

GHZEN: GUH-zen

HEBRINGG: heh-BRING

JIMENA: HIM-en-ah

KUCCESH: coo-KESH

LUOMNILI: loo-ohm-KNEE-lee

MIHSOI: ME-soy

NACHNUII: knock-NEW-ee

NAVDA: NAHV-duh

QADA: KAY-duh

RACHA: RA-kah

SAELVIA MAAĴKA: sal-VEE-ah mah-SH-ka

SAVACH: SAW-vah-kh

TAE: TAY

TALLEY: TA-lee

TASHUL: tah-SHOOL

YLAA: YUH-lah

Acknowledgments

I can't begin to thank the wonderful people in my life enough for getting me to this point. Publishing a novel has been a dream of mine since I started writing creatively in elementary school (although at that time it seemed more like magic than an intricate process that takes a lot of time and dedication). I wouldn't have made it this far were it not for the unending support from my parents who always believed in me and encouraged me to grow my writing skills. Thank you for always being willing to listen to me talk about my work and being excited to read my short stories and manuscripts. I love you so much.

Next, I have to thank my beta readers, both those I hired and my friends Mairi and Abby who took the time to read my drafts and give me feedback. It has changed so much since they have read it, and that is all I could have hoped for! Fresh eyes and opinions are incredibly helpful for someone who has read the words what seems a million times over. I was beginning to think it was a boring, unoriginal work, but the truth is, I could probably just recite this novel from memory.

A special thanks has to go to my freshman college roommate Shaela who actually gave me the idea for this book. I remember we were talking about time travel and pirates and I actually took some notes on that conversation. Later that night, I started drafting out a plotline! It's hard to believe this started as a time-traveling novel. It's nowhere near what we were discussing that night but without her this novel wouldn't have been created, let alone come to fruition.

To my friends who talked to me about writing and bouncing ideas off of each other, thank you for helping me grow as a writer and make my novel (and worldbuilding especially!) so much better.

To Coral, my amazing roommate who has been my lifeline more times than I can count. Thank you for always being there.

Lastly, but certainly not least, thank you to Carina, my ride or die, who has always believed in me and my writing. You are such a good hype-man and I would not be here without your encouragement.

Thank you, all of you, for being a part of my writing journey. I couldn't have done this without you wonderful, wonderful people.

www.ingramcontent.com/pod-product-compliance
Ingram Content Group UK Ltd.
Pitfield, Milton Keynes, MK11 3LW, UK
UKHW040022200726
13854UKWH00001B/314